A PLUME BOOK

MRS. LINCOLN'S RIVAL

Steven Garfinkel

JENNIFER CHIAVERINI is the *New York Times* bestselling author of *Mrs. Lincoln's Dressmaker*, *The Spymistress*, and the Elm Creek Quilts series. A graduate of the University of Notre Dame and the University of Chicago, she lives with her husband and two sons in Madison, Wisconsin.

Mrs. Lincoln's Rival

A Novel

JENNIFER CHIAVERINI

A PLUME BOOK

PLUME
Published by the Penguin Group
Penguin Group (USA) LLC
375 Hudson Street
New York, New York 10014

USA | Canada | UK | Ireland | Australia | New Zealand | India | South Africa | China
penguin.com
A Penguin Random House Company

First published in the United States of America by Dutton, a member of Penguin Group
(USA) LLC, 2014
First Plume Printing 2014

THE LIBRARY OF CONGRESS HAS CATALOGED THE DUTTON EDITION AS FOLLOWS:
Chiaverini, Jennifer.
Mrs. Lincoln's rival : a novel / Jennifer Chiaverini.
pages cm
ISBN 978-0-525-95428-6 (hc.)
ISBN 978-0-14-218132-4 (pbk.)
1. Lincoln, Mary Todd, 1818–1882—Fiction. 2. Sprague, Kate Chase, 1840–1899—
Fiction. 3. First ladies—Fiction. 4. Children of politicians—Fiction. 5. Governors'
spouses—Fiction. 6. Washington (D.C.)—Social life and customs—19th century—
Fiction. I. Title.
PS3553.H473M78 2014
813'.54—dc23
2013035542

Printed in the United States of America
1   3   5   7   9   10   8   6   4   2

Set in ITC New Baskerville Std
Original hardcover design by Elke Sigal

To Marty, Nick, and Michael,
with love and gratitude

Mrs. Lincoln's Rival

Prologue

On the occasion of President Lincoln's first state dinner, carriages, carts, and hundreds of men on foot crowded the circular drive in front of the White House nearly all the way to Lafayette Square. Kate Chase studied the scene through the window of her father's carriage, forgetting, for the moment, her misgivings that she was attending the event as a guest rather than the hostess. The crush of people forced their horses to slow to a walk long before they reached the bronze statue of Thomas Jefferson in the center of the driveway, and the tall white columns of the front portico suddenly seemed to be an interminable distance away.

"Father," Kate said, touching his hand where it rested on the black leather seat between them. "Didn't you say that the president and his wife had invited only cabinet members, a few dignitaries, and their wives to tonight's dinner?"

"Wives or daughters, as the case may be."

"Or daughters," amended Kate, smiling. "I ask because if the size of this crowd is any indication, it would seem that either you were misinformed, or the vast population of Washington City was."

"I trust I didn't misunderstand the president's invitation," her father replied. "No, my dear Katie, what you see before you is the capital's most persistent plague—patronage seekers. They know they won't be allowed past the doorman tonight, but that won't stop them from clutching at the sleeves and pleading in the ears of any unfortunate official whom they can accost on the way to the door."

Kate lowered her voice to a conspiratorial whisper. "Then we shall have to be quick and clever to avoid them."

"Yes, and we'll keep the distance from carriage to threshold as short as possible." Salmon P. Chase frowned out the window. Impeded by the throng, the carriage had slowed to a crawl until it finally halted several yards away from the portico. "Although that might prove difficult."

"I'm sorry, Mr. Secretary," the driver called down. "I can't get any closer until those other drivers clear away."

Kate had no desire to spend any more of that lovely spring evening gazing longingly at the brightly lit White House through a carriage window and imagining all she was missing within. "Let's brave the gauntlet," she proposed. "The president and his wife are expecting us."

Her father nodded, more impatient than she to join the gathering inside. He deplored tardiness and did not tolerate it in himself or anyone else. "This will do, George," he called to the driver. "We'll walk from here."

Her father helped her down from the carriage, and as she took his arm, she felt a glow of warmth and happiness fill her heart despite the small, sad ache of disappointment that had nagged her ever since the Republican Party had selected Mr. Lincoln rather than her father as its candidate. If not for the perfidy of the delegates from his own state of Ohio, her father surely would have been sworn in as president earlier that month rather than as secretary of the treasury, and Kate, as the widower's eldest daughter, would have become First Lady.

Salmon P. Chase was, Kate knew to the very core of her being, the better man—better educated than Mr. Lincoln, more experienced, more committed to the noble cause of abolition, and vastly more qualified. Father had been a senator and governor, while Mr. Lincoln—well, Kate liked him, but if she set sentiment aside and forced herself to be strictly objective, she had no choice but to admit that a kindly country lawyer from the West with but one term in Congress to his credit was ill prepared to steer the ship of state, especially through the rough waters the nation faced. Any observer could see that, and in fact, many had, and had said so in the streets and in the press. No one expected much of the new president, and they expected even less of his overeager, overanxious wife, a matron in her midforties who had thus far failed to make a favorable impression on Washington's social elite.

Fortunately, Mr. Lincoln would have Salmon P. Chase to advise him. As for Mrs. Lincoln, for the good of the nation and the Republican Party, some kind lady ought to befriend her, become her confidante, and help her navigate the thorny maze of Washington society.

Kate resigned herself to the likelihood that no one was better suited for the role than herself, though she was more than twenty years younger than Mrs. Lincoln.

"Mr. Secretary," a voice rang out. Glancing to her left, Kate glimpsed a freckled young man in a brown suit two sizes too large for his bony frame, waving a handful of papers and grinning hopefully. "Mr. Secretary, a moment of your time, if you please."

"He's no one," Kate murmured, not unkindly. Her father was terribly nearsighted, but he hated to wear his spectacles in public and often relied upon Kate to identify people at a distance. He had been known to pass good friends and acquaintances on the sidewalks or halls of Congress without recognizing them, an unfortunate habit that contributed to his reputation as being aloof and uncongenial.

As other eager, avaricious faces turned their way, Father offered Kate his arm. "Let's make haste."

Quickly Kate slipped her hand into the crook of his elbow and hurried off beside him. "Perhaps you should throw a few minor treasury appointments after us to distract them," she teased, breathless. "Rather like Aphrodite's golden apples, but in reverse."

"I'll have no Hippomenes catch my Atalanta," her father declared, quickening his pace as he guided her through the crowd. Laughing, Kate did her best to keep up with him, though she was shorter than her father by nearly half a foot and encumbered by her corset and hoopskirt.

At last they reached the portico, where the burly, white-haired doorman greeted them in an Irish brogue and admitted them into the vestibule. They passed through the main hall into the Blue Room, a graceful ellipse with tall windows overlooking the south lawn and the Potomac River. It seemed to Kate to be in better repair than the other public rooms of the Executive Mansion, which were shabbily furnished with threadbare and tobacco-stained rugs, broken furniture, torn wallpaper, and ruined draperies, from which souvenir collectors had snipped pieces until they hung in tatters. Here, however, all was in elegant order. The chairs and settees were upholstered in rich blue and silver damask, the woodwork brilliantly gilded. Ornate mirrors on the marble mantel reflected the light from the chandeliers hanging high above from a frescoed ceiling of cerulean blue, beneath which men of influence clad in evening black and their ladies in elegant gowns of every hue mingled and chatted, the soft blue-and-white carpet muffling their footsteps.

Before passing from the brightly lit hall into the Blue Room, the Chases paused in the doorway, long enough for almost thirty pairs of eyes to turn their way. Conversations paused as the guests took in the newcomers, and as Kate smiled warmly and nodded gracefully to one acquaintance after another, she drew herself up proudly, knowing how she and her father looked to them. Salmon P. Chase—tall, broad-shouldered, and powerfully built, his features strong and regular beneath a high, clear brow projecting intelligence, courage, and dignity—was the very image of a statesman. And Kate herself—auburn-haired, hazel-eyed, young, slender, vivacious, becomingly attired in a gown of pale-yellow silk, her hair arranged in a simple, elegant twist and adorned with white flowers—was the very ideal of the accomplished, dutiful daughter. "You look like the king and queen of Washington," her younger sister, Nettie, had sighed wistfully upon their departure from home. Father had taken a moment to lecture his youngest child on the superiority of American democracy to European monarchy, which she accepted with a good-natured shrug, with none of the shame and remorse Father's admonishments evoked in Kate.

As John Nicolay, the president's private secretary, made the customary introductions, Father escorted Kate across the room, where Mr. and Mrs. Lincoln waited to receive their guests. The president's gaunt features became warmer, his eyes brighter, when he smiled, as he did when he shook Father's hand and then Kate's. "How is little Nettie?" Mr. Lincoln asked, his thick, dark brows rising quizzically, an amusing complement to the high, thin quality of his voice.

"Very well, thank you," Father replied formally, bowing to Mrs. Lincoln.

Seeing her father and the president together, Kate almost laughed aloud, taken anew by the remarkable distinction between them. If Father looked every inch a statesman, Mr. Lincoln resembled a frontier schoolmaster with no wife to remind him to brush his hair and straighten his coat. "Nettie is indeed well"—she amended her father's reply—"but I confess she was disappointed to be left at home."

"Why didn't you bring her along?" Mr. Lincoln asked, genuinely perplexed.

"Oh, Mr. Lincoln," his wife chided him, laughing shortly. Her eyes were sharply blue, her complexion white and smooth, her neck and arms elegantly molded, but she was otherwise plain and tended toward stoutness, which her short stature and her husband's great height unfortunately exaggerated. "Children, at a state dinner for the cabinet? Not even Tad and Willie will be in attendance tonight."

Mr. Lincoln smiled benignly down upon his wife. "I'm fortunate to have you here to remind me of such things." He turned back to the Chases with a self-deprecating shrug. "When I consider the reams of paper piled upon my desk, which are almost certainly accumulating greater heights even as we speak, I can only hope that an instructive book on presidential manners lies at the bottom."

"At the *very* bottom, do you mean?" teased Kate, detecting an ironic note in his tone. "So deeply buried that no one can expect you to unearth and to read it?"

Mr. Lincoln's laugh rang out, rich and full. "Why, yes, Miss Chase. You understand me perfectly."

Father beamed proudly, but as she shook Mrs. Lincoln's hand, Kate detected a flicker of annoyance in the First Lady's eyes above her gracious smile, and she was not sorry to move on. There were wives and daughters to befriend, gentlemen to charm, and people of influence to impress, but as she and her father made their way around the room, Kate often thought she still felt Mrs. Lincoln's blue eyes upon her, taking her measure with scrupulous, unforgiving precision.

Kate soon forgot Mrs. Lincoln's displeasure, swept up in the pleasure of making new acquaintances and engaging in lively conversation that occasionally, and rather delightfully, leaned toward debate. United States attorney general Edward Bates, black-haired and white-bearded, spoke longingly and endearingly of the Missouri home he had only recently departed, while General Simon Cameron, with his keen, deep-set eyes and thin mouth, struck her as insistent and shrewd. One by one Kate addressed them all, and the ladies who had accompanied them, complimenting their attire and inquiring about their children. Kate especially liked the wife of the secretary of state, Frances Seward, whose dark, intelligent eyes belied the frailty of her form. Unfortunately, Mrs. Seward spent little time in Washington City, preferring her gracious family home and more temperate climate of Auburn, New York—but her frequent absence, and that of the vice-president's wife, did leave Kate the second-highest-ranking woman of the executive branch according to protocol and tradition, behind Mrs. Lincoln, who never let her forget it.

A moment came when Kate found herself unaccompanied, but just as it occurred to her that they should have been called in to dinner by then, Mrs. Lincoln appeared at her side. "Dinner will be delayed somewhat longer," the First Lady explained, drawing her apart from the others. "General Scott has not yet arrived."

"Oh, of course we must wait for him," Kate replied. "I hope he wasn't swallowed up in the crush outside."

"I'm sure he wasn't. A crowd of patronage seekers is no match for a gentleman who commands entire armies."

Kate smiled. "I'm sure you're right."

"Be careful what you say in this city, even in jest," Mrs. Lincoln cautioned, linking her arm through Kate's and strolling away from the other guests so that Kate was compelled to come along. "Rumors fly so swiftly in Washington that if I were to cross this room right now, I would not be surprised if the people on the other side greeted me with the dreadful news that General Scott met his demise at the hands of a mob on our front doorstep."

Kate laughed easily. "Thank you for the warning. I'll take heed, I assure you."

"Speaking of rumors." Mrs. Lincoln halted, slipped her arm free from Kate's, and fixed her with an inscrutable look. "You do know the rumors circulating about us, don't you?"

"Why, no," said Kate. "Why should there be any rumors about you and me?"

"Because people enjoy gossip even more than they relish believing that accomplished women cannot get along." Mrs. Lincoln smiled, but she glanced past Kate's shoulder as if wary that they would be overheard. "They say that you and I are embroiled in a terrible feud."

Kate was so astonished she laughed. "And what reason do they give for it?"

"My overwhelming jealousy at the attentions my husband showed you at the military ball given in his honor when we stopped in Columbus in February on our way to Washington." Mrs. Lincoln's smile tightened as she nodded to a cabinet official passing nearby. "They say he danced with you more often than was seemly and showered you in compliments, while I looked on, weeping by some accounts and seething according to others."

"That's nonsense," Kate exclaimed, quickly lowering her voice. "I wasn't even in Columbus when your train passed through."

"Why, no, you weren't, were you?" mused Mrs. Lincoln as if she had only just remembered—although an edge to her voice immediately told Kate that the perceived slight had been in the forefront of her thoughts all evening. "You knew the president-elect and his wife and sons would be passing through your own city, and yet some urgent business of far greater importance compelled you away."

"Not of greater importance, but essential nonetheless." Kate drew herself up to her full height and regarded the First Lady steadily. "Governor Dennison had appointed my father a state delegate to the Peace Convention. My family had already come to Washington City by the time you reached Columbus, or I would have been there to meet you. I trust Governor Dennison's wife welcomed you as well as I would have done."

Mrs. Lincoln's smile deepened and hardened. "Or better, perhaps. Almost certainly better."

With that, she moved off in a swirl of silk skirts, leaving Kate watching after her, utterly astonished.

Soon thereafter, word came that General Scott was ill and would not be able to join them after all. Mr. Nicolay signaled for the Marine Band to strike up a spirited march, and as the brisk, merry tune played, Kate quickly composed herself, found her father, and let him lead her into the state dining room. Mr. Lincoln's place was in the middle of one side of the long table rather than at the head, while Mrs. Lincoln sat opposite him, and the others were seated all around according to rank. Kate found herself across the table from a Mr. William Howard Russell, a correspondent for the *London Times*, who seemed as charmed by Kate's conversation as she was by his wit and accent.

The food was excellent, the talk around the table bright and lively and quick, but whenever Mr. Lincoln spoke, all other voices hushed and all faces turned to him expectantly as he spun an amusing tale or made a point with a clever witticism. From the first course to the sweets, Mrs. Lincoln was so merry and chatty and smiling that Kate found herself wondering if she had imagined the strange confrontation in the Blue Room.

After the meal, the gentlemen withdrew to the Red Room, but just before the ladies were led off to an adjoining drawing room, Kate observed Mr. Nicolay whisper in her father's ear, and then in Mr. Seward's, and on to each member of the cabinet in turn. Just before a servant closed the door between the rooms, Kate glimpsed Mr. Lincoln and his cabinet quietly disappearing into another chamber while the other gentlemen lit cigars and poured brandy, apparently oblivious to their quiet departure.

Kate frowned at the closed door. Her curiosity would have to remain unsatisfied until the drive home, when her father would surely tell her everything.

She chatted easily with the other ladies, even Mrs. Lincoln, but her thoughts were with her father, wondering what intriguing subjects of national importance the men were discussing. Had the president finally decided whether to send provisions to Major Anderson's men holding Fort Sumter in Charleston Harbor? Had Virginia at last declared its intention to remain in the Union or to secede with the South? How she wished she could put an ear to the wall and listen. Her father was open and frank when he confided to her the substance of such clandestine conferences, but sometimes he missed the subtleties of tone and implication and expression, and thereby a significant amount of any conversation. He relied upon her for those observations, and for a great deal more besides.

She managed to stifle a sigh of relief when at last the gentlemen rejoined the ladies. She sensed a new tension in the air as she studied the cabinet secretaries and tried to read their expressions, but like her father, they were careful to maintain a facade of the former joviality of the party. She noticed that Mrs. Lincoln's keen gaze was often upon the president's face, and she knew that Mrs. Lincoln was as eager to hear his account of the secret meeting as Kate was to hear her father's.

When the evening at last drew to a close, Kate slipped on her shawl, took her father's arm, and bade Mr. and Mrs. Lincoln good night. "I do hope we will prove all the rumors false and become good friends," Kate told the First Lady quietly while her father and the president were otherwise distracted. "There is already too much division in our country for us to contribute to it. If malicious gossips are eagerly anticipating a fight between us, let's conspire to disappoint them."

"Why, I hope we will become good friends too," Mrs. Lincoln replied grandly, too loudly and too brightly, not for Kate but for everyone else. For Kate she reserved a private, haughty glare that announced she meant not a word of it. "I shall be glad to see you at any time, Miss Chase."

Kate's temper flared. She had spoken with utter frankness and sincerity, but Mrs. Lincoln was determined to be disagreeable. "Mrs. Lincoln," she said, smiling graciously, "I shall be glad to have *you* call on *me* at any time."

Mrs. Lincoln's eyes widened with shock at her impudence, but Kate's smile only deepened as she turned and left the White House on her father's arm.

Those who had overheard the exchange might conclude that Kate had innocently misspoken, that because of her youth and inexperience she was unaware of the custom that decreed that the First Lady did not call on others. Mrs. Lincoln was first in Washington society by virtue of her husband's exalted position, and so, as an inviolable rule, others came to her. But it had been no girlish mistake. Kate understood precedent perfectly well, and she knew that by assuming that Mrs. Lincoln would call upon her like any other lady of Washington society might, she was claiming a higher rank than the First Lady.

Kate knew it, and Mrs. Lincoln knew it too.

Kate had tried to befriend her, but she had been coldly and unreasonably rebuffed. She would not try again.

If Mrs. Lincoln was determined to have a rival, Kate would be happy to oblige.

Chapter One

MARCH 1858

*O*n a bright Saturday afternoon in Ohio, with sunlight and birdsong outside her window setting an appropriately joyful scene for her errand, Kate dressed with care in her best blue riding dress and gathered her long auburn locks into a hairnet. Her father had entrusted to her a most important task— nothing less than the redemption of an innocent man— and she must show due respect to the occasion.

The previous evening, after her father had finished his customary program of study and prayer, he had found himself with an idle hour, which, disapproving of idleness, he had sought to fill. Kate immediately proposed a game of chess, and as they studied the pieces and predicted each other's next moves, Father had told her about the prisoner, an aged Polish immigrant who had fought bravely for his adopted country in the War of 1812 but sometime thereafter had been convicted of burglary. For years he had patiently served out his sentence in Hamilton county without the consolation of friends or any hope of reprieve, but in the course of a transfer to the state penitentiary in Columbus, new facts had come to light suggesting that he could not have committed the crime. "I have become convinced that because of his years and declining health," Father said as he captured Kate's rook, "justice would be better served if I grant him a pardon rather than await the outcome of a new trial. I've made up my mind to sign the papers tomorrow afternoon, and as soon as they're delivered to the warden, the poor old fellow shall walk through the prison gates a free man."

Kate felt such a rush of joy and pride that she nearly overlooked that her father was two moves away from placing her in check. "Let me deliver the pardon for you," she implored, moving her bishop to defend her king. "What a blessing it would be to carry such good news, to help deliver an innocent man from unjust captivity."

"And what an honor and comfort it would be for the old gentleman," her father said, nodding approvingly, "to have his liberty restored to him by a compassionate young woman, the governor's own child, rather than an anonymous clerk."

They agreed that Kate should retrieve the signed document from her father's office in the capitol the following day, as soon as it could be prepared. Then her father wondered aloud if Kate ought not to travel unescorted. "Perhaps Aunt Alice should accompany you."

"I'd prefer to go alone." The noble mission was Kate's idea and she intended to carry it out herself. "Besides, Aunt Alice will be busy with Nettie."

For a moment she feared she had miscalculated, and that her father would next decree that both Aunt Alice and ten-year-old Nettie should accompany her, but instead he reluctantly agreed. "Do not acquire any unsuitable companions along the way," he instructed her, and as she nodded, she felt her cheeks flush with embarrassment. Would he never forgive the foolish mistakes of her girlhood? She knew she had erred in the past, that she had allowed herself to fall under the heady spell of men's admiration and flattery, but no lasting harm to her person or reputation had been done, and they ought to let the incidents fade into history. She had resolved never to repeat them, and she was not a guileless girl anymore but a woman grown, almost eighteen. She ran her father's household as skillfully as her mother or Nettie's mother or his first wife would have done, had they lived, and she had become what he had raised her to be—an educated young woman, "qualified to ornament any society in our own country or elsewhere into which I may have occasion to take you," as he had written to her so many years before when she was a lonely, motherless girl at boarding school in New York. He had relentlessly urged her to pursue her studies diligently, to cultivate her manners, to establish sound moral and religious principles, and all this she had done, the better to help him achieve his noble ambitions.

She knew too that if she made herself indispensable to him, he would never again send her away to boarding school—nor would he find it necessary to seek a fourth Mrs. Chase.

The memory of her father's warning dimmed the brilliance of the day, but only for a moment, and soon she was flying down the stairs as lighthearted as a child and searching the house for her aunt and sister. She found them in the parlor side by side on the settee, Aunt Alice nodding patiently as Nettie stumbled through her Latin recitations. Nettie glanced up from her work eagerly upon Kate's arrival, glad for any excuse to set her studies aside. She would much rather be drawing, or composing little stories in English, or flitting about in the garden. Little golden-haired Nettie resembled their strong-featured father too much to be truly pretty, but her sweet manner and cheerful spirits inspired affection from all who met her. "Nettie is a sweet child and everyone seems to love her," her father had praised his youngest living child in a letter when Kate was eleven years old. He had never used such phrases to describe Kate, but it was certainly true about Nettie. Even Kate was not immune to her charms. Kate, who knew she inspired admiration and envy rather than affection, who might properly have been jealous of a much-adored younger sister, loved Nettie too much to resent her.

She bade her aunt and sister good-bye, and endured her aunt's sad-eyed warning to be cautious in her choice of companions, silently fuming as she smiled and assured her that she would be wary of strangers. Two years had passed since her impropriety, two years without another such transgression, with scarcely anything worse than unsatisfactory marks in school, poor penmanship, and overdue replies to letters to give her father and aunt reason for complaint. She could only imagine how they would react if she did something truly, irreparably scandalous. The shrieks and lamentations would rival those of the Egyptians suffering the twelve plagues.

A giggle escaped her throat before she could contain it, so she feigned a cough, which tickled her throat so uncomfortably that she began to cough in earnest. "It's nothing," she managed to say as Nettie and Aunt Alice peered up at her, concerned. "Just a little—" Her words broke off in another fit of coughing.

"My dear Katie, are you quite all right?" her aunt queried, her brow furrowing. She had good reason to worry. Both Kate's mother and Nettie's had died of consumption, and Kate had been troubled with respiratory ailments nearly all her life.

Kate took a breath and cleared her throat. "I'm fine," she said, smiling to reassure them. "I'll be home soon."

She hurried off to the stable before her aunt could offer to feel her forehead or dose her with castor oil.

Ohio had no official residence for its governor, but the stately Gothic residence on the corner of State and Sixth streets with its peaked roofs, towers, and numerous chimneys was mansion enough to satisfy Kate. The family had moved to the fashionable neighborhood from rented lodgings the previous December, after Father's election to a second term convinced him that they would reside in Columbus long enough to warrant more permanent lodgings. He had delegated the task of furnishing the home to Kate, and she had delighted in traveling to Cincinnati, Philadelphia, and New York to purchase carpets and draperies, sofas and china, all to her father's exacting standards. To be sure, he had sent her off with strict instructions and had inundated her with letters throughout her excursions, but for the most part she had been on her own, meeting with merchants, comparing the cost and quality of materials and workmanship, and making the final decisions. She had never felt so necessary and yet so free and independent. Naturally, Father fretted over the bills and warned her time and again about spending too much for too little, but when she had finished, he was well pleased with his comfortable, gracious home and the grand impression it made upon visitors.

The groom helped her saddle Honeysuckle, her beloved bay mare, and soon she was on her way to the capitol, where her father kept his offices and the legislature met. Though it was not yet complete, the magnificent Greek Revival edifice, with its tall, white Doric columns framing each entrance and large cupola on top, shone with grandeur.

Kate left Honeysuckle at a hitching post and swept up the front steps to the portico. Inside, clerks and citizens greeted her in passing, some of whom she knew, others she did not but who could not fail to recognize the governor's eldest daughter. When she reached her father's offices, his secretary welcomed her in the anteroom and promptly ushered her to his chamber. "My dear Katie," he greeted her, rising from his chair and bending to kiss her cheek. "I expected you earlier." From his orderly desktop he retrieved a single document, folded and sealed, and placed it into her hands. "Deliver this to the warden as quickly as you can. An innocent man has already spent too much time wrongly imprisoned."

"I will go with all speed," Kate promised, smiling to hide her disappointment. She had hoped to witness her father signing the pardon, and perhaps linger for a bit of chat, but of course Father did not have time to spare, and the poor prisoner should not be kept waiting a moment longer.

She bade him good-bye, rising on tiptoe to kiss his cheek, and hurried on her way, the precious document carefully tucked inside her reticule. She and Honeysuckle had traveled scarcely two blocks from the capitol when she heard a horse's hooves on the road behind them, swiftly closing the gap.

Resisting the urge to glance over her shoulder, she held Honeysuckle to a steady gait as a man on horseback pulled up alongside. "Good afternoon, Miss Chase," he greeted her. "A lovely day for a ride, wouldn't you agree?"

"Why, Leonard Hillington," she exclaimed. "Aren't you supposed to be away at college?"

"I should be, but I came home to attend to some business of my father's."

His father, she knew, was a prominent businessman who also served in the legislature. She wondered what urgent matter had compelled Leonard to travel so far in the middle of the term. "I do hope all is well at home."

"Oh, yes. It's just a routine matter, accounts to examine, paperwork to sign." He held her gaze in a friendly way as they trotted along. "To be frank, I was glad to escape my studies for a while."

"Escape?" Kate echoed archly. "My father rather enjoyed his years at Dartmouth, and he continues to study on his own every evening without fail."

"Your father is a giant among men," said Leonard. "We mere mortals need occasional time away from our books."

Kate smiled, her eyes on the road ahead. He sounded sincere, but he surely realized that praising her father was the most certain way to rise in her esteem. "He sets a fine example for us all."

"Indeed he does." After a moment, Leonard said, "If it's no intrusion, may I ask where you're going? Your manner seems too purposeful for someone merely taking her exercise."

"I'm on my way to prison, of course."

He was so astonished he laughed. "To prison?"

"That's right."

"With what crime have you been charged? Whatever it is, I shall stand as a character witness in your defense."

Kate smiled. "How very good of you."

"What is it, then? Petty theft? Breaking and entering? Or breaking hearts?"

Kate laughed and groaned together. "Oh, Leonard, really."

"On the other hand, perhaps breaking windows is more likely," he mused. "I do recall a certain auburn-haired schoolgirl hurling rocks at my friends and me on the sidewalks of Columbus years ago."

"You deserved nothing less for the horrid insults you shouted."

"Perhaps you're right. I wouldn't dream of shouting insults at you now."

"Dartmouth has greatly improved you, then," she teased. "Perhaps you should hurry back so they may polish away the rest of your rough edges."

His laughter rang out, and it occurred to Kate that Leonard had learned confidence as well as flirtation in his time away from Columbus. He never could have summoned up the courage to banter with her before.

She explained the true nature of her errand as they rode along, and when they reached the prison, he offered to wait and escort her home afterward. She hesitated, dismayed by the hope in his eyes. Next he would be asking to call on her, and for permission to exchange letters with her upon his return to Dartmouth. He was kind and intelligent and handsome in a boyish way—and most important, he was unmarried—but she had no time for beaux. So she thanked him but assured him she would make it home perfectly well on her own, and sent him on his way, disappointed.

At the front gate she dismounted, gave her name to the guard, and asked to be taken to see the warden. "I have come on an important errand from Governor Chase," she said grandly. Looking rather startled, the guard promptly escorted her inside, taking a long, circuitous route designed, she suspected, to prevent a glimpse of the prisoners too shocking for a young lady's gaze. At last they came to the warden's office, but he was not alone; after welcoming her, the warden introduced her to his companions, Reverend Myers, a stout, black-haired man in a black suit and minister's collar, and Mr. French, a sandy-haired man in a rumpled suit carrying a notepad with ink-stained fingers. A clerk, Kate decided, and turned a disarming smile upon the warden. "I believe you know the reason for my visit," she said. "Would you please take me to Mr. Malecki?"

The warden and the minister spoke over themselves in their haste to inform her they had made more suitable arrangements, and with Mr. French trailing along behind, they escorted her to a simply furnished but comfortable sitting room, which she gathered was reserved for dignitaries and was not the usual place visitors met prisoners.

Before long a guard brought in a white-haired man, who shuffled with head bowed to stand before the warden. Kate's smile faded as she took in a face lined with misery, a back stooped from grief and hard toil, scrawny limbs from which pale, weathered skin hung loosely, like an old, wrinkled suit that had once fit a younger, heartier man.

Her throat constricted as the warden announced her and the prisoner lifted his head to regard her warily. She should have come earlier. She should have begged her father to have the documents signed first thing in the morning. She should have sped Honeysuckle from the capitol to the prison at her fastest clip rather than allow this poor man to suffer a single moment longer than necessary.

"Would you like a chair, Miss Chase?" the warden asked.

"Yes, indeed," Kate quickly replied, "not for myself but for this gentleman."

Looking a trifle put out, at a nod from the warden the guard left the room and returned with a wooden chair, which he set down with an impatient flourish and gestured for the prisoner to take. After a moment's hesitation, and after a murmur of encouragement from the minister, Mr. Malecki carefully seated himself, slowly folding up his bony limbs as if it pained him to move.

Kate took a quick breath to steel herself before approaching him. "Mr. Malecki," she said steadily, managing a warm smile, "it is my great honor to present to you this pardon from my father, the governor, which he offers with his regards and his certainty of your innocence."

The man's watery, hooded eyes flicked from the document she held out to him to her face and back again. He did not move to take it from her.

"Malecki," the warden said sternly, "you owe this young woman the courtesy of a reply."

"He owes me nothing," Kate said evenly, breaking the seal, unfolding the paper, and placing it in his hands on his lap. "This must be quite unexpected, sir, but I assure you, everything is in order."

She held her breath as his gaze skimmed the page, taking in the printed script, the official seal, her father's angular handwriting. He looked up, his face a study in wonder. "I'm a free man?"

"Yes, you are," Kate assured him.

Mr. Malecki glanced up at the warden. "But what about my—my new trial?"

"Unnecessary now," the minister told him, placing a hand on his shoulder.

Trembling, Mr. Malecki looked around the room, tears welling up in his eyes. A raw, aching sob burst from him, and he crumpled, resting his elbows on his knees and burying his head in his hands. Involuntarily, Kate stepped back, and a moment later the warden was at her side, offering her his arm and murmuring that she need not remain to witness the upsetting scene. Before she could protest, he had ushered her from the room. A quick backward glance revealed the minister bent over the weeping man, and Mr. French jotting notes on his pad as he followed Kate and the warden into the hall.

"That poor man," Kate managed to say as the warden escorted her to the exit. "What will become of him? Does he have any family, any friends?"

"No family in this country," Mr. French remarked, flipping through his notepad. "Any friends he might have had before he went to prison must have forgotten him by now."

"Reverend Myers has arranged a room for him in the boardinghouse of one of his parishioners," the warden assured her. "If, after a time, the old fellow can work, they'll find him a job. Until then, the church will provide for him."

Kate nodded, somewhat relieved. She managed to compose herself by the time they reached the exit, where she thanked the warden and nodded politely to Mr. French, who threw her a rakish grin and said, "No, Miss Chase, it is I who thank you. This was truly a fascinating episode."

Kate studied him curiously for a moment, but her attention was snatched away when the warden cleared his throat. "Miss Chase," he ventured, "I trust that you will assure your father that his wishes were carried out with the utmost expediency, and that you were protected at all times from any distress?"

"Of course. The governor will be pleased to hear how efficiently and faithfully you carried out your duties. And you, Mr. French?" she asked, turning to him. "Would you like me to recommend you to my father too?"

Mr. French frowned thoughtfully. "I suppose that wouldn't hurt. Perhaps if you spoke well of me, he'd allow me to interview him someday."

"Perhaps," Kate said faintly, keeping her smile in place. She nodded to both men and quickly turned to go, her knees trembling as she crossed the yard to the place where Honeysuckle waited, picketed and grazing.

A newspaperman, she thought as she rode away. A particular breed of man her father declared was a blessing when they spoke well of one and a curse every other day. The warden must have invited him to the prison, for her father certainly would not have done.

She decided not to mention Mr. French at home, and she fervently hoped that when he reviewed his notes and came to write his story, he would find nothing worth mentioning about her. But she knew her hopes were in vain. People always found something to say about Kate, for good or ill. Reviewing the scene at the prison in her mind's eye, she took comfort in knowing that her behavior had been exemplary, that she had neither said nor done anything that would reflect badly upon herself or her father.

That had not always been so.

Two years before, newly liberated from Miss Haines's School in Manhattan, she had come to Columbus, exultant with freedom—from the headmistress's demands, from loneliness, from the strictures of childhood. She had craved attention, admiration, love—things her pious and preoccupied father offered in frustratingly minute quantities. He relent-lessly admonished her for her faults, reminded her that her days on earth were limited, and urged her to pursue perfection—ceaselessly de-manding, forever unsatisfied. Was it any wonder that her heart and imag-ination were captivated by a man who admired her exactly as she was, who thought her perfect already?

He was a young man, though nearly ten years older than she, wealthy, handsome, and recently wed to a lovely woman from a prominent Co-lumbus family. Of course Kate was flattered when he paid attention to her whenever they met in society. Conversations in the midst of a watch-ful crowd led to earnest confidences shared in secluded nooks. He be-gan calling on her at home while her father was away, and then, more boldly, taking her on drives throughout the city, heedless and unmistak-able in an open chaise. Their illicit meetings went on so long and so pub-licly his wife inevitably learned of them. Whether she confronted her husband Kate did not know, but rumors whispered that the heartbroken wife would visit friends who lived across the street from the Chases and watch through the window day after day, tears streaming down her cheeks, as her husband helped the glowing young girl into his carriage and drove off with her alone.

When Aunt Alice told Kate's father, he scolded her so terribly that she wept, but she could not give up her admirer. Once she had experi-enced the heady rush of his limitless praise and adoration, the dizzying excitement of his presence, the terrifying allure of the forbidden, she could not go back to the dull, colorless, ordinary days she had known all her life before him.

She let him kiss her once, no more, but it was enough. He boasted to his friends of his familiarity with her, and unkind but not unprovoked gossip swirled about her. Furious, her father forbade her to see him again, shouted down her tearful pleas, and threatened to send her away to live with relatives until the scandal could be forgotten. Heartbroken, without a single sympathetic friend, she yearned for her admirer and lived for the days her father traveled away from the city and she could do as she pleased, free from his condemning scrutiny.

One day it was announced in the papers that her father intended to travel to Washington City, but on the appointed day he did not go, and so he was in his study reading when the man arrived to take Kate riding.

Alarmed by the sound of the governor's footfalls in the hall, he scrambled beneath a sofa, where Father quickly found him, hauled him to his feet, and beat him soundly with the whip from his own buggy, rendering him so bruised and bloodied that he could not go out in public for several days. He never again appeared on the Chases' doorstep, and when Kate plummeted into a dark pit of melancholy, forlorn and abandoned, her father sent her east to stay with family until she came to her senses.

After many long weeks, separation and silence from her would-be lover accomplished what all her father's warnings and punishments had not. Remorse overcame her, and shame, and regret, and when she thought of the anguish she had put his poor wife through she could hardly bear it. Time passed, and whenever Kate thought back on those strange, intoxicating times, she remembered feeling passion and desire and love, but she could not summon up those feelings anew. She did not know what had come over her, why she had risked her reputation, her father's respect, and all her future happiness upon someone who, it must be said, was no more than an ordinary man. In fact, his behavior marked him as *worse* than an ordinary man, for he had been willing to sacrifice two innocent women to his carnal desire—and he had left one less innocent than before.

Kate knew her father would be displeased to find her the subject of gossip once again, even if it were inspired by a good deed done on his own behalf rather than the reckless actions of a foolish girl who thought she was in love.

More than a week later, just as Kate had stopped dreading the delivery of the morning paper and had begun to hope that Mr. French would write nothing of the events at the prison, or that he had already done so but had not mentioned her role in them, her father came home from the capitol agitated and scowling. She felt herself shrinking inwardly as she waited for the storm to burst, wondering whether he would reprimand her at dinner in front of Nettie and their aunt or if he would take her aside and scold her alone. She hardly knew which she would prefer.

He chose breakfast the next morning, slapping upon the center of the table a newspaper folded open to the headline, "A Pardon Scene—Miss Chase." As he lectured her on the dangers of putting herself forward in public, she nodded, half-listening, as she read the article, fearing the worst. "On Saturday afternoon," Mr. French had written after a brief account of the unnamed prisoner's ordeal, "Governor Chase's daughter, a fair and noble girl of seventeen or eighteen summers—and who in her person proves that the generally accepted truth that 'great men never have great sons,' does not reach daughters—takes the Pardon and makes her way to the Prison." A dramatic and somewhat embellished description of the prisoner's response to his pardon followed, and the piece concluded on a note of apology: "The fair and modest heroine, I know will shrink from this public recital; but one cannot forbear telling so beautiful an event."

"That wasn't as dreadful as I had feared," Kate said as she passed the newspaper on to her aunt. At one warning glance from her father, she quickly amended, "Although I *do* shrink from publicity, and I wish the reporter had shown forbearance."

"A lady should strive to keep her name out of the papers," her father admonished. "She should be mentioned only upon the occasions of her marriage and of her death."

"Twice more only for me, then," Kate replied cheerfully, immediately regretting it when her father's scowl deepened. "Father, you must know that I didn't seek out this attention."

"The press is a tool to be used judiciously to achieve a worthy goal," her father said, rapping on the table for emphasis. "Do not let *it* use *you*."

"I had no idea Mr. French was a newspaperman until it was too late," Kate protested. "I thought he was a clerk."

"He should have identified himself," Aunt Alice said. "He should have made his intentions clear from the beginning."

Kate threw her a grateful look.

Her father heaved a sigh of resignation. "You must be more cautious in the future," he scolded, but more gently than before. "Anything you do or say could be remarked upon by others. You must be irreproachable, not only in your conduct but also in your private thoughts, though only you and God will know them."

"I understand," Kate replied, and she promised to do all she could not to displease him again.

The meal ended, and Father disappeared into his study to read pending legislation and write letters. Kate knew better than to attempt to cajole him into a game of chess, but she was pleased when, as he called the family together for their customary evening prayers, he smiled fondly to show her that all was forgiven. "Would you put the Bible away, my dear Katie?" he asked afterward, and she knew it was his way of telling her that she had not lost his trust.

Alone in his study, she hesitated before returning the holy book to its shelf, and instead turned to the family memoranda her father recorded in the blank pages bound in at the end. She had read the passage noting the day of her birth so often that the book fell open readily at the proper place, and almost involuntarily, she read again the lines that were forever engraved upon her memory.

"The babe is pronounced pretty," her father had written mere hours after she had taken her first breath. "I think it quite otherwise. It is, however, well formed, and I am thankful. May God give the child a good understanding that she may know and keep his commandments."

It had not taken her long to disappoint him, Kate reflected, and she had spent nearly every day afterward trying to make up for it. Someday, perhaps, she would.

Gently she closed the Bible and returned it to the shelf.

Chapter Two

In the months that followed, Kate redoubled her efforts to make herself indispensable to her father, and when she proved to be efficient, intelligent, and more devoted to him than any clerk or secretary he could ever hire, he entrusted her with more, and more important, duties. She managed his correspondence, scheduled appointments, attended official functions, and offered a willing ear when he needed to privately air his grievances with the legislature or party politics, or when he practiced a speech. Though in writing he was an eloquent rhetorician with moments of brilliance, he was less confident in speechmaking. His handsome face and tall, powerful form gave him a majestic presence when he stood before an audience, but he spoke with a slight though unmistakable lisp and his voice had a deep, throaty quality that rendered him too self-conscious to achieve the air of effortless eloquence. Diligent practice helped, and so did Kate's tactful reviews.

Kate relished the role of his official hostess, which her more reserved Aunt Alice gladly ceded to her. Dressed in flattering gowns, her hair parted in the center and gathered in a simple, elegant knot at the base of her graceful neck, she presided over receptions and dinners and teas for legislators, political friends, potential allies, and influential businessmen and editors traveling through Ohio. Gatherings at her father's house became renowned for their elegant surroundings, convivial atmosphere, and stimulating conversation, and the consensus was that the governor owed all due credit to his eldest daughter. She was confident and outgoing where her father could seem aloof, and she wielded tact and charm with the skill of an experienced diplomat in fraught situations where her father tended to trample unwittingly over other people's feelings. Though her father still dispensed criticism freely but held on as tightly to praise as a miser did coin, she knew he appreciated her efforts, and she glowed with happiness when she saw how puffed up with pride he became whenever his colleagues commended her to him.

Kate became the lady of the house in fact as well as practice in the sorrowful aftermath of Aunt Alice's death.

On a frosty evening in mid-February 1859, she and her father were in his study, contemplating his political future over a game of chess. A month before, he had received a discouraging letter from a longtime friend and trusted political ally, Mr. Gamaliel Bailey, former editor of Cincinnati's abolitionist paper the *Philanthropist* turned publisher of the *National Era* in Washington. After observing the ebb and flow of public opinion and studying the signs of the times, Mr. Bailey had concluded that although there was no man he would rather see in the presidential chair than Salmon P. Chase, he thought it best to support New York senator William H. Seward for the presidency in 1860.

"Bailey himself admits that Seward and I are the two most prominent men of the Republican Party," her father said mournfully, still brooding over the letter, which lay unfolded on the table beside the chessboard. "But Seward is older than I, he emphasizes, as if that matters. How can age alone be reason to prefer one candidate to another, especially when the other is not only eminently qualified but also a longtime friend?"

Kate shook her head sympathetically, her fingertips resting on a pawn. "I had always credited Mr. Bailey with sounder judgment."

"So had I, until now. How can he concur with Seward's friends that it is 'now or never' with him, and that 'to postpone him now is to postpone him forever'? And then to attempt to conciliate me with assurances that I, the younger man by seven years and still in the prime of life, will have many more opportunities to seek the presidency"—Father shook his head—"it is ridiculous."

"That last part is not ridiculous," Kate protested. "You're not only younger than Mr. Seward but also more vigorous, and you will indeed have many more opportunities to run for president—although I firmly believe that *this* opportunity remains well within your reach."

Her father's gloom seemed to lift slightly, but he was not yet ready to put the subject aside. "A considerable body of the people, including not a few who would adamantly refuse to vote for any Republican candidate but myself, seem to desire that I should be nominated in May," he said. "No effort of mine or of any of my closest friends has created this feeling. It seems to be of spontaneous growth, an appeal for me to serve that I did not seek and yet cannot ignore."

"Of course it is," said Kate placidly. She of all people knew how badly her father craved the highest office in the land, and how he had devoted years to building his national reputation and constructing a political machine that would, if all went as they intended, carry him to the White House. He wanted to believe that his driving ambition was instead a dutiful response to the demands of the public, and since she wholeheartedly believed the country needed him, she saw no reason to disabuse him of the notion.

Father's knight took her pawn. "Perhaps if I wrote to Bailey and reminded him—"

A strange, unearthly groan snatched Kate's attention away. "What was that?"

"What was what?"

"That noise. A moan, coming from outside."

Her father shook his head, brow furrowing. "I heard nothing."

He had barely finished speaking when the sound came again, louder this time, sending chills racing down Kate's spine. She and her father bolted to their feet, hurried to the front door, and tore it open to discover Aunt Alice crumpled on the front porch with her limbs splayed, eyes tightly shut, a groan of anguish choking out through clenched teeth.

Swiftly bending over his elder sister, Father shouted for servants to come to their aid. They carried her inside to her bedchamber, where she lay upon the coverlet, insensible. Father sent the coachman racing for the doctor, and while they waited Kate tried to revive her aunt with smelling salts and cool water sprinkled on her face, all to no avail. When Aunt Alice had left for church earlier that evening, she had seemed in perfect health, but when the doctor finally arrived and examined her, he concluded that she had suffered an apoplexy.

For four days she drifted in and out of consciousness, plagued by terrible headaches and garbled speech, but on the twentieth of February she passed away, released from her suffering. Kate and Nettie were heartbroken, but Father was even more disconsolate. He had buried three wives, four young daughters, and several siblings, and the sudden death of his sister on his doorstep shook him badly. "Death has pursued me incessantly ever since I was twenty-five," he murmured as Aunt Alice's casket was lowered into the ground. Speechless from grief, Kate reached for his hand, but he seemed unaware of her touch and did not fold her small, soft hand inside his larger one.

Aunt Alice had been gone less than a year when Father's second term as governor ended in January 1860; he had not sought a third. Less than a month later, in a joint convention of its two houses, the Ohio legislature had elected him as United States senator for a term beginning on March 4, 1861. Kate was excessively proud of him and thrilled by the thought of moving to Washington City. She had visited him all too infrequently there during her father's first term in the Senate, for the headmistress had frequently denied her permission to leave school as punishment for one small infraction or another.

Father was eager to return to Washington too, but not as a senator. Mr. Bailey's letter had disappointed him, but it could not dissuade him from pursuing the even higher office to which he aspired.

In his travels and through his correspondence, Father learned that he had strong support among northerners who adamantly objected to allowing slavery to spread to new states and territories, and yet he was not seen as a radical abolitionist, which made him more appealing to conservatives. He also knew that Mr. Bailey's choice, William Seward, was widely regarded as the man most likely to capture the Republican nomination, but that other intriguing contenders had recently emerged: prominent St. Louis attorney Edward Bates, the venerated judge and elder statesman from an important border state; and Abraham Lincoln, an up-and-coming lawyer and one-term congressman from Illinois.

Both gentlemen's names were familiar to Kate, but she was surprised to find the latter included in such company, although perhaps she should not have been. Two years before, Father had been so impressed by what he had read of Mr. Lincoln and his debates with Stephen Douglas that he had campaigned for Mr. Lincoln in his bid for the Senate, mustering support among prominent Illinois Republicans and urging cheering crowds to turn out at the polls on his behalf. Despite Father's best efforts Mr. Lincoln had lost the election, but his graciousness in defeat had apparently made a good impression upon party moderates. Kate knew too that he had given nearly two dozen speeches in western states in late 1859, and that he had recently accepted an invitation to speak as part of a lecture series in Brooklyn, an engagement that had first been offered to her father—and which, to her chagrin, he had declined.

Mr. Lincoln clearly intended to introduce himself to the voters of New England. Kate had no doubt he would meet with great acclaim there, having witnessed his rhetorical powers at work the previous September when he had visited Columbus and had spoken from the capitol steps to a large, admiring crowd who had hung on his every phrase throughout his two-hour address. Mr. Bates too could boast of many admirers, and as a candidate from a slave state, he could expect stronger support from the South than any other Republican in contention. But Mr. Seward remained her father's strongest rival, despite concerns within the party that he was too radical to win a national election.

In Kate's opinion, if her father were to have any chance at wresting the nomination away from Mr. Seward, he first needed to affirm the loyalties of Ohio's delegates, so that he could be confident of their votes at the upcoming convention. Next, he must win endorsements from influential Republicans across the country in order to shatter the illusion that the party was united behind the senator from New York.

Father was confident that Ohio's delegates were securely his. How could they fail to vote for one of their own, a man who had done more for the noble cause of abolition than any of the other candidates, a man who had served their beloved state so well for so long? His faith seemed confirmed when the state Republican convention, meeting in Columbus on March 1 to appoint committees and elect delegates, passed a resolution stating that while Ohio's delegates would give their united and earnest support to whatever nominee was chosen at the national convention, Salmon P. Chase was their first choice and their recommendation. Although the vote was not unanimous, Father was so confident that Ohio was behind him that he set himself to writing letters to prominent men from elsewhere in the nation, men he hoped to win to his side.

Included among these men was the Prussian-born Carl Schurz, a staunch advocate of abolition and democracy whose opinions swayed voters in his home state of Wisconsin and throughout the northwest, especially those of German immigrant heritage. When Father learned through a mutual acquaintance that Mr. Schurz would be traveling through Ohio on a speaking tour, he immediately wrote to invite him to stay at the Chase residence when he visited Columbus.

Mr. Schurz accepted by return mail, and for several days the house fairly hummed with excitement as Kate prepared to welcome their honored guest. On the night before he was due to arrive, Kate went off to bed satisfied that she had everything well in hand, but the next morning, her maid shook her awake early with the startling announcement that Mr. Schurz had arrived, and that her father was entertaining him in the breakfast room.

"Mr. Schurz is here *now?*" Kate threw back the coverlet, bounded out of bed, and filled the washbasin from the pitcher. "We weren't expecting him until midafternoon!"

"He knows that, miss," Vina said, snatching up a towel and holding it at the ready. "He stood on the doorstep apologizing for ages until Mr. Chase convinced him it was all right and that he should come in."

When Kate finished washing, Vina quickly helped her dress and arranged her hair, and soon Kate was darting down the stairs, catching her breath at the bottom, and walking sedately into the breakfast room as if nothing were amiss.

She found her father and Mr. Schurz—a wiry brown-haired man of about thirty years with a scholarly brow and pince-nez spectacles—seated at the table and sharing a pot of coffee, a rasher of bacon, and a basket of hot biscuits with sweet butter and marmalade. "Mr. Schurz, I presume," she greeted him warmly, and when he rose and bowed, she smiled in return, kissed her father on the cheek, and settled gracefully into the chair at his right hand. "How was your journey to Columbus?"

"Unexpectedly swift, Miss Chase," he said, his German accent charmingly formal. "Hence my early arrival. I must apologize for disturbing you at such an unforgivable hour."

"No apologies are necessary," Kate assured him. "You certainly didn't disturb me, and my father is an early riser, so I'm sure you didn't disturb him either."

"Not at all," her father remarked. "I was reading the papers and drinking coffee, which is always more enjoyable in good company."

"You're very kind," Mr. Schurz said.

Concluding that they had exceeded the requisite amount of apologies and reassurances warranted in such circumstances, Kate lightly led them on to other matters—the progress of Mr. Schurz's speaking tour, the differences in climate between Wisconsin and Ohio, the opinions of the German immigrant community on various issues of the day. Naturally, the subject soon turned to abolition and to politics, and Kate deftly directed the conversation to show her father to his best advantage, and to allow Mr. Schurz to discover for himself how many beliefs they held in common.

After breakfast, they continued their conversation in Father's study, where Father showed Mr. Schurz a few of the most prized volumes in his library. Observing them from the corner of her eye as she poured coffee, Kate was pleased to see that her father's public bearing—which his critics derided as cold, haughty, or distant, when she knew it to be a natural reserve, a dignified shyness—had fallen away as it did usually only among close friends and family, allowing his goodness and warmth to shine through.

When the men settled down with their cups into comfortable chairs, Kate had barely enough time to smooth her skirts and seat herself when her father somewhat abruptly broached the subject of the upcoming Republican Convention. "I will tell you frankly that I have an ardent desire to be president of the United States," her father told their guest, who seemed startled by the admission. "You will undoubtedly be sent by the Republicans of Wisconsin as a delegate to the convention in Chicago, and I wish very much to know what you think of my candidacy."

Mr. Schurz hesitated, drank deeply of his coffee, and frowned briefly at the carpet. "It would give me sincere happiness could I answer with a note of encouragement," he eventually said, "but I cannot, and I esteem you too highly to flatter you or dissemble with ambiguous phrases."

Though she had expected as much, Kate nevertheless felt her heart sink, and the look of surprised sadness on her father's face pained her.

"You'd honor me most by offering the plain truth," her father said, taken aback. "Please, speak freely, with no fear of embarrassment."

With a pensive sigh, Mr. Schurz set his coffee cup on the table and met her father's gaze squarely. "I'm too inexperienced in American politics to estimate the number of votes you might command at the convention, but I have formed a general judgment of the situation."

"And what is that?" inquired Kate pleasantly, as if they were discussing gardening or poetry rather than her father's political future.

Mr. Schurz offered her a regretful smile before turning back to her father. "If the Republicans at Chicago have courage enough to nominate a strong antislavery man, they will nominate Seward," he said in a voice that allowed no doubt. "If they lack that courage, they will not nominate you."

He said it as kindly as he could, but her father fell silent for a long moment, stunned. "Thank you for so straightforwardly giving your opinion," he managed to say, "which, possibly, might be correct."

Mr. Schurz inclined his head in polite acknowledgment that it might not.

"But without impugning Seward's character and past service to the country," Father continued in a sudden rush, "I don't understand why strong antislavery men should place me second in order of leadership instead of first."

"I hardly wish to argue the point," Mr. Schurz replied, his broad brow furrowing slightly. "Senator Seward has mustered strong support for his candidacy—strongest in the East, of course, but widespread."

"He has detractors," Father countered. "Some say he's too radical, and they worry that if he's nominated, it'll hurt Republicans in local elections."

Mr. Schurz conceded that some men did indeed hold that opinion, but he did not count himself among them.

Sensing that the discussion would soon devolve into argument if she did not intervene, Kate quickly brought the conversation back to safer ground. Her father could not conceal his disappointment, but he nonetheless maintained a cordial demeanor, and before long, most of the men's earlier conviviality had been restored.

Soon thereafter, Mr. Schurz retired to the room they had prepared for him to rest after his long, wearying journey. When he emerged from his chamber hours later, they enjoyed a pleasant luncheon, after which Father, Kate, and Nettie took him on a carriage tour of the capital city, showing him the sights and introducing him to many of their most notable citizens. At eight o'clock that evening, Father and Kate escorted Mr. Schurz to the Congregational Church, where an eager audience had gathered to hear his lecture titled "France Since 1848." Mr. Schurz proved to be an energetic, knowledgeable speaker, and while he was at the podium, Kate was able to forget her father's disappointment for a little while.

The following morning after breakfast, Kate accompanied Mr. Schurz in the carriage to the station, where he would board the train for Cincinnati, the next city on his tour. As she bade him farewell, he lingered to apologize for offending her and her father with his blunt assessment of Father's prospects at the upcoming convention.

"There was no offense taken," Kate assured him. "It is never a disservice to speak the truth. You would have done my father no favors if you had falsely raised his expectations instead of telling him plainly what obstacles lie in his path."

"It is a path I see he is determined to follow," Mr. Schurz replied, with obvious regret. "I have studied this country enough to know that 'presidential fever' is a troublesome ailment, and sometimes fatal to the peace of mind and moral equilibrium of men afflicted with it. Your father seems to me to be one of the noblest men suffering from that disease."

Kate managed a laugh. "Suffering has never looked so hale and hearty."

"I feel obliged to warn you, Miss Chase, that I have never before met anyone so strongly possessed by the desire to be president, to the extent that he believes he owes it to the country and that the country owes it to him that he should assume that high office."

"Perhaps he is correct in his beliefs," Kate said lightly, keeping her smile in place. "Many others share them."

"Perhaps not as many as you think," said Mr. Schurz carefully. "I have no doubt that your good father will never allow his ambition to corrupt his principles, but I am concerned that repeated disappointments will pierce him like poisoned arrows, and that in the years to come he will be incessantly tortured by feelings that his country did not do justice to him."

"My father has overcome disappointment before," Kate reminded him. "Let's not forget too that it's entirely possible he won't find his great ambition thwarted."

"Of course, you're right." Mr. Schurz offered her a small, apologetic smile. "You're a true and loyal daughter. Your father is richly blessed."

"Thank you. I'll be sure to remind him."

Mr. Schurz laughed aloud, and so despite his foreboding words, they parted as friends.

Father quickly rebounded from his disappointment, and before the week was out, he told Kate that he still hoped to win the influential German to his side. "I believe Mr. Schurz has settled firmly in Mr. Seward's camp," Kate cautioned him, but her father's optimism did not waver. His hopes were buoyed by laudatory articles in the *Ohio State Journal*, Columbus's Republican newspaper, which praised him almost daily and suggested that his nomination in May was all but certain. "No man in the country is more worthy, no one is more competent," the editor declared, praising Father's "steady devotion to the principles of popular freedom, through a long political career," which had won him "the confidence and attachment of the people in regions far beyond the State."

Kate believed her father deserved every word of the *Journal*'s praise, but the steady stream of encouragement filled her with misgivings. Her father seemed too determined to believe that everyone shared the *Journal*'s opinion, ignoring the more derisive reports that appeared in the *Daily Statesman* and elsewhere.

As the national convention approached, her worries grew. Her father had no strong advocate organizing his campaign, as Mr. Seward had in the political impresario Thurlow Weed. Father had not mended fences with rivals in Ohio, but preferred instead to exchange letters with his most ardent supporters, men who no longer needed convincing. When Kate mentioned troubling signs—reports of Mr. Seward's firm grasp on the delegates from numerous states other than his own, Mr. Lincoln's rising reputation in the East in the wake of his wildly successful speech at the Cooper Union, an engagement her father never should have declined—her father dismissed them. "If the cherished wishes of the people prevail," he assured her, with an irritating note of condescension to which she tried not to take offense, "I will be the nominee in Chicago in May."

Kate feared otherwise, and after much delicate cajoling—and at the urging of her father's successor, Governor Dennison, and a handful of supporters back East—she managed to convince him that he should travel to Washington City to reinforce his support among the congressmen and senators there, and to remind everyone of his national prominence.

A few weeks before the convention, Kate, her father, Governor Dennison, and his wife boarded a train for Washington City, leaving Nettie forlorn and unhappy at home in the care of an older cousin. After a long, wearying ride spent poring over newspapers and planning a strategy of whom to meet, they arrived at the capital late in the evening and took rooms at the celebrated Willard Hotel on the corner of Fourteenth Street and Pennsylvania Avenue, an establishment Kate and her father knew well. A year before, they had been among 1,800 guests at the Willard for an elegant, extravagant farewell dinner and ball in honor of the British ambassador, Lord Napier, who was returning to his native country. How different the purpose for their visit this time, Kate reflected as she settled into her room. She could see the White House from her window, luminous and tantalizing in the moonlight on the other side of Lafayette Square.

The next morning, Kate and her father embarked upon a program of meetings, receptions, and dinners, a whirlwind of activity that delighted Kate but, not surprisingly, proved to be an uncomfortable exercise in forced affability for her father. Fortunately she was nearly always at his side to ease the flow of conversation, to calm impatient congressmen, to soften her father's stoic demeanor with her own warmth and charm. For the most part, as the days passed, their efforts seemed to make headway against the current sweeping toward Mr. Seward, but on other occasions, her father stumbled. He tried to convince Benjamin F. Wade, the senior senator from Ohio whose name had been bandied about as a possible presidential nominee, to withdraw his highly improbable bid rather than risk stealing votes away from himself, but was coldly and rudely rebuffed. He courted favor with the influential editor of the *New York Tribune*, the staunch abolitionist Horace Greeley, who concurred with Mr. Seward on almost every relevant issue but had never forgiven him for blocking his appointment to a state office years before. Rather than giving Father his endorsement, however, Mr. Greeley declared himself for Missouri's Judge Bates, dumbfounding both father and daughter. "If Greeley's guiding principle is to promote anyone but Seward," Father wondered aloud in the carriage on the way back to the Willard, "how could he, an abolition man, choose Bates over me?"

Kate had no logical explanation to offer him.

On some occasions, while her father mingled with congressmen elsewhere in the yet-unfinished Capitol, Kate went alone to the Senate gallery, where she watched the debates with intermingled feelings of excitement and dread. The tension in that venerable chamber was more brittle and electric than she remembered, the men's expressions gloomier, the insults more biting, the debates more vitriolic. Her father had been engaged in the battle against slavery so long that she took for granted the fierce disagreement between the North and the South, but to witness elected representatives from opposing states argue and shout threats, to glimpse the ominous shape of firearms beneath their coats, to hear talk of duels and of war—the new temper of Washington City startled and troubled her.

The animosity was not confined to the halls of Congress either. It spilled over into the ballrooms and fashionable parlors of the city's social elite, where for decades a mutual regard for protocol and decorum had enforced civility even when fierce debates waged in the House and Senate. Now the Buchanan administration was in its final year, and no one knew what would replace it, for cracks had begun to appear in the foundation of all they had once accepted as true and immutable.

Kate had made friends on both sides during her visits to the nation's capital through the years, and she did her best to navigate this new, unsteady terrain without damaging her father's prospects by favoring one faction over another, and without abandoning her principles.

One day, while her father and Governor Dennison were ensconced at a club favored by Republicans and Whigs, Kate called on Miss Harriet Lane at the White House. Though nearly a decade separated them in age, they had become fast friends during one of Kate's previous visits to the capital, and even after her bachelor uncle's election to the presidency elevated her to great prominence as his official hostess, Miss Lane had always graciously received Kate whenever she was in Washington.

Mr. Buchanan, a Democrat of Pennsylvania, had vowed in his inaugural address four years earlier that he would not run for a second term, so Kate's visit was blessedly free of the inevitable tension that would have come between them were Miss Lane's uncle and Kate's father contending for the same post. In the family library on the second floor of the Executive Mansion, Miss Lane embraced Kate as fondly as she would a younger sister, took her by the hand, and led her to the sofa, where she prompted Kate with questions about Columbus, her father's ambitions, and her opinion about his prospects. Too loyal to confess her doubts even to a trusted friend, Kate touched lightly on his setbacks and instead emphasized recent favorable developments—the resolution of the Ohio Convention naming Father as their first choice; the strong support offered by Joseph Medill, the publisher of the *Chicago Tribune*; and the promises of various officials they had met during their visit. "But what about you?" Kate asked, clasping Miss Lane's hand. "I can only imagine how it has been for you these past few months, contending with such unrelenting animosity."

Miss Lane, ever self-possessed and dignified, shook her head as if there were no words for her difficulties, lifting a hand and letting it fall to her lap. "Seating arrangements at official events have become something of a geometric puzzle," she said, smiling at the profound understatement. "I must place everyone with utmost care, paying due deference to rank while keeping foes apart." Her smile faltered. "Their differences run far deeper than disagreements over a budget or a bill. I don't see how the North and South will be able to restore any sort of harmony to the country when they can barely sit around the same dinner table without erupting into angry shouts, or proposing duels, or worse."

"The country will never know peace as long as slavery exists within its borders," said Kate.

"I know that's what you and your father believe, but we've managed nearly a century half-slave and half-free."

"I wouldn't say that we've managed particularly well," Kate countered. "Or, thanks to the Fugitive Slave Law, that we're even half-free. Even in the North the law compels us to return fugitive slaves to their enslavers."

"That law is ignored as often as it is obeyed."

"If the Southern slave powers have their way, that will no longer be so." Kate shook her head, sighing. "No, this confrontation has been awaiting us ever since the founding fathers failed to forbid slavery in the new nation they created. It was and has always been inevitable. I only pray that this confrontation, when it finally breaks, will be a battle of laws and legislation and not one of muskets and cannon."

"I hope the same, with all my heart," said Miss Lane fervently. "The more men talk of war, the easier it becomes to move closer to the edge of that precipice. I confess I don't envy the man who will take my uncle's place next year, and I envy only very little the woman who will take mine."

"I hope that woman will be myself," Kate admitted, although Miss Lane surely knew that already. "For my father's sake, of course, and for the nation's."

Miss Lane smiled. "Not for your own, not even a little?" Then her expression grew somber. "I wish I could promise you my uncle's support. He admires your father, but he would prefer a conservative Democrat to succeed him. He'll support the party's nominee, whomever that shall be."

"I understand," Kate said, "and I promise that I won't let politics interfere with our friendship."

"Neither shall I," Miss Lane promised in return.

There were others in Washington, Kate knew, to whom Miss Lane could not make that promise. Miss Lane was embroiled in a bitter feud with another lady Kate greatly admired, Adele Douglas, wife of the same Stephen Douglas who had defeated Abraham Lincoln in the 1858 Senate race. Although as the president's niece and official hostess Harriet Lane held the highest rank in society, it was Adele Douglas who was called the Belle of Washington, her invitations that everyone in the capital eagerly awaited, her style that other ladies imitated, and her beauty and elegance that won praise and admiration from all who met her.

The discord between Miss Lane and Mrs. Douglas originated not in any insult one lady had inflicted upon the other, but rather the longstanding animosity between Miss Lane's uncle and Mrs. Douglas's husband, an intense hatred sparked by political attacks and profound disagreements over policy. Each lady knew that Kate was friends with the other, but neither rebuked her for it or demanded that she choose one over the other. For that Kate was grateful, but as much as she liked both women, she found their rivalry petty and pointless. It bewildered her that the otherwise sympathetic Mrs. Douglas would so publicly adopt her husband's quarrels as her own, and that the dignified Miss Lane would descend to open conflict with anyone. Why two such intelligent, refined women did not instead set aside their mistrust and work together, discreetly, to mitigate the harmful effects of their gentlemen's disputes, Kate could not understand.

She called on Mrs. Douglas not long after she visited Miss Lane, and learned that Mrs. Douglas too was alarmed by the splintering of the capital into hostile factions along geographic lines. She shared what she knew of Mr. Lincoln, knowledge gleaned from her husband's hard-fought Senate campaign and the rhetorical battles that had formed such a significant part of it. Kate passed the information on to her father, who thanked her but noted that Mr. Lincoln would likely figure little or not at all in the upcoming convention. By all accounts Mr. Seward retained his significant lead, and it was he whom her father must pursue and overtake.

If Mr. Seward considered Father any sort of threat, his behavior toward the Chases during their visit concealed his anxieties entirely. To Kate's surprise, the senator from New York hosted a dinner party in their honor, a remarkably congenial event considering that all sides—North and South, Conservative and Radical, Democrat and Whig, and Republican and Know-Nothing—were represented in fairly equal numbers. The next evening, a former Ohio congressman held a party to recognize both the former and current governors of his home state, and this gathering too Mr. Seward attended. Nearly sixty years old and slight of build, he nevertheless possessed an imposing presence that somehow made other men seem smaller when they stood near him. His eyes were sharply intelligent above a hawk-like nose; his gaze keen and appraising; his ears, almost comically large; his eyebrows bushy and fading, like his hair, from red to straw. That evening he was as convivial a guest as he had been a host, and afterward Father admitted that the senator had been kinder to him than he had expected. Even Kate could not help enjoying the few conversations they shared, and she laughed despite herself when he jokingly confessed, "I find much comfort in the discovery that Ohio is home to at least three candidates for the presidency, all eminent and excellent men, but each preferring anybody out of Ohio to his two rivals within."

On their last night in Washington, Kate and her father met Mr. Seward a third time, at a lavish party for the Ohio contingent hosted by the prominent Blair family at their country estate in Silver Spring, Maryland. It was a delightful evening, though news and rumors from the Democratic National Convention recently opened in Charleston dominated conversation. Mr. Douglas was considered most likely to receive the nomination there, and Kate could well imagine how displeased Miss Lane would be to think that Mrs. Douglas might succeed her.

For reasons other than her friend's satisfaction, Kate resolved to do all she could to prevent that from happening.

The next day, the Chases and Dennisons boarded the train home to Columbus weary but satisfied with the results of their excursion, which in Kate's estimation had encountered more success than disappointment. If nothing else, her father seemed to have been roused from his complacency. He had discovered for himself that Senator Seward was a formidable opponent whose affairs were well managed by the shrewd Thurlow Weed, that Judge Bates of Missouri was the fortunate beneficiary of Horace Greeley's endorsement, and that even Mr. Lincoln's star was on the rise thanks to his astonishingly successful lecture tour.

Her father had expected to leave Washington with his prospects more secure, but to Kate's relief, he at last seemed to understand that he must marshal his forces swiftly if he hoped to win the nomination.

Chapter Three

---

*B*efore the train pulled into the station in Columbus, Kate's father had already penned numerous letters to supporters from Ohio to New York thanking them for their promises to stand firm for him at the upcoming convention and asking them to rally more out-of-state delegates to his side. With the Democrats too divided and distracted even to choose a nominee at the party's national convention in Charleston, unity became the watchword among Republicans. In the second week of May, news came from Decatur that the Illinois Republican Convention had not only nominated Mr. Lincoln—dubbing him the "rail candidate for president" and with great fanfare carrying into the hall two fence rails he had supposedly split as a youth—but had passed a resolution stating that "the delegates from this State are instructed to use all honorable means to secure his nomination by the Chicago Convention, and to vote as a unit for him." No such resolution bound Ohio's delegates to Father, but he trusted that they would stand unified behind his candidacy if for no other reason than he was the designated choice of the state convention. It was evident that his success depended upon their support. Father knew he would not win the nomination on the first vote—Seward's stature was too great for that—but delegates from other states might rally to him as an alternative to the front-runner if he survived the first ballot. Everything depended upon a unified vote for Salmon P. Chase from the

Ohio delegation—an outcome Father expected but that was hardly guaranteed.

At the last moment, Father chose his brother Edward as his unofficial representative to the convention; but while Uncle Edward was loyal and true, he was essentially a political novice, lacking political connections, deal-making skills, and access to the back rooms where such deals were made. Father trusted him implicitly, however, and since he intended to follow the established custom of not attending the convention himself, Uncle Edward's trustworthiness more than compensated for any deficiencies of political savvy.

Uncle Edward sent a telegram upon his arrival in Chicago on May 15, briefly describing the illuminated city, the crush of delegates traveling to the convention from all corners of the nation, the spectacular displays of skyrockets and nine-pounder brass cannon firing over Lake Michigan, the free-flowing alcohol and brass bands everywhere else. He promised to go early the next day to the Wigwam, the enormous structure of rough pine boards and rafters on the corner of Lake and Market streets built in a rustic imitation of New York's Crystal Palace expressly for the convention. From there he would telegraph reports as events warranted.

Thus apprised, Father, Kate, and the rest of the Chase household settled themselves down to what they knew could be a long and apprehensive wait.

On Wednesday evening, May 16, Uncle Edward telegraphed a single report, frustrating in its brevity: "Preliminaries concluded. Various committees formed. Adjourned till 10 AM tomorrow. All is well." The following evening, his single telegram was only slightly less taciturn: "Platform favorable to Northern interests adopted. Provision requiring two-thirds vote failed. Simple majority sufficient to nominate. Adjourned till 10 AM tomorrow."

"Uncle Edward didn't say, 'All is well,' this time," Nettie noted.

"That doesn't mean all is *not* well," said Kate, absently stroking her sister's fine golden curls. "Uncle Edward said all was well yesterday, and since he hasn't said otherwise, we can assume that is unchanged. If something had gone wrong, he would have told us."

But although it escaped Nettie's notice, something had. The ruling that the nominee could be chosen by a simple majority rather than two-thirds of the votes benefited no candidate but Mr. Seward, who might have commanded a majority of the delegates even before they stepped off the train in Chicago.

"We'll know more when he telegraphs again," said Father resignedly. He opened his Bible, summoned the servants, and brought the household together in the library for their customary evening prayer. The ruling had been made; there was nothing they could do to change it.

Kate slept poorly that night, but she rose on the morning of the third day of the convention energetic and full of anticipation. She dressed and bounded lightly downstairs to the front sitting room, where the household gathered every morning—family, guests, and servants alike—for Father's solemn scripture reading. Then the family sat down to breakfast, as if it were an ordinary day, except that the meal was interrupted by the arrival of a telegram from Uncle Edward. "Chase submitted by Cartter to thunderous applause," he reported. "Others named—Seward Lincoln Dayton Cameron Bates McLean by Corwin. Delano seconded Lincoln. Cannot leave Wigwam now. Will send mssgr to telegraph news."

"Mr. Corwin," said Kate, disbelieving. "Mr. Corwin nominated Mr. McLean."

"And Mr. Delano seconded Lincoln instead of me," said her father grimly. "Two Ohio delegates have forsaken me before the first ballot."

Nettie looked from her father to her sister and back. "How could anyone from Ohio vote for anyone but you?"

"The vote hasn't been taken yet," Kate explained. "These are merely the nominations."

"A delegate is hardly likely to nominate or second one man and vote for another," Father said grumpily.

Nettie threw Kate an anxious look, and she returned what she hoped was a reassuring smile. "Politics is a strange business," she reminded her father. "That may be a ploy to draw delegates away from Mr. Seward so he doesn't win on the first ballot."

Her father made no reply, but at least he did not disagree.

Restless and craving fresh air and distraction, Kate had Honeysuckle saddled and went riding through the fashionable districts along State and High streets and around the magnificent capitol. She exchanged greetings in passing from friends and acquaintances, and politely accepted premature congratulations from others. Here and there she observed signs of the great celebration planned for the evening should her father receive the nomination. Brass bands were rehearsing, a sturdy cart had been procured to haul an enormous cannon to the statehouse to announce the good news with a thunderous salute, and somewhere, Kate knew, fireworks were being made ready. She fervently hoped that the city's preparations would not be in vain.

Less than an hour after she returned home from her ride, another telegram arrived from Uncle Edward: "First ballot," Father read aloud, holding the paper close to his eyes. "Seward 173½, Lincoln 102, Cameron 50½, Chase 49, Bates 48, McLean 12, Collamer 10, Wade 3, Sumner 1, Fremont 1."

Kate's heart sank as she and her father read the telegram together in silence, once, twice, and yet again. The delegates of Ohio had not rallied around Father. Mr. Seward was first, as all had expected, but somehow Mr. Lincoln had emerged as the second favorite, with General Simon Cameron of Pennsylvania inexplicably ranked third, ahead of Father. "How can this be?" Father wondered aloud, wounded. "Not even second, but a distant fourth?"

"Not too distant," Kate quickly replied. "We all knew Mr. Seward would take the first ballot, but he has not yet taken the nomination. Now that the delegates know how matters stand, and that some candidates have no chance at all, there will be a shifting of votes."

"Yes, but will two hundred and thirty-three votes shift to me?"

Kate found herself at a loss for a satisfactory reply. All they could do was wait for Uncle Edward's next telegram.

It was not long in coming, and when Father carried it into the library to read in seclusion, Kate followed close behind and read over his shoulder. "Second ballot," Uncle Edward had tersely announced. "Seward 184½, Lincoln 181, Chase 42½, Bates 35, Dayton 10, McLean 8, Cameron 2, Clay 2. Third ballot forthcoming."

Mr. Seward had gained a little ground, but although Father had overtaken General Cameron in the ranking, he had garnered fewer delegates than on the first ballot. The shifting of votes had gone mostly Mr. Lincoln's way.

"It is finished," Father murmured, letting his brother's telegram fall to the desktop.

"It is not yet finished," Kate protested. "It's not finished until one man has two hundred and thirty-three delegates."

"Katie, dear child," her father said, reaching for her hand. "Barring some miracle, it is finished for me. Even if I claimed the votes of every candidate lower in the polling than myself, I would not have enough to catch up to Seward and Lincoln."

"There are more delegates who *don't* want Mr. Seward than do," Kate countered. "Now that they've seen he's vulnerable, they would be wise to shift their votes to you so that you may overtake him before he collects enough to win the nomination."

"If Seward's enemies consolidate their votes behind someone else to block him, why would they choose me instead of Lincoln?"

It was a rhetorical question, resignedly posed, but Kate decided to respond as if he meant it. "Mr. Lincoln is not as well-known as you outside his home state, and therefore less likely to prevail in November. That alone makes him a risky nominee, but in his case it is doubly true because the Democrats are likely to choose Mr. Douglas, who has defeated him before, and rather recently. You are the more prudent choice."

Her father brooded for a long moment in silence, which he broke, at last, with a heavy sigh. "Perhaps you're right," he said wearily. "The third ballot will decide it."

It seemed hours until Uncle Edward's next telegram proved him right. The next time the messenger knocked on the door, Kate and Nettie flew to answer it, with their father and the rest of the household close behind.

"Read it, Katie," her father instructed.

Holding the paper with trembling hands, Kate took a deep breath and said, "Uncle Edward writes, 'Third ballot. Lincoln 231½, Seward 180, Chase 24½, rest to others. After ballot Cartter—" Her voice faltered, but she steeled herself and plunged ahead. "Cartter switched four Ohio votes to give Lincoln majority. Great enthusiasm and rush to switch votes to make unanimous. My sincere regrets."

All eyes went to Father, who stood pale and tall and stoic in their midst. "It comes down to Ohio again," he said in a voice devoid of emotion. "If they had been true from the outset, and remained true throughout—" He fell silent, opened his mouth again as if he would say more, but then he shook his head and slowly walked off alone. A moment later Kate heard the study door close behind him.

Tears streamed down Nettie's fair cheeks. "It's not fair," she said, balling up her skirts in her fists. "It's not right. There must be some mistake. They counted wrong."

"Nettie," Kate soothed, embracing her. "There is no mistake. Uncle Edward would not have gotten it wrong."

A catch in her throat silenced her. She was close to weeping too, but she refused to break down in the foyer with all eyes upon her. Her father needed them to be strong, loyal, and reassuring as he prepared for a future far different from his expectations, and the rest of the family would follow her lead. She would grieve later, alone, where no one could see.

Later that day, as word of her father's defeat and Mr. Lincoln's triumph diffused through the city, a muted ceremony to honor the nominee took place. The brass bands and fireworks were canceled, but the cannon fired once at the corner of Third and State streets, and then it was over. Kate, who had hoped to attend a grand celebration at her father's side, instead heard the thunderous salute from her father's library, where she had set up the chessboard and invited him to play. After halfheartedly capturing a few of her pawns and losing a knight, he apologized and told her he felt a headache coming on and wanted nothing more than to lie in the quiet darkness of his bedchamber and rest his eyes.

In the days that followed, Kate stifled her indignant anger as she read how the delegates in Chicago had celebrated after making their choice—the wrong choice—and how cannons had been fired and nearly thirty thousand people had filled the streets, shouting and cheering, how the *Press* and *Tribune* buildings had been illuminated from foundation to rooftop, and how bands had played triumphant marches as Republicans paraded through the streets with fence rails on their shoulders in a nod to Mr. Lincoln's humble origins.

"Fence rails again," Kate muttered, shoving the papers aside in disgust. The people could have chosen as their champion a truly wise and good man, a brilliant governor, a courageous defender of the Negro, a tireless enemy of slavery, but instead they had settled for an unpolished, untried country lawyer, a one-term congressman from the wilds of Illinois—all because he told entertaining stories, could make a good speech, and wasn't William H. Seward.

The people would realize their mistake in due course, but by then it would be too late.

Where Kate was disappointed and indignant, her father felt betrayed, bitter, and hurt. In the immediate aftermath of the convention, he could not conceal his fury at the delegates of Ohio for refusing to rally behind him unanimously. "When I reflect upon what Illinois did for Lincoln, what New York did for Seward, and what Missouri did for Bates," he told Kate one morning as they strolled through the garden, her arm through his, "and then when I consider the actions of the Ohio delegation, I confess it wrenches my heart."

"There is no excuse for their treachery," Kate said hotly. "The outcome would have been entirely different had they been true."

Although Father was tormented by thoughts of what might have been, he nevertheless mustered up the good grace to send his best regards to the victor. "I congratulate you most heartily on your nomination," he wrote to Mr. Lincoln in Springfield, "and shall support you, in 1860, as cordially and earnestly as I did in 1858." He praised the platform adopted at the convention and the selection of Hannibal Hamlin, "that true & able man," as the nominee for vice-president. "They will prove, I am confident, as auspicious to the country as they are honorable to the nominees."

Soon thereafter, Mr. Lincoln responded with a gracious letter of his own. "Holding myself the humblest of all whose names were before the convention," he wrote, "I feel in especial need of the assistance of all; and I am glad—very glad—of the indication that you stand ready."

Mr. Lincoln's sincere humility mollified Kate's anger somewhat. "At least he realizes that he needs your help," she said, returning the letter to her father. "Will you, as he puts it, 'do service in the common cause'?"

"Of course," Father responded solemnly. "No amount of personal disappointment could compel me to forsake my duty to my country."

Kate had never been more proud of him.

Mr. Lincoln was right to admit that he needed help if he were to win the national election, and some help came to him unwittingly from an unlikely quarter—the Democratic Party. After their convention in Charleston had ended in shambles, the Southern delegates who had walked out were replaced by other men from their states when the Democrats officially reconvened in Baltimore on June 18. There, to no one's surprise, Mr. Douglas was chosen as the party's nominee. Five days later, elsewhere in the city, the excluded Southern delegates defiantly held their own convention, where they nominated former congressman and current vice-president John C. Breckinridge, a Kentuckian who adamantly insisted that the Constitution permitted slavery throughout the states and new territories. Further crowding the slate of presidential candidates was Mr. John Bell of Tennessee, the nominee of the Constitutional Union Party, an alliance of conservative Know-Nothings and Whigs whose simple platform suggested that their approach to the slavery question was to ignore it altogether. With the Democrats splintered, the outlook for a Republican victory in November seemed promising, although Kate and her father agreed that the battle for electoral votes would likely break along geographic lines, with Mr. Lincoln battling Mr. Douglas for the Northern states and Mr. Breckinridge and Mr. Bell for the Southern. But as Kate had noted on the last day of the convention, Mr. Douglas had trounced Mr. Lincoln before. The Republicans could take nothing for granted.

His loyalty to the party stronger than its loyalty to him, Father kept his promise and campaigned on behalf of his former rival in midsummer and into the fall, just as he had when Mr. Lincoln ran for the Senate in 1858.

In September, Father decided to take time away from his electioneering for a trip to Cleveland to attend the dedication of a monument to Commodore Oliver Hazard Perry, the "Hero of Lake Erie," who had commanded the American naval forces in tremendous, unprecedented victories against the Royal Navy in the War of 1812. Father's good friend Richard Parsons, a Cleveland attorney and the Speaker of the state House of Representatives, had invited the Chases to be his honored guests during their visit.

"A trip to Washington would be more fruitful," Kate urged. "In half a year you will be in the Senate again. There is no time like the present to begin building a coalition."

"It will not look well if I don't go to Cleveland," Father said, surprised by her reluctance. "The people will think I sulk at home, or that I begrudge a hero his accolades. No, Katie, I must go, and I would have you come with me."

"Take Nettie instead."

"I wish to take you both." His brow furrowed. "You usually relish this sort of pageantry. Why don't you want to go? Is it because Columbus didn't celebrate for me back in May?"

"No, it's not that." Kate had not even thought of the canceled fireworks and the muted bands and the melancholy single-cannon salute since the last night of the Republican Convention. "Every notable Ohioan will be in Cleveland, and I confess I haven't forgiven those who betrayed you in Chicago."

"Dear Katie." Her father held her at arm's length and studied her sympathetically. He did not have to incline his head far to meet her gaze; for most of her life he had seemed to tower over her, a powerful figure taking up most of her small sky, but now he did so only in her heart and memory. "You must be brave, brave and practical. When I return to the Senate in March, I'll need friends if I am to push through the good works I intend to accomplish. We must show them we are not cowed, and that we are not broken. They will remember how I bear this disappointment four years hence."

She knew he was right, and that it was folly to hold a grudge against the people upon whom her father's political future might depend.

"Come, now," her father cajoled. Suddenly she realized that he did not want to go without her; he would if he must, but he would not impress voters and dignitaries half as well without her by his side. "There will be a ball, and you may buy a new dress. Silk, if you wish."

"Oh, well, that's a different matter entirely," she replied, managing a smile. Whereas other women of their class adorned themselves in silk and jewels on special occasions, Kate wore white linen and flowers. Others praised her simple, elegant style, saying that it suited her youth and did not distract from her own natural beauty. What they did not know was that linen and flowers were the best her father could afford, and she happily would have bedecked herself in diamonds if permitted. "You didn't tell me I could have a new silk dress."

He smiled back, greatly relieved, although he promptly began to caution her not to spend too much on her gown. She tolerated his warnings fondly. Despite her father's political stature, he was not a wealthy man. They had invested a great deal of money in their home and had filled it with the trappings of success, but much of their extended family depended upon Father's support, and he often found himself short of funds. He abhorred debt nearly as much as drunkenness, but the life he had chosen demanded certain unavoidable expenditures.

Kate dutifully—but not unwillingly—ordered a new gown from her favorite New York dressmaker, who knew her measurements and her tastes and could be relied upon to work swiftly. Two days before their departure, the gown arrived—a lovely pale-green silk trimmed in exquisite lace, with a flatteringly snug bodice embellished with mother-of-pearl buttons up the front and a modest train. Nettie was pleased with her pretty frock too, a fine blue wool dress adorned with white ribbons that had once belonged to Kate but had been let out in the waist and hemmed. Father, as always, would dress impeccably, in a well-fitted gray suit and a new waistcoat of burgundy brocade.

It rained heavily on the evening they traveled with Governor Dennison's party north to Cleveland on the shores of Lake Erie. Mr. Parsons, an energetic lawyer in his early thirties, was among those who met them at the station, and while the Committee on Arrangements escorted his entourage to the Angier House on the corner of Bank and Saint Clair streets, Mr. Parsons took the Chases home to his charming residence on Prospect, where his wife, Sarah, welcomed them warmly at the door. The rain had stopped but the heat of the day remained, so they took supper in the shady garden. Afterward, while the Parsons' two young children, a girl and a boy, played nearby and Nettie wandered off with a sketchbook and pencils to draw a bird's nest she had found nestled in the crook of a tree, Kate and her father and the Parsonses talked politics. While Mr. Parsons would have preferred to vote for Father in November, he and his wife found Mr. Lincoln a satisfactory and even appealing alternative, but reports of increasing rancor between North and South troubled them deeply. "Mr. Lincoln must win," Mr. Parsons said, "and yet, if he does, I cannot imagine that the South will not respond with violence."

"*When* Mr. Lincoln wins," Father replied, with decisive emphasis, "the slave powers will discover that their influence in Washington City has diminished precipitously. They will have no choice but to abandon slavery—immediately, as I would have it, or gradually and with compensation for their financial losses, as Mr. Lincoln seems more inclined to do."

"There is another choice," Mr. Parsons reminded him. "War."

Father shook his head. "The South would have to be a conglomeration of fools to start a war they have no chance of winning. They lack the resources, the men, and the will to go to war. Generations of slaveholding have rendered them soft and self-indulgent. They preen and polish their swords and threaten duels, but they will not go to war."

"Then let us not even speak of it," urged Mrs. Parsons, shaking her head so that the chestnut-brown curls framing her face bounced lightly. "It is too dreadful a subject to contemplate on such a fine autumn evening, with so many delightful events awaiting us."

The gentlemen nodded politely and agreed, as did Kate, although she happily would have discussed politics all evening and well into the night. Some women considered a keen interest in politics unbecoming in a lady, but thankfully, Father had no such prejudices.

The rain resumed overnight and continued throughout the next day, which Father devoted to meeting with acquaintances and potential allies from the realms of business and politics, not only to support Mr. Lincoln's candidacy but also to prepare for his return to the Senate. Kate knew that he had been right to insist that they come. The city hummed with excitement and possibility, and as she made her own round of calls escorted by Mrs. Parsons, she made sure to court old acquaintances as well as to arrange for introductions to the wives and daughters of gentlemen who might have occasion to help her father someday. She and her father were a formidable team, she thought, even when they toiled separately.

Sunday morning dawned bright and promising, the downpours and oppressively sultry air of the previous two days at last giving way to the cool, clear breezes of autumn. The heavy rains had wet down the streets sufficiently to keep down the dust, and yet not enough to make them impassible rivers of mud, so after breakfast Mrs. Parsons took Kate and Nettie out driving to view the preparations for the next day's celebration.

Numerous military regiments that would march in the grand parade had bivouacked at Camp Perry on the county fairgrounds, where their brilliant regalia, shining brass, and neat rows of white tents lent a thrilling martial air to the scene. There Mrs. Parsons and the Chase sisters left the carriage, lifted their skirts to pick their way across the soft, damp grass, and joined the throng of admiring onlookers lining the parade grounds as the soldiers marched and drilled in preparation for the grand procession. When a cavalry regiment passed swiftly by, hooves flashing and manes tossing and banners flying, Kate was rendered breathless from excitement.

As the cavalry regiment circled and passed again, Kate's gaze flew to the young, dark-haired officer in the lead. "Who is he?" she heard herself ask. He sat his horse as naturally as if he had been in the saddle all his life, and despite his youth, his bearing was one of a man accustomed to command.

"That's William Sprague, the governor of Rhode Island." Mrs. Parsons watched him pass. "They call him the Boy Governor. He's no more than thirty."

Astonished, Kate kept his eyes fixed on his back as he rode away. "A governor, and a cavalry officer, at thirty?"

"And an extraordinarily successful man of business too. He and his brother—I think it was an elder brother, but perhaps it was a cousin—founded the A. & W. Sprague Company. Have you heard of it?" When Kate shook her head, Mrs. Parsons continued. "They run cotton mills in Rhode Island. That remarkable young man is worth millions."

Kate felt her cheeks grow warm as the Rhode Island regiment passed again, and she deliberately tore her gaze away from the gallant figure on horseback to face Mrs. Parsons. "Commodore Perry was a native son of Rhode Island, if I recall," she said. "I suppose that's why so many Rhode Islanders have made the long journey west for this occasion. Soldiers, politicians, newspapermen—and I see many of them have brought their wives and children."

"Yes, indeed." An amused smile played in the corners of Mrs. Parsons's mouth. "But Governor Sprague did not, because he is not yet married."

"I wonder why," Kate said, as if she were only vaguely interested. "Too busy, I suppose. Businessman, governor, officer—any one of those occupations is usually enough for one man, and he is trying to do all three."

Mrs. Parsons looked as if she was struggling not to laugh. "Trying, and from what I hear, succeeding tremendously."

Kate shaded her eyes, deliberately looked in the other direction, and resisted the urge to ask what else Mrs. Parsons had heard of the gentleman from Rhode Island. "Nettie, look how neatly and precisely arranged the soldiers' tents are. How do you suppose they do it? With a peg and a long piece of string to mark a straight line?"

Nettie tore her gaze away from the horses to peer up at her sister. "I don't know," she said, in a tone that implied it was her sister's manner and not the question that baffled her.

The next morning the sun rose brilliant in a sky of white-puffed blue, with no threat of rain. Governor Dennison had invited Father to ride in the parade as a member of his contingent, but he had declined, explaining that he would see very little of the glorious procession if he were in it. Kate knew that was not the only reason, if only because without his spectacles, Father would see very little of the parade no matter where he was. Some politicians—Mr. Lincoln, perhaps—might enjoy waving and smiling and nodding graciously on public display for hours at a time, but Father would find it a painful ordeal. Instead the Chases joined the Parsons in an excellent spot on the public square in the viewing stands reserved for honored guests.

And what a glorious procession it was, and what a perfect view they had of every band, every regiment, every gray-bearded veteran! First came the parade marshals and assistant marshals and their staffs, followed by a band playing a spirited march, then the First Regiment of Cleveland Light Artillery, the pride of the city, and the Brooklyn Light Artillery and the Cleveland Light Dragoons. Rousing cheers for the local boys had scarcely begun to fade when another band marched proudly past in time with their exuberant tune. Next came General Wilson of Pennsylvania and his staff accompanied by the Hibernian Guards, the Cleveland Grays, and other military corps. The Union Cornet Band followed, and more Pennsylvania regiments, proudly and neatly attired, and a contingent of politicians and other officials, including Governor Dennison and his staff, and then—Kate felt an electric jolt of recognition—Governor Sprague, seeming even younger and bolder and more handsome surrounded by a distinguished company of legislators and other dignitaries from Rhode Island.

Watching them approach, Kate felt an unsettlingly, dizzying mixture of euphoria and dismay. "There's the governor now," Father said, recognizing him later than his more keen-eyed daughters. He meant Ohio's governor, of course, but Kate nodded and applauded along with everyone else, her gaze fixed on the Boy Governor following close behind Mr. Dennison. And then, just as the Rhode Island company reached their viewing stand, Mr. Sprague glanced up into the throng of onlookers and his eyes met Kate's. He smiled, removed his hat, and bowed in her direction—although even as she inclined her head in gracious acknowledgment of his salute, she told herself that she might have only imagined that the gesture was meant for her, when of course he could have intended it for any one of the dozens of people around her, or indeed, the entire crowd.

She felt an elbow in her side, and when she started and tore her gaze away from Governor Sprague, she found Nettie grinning up at her. Kate sighed and gazed heavenward, but as Nettie giggled, she returned her attention to the procession only to find that the Rhode Islanders had passed and that a bright brass band had taken their place.

It was a sublimely beautiful scene after the procession ended and the Reverend Doctor Perry of Natchez took the stage and commenced the inauguration with a solemn prayer—golden sunlight streaming through the green trees upon the vast sea of humanity; the fountain cascading behind the platform, its dancing waters sparkling and casting rainbows upon the onlookers. After the reverend closed his lengthy invocation and the vast crowd replied with a reverential amen, Mr. Walcott the artist came forward, nervous and pale, and removed the starred-and-striped draping from his marble creation. A long, silent moment of anxious, eager gazing and expectant half holding of breaths followed, and then from tens of thousands of throats came such a roar of approval that the air and earth seemed to reverberate with the joyful sound. The applause and cheering went on and on, but when it began to subside, Mr. Walcott, looking tremulous but much relieved, came forward to thank them for the kind expression of their favor and to explain the inspiration for his design. "No sculptor ever had a nobler subject," he declared, and was met with shouts of agreement.

The mayor of Cleveland spoke next, and after a band played, the Honorable George Bancroft addressed the crowd. Other speeches, more stirring music, and the performance of Masonic rites followed, and the ceremony concluded with the performance by the Masonic Choir of an original song composed for the occasion whose lyrics included Commodore Perry's memorable declaration, "We have met the enemy and they are ours!"

Entranced by the glorious pageantry of the day, Kate nevertheless found her gaze stealing, from time to time, to Governor William Sprague, but he—to her relief and dismay and confusion—did not look her way again.

That evening, Kate dressed with special care, bathing and applying a subtle scent, enjoying the feel of the pale-green silk as it slipped over her skin. The maid arranged her auburn locks in a simple, elegant twist adorned with jasmine, her only jewelry a pearl pendant that had belonged to her mother. "You will be the loveliest girl at the ball," the maid gushed, proud of her handiwork. Kate smiled when she thanked her, but when the maid turned away she frowned critically at her reflection in the mirror. She had been blessed with thick hair in a rich auburn hue, entrancing hazel eyes that could seem green or brown or even amber depending upon the light and the color of her attire, and smooth, fair skin that at the moment fairly glowed with anticipation, but her nose turned up pertly, not unattractively so but just enough to prevent her from being truly beautiful in the classic sense. She liked her nose perfectly well and usually dismissed criticism of her most obvious flaw as the spiteful ramblings of the jealous, and it annoyed her that she should suddenly worry and fret about it on that of all nights.

Nettie, who was not yet out in society, settled resignedly down to her sketch pad and pencils as Father escorted Kate outside to the carriage where Mr. and Mrs. Parsons waited. It was a short drive to the grand ballroom in the heart of the city, but progress through the crowded streets was slow. The roads were packed with carriages and men on horseback, the sidewalks lined with the envious and admiring who had not been invited but could not resist turning out to glimpse the gleaming carriages and splendid attire of the more fortunate.

When their driver finally halted before the front portico, Kate was thankful for her father's imposing size and commanding manner as they made their way through the press of eager onlookers to the front door. Inside, the vast, airy space had been sumptuously bedecked in flowers and bunting in patriotic hues and silk banners illustrated with scenes from the Battle of Lake Erie, naval insignia, or symbols of the great states of Ohio and Rhode Island. After the usual perfunctory greetings were made to all the appropriate people, Kate surrendered entirely to the delights of the evening. The orchestra was in excellent form, the music enchanting, the ladies brilliant in their jewels and finest gowns, the gentlemen attentive and charming. She was never without a partner for the dance unless she wanted to rest, and as she whirled about the ballroom, smiling and laughing and chatting easily with agreeable young men, she felt a rush of exhilaration knowing that she was one of the most graceful, intriguing, and desirable women in the room. It was intoxicating, the constant outpouring of admiration from young officers and mature statesmen alike. In a moment of wistful reflection, it occurred to her that she had probably received more praise from other gentlemen that evening than she had received from her father over the course of a lifetime.

The evening was nearly half over when the moment she had been expecting and dreading arrived at last—she turned from a pleasant chat with a myopic dowager to find Mr. Parsons and the dashing young governor of Rhode Island standing before her, smiling. "My dear Miss Chase," Mr. Parsons said, "I beg to introduce to you one of our honored guests—Mr. William Sprague, the governor of Rhode Island. Governor, allow me to present Miss Kate Chase, the daughter of the former governor of Ohio, Mr. Salmon Chase, who is also our former and future senator."

"Yes, of course," said Kate, adding a note of surprise to her voice as she extended her hand gracefully, as if she had not been surreptitiously watching him throughout the evening. "I recognize you from the procession. I congratulate you, Governor. What a magnificent company of men you command."

"Thank you, Miss Chase." He took her hand, smiling, and she felt the warmth of his skin through her glove. He was of slighter build than he had seemed on horseback, but his dark eyes were more compelling than at a distance, his smile more stirring. "They're the pride of Rhode Island. Have you ever visited our beautiful state?"

"I'm sorry to say that I have not."

"You must come when you return to Washington City, you and your father. It would be my great pleasure to show him our statehouse and speak with him, governor to governor, so that I might benefit from his wisdom and experience."

"I'm sure he would enjoy that," Kate replied. "As for his wisdom, I benefit from it daily, but he possesses it in such abundance that I am not too miserly to share."

Mr. Parsons chuckled, and as the orchestra and dancers finished a quadrille, Governor Sprague started as if he had suddenly remembered something previously overlooked. "Miss Chase, may I have the honor of the next dance?"

Graciously she agreed, bade Mr. Parsons good-bye for the moment, and allowed Governor Sprague to lead her to the dance floor. The orchestra struck up a sweet, slow waltz, and he took her in his arms and into the dance. Their eyes were nearly level, and he held her gaze with such self-assurance that she needed all her strength to fend off a sudden bout of shyness. "Tell me, Governor," she asked, "how did the procession appear from your perspective?"

And so, in the most modest and amiable terms, he told her what he had seen, praising the fine weather, the charming city, and the enthusiasm of the citizens who had come out to watch and cheer and honor one of Rhode Island's most illustrious and beloved sons. When the waltz ended, since their conversation had not, they lined up for the schottische together by mutual, unspoken agreement, although that was not strictly proper. One dance led to another, followed by a respite to refresh themselves with a glass of punch for her and wine for him, and then they danced again, chatting easily all the while.

When they had exhausted the subject of the day's ceremonies, the young governor confessed his admiration for her father, and it soon became evident that his knowledge of Salmon P. Chase's political and legal achievements rivaled her own. Governor Sprague was a stalwart abolition man—yet another virtue—and he spoke admiringly about her father's legal work in Cincinnati on behalf of the Negro, including the defenses of numerous slaves who had found themselves in the free state of Ohio and had desperately desired to remain. "There was a case of a young slave woman," he recalled, "the daughter of her master—"

"Matilda," Kate offered when he could not remember the name. She would have been too young to remember the celebrated—or as some regarded it, infamous—trial, but she had read the proceedings and knew them by heart.

"Matilda. Yes, of course. To argue that the Fugitive Slave Law did not apply in her case, because she was no fugitive as her master had brought her to Ohio himself"—Governor Sprague shook his head admiringly as the music ended and he led her off the dance floor—"that was a stroke of genius."

"It didn't work," Kate reminded him. "My father lost that case. Matilda was returned to her master and carried off back to the South." Her father had never learned what had become of the young woman he had so fiercely defended, and her unknown but surely unhappy fate haunted him to that day.

"Even so, it was an ingenious tactic, and it struck another blow to the legal justification of slavery. Enough such strikes, and the foundation will crumble."

The governor's sincere and enthusiastic admiration for her father pleased her, and yet she found it vaguely upsetting that although they had spent every moment of the ball together since Mr. Parsons had introduced them, they had spoken of little else but the procession, the beauties of Rhode Island, and Salmon P. Chase. "Governor Sprague," she said lightly as he offered her his arm, pretending not to notice the naval officer who was quickly approaching, evidently eager to engage Kate before she was whisked off again, "I would almost think that you would rather dance with my father than myself, you speak of him with such constant admiration."

"Certainly not," he protested as the orchestra struck up a lively polka. "He's much too tall for me."

Kate burst out laughing. "Governor, you are . . ."

"What?" he prompted, smiling and pulling her closer than was necessary for a polka.

"Let me think." She pondered her words as they whirled about. "You are unlike any other man I've ever met."

His brows rose. "In what way?"

He was not transformed into a dazed, blathering fool by her mere presence, for one, but she certainly could not tell him that. "I have not been in society long, but I have discovered that men seem to enjoy telling me about my beautiful eyes, my rosebud mouth, my glorious crown of auburn hair, my swanlike neck—have I left out anything?"

"Your graceful, sylphlike figure?" he suggested helpfully.

"Yes, of course. How could I have forgotten that? *They* never do. But you, Governor, you have not spoken a word about any of that all evening."

"Why should I have done?" he asked, making a show of being genuinely puzzled, although she did not believe it for a moment. "I presume you own a mirror and that your eyes are functional as well as enchanting. You should not need me to describe you to yourself."

"Ah! And yet here you have done it at last," she remarked, strangely triumphant. "You have called my eyes enchanting."

"As indeed they must be, because you have charmed a compliment out of me, when I have been doing my very best to stand firm and to reveal nothing." Suddenly he pulled her close until his mouth brushed her ear, his breath warm on her cheek. "You should settle for the compliment to your eyes, for if you were to conjure the entire truth out of me, you would learn that I find you the most alluring, intoxicating woman I've ever met, and that if we were alone and you were mine, I would caress your face and kiss you until we were both breathless from desire. And that confession, Miss Chase, is not fit for an innocent young lady to hear."

His tight hold upon her loosened, and she instinctively pulled away, but his right hand was pressed firmly against her back and his left clasped around hers, so she could not go far. He smiled benignly as if he had said nothing untoward, but she knew that was a show for anyone who might be watching and that he had meant every word. She was still too shocked to do anything but stare at him, speechless, and when he held her gaze too long she felt a tremor of warmth spreading through her until she could barely finish the dance, which mercifully ended soon thereafter.

When the last merry notes faded away, the governor escorted her to the edge of the dance floor, where he bowed to her politely and walked away. Within moments the naval officer appeared and asked her for the next dance, but she scarcely heard him. When he asked a second time, she managed a smile and a nod, but she felt clumsy and stiff in his arms, and she could barely hold up her end of the conversation. Afterward, the lieutenant led her from the floor and thanked her courteously for the dance, but he was clearly disappointed and he did not ask her again.

Nor did Governor Sprague. As the ball came to a close, Kate glimpsed the governor on the dance floor with other smiling young belles in his arms, and once she was startled to discover him engaged in earnest conversation with her father as if he had not been murmuring indecently into his daughter's ear not long before. But he did not speak to Kate again, neither to apologize nor to bid her good night.

It was not embarrassment or shame that kept him from her. She knew that, though she could not say how she knew, nor what it was that restrained him.

Chapter Four

*K*ate thought she might hear from Governor Sprague before the Chases left Cleveland, but he sent no word to her at the Parsons residence, nor did he write to her in Columbus upon her return home. Bewildered, she tried to put him out of her mind, and to forget the strange, unsettling effect he had upon her. He intimated that she had enchanted him, and yet she felt as if he had worked some sort of mesmerism upon her instead. She had not found a man so distracting since the shameful episode of her youth she had tried so hard to expunge from memory. It was a relief and a blessing, she told herself as she resumed the familiar routines of home, that half of a continent separated them, and that it was not likely she would see him again.

As the vivid hues of autumn stole over the forests and fields of Ohio, political fervor seized the nation. Father resumed his electioneering for Mr. Lincoln, and he soon learned that he was not the only former candidate for the Republican nomination to come out in support of the man who had unexpectedly defeated him. Mutual friends confirmed rumors that Mr. Thurlow Weed, Mr. Seward's longtime political advisor, had visited Mr. Lincoln in Springfield and had come away much impressed with his intuitive knowledge of human nature and the virtues and caprice of politicians. Mr. Weed began to work quietly on Mr. Lincoln's behalf, and eventually, although Mr. Seward had been rendered so dejected by his upset in Chicago that he had contemplated resigning from the Senate and retiring to his estate in Auburn, he too campaigned for Mr. Lincoln, embarking on a lengthy speaking tour on his erstwhile rival's behalf. Judge Edward Bates penned an open letter published in newspapers both Northern and Southern in which he extolled Mr. Lincoln's virtues and conservative values, and declared that he intended to support the Republican ticket. He praised especially Mr. Lincoln's fairness, his commitment to nationalism rather than sectional politics, and his "high reputation for truth, courage, candor, morals and ability."

Kate understood well that Father and his fellow newly made Lincoln-ites had their work cut out for them. In order to win the election, Mr. Lincoln would have to capture at least 152 of the 303 electoral votes. Since he was unlikely to pick up any in the slaveholding South—in some Southern states he would not even appear on the ballot—he would have to take almost the entire North. That would be no small feat, considering that in some of the most important Northern states—Ohio, Indiana, and Pennsylvania—Mr. Douglas was quite popular in border counties where many natives of Southern states had settled.

It did not help that Mr. Lincoln was a stranger to a vast number of men he urgently needed to vote for him. He was so little known even within his own party that after the convention, there had been some confusion within the Republican press whether his given name was Abraham or Abram. In Washington City, news of his nomination had been met with general incredulity, and Democratic newspapers gleefully ridiculed his humble origins, calling him a "third-rate Western lawyer"—a sentiment Kate herself had been guilty of harboring—and a "fourth-rate lecturer who cannot speak good grammar" and whose illiterate speeches were "interlarded with coarse and clumsy jokes"—a claim she knew from her own experience was patently untrue. Not surprisingly, the Southern press provided the most blistering vitriol, mocking not only Mr. Lincoln's intellect, which they wrongly assumed to be quite insignificant, but also his appearance. "Lincoln is the leanest, lankest, most ungainly mass of legs, arms and hatchet-face ever strung upon a single frame," the *Houston Telegraph* declared with fascinated horror. "He has most unwarrantably abused the privilege which all politicians have of being ugly." Remarking upon Mr. Lincoln's image in *Harper's Weekly*, the *Charleston Mercury* proclaimed, "A horrid looking wretch he is, sooty and scoundrelly in aspect, a cross between the nutmeg dealer, the horse swapper, and the night man, a creature fit evidently for petty treason, small strategems, and all sorts of spoils." Kate found such lurid prose utterly unfair; Mr. Lincoln might not be what most people would consider handsome, but he was not the grotesquerie depicted in the papers, either. There were enough legitimate reasons to criticize Mr. Lincoln without inventing fictions.

Someone—the indefatigable Mr. Weed, perhaps, or another Republican ally, or even Mr. Lincoln himself—must have carefully crafted a response, because as the weeks passed, more favorable reports began to appear in the press, at least in the North. Mr. Lincoln's friend published a brief, modest, and yet compelling biography about him, which sold more than a million copies. At his home in Springfield Mr. Lincoln met with reporters, who invariably departed with favorable impressions, which they expressed in glowing phrases to their readers back home. His life, home, and habits came under scrutiny, but none held more fascination for Kate than the accounts of his wife, Mary Todd Lincoln. She was said to be as graceful as her husband was awkward, her family as distinguished as her husband's was humble. Mrs. Lincoln was well educated and refined, the reporters enthused; self-assured, vivacious, and handsome; fluent in French; and a fascinating conversationalist. She was a devout member of the Presbyterian Church and the mother of three living sons, of whom the eldest, Robert, was a student at Harvard College. Kate was as curious about Mr. Lincoln's wife as everyone else, and she concluded that if the newspaper reports were reliable, Mary Lincoln would be an asset to her husband and bring dignity and grace to his administration.

Kate suspected that in Washington City, Adele Douglas was following the newspaper reports too, sizing up her newest rival. As much as Kate liked her friend and wished for her happiness, she would rather see Mrs. Lincoln assume the role of First Lady if it meant that Mr. Douglas had been denied the White House. Mr. Lincoln was not as ardent an abolitionist as her father, but he was far better on the issue than Mr. Douglas, who seemed content to let the poison of slavery spread across the continent if it would appease the South.

As November approached, the results of early fall elections boded well for Mr. Lincoln, with sweeping Republican victories in local and state elections in Vermont, Maine, Pennsylvania, Ohio, and Indiana. Then, at long last and yet before Kate felt quite prepared for it, Election Day arrived.

On that momentous morning, Kate and Nettie accompanied Father to the polls and proudly stood by as he cast his ballot. "I hope you wrote in your own name," Kate murmured as they walked home, and her father rewarded her with a smile.

It was a long, anxious day, painfully reminiscent of the time in mid-May when they had waited with dwindling hopes for the results from the Republican Convention. Father had arranged for a messenger, the fifteen-year-old son of one of his clerks from his time as governor, to wait at the telegraph office and bring him the election returns as they came down the wire. By early evening, the boy had come by to announce that Mr. Lincoln had won the New England states. An hour and a half later he returned, and when Will, Father's servant, escorted him to Father's study, he was out of breath and so wild-eyed that Kate's heart plummeted and she was certain he would announce that Mr. Douglas had won the presidency. Instead he gasped out, "Mr. Lincoln won Pennsylvania, and the Neil House is on fire!"

Father bolted from his chair. "The alarm," he muttered. Not long after he had sent Nettie to bed, he and Kate had heard the bells pealing, but they had taken it as an announcement that the polls would soon close, and had attributed the faint odor of smoke to the bonfires and torches of the Wide Awakes, Republican men who marched in the streets clad in uniforms of full capes and black glazed hats and kept vigil at polling places.

"How bad is the fire?" Kate asked the messenger boy. The Neil House, the largest and most elegant hotel in Columbus, occupied an entire block on High Street across from the capitol and had hosted countless visiting dignitaries since it was built in 1842. It was impossible to imagine the city landscape without it.

"Terrible," he said eagerly, edging toward the door as if he needed all his willpower to not to break into a run.

"Don't linger to gape at the scene," Father admonished him sternly. "I need you at the telegraph office."

"Yes, sir, Mr. Chase," he said, and darted off without waiting for Will to show him out.

Kate pressed a hand to her stomach and inhaled shakily. "I hope all the guests escaped unharmed."

"Yes," said Father distantly. He had stayed at the Neil House numerous times while traveling on political and legal business before becoming governor, and in the years since, he had attended more meetings and luncheons there than Kate could count. Its public rooms were so lively with political activity that some wags claimed it was the real capitol. If the blaze was as bad as the messenger said, at that moment, a significant part of Columbus history was turning to ashes.

Abruptly Father turned and strode from the library.

"Father?" Kate called, hurrying after him. She caught up to him in the front foyer, where he had summoned Will to bring his coat. "Where are you going?"

"To observe the progress of the fire."

"I'll come with you."

"No, Katie." He slipped his arms into the coat as Will held it open. "It's too dangerous."

"I'll stay well back from the flames." She gestured to Will to fetch her wraps too, but he hesitated, glancing from her to Father and back, unwilling to displease either of them.

"I was referring not to the flames but to the thick smoke, and its effect on your weak lungs."

"I don't have weak lungs," Kate replied, a trifle sharply. She had suffered more than the usual childhood ailments, perhaps, but that was years ago, and her lungs were as robust as anyone's. "I need a distraction as much as you."

"Katie—" Father broke off and regarded her with mild exasperation. Then he relented, and after admonishing her that she must cover her nose and mouth with a handkerchief and be certain not to get in the way of the men fighting the blaze, he told her to put on her wraps. She did so, and within minutes they were hurrying off down State Street west toward the capitol.

From a distance, they saw dark smoke rising above the trees and rooftops and churning into the night sky. As they hurried closer, they heard the roaring and snapping of the blaze. Shock brought them to an abrupt halt when they reached the corner of State and Third, for across the Capitol Square grounds they saw the Neil House engulfed in flames.

All the fire companies had come out, dozens upon dozens of men racing to subdue the blaze, but it seemed impossible that they could succeed. Five stories of black walnut, Kate thought numbly. More than three hundred suites. Beautifully appointed lobbies and sitting rooms, the site of countless political debates and negotiations and immeasurable intrigue. Ashes to ashes, she thought. Dust to dust. So everything ends.

Her eyes stinging from smoke, she turned her head away to blink and to clear her throat, and it was then that she noticed the men milling about on the capitol grounds, a few in their nightclothes, and several women and children too. An aged woman wept and clung to a white-bearded man, likely her husband, but as Kate took an instinctive step toward her, a woman in her middle years ran up and embraced them both, her face a study of fright and relief.

"It is both glorious and terrible, is it not?" her father said at her side.

Kate glanced up at him, startled, uncertain whether she had heard him correctly. She saw nothing glorious in the destruction and terror roaring like a monstrous, ravenous beast in the heart of the city. "How do you mean?"

"It is grand to see the fire gradually prevail over the enormous ruin," he said, his gaze fixed on the conflagration. "It is sickening to feel human impotence to avert the devastation. See, look there—burning embers are drifting on the hot wind raised by the flames, and they fall upon the roof of the Odeon Theater. The Neil House is lost. All we can hope now is that the fire will be extinguished before it spreads."

Kate stared at him a moment before turning her gaze back to the inferno. "You don't suppose . . ." She hesitated. "Surely this was an accident?"

He threw her a curious look. "We have no reason to believe it was not. When the fire is extinguished, the authorities will examine the ruins and determine the cause." He tucked her hand through his arm. "You needn't fear that a mad arsonist is on the loose."

"It just seems so . . . strange, that this should happen tonight, of all nights."

"Pure coincidence," Father said firmly. "If it were meant as an act of intimidation to keep voters from the polls, your mad arsonist would have struck earlier in the day, and the statehouse itself would be burning."

"And the polling places too," added Kate dubiously, not entirely believing it.

Her throat tightened and she coughed to clear it, just a small, barely audible cough, but enough to convince her father that she had spent quite enough time gazing, stunned and horror-stricken, at the fiery death throes of the celebrated city landmark, the stately edifice that represented, perhaps second only to the statehouse itself, the bringing together of divergent voices in the marvelous experiment of democracy.

"It's difficult not to see a foreboding portent in this," Kate said as they walked along State Street to home, weaving their way past the men and boys hurrying in the opposite direction toward the fire.

"Do you mean as a fearsome warning that Mr. Lincoln will lose the election?" Father shook his head, frowning impatiently. He abhorred superstition and fortune-telling, the sort of popular spiritualism that seized hold of the weak-minded and unfaithful, tempting them away from Christian truth.

"No, not that," said Kate, quickly adding, "and I don't mean that I believe it to be an omen, but rather a symbol, a dreadful sign of what might become of the country after Mr. Lincoln takes the White House."

"It is just a fire," said her father. "A terrible fire, but no more than that. There is no divine message, no demonic cause in it."

"I know." She held tighter to his arm, wishing she could shut her ears to the roar and snap of the inferno, that she could close her nostrils to the terrible scorched odor of smoke and ember. "I pray no one was hurt."

When they reached home, she washed her face and hands and brushed her hair and changed clothes, but the smell of smoke lingered as if she had taken it into herself. Soon thereafter, the messenger returned with the news that the Odeon Theater had caught fire, and that Mr. Lincoln had won the Northwest and Indiana. Kate quickly calculated that he still needed New York to claim a majority of the electoral votes, and the realization set her heart pounding with trepidation. New York City's substantial Irish population, strongly Democrat, was likely to go for Mr. Douglas.

By ten o'clock, Father had begun intermittent pacing in his office, and Kate had recited all the prayers she knew and had begun, reluctantly, to compose a congratulatory letter to Mrs. Douglas in her head. And then, just before eleven o'clock, the weary young messenger brought word from New York that Mr. Lincoln had made steady and promising gains throughout the state, but the results from New York City had not been tallied in sufficient percentages for the Republicans to claim victory.

"But the returns from the city will decide it," Kate said, her father's vigorous nods indicating that he shared the same thought. "Without that, the state returns are meaningless. If Mr. Douglas builds up a sufficient majority in the city, he could easily overcome Mr. Lincoln's lead elsewhere in the state."

And without New York's precious thirty-five electoral votes, Mr. Lincoln would fall seven short of a majority.

Father urged her to bed, but Kate demurred, noting that she was too anxious to sleep anyway. She fixed them a pot of tea, and prepared a tray of cream and sugar and sweet buns, and when she returned to the library she found that her father had set up the chessboard. "I thought we could have a game to distract ourselves," he said, his exhaustion and worry etched in lines and shadows on his strong, handsome face.

They had finished one game and started another when, shortly after midnight, church bells began to peal—first one, and then another, until it seemed that all the steeples of Columbus rang with the news that a president had been chosen. But whom? Father and daughter exchanged a silent, hopeful, anxious look, and then, the game forgotten, they hurried to the foyer to await the messenger.

He arrived soon thereafter, breathless from his mad dash through the streets of Columbus, and yet he seemed exultant, knowing he was sure to receive a generous gratuity for the happy news he carried.

New York had gone to Mr. Lincoln, and Mr. Lincoln would go to the White House.

The response of the press to Mr. Lincoln's election was swift and unsurprising. One Kansas paper referred to the news of his victory as "glorious tidings," while the *Richmond Dispatch* gloomily intoned, "The event is the most deplorable one that has happened in the history of the country." A Massachusetts editor was more sanguine, reassuring his readers that a Lincoln presidency would not "mean evil to any section of the country. It is not only regular and lawful, but is necessary to restore the old spirit and policy of the country, and give peace to the land." The *Courier* of New Orleans sharply disagreed, warning that the election had "awakened throughout the South a spirit of stubborn resistance which it will be found is impossible to quell." The *New York Enquirer* paid homage to the spirit of democracy and took a conciliatory approach, proclaiming, "Stretching out our hands to the South over this victory, we have no word of taunt to utter for the threats of disunion which were raised for our defeat. Let those threats be buried in oblivion." The editor of the *Semi-Weekly Mississippian* would have none of that, and beneath a headline declaring, "The Deed's Done—Disunion the Remedy," appeared a foreboding statement that Kate feared was echoed in hearts throughout the South:

> The outrages which abolition fanaticism has continued year by year to heap upon the South, have at length culminated in the election of Abraham Lincoln and Hannibal Hamlin, avowed abolitionists, to the presidency and vice presidency—both bigoted, unscrupulous and cold-blooded enemies of the peace and equality of the slaveholding states, and one of the pair strongly marked with the blood of his negro ancestry. . . . In view of the formal declaration, through the ballot box, of a purpose by the northern states to wield the vast machinery of the federal Government as now constituted, for destroying the liberties of the slaveholding states, it becomes their duty to dissolve their connection with it and establish a separate and independent government of their own.

"It never ceases to amaze me," Kate told her father, "how any reasonable person could believe that it is wrong to destroy the liberties of slaveholding states and yet perfectly acceptable to destroy the liberties of human beings. And to call for disunion so that they might persist in their cruelty"—she shook her head—"what good do they expect to come of this?"

Father reminded her that the South had been threatening to leave the Union for more than forty years, and that a certain amount of heightened agitation and a frenzied clamor for secession could be expected in the aftermath of such a hard-fought election. "Nothing will come of these calls for disunion," he assured Kate. "They will subside after Mr.

Lincoln's inauguration, just as they always have, and Congress will settle down to the usual squabbling and deal making."

Kate hoped he was right, but in the midst of the postelection turmoil, it was still unclear whether Father would be involved in that squabbling and deal making. No cabinet position had been offered him, and his queries to mutual acquaintances received inconclusive replies. It was known that Mr. Lincoln was forming his cabinet, but whether he meant to include Father was uncertain. And so Father prepared to return to the Senate, although he told Kate that the prospect of resuming his position there disheartened him, and he would happily decline and retire from politics altogether if he thought he could do so honorably. The admission would have greatly troubled Kate if she had not known that he was merely speaking his mood of the moment, and not the true desire of his heart.

In the meantime, Father's prediction that the outrage of the South would subside proved terribly, shockingly wrong. A few days before Christmas, at a state convention held at Saint Andrew's Hall in Charleston, the delegates of South Carolina voted unanimously to secede from the Union.

Although warnings of secession had appeared with increasing frequency in Southern papers after Mr. Lincoln's election, many people in the North, including Father and President Buchanan, were astounded when South Carolina finally made good on their threat. The stock market roiled, politicians debated what to do, and citizens North and South wondered with trepidation or eagerness which state would be next to secede. Any hopes that South Carolina could swiftly be restored to the Union through negotiation were dashed when its newly appointed leaders declared that the three federal forts within its borders fell within their jurisdiction. While President Buchanan dithered over the appropriate response, perhaps wishing that Mr. Lincoln could assume his high office sooner than scheduled, the federal officer in charge of one of the forts took action. On the night of December 26, Major Robert Anderson moved his troops from their vulnerable position at Fort Moultrie on the mainland to the more defensible Fort Sumter in Charleston Harbor. The next day, South Carolina militia seized Fort Moultrie and Castle Pinckney, and demanded Major Anderson's surrender. Major Anderson declined, and instead resolutely held his post while the South Carolina military settled in for the siege.

In the midst of unprecedented national turmoil and alarm, Mr. Lincoln was still obliged to continue the work of his fledgling administration. In the early days of what boded to be a tumultuous New Year, Father received a brief letter from Springfield.

> *Hon. S. P. Chase*
> *Springfield, Ill.*
> *December 31, 1860*
>
> *My dear Sir:*
> *In these troublous times, I would much like a conference with you.*
> *Please visit me here at once.*
> *Yours very truly,*
> *A. LINCOLN*

Kate's heart jumped when she read the angular script and discerned the urgency of the request. "When will you depart?"

"Tomorrow." Father's expression was a curious mixture of joy and apprehension. "He must want to name me secretary of state immediately so I may assist him in addressing this crisis."

Father wrote back to inform the president-elect that he would leave the following day on the morning train, which would put him in Springfield on January 4. Swiftly Kate helped him pack and prepare for the journey, wishing that she might accompany him. Indeed, she saw no reason why she should not, except that her presence might suggest to Mr. Lincoln that Father regarded the visit as a social call rather than a serious matter of state.

While her father was away, Kate followed the news from Fort Sumter and Washington in the papers and waited for a telegram from Springfield that never came. Tantalizing glimpses of her father's meetings with Mr. Lincoln appeared in brief newspaper reports noting his arrival in Springfield, the quality of his lodgings at the Chenery House, and the days, locations, and duration of his visits with the president-elect. Rumors about the nature of their discussions varied so wildly that she could trust none of them. They were almost lost too, amid the flurry of reports from the East. The day Father departed for Springfield, the *Herald* reported that a steamship called the *Star of the West* had set out from New

York en route for Charleston with supplies and troops to relieve Major Anderson at Fort Sumter. Other newspapers confirmed the story, noting where and when the merchant vessel had been spotted as it journeyed south along the coast. Kate would have felt more reassured by President Buchanan's decision to take action if she were not aware that the people of Charleston could get the news from Eastern papers as easily as she could. Surely their military forces would be ready and waiting when the *Star of the West* arrived.

When Father at last returned home, nearly a week after his departure, Kate flew to the door to welcome him and help him out of his coat, but his grim, bedraggled expression stopped her short. "What's wrong?" she asked as he stood on the doorstep stamping snow from his boots. "Did Mr. Lincoln not offer you the Department of State?"

"He offered me nothing."

"What?" They had assumed from the moment Mr. Lincoln's letter had arrived that he would not have summoned Father so urgently for anything less than a cabinet position. "Why on earth did he have you travel so far for nothing?" Her father's look was so full of woebegone misery that she immediately adopted a gentler tone. "You must be exhausted. Wash up and change if you like, and by the time you come downstairs again, I'll have a hot supper waiting for you."

Father obediently trudged off, his servant Will trailing after him with his suitcase. Kate summoned the cook and put the kettle on, and when Father came to the table, his gloomy expression cleared somewhat at the sight of the plate of eggs, ham, pickled asparagus, and toast spread thickly with butter. Nettie bounded in as he seated himself and queried him about the most trivial aspects of his journey—what he had seen through the train windows, whether Mr. Lincoln truly was as ugly as everyone said—with such innocent eagerness that his misery gradually dissipated. By the time he finished eating and Nettie danced off again, his manner had become relaxed, though subdued, and he seemed ready to talk.

"It was a bewildering interview," he told Kate when they were alone. "From the tone of Mr. Lincoln's letter, I had expected the offer of a cabinet position."

"As did I," said Kate.

"I cannot help thinking that he had intended to offer me a position, but that between writing the letter and meeting me at my hotel in Springfield, something happened to change his mind." Father sighed and ran a hand over his brow. "Upon my arrival I had sent him my card and a note saying I would call when convenient. I had scarcely settled into my room when the bellman came up and told me Mr. Lincoln was waiting for me in the lobby."

"Then it *was* an urgent matter."

"So it seemed. I went down promptly to see him, and he shook my hand and thanked me heartily for my efforts on his behalf leading up to the election, as well as the stumping I did for him in 1858."

"As well he should have."

"We talked at length about the issues of the day, when quite unexpectedly, he said, 'I have done with you what I would not perhaps have ventured to do with any other man in the country—sent for you to ask whether you will accept the appointment of secretary of the treasury, without, however, being exactly prepared to offer it to you.'"

For a moment Kate could only stare at him, dumbfounded. "He offered you the Treasury, and yet did *not* offer it?"

Father sighed wearily and nodded.

"He had you travel hundreds of miles merely to gauge your interest?" Indignant, Kate folded her arms over her chest and sank back into her chair. "This was not a question you could have answered just as easily through the mails?"

Father nodded again. "You understand, then, why I was less than enthusiastic in my reply."

Kate was almost afraid to hear the answer, but she asked, "What did you say?"

"I denied that I had sought any appointment whatsoever, and I implied that if I were to be offered a cabinet post, I would not accept a subordinate place. And there our interview concluded."

Kate's heart sank with dismay, but she kept her voice even. "But that could not have been the last word, or you would have come home sooner."

"Exactly so. We met again, several times over the next few days, and Mr. Lincoln eventually revealed that he intended to make Seward his secretary of state in deference to his status as the leader of the party."

"Mr. Seward enjoys a certain prominence, to be sure," said Kate, "but no more so than you. Your lifetime of service, your experience in governance, your devotion to the cause of abolition—all mark you as equally deserving of a senior position."

"Mr. Lincoln did say that if Seward had declined, he would have offered the State Department to me without hesitation."

It seemed odd that Mr. Lincoln was apparently able to offer the highest position in the cabinet to one man, yet was somehow prevented from giving the next most important post to another. "Did Mr. Lincoln mention anyone else he is considering for secretary of the treasury?"

"No, but—" He hesitated. "On the way to Springfield, I heard rumors that Mr. Lincoln had already offered the post to General Cameron, and that he had accepted."

Bewildered, Kate shook her head. "That makes no sense. That would make your entire journey to Springfield a cruel farce. Why measure your interest in a position that has already been filled?"

"There could be any number of reasons, and I believe I have contemplated every one of them."

"Keeping in mind that one cannot decline what has not been offered . . ." Kate hesitated. "Did you decline?"

"Not outright." As Kate breathed a sigh of relief, he added, "I told him I was unprepared to accept the position if it were extended to me. I reminded him that I had six years in the Senate to look forward to, and that I could be of service to him and to the nation in that capacity as well if not better than in the cabinet." He smiled ruefully. "He didn't dispute the point, but he didn't agree either."

In the days that followed, Father and Mr. Lincoln had met again, sometimes alone, sometimes with one or two other advisors, but always to confer at great length, earnestly and seriously. Father had come away from their interviews impressed with the president-elect's grasp of the complexities of the constitutional crisis facing the nation, his willingness to accept advice, and his warm, amiable nature. On Sunday Father attended church services with Mr. and Mrs. Lincoln, and on Monday morning Mr. Lincoln saw Father off at the train station with the parting request that he consult with trusted friends about accepting the Department of Treasury post, which Mr. Lincoln was still unable to offer.

"Will you?" Kate asked, trying not to sound too hopeful. "Consult with people you trust, I mean, and consider accepting the position, should it be offered?"

"I've already begun," Father admitted. "My pride is not too great for that. I wrote to several friends from the train asking them to speak well of me to Mr. Lincoln. I confess—and this is for your ears alone, daughter—that I would like to be offered a cabinet position, but not to seem to seek it—and I don't yet know if I will accept one if it is eventually offered."

Kate nodded, greatly relieved that her father's wounded pride had not compelled him to refuse to serve in Mr. Lincoln's administration. Although he would not be first in rank, he would command a great deal of authority and influence during a time of increasing national uncertainty. She knew of no better man—none wiser, none more ethical—to be at the president's side in a crisis.

And, she admitted to herself, it could only help him in four years' time if the nation learned now what a strong, intelligent leader he was, and would be.

The morning after Father's homecoming, the newspapers were ablaze with news from South Carolina. The previous day, while Father was writing letters to trusted friends from a jolting railcar, the *Star of the West* sailed into Charleston Harbor and was fired upon by militia and young military cadets. Struck in the mast but not seriously damaged, the steamer nonetheless was forced back into the channel and out to the open sea.

On that same day, far to the south, delegates in Mississippi voted in favor of secession. The next day, Florida seceded from the Union, and the next, Alabama. One after another they fell, like books carelessly arranged on an unsteady shelf, but just when Kate began to believe that no voice of reason and prudence remained in the South, former president John Tyler, living in retirement in Richmond, Virginia, published an appeal for a convention to make one last great effort to resolve the crisis. Two days later, Georgia seceded, and two days after that, five senators from Alabama, Florida, and Mississippi—some defiantly, others full of sorrow—rose to offer farewell speeches before resigning their seats in the Senate and leaving Washington for their homes in the South. The papers somberly described how Senator Jefferson Davis, the last to speak, reiterated his opinion that states did have the constitutional right to leave the Union, and that his home state of Mississippi had justifiable cause for doing so. Even so, he regretted the conflict that had divided them. "I am sure I feel no hostility toward you, senators from the North," he said. "I am sure there is not one of you, whatever sharp discussion there may have been between us, to whom I cannot now say, in the presence of my God, I wish you well; and such, I feel, is the feeling of the people whom I represent toward those whom you represent." He expressed his hopes that their separate governments would eventually have peaceable relations, and made his own personal apology for any pain he might have inflicted upon any other senator in the heat of discussion. "Mr. President and senators," he concluded, weary from illness and strain, "having made the announcement which the occasion seemed to me to require, it only remains for me to bid you a final adieu."

Five days later, Louisiana seceded.

Although to Kate it seemed a futile effort, plans were swiftly made to organize Mr. Tyler's Peace Convention. And in the final days of January, Father at last received an appointment, though not the one he had been hoping for.

Much to Father's chagrin, for he had long been an outspoken opponent of any compromise with the secessionist and slaveholding powers, Governor Dennison appointed him a delegate to the Peace Convention in hopes that the crisis could be resolved through negotiation before Mr. Lincoln took office. Father would be returning to Washington sooner than expected, and in a role he never could have imagined and did not want.

Chapter Five

*T*his is a mortifying embarrassment," Father grumbled as he paged through a sheaf of documents Governor Dennison had sent over from his office in the capitol. "I've stated very clearly, in person and in print, that I object to any conciliation with the secessionist states until after Mr. Lincoln takes office. Dennison knows that. *Everyone* knows that. It will seem the height of hypocrisy for me to sit down with these traitors now."

"It isn't hypocritical merely to meet with them, if you don't give in to their demands." Kate glanced over his shoulder at the papers lined up neatly on his desktop. The conference would open at the Willard Hotel in Washington City on February 4, she read, and former president John Tyler himself would be the chairman. "It isn't hypocrisy to represent the state of Ohio at the request of your governor, or to listen to what the secessionists have to say for themselves. Also, don't underestimate your influence, Father. You might achieve some good there."

"I can't imagine what. I doubt that most of the rebellious states will send delegates. Those who most need to listen to reason won't be present to hear it." Shaking his head, Father organized the papers into a neat stack and placed them into the leather satchel she and Nettie had given him for Christmas the year he became governor. "Our time would be better spent strengthening the capital's defenses against an attack from the South. There are fewer than a thousand federal troops and local militia stationed around Washington, and their loyalty to the Union is by no means certain."

"Couldn't President Buchanan summon troops from the Western frontier?"

"He could, but he won't. He's afraid that a show of military strength would only heighten the tensions, so instead he's determined to be the very model of inaction." Frowning, Father set the satchel aside and rose from his desk. "I'm also displeased to be obliged to depart for Washington sooner than I had intended. I expected to have another month to prepare, to close up the house here, to find a proper home for you and your sister there."

"I'll take care of matters here," Kate reminded him, tucking her hand through his arm and giving it a reassuring pat. "Once you're in Washington, you'll be able to find temporary lodgings for us, and that will do until I join you and can begin the search for a proper home."

So Father and Nettie packed and prepared and departed Columbus for Washington, arriving on February 1. On that same day Texas seceded from the Union, as if to mock Mr. Tyler's vain hopes for peace.

Upon their arrival, Father and Nettie first stayed with longtime friends, Elizabeth and Louis M. Goldsborough, the daughter and son-in-law of Father's mentor in his legal studies, William Wirt. A few days later, Father rented a suite of rooms at the Rugby House at the corner of Fourteenth and K streets. "It used to be a private boys' school but it is newly made a hotel," Nettie wrote to Kate the day they moved in. "It is brick and in a quiet part of the city and I like it very much. I have made a friend across the hall, a gentleman by the name of Nathaniel Hawthorne, and yes, I do mean the writer. He is very shy but he is nice to me."

Kate was pleased that at last Nettie had found something to like about Washington City. Her earliest letters had been full of homesick longing for their lovely, comfortable home, for her cousins and playmates, and for the pretty, bustling city of Columbus. Nettie's first incredulous, appalled impression of Washington City was that of a squalid rural village where cows, pigs, and geese roamed freely through the streets, which were cloudy with dust on dry days and ran thick with mud when it rained. Pennsylvania Avenue and a few adjacent blocks of Seventh Street were paved, but the cobblestones were broken and uneven, and mud oozed up between the cracks.

The 156-foot stub of the Washington Monument stood forlornly in the midst of an open field where cattle grazed, its construction halted by political squabbling, uncertainty, and vandalism. The Capitol too was unfinished, but there, at least, construction continued; the incomplete, truncated dome loomed above the landscape surrounded by derricks and scaffolding, flanked by bare, unadorned marble wings and surrounded on all sides by a scattering of workers' sheds, tools, piles of bricks, and blocks of marble. Citizens dumped refuse in the old city canal, which often spilled over into the marsh to the south of the Executive Mansion grounds, and throughout the city, foul outhouses abounded, giving off a fetid miasma that the hotel keeper cheerfully warned Nettie would only worsen come spring and summer.

Kate was somewhat taken aback by her sister's critical review of their new home. Although she couldn't dispute a single one of Nettie's observations, and honesty compelled her to admit that the capital did offer a peculiar mix of grandeur and squalor in close proximity, Kate had always chosen to focus on the city's more pleasant attributes—the elaborate mansions and lovely gardens of the wealthier residents, the grand estates in the surrounding countryside, the opulent marble edifices that housed the various federal departments, and the splendid, extravagant entertainments put on by the social elite. True, it did take a bit of care and practice to navigate the city as one made one's way from dignified residence to grand reception without ruining skirts and shoes in the mud, but Kate considered that a small inconvenience compared to the exciting, invigorating rush of Washington City, and she could not wait to return.

Kate and her maid, Vina—who was unmarried and quite willing to leave Columbus for the excitement and adventure of a strange new city—traveled by train to Washington, where her father and sister met them at the station. Nettie held her hand and pointed out sights they passed along the way to the Rugby House—the Center Market on the Avenue between Seventh and Ninth streets, its stalls heaped with fruit, vegetables, fish, and beef and swarming with flies; her favorite cake and ginger-soda stands at the foot of Capitol Hill; the broad swath of grass south of the Executive Mansion where the Washington Potomacs played the popular game from New York called baseball. Hiding her amusement, Kate allowed Nettie to believe that she was glimpsing the familiar sights for the first time rather than spoil her sister's pleasure.

Father saw them safely to the large, unpretentious Rugby House before kissing Kate quickly on the cheek and apologizing for his retreat to the Peace Convention at Willard Hall, which was proceeding as badly as he had expected. Only twenty-five of the thirty-four states had answered the opening roll call; none of the seven seceded states had sent delegates, nor had Arkansas, nor five western states. Meanwhile, on that same day far to the south in Montgomery, Alabama, representatives from the seceded states were meeting to organize a unified Confederate government. John Tyler's own granddaughter raised the Confederate flag at the opening ceremonies.

As the senior delegate from Ohio, Father had tried to organize the more radical delegates from other Northern states under his leadership. In his first major speech, he emphasized that restriction of, not war upon, the South's "peculiar institution" would be the policy of the new administration. "This goes against my personal beliefs," Father admitted to Kate later, who needed no reminder of her father's opposition to slavery wherever it existed. "But it is the Republican Party platform, and Mr. Lincoln has professed his intention to follow it." Factions were so divided that Father would consider the conference a success if its sole achievement was keeping the important border states in the Union until Mr. Lincoln took office.

In the days that followed, while her father toiled at Willard Hall, Kate paid calls and deftly provided noncommittal answers to questions about her father's role in the new administration. According to the Washington press, one day Father was certain to be named secretary of the treasury, the next he was unquestionably out of contention. To Kate's satisfaction, some editors ran lengthy appeals to Mr. Lincoln urging him to offer Father the Treasury. The newspapermen knew the future no better than the Chases did, but that did not stop them from making contradictory announcements and printing demands that Mr. Lincoln was likely to ignore.

As Kate made her social rounds and searched for a more permanent residence for the family, she was dismayed to discover how many old acquaintances had closed up their fine mansions and had departed the city for their homes in the South. Some ladies were glad to go, loudly and defiantly condemning the United States and the "Illinois abolitionist ape" who would soon take the presidential chair, while others were grief-stricken, longing to remain but obliged to obediently follow their husbands out of the city and out of the Union. The friends they had left behind told Kate sadly of tearful farewells and solemn vows that the conflict between their states would not sever their bonds of affection. Perhaps wives could not choose their own country, but they could choose whom they loved.

Other acquaintances intended to remain in the city only until after the inauguration, when a new regime would succeed them. One of Kate's first calls was to Miss Harriet Lane, who was so distracted by her beleaguered uncle's political struggles that she seemed to have given little thought to her plans after her departure from the White House. "I wish it were you who would take my place here," Miss Lane confessed with a sudden, unexpected passion, "and even more so, that your father would take my uncle's, although perhaps that is not a position I should wish on any man. I don't know what to think of this frontier Republican, or his wife. I can't imagine how either will be prepared for the roles they are so ambitious to undertake."

"I wish the same," said Kate solemnly, but then she smiled mischievously. "But only because then the question of where my family will reside would be answered without any more trouble on my part."

Miss Lane laughed, her enormous troubles forgotten for a moment, which was precisely what Kate had intended.

Although Kate could make light of her fruitless search for a proper home to amuse her friend, in truth, she found little humor in it. Few of the available properties met Father's strict criteria. Their new home must be a handsome, gracious residence, comfortable enough for a family and yet suitable for entertaining large numbers of guests in fine style. It must be an easy walk to the Capitol, where Father expected to work, but also to the White House, in the event that the appointment he still hoped for was finally offered. Most important, it must be within Father's means, not only the rent but the cost of upkeep, furnishings, and servants. Father was burdened with debt, how sizable he would not say and Kate dared not insult him by asking. Although he was trying to sell their home in Columbus as well as a few properties in Cincinnati, the real estate market was too depressed to tempt any buyers. Cost would be the most difficult criterion to satisfy, Kate thought ruefully, but she refused to believe that her father had given her an impossible task.

. . .

On February 11, Mr. Lincoln, his family, and various dignitaries, assistants, and trusted friends departed Springfield for Washington City in a special train car adorned with patriotic bunting and fitted with all the modern conveniences and luxuries befitting the status of its illustrious occupant. The train would follow a long, circuitous route through several cities and towns, both to allow the president-elect to greet as many supporters along the way as he could and to thwart anyone who might attempt to do him harm. Numerous threats had been made upon his life from the day he won the nomination, and they had steadily increased ever since, spiking after the election, the secession of South Carolina, and Mr. Buchanan's failed attempt to relieve Major Anderson at Fort Sumter. The most vile threats came from the Southern press, who brazenly printed their menacing declarations in shockingly lurid detail. Of course, Kate only assumed that these editorials were the most vile; it was entirely possible, even probable, that Mr. Lincoln received much worse through the post.

When Kate considered the effect of the threats upon Mr. Lincoln's family, how frightened and concerned for his safety his wife and sons must surely be, she felt a painful twinge of sympathy—and the barest breath of relief that her father had not become the target of such fierce hatred.

Despite the vitriol in the press, the labors of the Peace Conference continued, although Father rarely had any progress to report. Then, two days after Mr. Lincoln left Springfield, the Peace Convention set their work aside and adjourned shortly before noon so that the delegates could attend the official counting of the states' electoral votes.

Earlier that morning Kate had asked her father if she could accompany him, and he had agreed, so Kate dressed in a sensible, flattering dress of dark-blue wool trimmed in pale-yellow ribbon, strolled a few blocks down Fourteenth Street from the Rugby House to the Willard, and waited in the ladies' parlor for the delegates to emerge from the adjacent Willard Hall, a former Presbyterian church that the Willard brothers had transformed into a lecture and performance venue. The Willard, like the Neil House in Columbus, was not only the city's finest and largest hotel but also a nexus of Washington society and politics. Mr. Hawthorne had told Kate he thought it more justly called the center of Washington and the nation than either the Capitol, the White House, or the State Department, which was perhaps why he had taken rooms at the Rugby House instead. Recently the Willard brothers had gamely endeavored to maintain peace between contentious factions by assigning Southern guests rooms on a single floor and urging them to use the ladies' Fourteenth Street entrance, while Northerners were encouraged to use the main doors on the Pennsylvania Avenue side. Even so, they were bound to encounter one another in the hotel's public rooms, which were illuminated by gaslight and opulently furnished in rosewood, damask, lace, and velvet and smelled of cigar smoke and spilled whiskey—and were not, perhaps, quite the place for a well-bred young woman to sit alone.

Fortunately, her father soon arrived, greeted her with a kiss on the cheek, and offered her his arm. "Dare I ask how your morning went?" Kate asked as they hurried off.

"Nothing has been accomplished," said Father. "My fellow delegates are too easily distracted, and this day, especially, has offered distractions in abundance."

It was all too true. Aside from the joint session of Congress to which they were on their way, news of Mr. Lincoln's train journey was everywhere: descriptions of the cheering crowds that had greeted him the first two days; his eloquent speeches, which drew praise for their brevity and moderate tone; the threats upon his life, which had come to the attention of authorities in the cities along his route. Closer yet, a sense of apprehension hung over the city, provoked by fears that Vice-President Breckinridge, a known Southern sympathizer, would betray his duty to preside over the counting of the electoral votes that would confirm Mr. Lincoln's victory.

As was the custom, the official election certificates had been kept in the vice-president's personal custody since their arrival in the capital, but with animosities between North and South rising by the hour, the occasion presented a dangerous opportunity for a political coup. The stalwart General Winfield Scott, charged with the defense of the capital, had vowed that interference with the lawful count of the electoral votes would be firmly and decisively quashed. Any man who tried to interfere, he declared, whether by force or unparliamentary disorder, "should be lashed to a muzzle of a twelve-pounder and fired out of a window of the Capitol. I would manure the hills of Arlington with fragments of his body, were he a senator or chief magistrate of my native state!" The general backed up his words by ordering two batteries of cannon into position along First Street near the Capitol. Kate eyed them anxiously but found some comfort in their presence as she accompanied her father to observe the count.

The halls of the Capitol were jammed with onlookers, the mood tense and wary. The delegates to the Peace Convention had been invited onto the House floor to witness the proceedings, so while Father made his way into the crowd of lawmakers and special guests, Kate climbed the stairs to the gallery. "There's Miss Chase," she heard someone murmur excitedly, and the crowd parted as heads turned to look her way. She exchanged warm, cordial greetings with those who gave her welcome, and nodded graciously to others who peered eagerly her way but were too shy to address her. A vacant chair appeared for her in the front, and as she took her seat she searched the crowd below for her father, and found him easily, his tall, imposing figure regal and solemn amid the milling throng.

At noon the House was called to order, and after the chaplain led them in prayer, the previous day's journal was read and approved. A member from Illinois submitted a perfunctory resolution that the Senate should be summoned for the reading of the votes, a measure that swiftly passed. While the House awaited the senators' arrival, a lengthy communication from the Treasury Department about a crucial loan matter was read. Afterward, the chairman of the House Ways and Means Committee, Mr. Sherman, asked to introduce a bill allowing the president to issue bonds to help meet the imperative needs of the Treasury. Immediately following the reading of the bill, a voice rang out, "I object!"

A murmur went up from the gallery. Kate searched the House for the speaker and her gaze lit upon a clean-shaven man of about forty years glaring about defiantly—Mr. Garnett, a Democrat of Virginia.

"I trust the gentleman from Virginia will not object," Mr. Sherman replied, brow furrowing, "as the simple effect of the bill will be to give to the creditors of the United States coupon bonds as evidence of indebtedness. No new debt will be incurred."

"After the recent declaration of war by the president-elect of the United States," Mr. Garnett retorted, "I deem it my duty to interpose every obstacle to the tyrannical and military despotism now about to be inaugurated!"

A chorus of assent clashed with a roar of anger in the air above the House floor. "Declaration of war?" Kate overheard a woman exclaim from the back of the gallery. "What on earth could he mean?"

Below, Mr. Sherman tried again to introduce the bill, only to have a representative from North Carolina object. As voices rose in a clamor of proposals and objections, the Speaker struggled to regain control of the chamber, finally banging his gavel and declaring that in accordance with precedent, he ruled it out of order to conduct any other business until the votes were counted.

At twenty minutes past twelve o'clock, the doorkeeper announced that the Senate had arrived. The members of the House rose as the gentlemen filed solemnly into the hall, Vice-President Breckinridge and the sergeant-at-arms at the head of the procession. Kate's pulse quickened at the sight of the tellers carrying the two large cases containing the election results from each state. "Breckinridge could have opened them at any time," a man muttered somewhere to her left. "He was a candidate too, and don't you forget it."

"Are you suggesting he might have substituted forged ballots with his own name for Mr. Lincoln's?" another man jeered in an undertone. "After the results from the states were announced in the papers?"

"His name or someone else's," the first man retorted.

Other voices in the gallery hissed and snapped for the first two to be silent. Vice-President Breckinridge had taken his seat to the right of the Speaker of the House, while the senators occupied the seats that had been reserved for them elsewhere in the chamber. Kate's gaze was riveted on the three clerks, who set the sealed cases upon the clerk's desk and seated themselves.

"The two Houses being assembled," Mr. Breckinridge began, his voice clear but his visage grimly somber, "in pursuance of the Constitution, that the votes may be counted and declared for president and vice-president of the United States for the term commencing on the fourth of March, eighteen hundred and sixty-one, it becomes my duty, under the Constitution, to open the certificates of election in the presences of the two Houses of Congress." He paused and inhaled deeply. "I now proceed to discharge that duty."

An expectant, apprehensive hush fell over the chamber as Mr. Breck-inridge opened and handed to the tellers the record of electoral votes from each state, beginning with Maine. As each state's results were an-nounced, Kate compared the tallies to those listed in a newspaper clip-ping she had saved from the day after the election, and a rustle of newsprint told her that others in the gallery were doing the same. None of the numbers conflicted; no one stormed the clerk's table and stole the records at gunpoint. A little more than halfway through the list, the elec-toral votes from Ohio were credited to Mr. Lincoln; with a pang of re-gret, Kate stole a look at her father, whose face she could see in profile as he sat below, listening stoically. Ohio's votes should have gone to him. If only the Ohio delegation had been true at the Republican Convention—

Quickly she returned her gaze to the newspaper clipping. There was nothing to be gained by dwelling upon what might have been. She should think instead of what yet could be.

As Mr. Breckinridge continued to announce the electoral votes, a murmur rose from the galleries, and distantly, Kate heard it echoed in the halls outside the chamber, overcrowded with eager, unfortunate would-be witnesses who had been unable to squeeze their way inside. The vote was going exactly as expected without a single indication of the dreaded coup. This development, judging from the tone of the rising murmur of voices, had brought relief to many but disappointment and anger to an impassioned few.

California, Minnesota, Oregon—and then it was done.

"Abraham Lincoln, of Illinois," Mr. Breckinridge declared, "having received a majority of the whole number of electoral votes, is elected president of the United States for four years, commencing the fourth of March, eighteen hundred and sixty-one." An outburst of cheers from the Republicans interrupted him, but he raised his voice to be heard above it as he announced that Hannibal Hamlin, of Maine, had been duly elected vice-president.

The chamber was called to order again with some effort, and then, their joint session concluded, the senators departed for their own cham-ber. As the Speaker resumed conducting House business—the first mat-ter was a movement to adjourn, which was briefly argued before it was voted down—Kate joined the flow of spectators leaving the gallery and waited in the vestibule for her father, who was, as she had expected, delayed, most likely cornered by a series of congressmen with causes to champion or curiosity to satisfy. Everyone wanted to know whether Father intended to return to the Senate or join Mr. Lincoln's cabinet, Father most of all. At last she spotted her father's noble head above the crowd, and she smiled and waved to catch his eye. He was surprisingly ebullient as he offered her his arm and escorted her from the Capitol. "You apparently appreciated the show more than I thought you would," she remarked as they crossed the Capitol grounds on their way back to the Willard, where the Peace Convention was scheduled to reconvene within the hour.

"Why would I not have?" He sounded genuinely puzzled. "The legitimately elected candidate was verified according to law and protocol, with no malfeasance and, thank God, no violence." He halted and glanced down at her upturned face. "Because the votes were not for me?"

She nodded, her heart full of sympathetic indignation.

He sighed and resumed leading her down Pennsylvania Avenue. "It is the will of the majority of the men of this country that Mr. Lincoln should lead it for the next four years. More important, it must be God's will, for nothing happens that is not a part of His divine plan, although we cannot always fathom his design."

Kate nodded again, although she only partly agreed with him.

When they reached the corner of Fourteenth Street and Pennsylvania Avenue, Kate left her father at the Willard with a kiss and good wishes for a successful afternoon. Then she continued down Fourteenth Street to the Rugby House and upstairs to the family's suite, where she found Nettie entertaining the quiet, grandfatherly Mr. Hawthorne—a gentle, refined man with snow-white hair and a mustache, a youthful face, and large, soft, very dark eyes—chatting over tea as she showed him a series of whimsical sketches she had made to accompany his novel *The Marble Faun*. Kate had never met a shyer, more reticent man, and when she greeted him warmly and invited him to join the family for supper that evening, he begged off without bothering to invent an excuse. He left soon thereafter, but not until Nettie extracted his promise to have tea together again soon.

"You frightened him away," Nettie scolded after their celebrated guest hastily departed.

"I didn't mean to," Kate said, by way of an apology. "Nettie, dear, Mr.

Hawthorne is a very busy and very bashful man. Are you sure you aren't becoming a nuisance?"

"No, I'm not. Of course I'm not."

"No one who is a nuisance ever believes themselves to be one."

"Then why did you bother to ask me?" Nettie leafed through her drawings, smiling. "I'm not a nuisance. Mr. Hawthorne likes me. He says I have talent, and that if I nurture it faithfully, I might become an accomplished artist someday."

"Did he, indeed?" It was the fact that Mr. Hawthorne had strung together so many words at once rather than the content of his statement that surprised her. "I agree with him wholeheartedly. The question is, will you devote yourself faithfully to the task?"

Nettie didn't answer, for her attention had already turned elsewhere—to the drawings scattered across the table, to the renowned author's praise, to sketches she planned to begin as soon as she found fresh paper. Nettie had shown artistic talent from the time she could hold a pencil, a gift she had likely inherited from her mother, Belle. Kate remembered fondly the charming sketches her stepmother had included in the letters she had sent to Kate at boarding school, her affection for her stepdaughter evident in every stroke of the pen. Belle had loved Kate as dearly as if she had truly been her own child, until consumption claimed her life as it had Kate's own mother's.

The deaths of three young, beloved wives—that too, Father would say, was an inexplicable part of God's plan.

When Father returned later that evening for supper—a simple family affair since their reticent neighbor had declined Kate's invitation—the weariness of a long day had settled upon him, but he remained in good spirits. Mr. Lincoln and his family were in Columbus, he informed his daughters, and while attending a celebration in his honor at the state capitol, Mr. Lincoln had received the good news that the electoral votes had been counted and his election was official. "Soon thereafter," Father added, "Mr. Lincoln was presented at a reception for members of the legislature at Governor Dennison's home, and following dinner, he will attend a military ball." He glanced at the clock on the mantelpiece. "Perhaps he is there at this very moment."

"I wish we were too," sighed Nettie, ignoring the inescapable fact that she was not out in society yet and would have stayed home with Vina while her father and sister enjoyed the lavish ball. "It seems so strange, to think that Mr. and Mrs. Lincoln are in our city, while here we are, in theirs."

"Washington is our city now," Kate corrected her sister, "and Mr. Lincoln's rightful place is not this city but Springfield. It is there he will return in four years' time, you'll see."

One glance at her father's faint smile told her that her words had pleased him.

Apprehension and excitement rose in the nation's capital as the president-elect's train wended its way toward Philadelphia, with appearances in Harrisburg, Leamon Place, Lancaster, and Baltimore—a city full of Southern sympathizers in a slave state, well-known for mob violence and secessionist fervor—next on the route. A few days before Mr. Lincoln was due to arrive in Washington, alarming rumors swept through the city of threats that he would not leave Baltimore alive.

All of Washington seemed to hold its breath, awaiting word from Mr. Lincoln's travels with a dread unlikely to abate until he had safely arrived in the capital. The coup they had feared on the day the electoral votes had been read could yet come, with the swift, merciless strike of an assassin's bullet.

Kate prayed daily, urgently, for the president-elect's safety. She understood the necessity for elected officials to go out among the people, but if she were Mrs. Lincoln, she would urge her husband not to expose himself so heedlessly to danger, regardless of the possibility of souring public opinion. Perhaps Mrs. Lincoln did not exercise that sort of influence over her husband.

On the morning of February 23, Kate woke to a thrill of trepidation. President Lincoln was due to arrive in Washington City on the four o'clock train, but first he must safely pass through Baltimore. She rose, washed, and dressed, and went downstairs to the breakfast table, where her father already sat sipping his coffee and reading his Bible. Nettie soon joined them, smiling and cheerful, her face freshly scrubbed and hair neatly braided.

Vina served the meal, and while they were eating, Will brought in the morning papers. "Mr. Chase," he said, "I hear that Mr. Lincoln is in Washington."

"No, not quite yet," Father replied, glancing at the front page of the newspaper on the top of the pile. "His train isn't due until late this afternoon, and God willing, no street-mob violence will delay it."

"No, Mr. Chase, he's already here. He was seen breakfasting with Mr. Seward at the Willard not half an hour ago."

"Mr. Lincoln is in the city? Now?"

Will nodded. "That's what I heard."

"He must have passed through Baltimore on the night train," Kate said. Will was not one to spread unfounded rumors. "A prudent measure, I should think, due to the threats of violence."

"Prudent, perhaps, but it will look cowardly." Frowning, Father pushed back his chair and rose, his breakfast forgotten. "Of course, Seward has already cornered him."

"Perhaps Mr. Seward wished to apologize for that dreadful conciliatory speech he made in the Senate in January," Kate suggested.

Father shook his head. "Seward wouldn't concede any wrongdoing. No, his purpose is to exert his influence over the president-elect from the moment of his arrival. He thinks to become the power behind the throne, but I believe he'll discover that Mr. Lincoln is not as indecisive and biddable as Mr. Buchanan."

With apologizes for his haste, Father hurried off to the Willard, in hopes of welcoming Mr. Lincoln to Washington before reporting to the Peace Convention.

Kate and a small group of other Republican ladies had planned to greet Mrs. Lincoln upon the arrival of her afternoon train, and she regretted the unwelcoming impression the empty platform must have given her. Hoping to make up for their absence with a belated welcome, at midmorning Kate went to the Willard, where she charmed the front desk clerk into revealing that the president-elect had been given Suite Number Six, the hotel's very best, but that he was not there at the moment. "Perhaps his wife will receive me," Kate said, offering the clerk her card and a disarming smile. "It is indeed she whom I came to see."

"Mrs. Lincoln isn't here," he replied.

"She has gone out?"

"I haven't seen her at all," the clerk confessed, "but I'll be sure to deliver your card."

Puzzled, Kate thanked him and turned away. A few raindrops began to patter upon the dusty street as she walked back to the Rugby House, but lost in thought, she scarcely noticed them.

Later, when Father returned home for a quick supper, he reported that Mr. Lincoln had arrived in Washington at six o'clock that morning, having passed incognito through hostile Baltimore on the night train, with only a few companions in his retinue. Father had arrived at the Willard a few minutes too late to see him, for after breakfast, Mr. Lincoln and Mr. Seward had gone to the White House to call on President Buchanan. Ensconced with the other delegates at the Peace Convention, Father did not know how the president-elect had spent the rest of his day, but he had heard that Mrs. Lincoln and her sons had arrived as scheduled on the four o'clock train. Unaware that Mr. Lincoln was not on board, a large crowd had gathered in a cloudburst to welcome him. Mr. Seward—"It is always Seward," Father grumbled—had met the train, but after Mrs. Lincoln and her sons disembarked, and it became apparent that Mr. Lincoln was not with them, the people loudly voiced their displeasure, shouting, joking disparagingly, whistling, and swearing. Shaken by the unpleasant welcome, soaked from the downpour, exhausted and nervous from travel and threats to her husband, Mrs. Lincoln had leaned on Mr. Seward's arm and had begged to be taken to the Willard with all speed.

"At this hour Mr. Lincoln dines at Seward's home with his family and Mr. Hamlin," Father said, frowning at his plate with such glum worry that Kate knew he wished he had been invited. "I will see Mr. Lincoln tonight, however, when the Peace Conference delegates meet with him at the Willard."

"Might I come along?" asked Kate. "I tried to call on Mrs. Lincoln today, thinking she had arrived with her husband. The clerk told me that she was out, not that she had never arrived, and so I didn't know to meet her at the train station this afternoon."

"I don't know if Mrs. Lincoln will be present," her father replied.

"I'm happy to take that chance."

Father considered. "Very well. I'm sure she'd be delighted to meet you. Your kindness and charm will help her forget the unpleasantness of her arrival."

"Can I come too?" Nettie piped up.

"No," Father and Kate replied in unison, and Father added, "You are not out yet, and it will be past your bedtime."

Nettie lifted her chin. "I am thirteen now, and I think because you will be senator and will attend so many nice balls and things that I should be out now."

Kate laughed, astonished. "What an idea! No one is out at thirteen."

"Well, I should at least have a later bedtime."

"That is a discussion for another day," said Father wearily. Nettie frowned, disappointed, but she knew Father's moods well enough not to press her luck.

Shortly before nine o'clock, Father escorted Kate, dressed in the lovely green silk gown she had worn the previous September at the dedication of Commodore Perry's monument, to Willard's, where they discovered that many other Republican delegates had also brought their ladies. Like Kate, all were eager to meet the president-elect and his wife, about whom the newspapers offered such contradictory descriptions that it was impossible to form any true sense of her. One reporter corresponding from the Lincolns' journey east had written, "The entire female population are in ecstasies of curiosity to know who she was, what she is, what she looks like, what her manner is, and if she has a presence of the sort necessary in the exalted station to which she will soon be introduced." Kate had laughed ruefully when she had read the arch remark, recognizing herself. Soon, she hoped, many of her questions would be answered.

While the gentlemen delegates went off to call on the president-elect, Kate and the other ladies waited in the best parlor, hoping the Lincolns would put in an appearance, sharing what little information they had about the future First Lady, and sizing up one another as they chatted. Their patience was rewarded much later when the delegates escorted Mr. Lincoln to the parlor to meet them. Father was at his right hand, Kate noted with satisfaction as the gentlemen entered the room and joined their ladies. Mr. Lincoln took his place of honor at one end of the room, the ladies formed a line to pass in review, and as each pair approached the president-elect, each gentleman introduced his lady.

"Kate, dear," Father said when it was their turn, "may I introduce our president-elect, Mr. Abraham Lincoln. Mr. Lincoln, this is my eldest daughter, Miss Kate Chase."

"It is an honor to meet you, Mr. Lincoln," said Kate.

"The honor is mine," he replied, his voice warm and sincere. He was more handsome than his portrait, and when he smiled his melancholy look vanished and a gentle, interested, and compassionate expression took its place.

"Did Mrs. Lincoln not accompany you?" Kate asked. "I have been looking forward to making her acquaintance."

"Regrettably, Mrs. Lincoln has retired for the evening," Mr. Lincoln replied, turning a rueful smile down upon her from his great height. "She was fatigued from her travels, and to make matters worse, at supper an unfortunate waiter spilled coffee upon her gown, and so she withdrew to avoid embarrassment."

"How vexing," Kate remarked, wondering why Mrs. Lincoln had no other gown she could have put on instead. "Although I might have said that it was Mrs. Lincoln rather than the waiter who was unfortunate."

The president-elect smiled. "If you had witnessed his mortification, you would understand why I described him as I did."

Kate smiled in return. She could not help it; she liked him, although she remained annoyed at him for repeatedly dangling the Treasury before her father only to yank it out of reach. "Is there any way I can be of service to her?"

"That's very kind of you, but I believe she has the matter well in hand. Many ladies have recommended their favorite dressmakers to her, so she will have a new frock in time for the inauguration."

Kate's favorite dressmaker was in New York, and he did not work swiftly, so she could not curry favor by recommending him. "One of my dear friends employs a marvelous dressmaker," she suddenly remembered. "I've seen her work, and it is truly exquisite. If Mrs. Lincoln would like, I could get her name."

"Thank you, Miss Chase," said Mr. Lincoln. "I'm sure Mrs. Lincoln would appreciate that."

"My friend's taste is considered the most fashionable in Washington City"—then Kate started and gave a little laugh—"although perhaps Mrs. Lincoln, or you, would object on grounds utterly unrelated to her dressmaker's skill. My friend is Mrs. Douglas, the wife of your former and frequent rival, Senator Douglas."

"I assure you, Miss Chase, my rivalry with Senator Douglas was confined to the election," Mr. Lincoln said, amused. "Even today he brought the Illinois congressional delegation to call upon me, and he made clear his support of my administration and his commitment to preserving the Union. We bear no grudges against each other, and we'd never begrudge our wives the services of Washington's best dressmaker out of jealousy or spite."

"Nor, I think," Kate mused aloud, "would you begrudge the nation the services of such an excellent man simply because he had once been your rival."

His eyes shone with amusement. "You're speaking of Mr. Douglas, of course."

"Of course."

"Miss Chase, I intend to gather the best men of the country around me, regardless of past disagreements or discord," he said with endearing frankness. "The challenges facing my administration, and my duty to the country, require no less."

"I am very pleased to hear that," Kate said, equally sincere. "And so, I assume, will Mr. Douglas be."

Mr. Lincoln laughed again, but Kate had taken up more of his time than was strictly proper, and so she bade him a good evening, bowed, and moved on.

"That was very well done, daughter," Father told her later as they climbed aboard the carriage he had hired to take them home. The walk was short and pleasant enough in the day, but the hour was late, and dangerous street gangs were known to prowl the streets after dark. The hooligans usually did not venture near the Willard and the White House, but prudence would cost Father and Kate very little and might save them a great deal of distress.

"Thank you, Father." She was rather proud of the exchange, which had served to advocate for her father without overtly querying the president-elect and embarrassing them all. She hoped that Mr. Lincoln meant what he'd said, and that he realized her father certainly belonged among any assembly of the best men of the country. "How did Mr. Lincoln receive the delegates, and how did they receive him? Did the Southerners behave themselves?"

"They managed to contain their disgust, but only just barely." Earlier that morning, the convention had fallen into an argument over whether they should request an audience with the man some of them considered to be a vulgar tyrant. Mr. Tyler mollified the angry Southerners by entreating them to pay their respects to the office if not to the man. "Each delegate shook his hand, even those who had been calling him an ignoramus or a gorilla hours before. A few could not resist the temptation to harass him about their pet issues, but in the end Mr. Lincoln impressed everyone with his friendliness and sincerity."

"Do you include yourself among those who were impressed?"

"I confess I felt rather awkward instead. This was our first meeting since I visited him in Springfield, and by now I ought to know where I stand. If he doesn't want me for the Treasury, why does he not say so? Why has he not appointed someone else? And as the only man there who had met him before, it fell to me to introduce him to the other delegates. I was not expecting to assume that responsibility and I had prepared no remarks."

"I'm sure you did well even so," Kate assured him. "I do wish that I had been able to meet Mrs. Lincoln tonight. I hope she didn't feel slighted when there was no party of Republican ladies to meet her at the train." She shook her head, frowning thoughtfully. "Their arrival was so confused. I understand why it was necessary to change their plans, of course. The threats against Mr. Lincoln's life had to be taken seriously."

"I agree," said Father, and then he smiled so broadly that she could not miss it even in the semidarkness of the carriage. "Although I believe he already regrets sneaking into the city under the cover of darkness."

"I don't see why he should. He passed through Baltimore unmolested and arrived in Washington safely. Isn't that what matters most?"

"Certainly, but the ridicule and accusations of cowardice have only just begun. Have you heard the rumor that he crept aboard the train disguised in a plaid cap, Scottish kilts, and a long military cloak?"

"Scurrilous rumors, surely," Kate scoffed. "Such an outlandish outfit would only have attracted more attention to him, especially with his great height and lanky frame."

"I'm sure there's more fiction than fact to it," Father conceded, "and yet, I confess I'm looking forward to seeing how his costume and cowardice play in the papers."

Kate had to admit that she too would take a certain amount of guilty pleasure from some harmless mockery of her father's rival. It would serve Mr. Lincoln right to have to endure his share of frustration and embarrassment after all that his interminable, inexplicable delay had caused her father. That trial of waiting, at least, would have to end soon. Mr. Lincoln's inauguration was only days away, and he must have a cabinet.

Chapter Six

*H*aving inadvertently eluded Mrs. Lincoln for far too long, Kate resolved to meet her on the very next occasion Mrs. Lincoln accepted callers. Soon an ideal occasion arose, and since Father was preoccupied with the work of the Peace Convention, Kate invited Nettie to accompany her.

As they walked the four blocks to the Willard, Kate offered her sister emphatic reminders of how to behave, instructions she suspected Nettie scarcely heard in her excitement. "Remember, Nettie, be gentle, respectful, and polite," she said as they approached the Fourteenth Street entrance. "Mrs. Lincoln will probably be tired and nervous, for she has been through quite an ordeal since departing Springfield, but you must not remark about its effects on her appearance. Be sweet and sympathetic, and don't mention any unpleasantness you might have overheard."

"You mean how Father is annoyed with Mr. Lincoln about the Treasury?"

"Yes," Kate quickly replied. "That is a very good example of something to keep to yourself."

"What about the drawing of Mr. Lincoln dressed like a Scotsman that appeared in the paper yesterday?" Nettie asked. "May I tell Mrs. Lincoln that I thought it was unkind and very poorly drawn?"

"I know you would mean it in the nicest possible way, but no, Nettie, you should not mention that either."

Nettie frowned, perplexed, as if Kate had dismissed all possible topics of conversation and they would have nothing at all to say to Mrs. Lincoln other than "Good afternoon" and "How do you do?"

Entering the hotel, they made their way through the crush of patronage seekers, politicians, clerks, and newspapermen to the ladies' parlor, where dozens of becomingly dressed women sipped tea and nibbled delicate cakes while others waited in line for Mrs. Lincoln to receive them. The only gentleman in the room was seated at the piano, playing soft renditions of popular dance melodies at a volume loud enough to entertain but not to drown out conversation. Kate guided Nettie to the end of the queue, exchanging pleasant greetings with other ladies she knew while discreetly taking her measure of the room. A short, middle-aged, dark-haired woman who resembled the portraits of Mrs. Lincoln too much to be anyone else stood between the window and the fireplace, smiling as she chatted with the wife of a congressman from New Jersey. Two other ladies, probably relatives or close friends, stood solicitously on either side of her, nodding politely to the guests as they approached, ready to attend to Mrs. Lincoln however she might require. Suddenly Kate was struck by the realization that all the ladies present were Northerners, and only a very few—perhaps no more than three—represented the social elite of Washington City. Perhaps they had met Mrs. Lincoln at an earlier, more intimate gathering, but Kate suspected it was, in fact, a deliberate snub.

Before long, Kate and Nettie reached the head of the line, where introductions were easily and pleasantly made. "You are from Columbus, are you not?" Mrs. Lincoln inquired, smiling at the sisters. Her dress of blue, white, and tan plaid wool looked to be of a more expensive fabric than Kate's, though less skillfully made, but the exquisite pearls adorning her neck and earlobes dazzled the eye and drew attention away from any flaws in her dress and figure. Kate was conscious, suddenly, of her own lack of jewels and guiltily wished that her father could afford more enduring embellishments than flowers.

"Yes," said Nettie, beaming. "We're from Columbus."

"We were born in Cincinnati," Kate amended, "but, yes, we have most recently come from Columbus."

"I found it such a charming city when we passed through," Mrs. Lincoln said, her blue eyes keen and appraising. "Although I believe you try to spend as little time there as possible, Miss Chase, is that not so?"

"I beg your pardon, but that is most certainly not so," said Kate easily, smiling despite the odd phrasing of the question. "Please don't mistake my admiration for Washington City as an absence of feeling for Columbus. I am indeed very fond of it."

"As am I," added Nettie with gracious formality.

Mrs. Lincoln smiled indulgently at Nettie before returning a quizzical gaze to Kate. "I must have misunderstood. I had thought that you spent very little time in Columbus."

Kate could not imagine why Mrs. Lincoln would think such a thing, nor why she would belabor the point. "It's true that I spent many years at boarding school in New York City as a girl, but I have lived in Columbus from the time I was sixteen."

"So not very long at all, then," said Mrs. Lincoln grandly. "Well, I do hope your longing for Ohio does not pain you too much, and that you'll soon feel more at home here in Washington."

Understanding that the interview was over, Kate thanked her and bowed graciously—at her side, Nettie quickly did the same—and moved along. She kept her expression perfectly pleasant as she led Nettie to the punch and cakes, but inside she held a flurry of confusion and insult. What a strange inquiry Mrs. Lincoln had subjected her to, but perhaps she had meant no offense. Perhaps in Kate's haste to assure Mrs. Lincoln that she was fond of Columbus, she had seemed overly wistful or melancholy, and Mrs. Lincoln had meant only to comfort her. And yet, even accounting for the quirks of western manners, Mrs. Lincoln's words rang somewhat out of tune, as if Kate were the newcomer and needed reassurance and guidance in a strange new city. As far as Kate knew, she had spent more time in Washington through the years than Mrs. Lincoln had despite the vast difference in their ages, and even if she had not, Kate was not a timid young girl tentatively venturing out into the larger world for the first time. She had lived half her life in New York City, and Washington was an up-and-coming rural town compared to Manhattan.

Whatever Mrs. Lincoln had heard or thought she knew of Kate, she was quite mistaken.

Kate left the reception as soon as it was not unseemly to do so, although Nettie gladly would have remained to listen to the piano music and taste more of the pretty cakes. "I liked her," Nettie remarked as they strolled home. "Didn't you?"

"She's quite interesting," Kate said, avoiding a proper answer. "She was not what I expected."

"Nor I. She did not seem at all tired or nervous. She seemed quite happy."

Indeed she had, especially when she was querying Kate. What had happened to the nervous, anxious woman who had clung to Mr. Seward's arm upon her arrival at the train station, drenched by rain and startled by an ungracious crowd who much preferred her husband? Who was this shrewd, handsome, sharp-eyed woman who had taken her place?

As February drew to a close, the Peace Convention adjourned for the last time. The following day at noon, General Scott ordered a company of artillery stationed at the City Hall lot to fire a one-hundred-gun salute "in honor of the pacification agreed on, and recommended to the Congress by the Peace Convention."

"That's for you, Father," Nettie exclaimed, covering her ears as the booms rattled windows and crockery in their rooms and probably in homes and boardinghouses throughout the city.

"Not for me alone," Father said, and to Kate he added, "One hundred guns are hardly warranted for such a dubious accomplishment."

"Perhaps fifty would have been more suitable?"

"Perhaps fifteen."

Father, who had long ago resigned himself to the fact that the time for compromise between North and South had passed, did not feel like celebrating. He was glad the fruitless ordeal was over, regretful that it had not reconciled the divided nation, and proud of its one lone accomplishment, which he had brought about: Virginia and the other border states would remain in the Union when Mr. Lincoln took his oath of office.

That day was rapidly approaching, and the population of Washington City swelled as visitors arrived from across the country to enjoy the festivities. Every hotel was booked beyond capacity, and even the modest Rugby House was in such demand that the proprietors arranged cots in the parlors to transform them into dormitories for single gentlemen.

The Kirkwood House and Brown's Hotel were even more jammed, and the Willard was so overcrowded that the proprietors scrounged up nearly five hundred mattresses, laid them upon the floors of every corridor and public room from cellar to roof, and still did not have enough to accommodate all who begged for a place to sleep.

The streets were full of so many strangers that Father did not like Kate and Nettie to go on even the simplest errands without him. When Kate did venture out, she rarely saw a single familiar face among the thousands, even walking the four short blocks from the Rugby House to the Willard. Here and there she spotted evidence of out-of-town visitors who had abandoned hope of finding accommodations in the city's packed hotels and had instead set up camp on the streets—a makeshift bed on a pile of lumber, men in rumpled suits dozing on market stalls using their coats as blankets and satchels as pillows, others shamelessly washing up at public pumps and horse troughs. One hundred street sweepers had been hired to keep the Avenue tidy and presentable, but although they toiled ceaselessly, they barely kept the litter at bay.

Father had told Kate that dispersed throughout the crowds were detectives and policemen in plain clothes, inconspicuous among the thousands of strangers but watchful and prepared to thwart anyone who might attempt to harm Mr. Lincoln. When the inaugural procession carried him from the Willard Hotel to the Capitol, riflemen would take up positions on the rooftops along the route and cavalry would guard every intersection. An entire battalion of District of Columbia militia would be stationed around the Capitol steps and sharpshooters would stand alert at the windows of the wings. "Every precaution will be taken to protect the president," Father assured Kate and Nettie, and Kate prayed it would suffice.

On the night before the inauguration, Mr. Lincoln hosted a dinner for Mr. Seward, Mr. Gideon Welles, Mr. Montgomery Blair, General Simon Cameron, Mr. Caleb B. Smith, Judge Edward Bates, and Father—all men who would comprise his cabinet, with the exception of Father. Kate hoped that her father would return from the gathering with the Department of the Treasury appointment finally and firmly in his grasp, but instead he came home empty-handed, disgruntled, and confused. "Was this an exercise in public humiliation?" he asked wearily as he settled down in the rented room's best chair and put his feet up. "Is Mr. Lincoln mocking me?"

"At the very least, he's wrongly testing your patience," Kate said, putting on a shawl before hurrying downstairs to fetch him some tea. What could Mr. Lincoln be thinking, to invite Father to a dinner for his cabinet, of which Father was conspicuously not a member? It was insulting, it was provoking, and it was spiteful behavior that until that moment she would have thought beneath him.

She brought her father his tea and sat on the footstool listening as he drank his tea and recounted the evening to her. "Not all is lost. I can do much good in the Senate," he said stoutly as he set the cup aside.

"You can, and you shall," said Kate fiercely. "Tomorrow, when you take the oath of office, I will be the proudest daughter in the audience—no, the proudest in all the country."

"Nettie may contend with you for that title," her father said as he rose to retire, a small bit of levity that assured her he was not too dispirited to fulfill the enormous tasks that awaited him in the Senate. The country needed his wisdom, his courage, his integrity—the country needed *him*, and Mr. Lincoln needed him, although the president-elect seemed not to realize how much.

On the morning of Abraham Lincoln's inauguration Kate rose early, a thrill of pride and excitement chasing away her slumbers as surely as the first pale rays of dawn through her windowpane and the tread of many feet on the street below. She washed and dressed quickly, and woke Nettie and urged her to do the same, lingering in the doorway until her sister dragged herself from bed and stumbled drowsily to the washbasin. Father was as she found him every morning—the first of the household to wake, sipping coffee and reading his Bible at the breakfast table—but that morning he was dressed in his finest suit and waistcoat, dignified and handsome. She felt a pang of pride and regret as she observed him. He had been denied the presidency and then the cabinet post that should have been his just reward for his loyalty to the Republican Party, his service to the nation, and his services to Mr. Lincoln in particular, and yet he did not sulk or lament. Instead he remained faithful to the Lord, devoted to his country, and dedicated to the noble cause of abolition.

When the household gathered for their customary morning scripture reading and prayers, the mood was both more solemn and more joyful than usual. The morning had broken chilly, damp, and overcast, but as the hours elapsed, a gusty, intermittent wind blew away the clouds and stirred up dust on the streets, already jammed with spectators. When Nettie begged to see the preparations for the grand procession, since they would be unable to witness the procession itself, Father agreed that Kate could take her out for a little while.

Even at that early hour, crowds had already begun to line the parade route. Military regiments splendidly attired in dashing uniforms with sashes and sabers drilled in open fields, while brass bands tuned their instruments and rehearsed their stirring melodies. Workers raced to put finishing touches of bunting, flowers, and banners on parade floats; Kate and Nettie's favorite, a Republican creation betokening the Constitution and the Union, would carry thirty-four young girls dressed in white to represent all thirty-four United States, including those that had seceded. The mood was celebratory, expectant, joyous, but Kate noticed stern-faced soldiers on horseback studying the crowds. And while some bunting-festooned balconies were already full of spectators and most windows were thrown open to offer a better view of the revelry outside, elsewhere other balconies were empty and bare, the windows closed, the curtains drawn tightly shut. Kate imagined Southern sympathizers on the other side, their eyes squeezed shut and fingers jammed in their ears to block out what were to them the offensive sights and sounds of Mr. Lincoln's triumph.

After an hour or so of strolling about and admiring the patriotic display, Kate and Nettie returned to the Rugby House to dress for their father's swearing-in ceremony.

At eleven o'clock, Father, Kate, and Nettie departed in a gleaming black barouche for the Capitol. A cheering crowd of well-wishers sent them off, and Kate was pleased to hear a man shout, "Chase for president!" Although Father merely smiled and raised his hand in reply, Kate knew he was pleased as well. Still, it was both too late and too early for that particular refrain.

When they reached the Capitol, they left the barouche and passed through an enclosed temporary walkway constructed of heavy lumber to enter the building, magnificent in glorious marble despite the incomplete dome. They parted at the rotunda, Father to his reserved seat on the floor, Kate and Nettie for the gallery. The Thirty-Sixth Congress was still in session as the sisters found chairs up above, and after exchanging whispered compliments with friends and acquaintances, they settled in to wait, observing the passage of a bill for the relief of Bloomfield College and another for the protection of certain guano discoveries, followed by a reconsideration of a metropolitan gas bill.

Meanwhile, Mr. Lincoln, Mr. Buchanan, the chief justice and associate justices of the Supreme Court, and several foreign ministers had entered the chamber and seated themselves in the front, below the secretary's desk. Kate felt an elbow nudge her side. "There she is," Nettie whispered excitedly, and nodded toward the diplomatic gallery, where Mrs. Lincoln, resplendent in an ashes-of-rose sateen gown, had taken her seat among her sons and sisters. She wore an elaborate headdress of flowers and ribbon, and diamonds sparkled from her ears. Her downturned gaze was fixed on her husband, her eyes moist with tears of pride and affection.

Kate frowned, inhaled deeply, and returned her gaze to the Senate floor, where Mr. Bright of Indiana continued to pontificate about the gas bill, his discourse having become neither more interesting nor, apparently, significantly nearer its conclusion, much to the amusement of his fellow senators and the annoyance of the spectators, who had expected more elevating oratory on such an auspicious day. He rambled on until noon, when he was obliged to cease, for at that hour, the Thirty-Sixth Congress expired and a new era must begin.

An expectant hush fell over the chamber as outgoing vice-president Breckinridge rose and offered a pleasant farewell address to the Senate. "He is a cousin of Mrs. Lincoln's," Kate murmured to Nettie after he finished and bowed graciously to generous applause. "Beginning today, he will serve with Father in the Senate."

Nettie nodded, her eyes fixed on the scene below as Mr. Hannibal Hamlin joined Mr. Breckinridge, who administered his oath of office. Applause and cheers filled the chamber as the new vice-president took the chair and called the Thirty-Seventh Congress to order. The clerk read the proclamation Mr. Buchanan had issued back in February calling for the special session, and thus it was convened.

Kate touched Nettie's hand, and Nettie nodded, bouncing a trifle in her seat from excitement, understanding that their father's moment would soon be at hand.

Mr. Breckinridge had not needed to wander far, for he was the first of the newly elected, or in some cases reelected, senators to take the oath of office. Then it was Father's turn. As was the custom, Senator Benjamin Wade, the other senator from Ohio, escorted Father down the aisle to Vice-President Hamlin, and Father's voice rang out strong and true as he declared, "I do solemnly swear that I will support the Constitution of the United States." No one who observed him could doubt that he meant every word of his oath.

Kate watched proudly as Father and Mr. Wade returned to their seats. The other newly elected senators echoed the simple, powerful words of the oath, which perhaps had never carried more meaning than at that moment as the nation stood on the brink of an unfathomable gulf, with seven of their number having already flung themselves over the edge and threatening, with the unbreakable bonds that united them, to pull the rest of them down after.

When the last of the senators had been sworn in, and the hour for their daily meeting had been fixed at one o'clock, the entire company proceeded outside to the eastern portico. Kate had planned on making a swift exit, and she timed it so perfectly that she and Nettie, hand in hand, were able to leave the gallery quickly and claim the places Father had secured for them on one side of the platform that had been erected for the ceremony. Father, she knew, would be seated at the front in a place of honor with Mr. Lincoln, Mr. Buchanan, Supreme Court chief justice Roger Taney, and Senator Edward D. Baker of Oregon, shaded beneath a wooden canopy near a small table where Mr. Lincoln would stand to address the crowd. Roughly thirty thousand people had packed the muddy Capitol grounds to witness the historic occasion, and as they waited eagerly for the new president to appear, they were entertained by the lively music of military bands, so they did not become too restless.

The sky had cleared, the sun shone brightly down upon the crowd, and shortly before one o'clock, Mrs. Lincoln emerged through the central door with her sons, sisters, and several gentlemen. Soon after they seated themselves upon the platform, the portly clerk of the Supreme Court appeared, carrying a Bible in one hand and leading the elderly, frail Supreme Court chief justice Roger Taney with the other.

When Mr. Lincoln appeared upon the platform, with Mr. Buchanan pale, sad, and nervous at his side, deafening cheers greeted him, going on and on nearly until the entire Senate and other dignitaries had taken their places. Kate and Nettie applauded loudest of all for Father, who took his seat with becoming dignity. Then Senator Baker, a longtime friend of Mr. Lincoln's, came forward and announced, with profound simplicity, "Fellow citizens, Abraham Lincoln, president of the United States, will now proceed to deliver his inaugural address."

Mr. Lincoln rose, serene and calm in his manner, and put on his spectacles as he approached the canopy. He removed his hat, and then suddenly halted, looking about with a self-deprecating smile as if he had realized only then he had no place to put it while he took his oath. His former rival, Senator Douglas, promptly came forward and took the hat, which he held on his lap while Mr. Lincoln addressed the crowd.

And what an address it was. In spite of herself, Kate was moved by the simple eloquence of his words, the clarity and compassion of his thought. He attended first to the fears of the Southern people, stating emphatically that he had no intention of interfering with slavery where it existed, and that even though the Fugitive Slave Law was offensive to many, he felt bound by the Constitution to enforce it. Though as an ardent abolitionist Kate was displeased by that position, his next subject almost made her forget her dissatisfaction with the first. Step by logical step, with simple, articulate, evocative phrases, he asserted that despite the claims of certain parties, according to the Constitution and the law, the Union was not and could not be broken. "I shall take care, as the Constitution itself expressly enjoins upon me, that the laws of the Union be faithfully executed in all the States," he vowed. "Doing this I deem to be only a simple duty on my part, and I shall perform it so far as practicable, unless my rightful masters, the American people, shall withhold the requisite means, or, in some authoritative manner, direct the contrary. I trust this will not be regarded as a menace, but only as the declared purpose of the Union that it will constitutionally defend and maintain itself." The North and South could not physically separate, he reminded them, and must not spiritually. "We are not enemies, but friends," he said, with lyrical power that spellbound his listeners. "We must not be enemies. Though passion may have strained, it must not break our bonds of affection. The mystic chords of memory, stretching from every battle-field, and patriot grave, to every living heart and hearth-stone, all over this broad land, will yet swell the chorus of the Union when again touched, as surely they will be, by the better angels of our nature."

All around her, and throughout the grounds of the Capitol, men raised their hats, women waved their handkerchiefs, and everyone roared their approval—but Kate, riveted by the unexpected power of Mr. Lincoln's words, sat motionless, transfixed. She watched in perfect stillness as Chief Justice Taney made his slow and unsteady way to the little table where Mr. Lincoln stood. There the elderly jurist conducted the ritual as he had six times before, and Mr. Lincoln placed his hand on the Bible, recited the oath of office, bowed, and kissed the holy book.

It was done. A fanfare of brass and a thundering of cannons announced that Abraham Lincoln had become the sixteenth president of the United States.

Afterward the president and his retinue returned to the White House in an open carriage surrounded by a cavalry escort, cheered along the way by tens of thousands of raucous well-wishers, who filled the sidewalks and clogged the dusty streets. The Lincolns would have little time to rest or to settle into their new home, however; Kate knew that in one of her final acts as Mr. Buchanan's hostess, Harriet Lane had arranged for an elegant dinner for the president, his wife, and enough friends and relations to make up a party of seventeen.

The Chase family, after finding one another in the crowd, summoned the rented barouche and returned to the Rugby House. From the corner of Fourteenth Street and Pennsylvania Avenue, they saw thousands of people milling about in the circular drive in front of the White House, cheering, chanting slogans, and shouting for the president to come out and address them again.

"Let the man rest," Father muttered as their carriage pulled away. "A heavy burden was just hefted upon his shoulders. Let him balance that before adding to the load."

Mr. Lincoln might not be permitted to rest, but Kate and her father were determined to. After a simple dinner that Vina, with her impeccable timing and good sense, had ready only minutes after they crossed the threshold, the Chases lingered at the table discussing the events of the day but then parted company to rest before the evening ball. Nettie begged again, halfheartedly, to be allowed to go, knowing she would be refused as she had been before. This time Kate softened the blow by adding, "In four years' time, you will be old enough, and I see no reason why you should not expect to attend the Inaugural Ball."

Especially if it was Father's inauguration they would be celebrating, Kate added silently.

Her mind was too full of memories and sensations to sleep easily in midday, so she lay in bed with the curtains drawn, a handkerchief over her eyes to block out the light, willing herself to rest. Eventually she drifted off, and dreamed of sharpshooters on rooftops and thousands of cheering admirers, stirring up so much dust on Pennsylvania Avenue as they marched to the strains of martial music that she bolted awake, coughing and gasping for breath.

She sat up in bed, sipped some water, and waited for her disorientation to clear. Dusk had fallen, she realized, and it was time to prepare for the ball.

Her fatigue and lingering disappointment fell away as she washed and dressed and sat perfectly still as Vina arranged her hair, all unhappiness replaced by a familiar anticipation and vitality. It was not vanity to acknowledge to herself that she was at her best on such occasions, when the stage was ideally set for her to wield her beauty, grace, intelligence, and wit to charm the elite and powerful to her father's advantage. She knew she looked resplendent in her white satin décolleté gown with puffed sleeves and an overskirt of cherry silk adorned with white satin roses. She wore matching flowers in her headpiece, a simple, elegant crown, and when she studied herself in the looking glass, her skin glowed and her hazel eyes were bright with excitement and pleasure.

The Union Ball would commence at ten o'clock, and Father, with his customary dislike of tardiness, made certain their carriage would arrive shortly thereafter. A large hall spacious enough to accommodate three thousand guests had been constructed on Judiciary Square especially for the occasion. Dubbed the "White Muslin Palace of Aladdin," the ballroom was actually a temporary yellow pine wood–frame and canvas structure, divided into rooms for dancing and for supper, and dependent on the adjacent City Hall for dressing rooms—ladies in the Common Council chamber and gentlemen in the courtroom. Within, the palace was beautifully decorated with red and white muslin drapings and colorful shields bearing the arms of the United States, brilliantly il-luminated by gaslight chandeliers.

Upon her arrival, Kate gracefully entered the inaugural palace on her father's strong arm, aware of the many heads that turned their way, the admiring looks, the excited whispers. Many handsome gentlemen, some whom she had met before, others who quickly arranged the appro-priate introductions, engaged her for dances. The ladies were dressed in their finest gowns and jewels, the gentlemen were at their most gallant and courteous, and as they mingled and chatted and laughed and re-counted the events of the day, they glanced often to the entrance, await-ing the arrival of the new president and his retinue. It was not strictly proper for the dancing to begin without them, but as the minutes ticked away and they still had not appeared, some impatient youths persuaded the band to begin.

Kate danced the first set, a quadrille, with Lord Lyons, the British ambassador who had once courted Miss Harriet Lane despite being a year older than Father. A much younger gentleman partnered her for the lancers that followed, and Father claimed her for the Strauss waltz that came next, after which a handsome, amusing captain whirled her about in a lively polka. Being then not engaged, having sensibly planned for a rest, she accepted the captain's escort to a chair, where she caught her breath and chatted pleasantly with other ladies who were sitting out the second quadrille.

She had not been resting long when her companions' conversation trailed off at a gentleman's approach. Kate glanced up—and her heart thudded when her gaze met a pair of dark, compelling eyes within a fa-miliar handsome countenance.

"Good evening, Miss Chase," Governor Sprague greeted her, and to her companions, said, "Good evening, ladies."

The other ladies bowed in acknowledgment, and a few offered him winning smiles, but his gaze, warm and amused, was fixed upon Kate. "Miss Chase, I see that you are not at present engaged, and I wondered if I might have the pleasure of this dance."

"Thank you, Governor," Kate replied smoothly, although her heart was pounding with a strange, annoying anxiety, "but I have danced every set so far and I am much in need of a rest. Besides, the quadrille has al-ready begun and we'll upset the pattern if we fling ourselves into it now."

He accepted the rejection with a smile and a gracious nod, and as she deliberately turned back to her companions, she saw a few of them exchange knowing glances while others straightened in their seats becomingly, perhaps hoping that the Boy Governor would invite them instead.

"After you have rested, then," Governor Sprague suggested, with no indication that he had sensed a rebuff. "I would enjoy any dance in your company, so when are you next not engaged?"

Kate knew already, but she glanced at her dance card anyway. "I am not engaged for the next dance," she admitted. A lady could not politely refuse a gentleman unless she already had a partner or sincerely needed to rest, and no one would believe that the vivacious Miss Chase needed to sit out two dances in a row.

"Do you think you shall be sufficiently recovered by then?" Governor Sprague inquired.

"I am certain I shall be."

He smiled, amused and knowing. "Then it would be my honor to escort you."

She managed to smile in return, hoping fervently that color was not rising in her cheeks, as she handed him her dance card. He wrote in his name, returned the card to her with a bow, gave his compliments to the ladies, and strolled away, only to return a few minutes later to claim her for the dance she had promised.

It was another lancers, and the movement of the figure was such that it was blessedly difficult to converse. He seemed perfectly content to hold her hands and whirl about or step to this side or the other as the figure required, judging by his smile, warm and amused and almost too familiar. She smiled back, polite but aloof, and as they danced, she began to feel annoyed, but she could not have said whether his behavior or hers provoked the feeling. Instead of asking her to dance, Governor Sprague should have apologized for his ill-mannered behavior at the ball in Cleveland. Instead of allowing him to engage her, she should have pretended that her dance card was full, except for necessary rests, and ignored him for the rest of the evening. It bothered her that he disconcerted her so, she who conversed easily with the greatest political minds of the age, her father's allies as well as his rivals, impressing them with her wit and intelligence. Why did this so-called Boy Governor fluster her, and fascinate her? She ought to be too offended to speak to him, but instead, knowing and not quite believing how he had already crossed the line of propriety so brazenly and without remorse, she was compelled to see what he might do next. It was as if she expected and dreaded that something even more shocking might yet unfold and could not tear her eyes away, as if she were watching a carriage crash from a great distance.

She was not sure whether she was more disappointed or relieved that he conducted himself as a perfect gentleman. She almost began to wonder if her mind had played tricks on her the previous September, if she had merely imagined him pulling her close and murmuring in her ear, but before she could frame a question she noticed a commotion near the front entrance. The music quickly died away and dancing was abruptly suspended as word swept through the ballroom that the president had arrived. Everyone turned expectantly to the doorway, and soon President Lincoln appeared, accompanied by Vice-President Hamlin and Senator Anthony of Rhode Island. A burst of applause greeted them, and the band struck up "Hail, Columbia."

Following the president and his companions was Mrs. Lincoln, escorted, Kate was surprised to discover, by none other than Senator Douglas. The end of their campaign rivalry, implied by Mr. Douglas's courteous holding of the president's hat earlier that day, could not have been more firmly or convincingly expressed than by this great honor. Mrs. Lincoln looked almost radiant in a low-necked blue silk gown of an exquisite hue, perfect fit, and evident richness, embellished with point lace. Her necklace and bracelets were fashioned of gold and pearls, flowers adorned her headdress, and every element of her costume spoke of refinement and taste.

"The president is infinitely a better-looking man than he has been represented," Governor Sprague remarked, "but I am pleasantly disappointed in Mrs. Lincoln. She is not at all as coarse, ignorant, or unfashionable as I had been led to believe."

Although privately Kate agreed, and ordinarily enjoyed a bit of gossip, she pretended she had not heard him over the applause rather than compose a clever reply he might carry elsewhere. She did not trust him to keep her confidences.

Other dignitaries and family members completed the presidential entourage, and after a brief promenade, President Lincoln and Mr.

Hamlin took stations at the upper end of the room, where many guests promptly availed themselves of the opportunity to be presented to Mr. Lincoln, who cordially shook hands with one and all.

"Would you like me to introduce you to the president?" Governor Sprague offered.

"Thank you, but we have already met," Kate replied. "I will, of course, pay my respects, but later, after the line diminishes."

"Then may I request the honor of another dance, especially since our first was cut short?"

The band had begun another refrain of "Hail, Columbia" and nearly everyone had left the dance floor. "I don't think dancing will resume until after supper," Kate said. "And forgive me, but should you engage the same lady for two dances, when there are so many other ladies present?"

"We have had only three-quarters of a dance," the governor protested. "And in any case, I doubt that anyone is keeping count."

Incredulous, Kate had to laugh. "I assure you, a great many people are. For some it will be their favorite entertainment of the evening."

"Well, then, if it will give a few vinegary dowagers pleasure to perceive scandal where there is none, it would be unkind of me to disappoint them." He raised his eyebrows and extended his hand, and she knew it to be a challenge. Annoyed, and yet somehow also amused, she gave him her dance card again, with only the barest, almost inaudible sigh of exasperation. He signed his name on one of the few remaining unclaimed lines, and when he returned it to her, she slipped it into her reticule without troubling herself to see which dance he had chosen. His smile deepened knowingly as he escorted her to a chair, bowed, thanked her, and departed.

She did not see him again until half past eleven, when the guests promenaded into the supper hall, and that was only from across the room—one brief, shared glance before the gentleman seated at Kate's right distracted her with a question. The meal was excellent, and afterward the dancing resumed. She was never without a partner unless she chose to be, and among the gentlemen whose company she enjoyed most were Senator Sumner, a friend of her father's she had long admired; Colonel Elmer Ellsworth, a very dear but much younger friend of Mr. Lincoln's from Chicago, who looked gallant in his red-and-black Zouave uniform and spoke with endearing earnestness about his pretty fiancée back home in Rockford; and Mr. John Hay, the handsome, debonair, and very charming assistant private secretary to the president. She enjoyed Mr. Hay's company so much that she allowed him to a second dance, and when he asked if he might call on her on another occasion, she graciously agreed.

But it was the governor of Rhode Island whom she most desired to dance with again, though when the time came, she endeavored to show no more eagerness for his company than any other gentleman's. It was a waltz, and Kate felt the heat rising in her chest as she remembered that other waltz, and what he had done and said, and part of her dreaded that he would do the same again, and part of her could not believe that he would be so brash as to attempt it in such illustrious company.

She had worked herself into such a state of suspense that when he behaved with perfect courtesy, she was almost disappointed.

The dance ended, and as he escorted her from the floor, Governor Sprague asked, "May I call on you and Senator Chase before I return to Rhode Island?"

She felt a crushing disappointment. Of course he wanted to speak to her father more than herself, and of course he would not remain in Washington long; he had a state to govern. "You may," she replied, slightly aloof. "I'm sure Senator Chase would be pleased to speak with you again."

He recognized the chill in her tone, but misunderstood her reason, or pretended to. "Did I offend? Perhaps I should have said *Secretary* Chase instead?"

"Not at all," she said evenly. "My father was sworn in as a senator of Ohio earlier today. Perhaps you heard something of the event?"

"Oh, yes, I do recall hearing something about a rather large gathering at the Capitol." He lowered his voice conspiratorially, and for a moment her heart pounded again, but when he leaned closer, all he said was, "I have heard other things too, and I am not certain your father will remain long in the Senate."

And with that, he transformed his intimate bend into a formal bow, straightened, and left her staring after him, utterly astonished.

The dancing and celebrating continued until the small hours of the morning, but President Lincoln left before two o'clock, visibly exhausted and, Kate supposed, mindful of the arduous duties that awaited him in the morning. Father had not wanted to leave before the president, but as soon as he departed Father found Kate and told her it was time to go. Concealing her reluctance, Kate collected her wraps, found Adele Douglas in the throng and bade her good night, and took her father's arm. She hated to leave while Mrs. Lincoln was still whirling about on the dance floor, clearly having the most wonderful night of her life.

"You were the brightest star of the evening, my dear," Father said as they drove home, his voice heavy with weariness.

Kate thanked him, but she knew she had not been. Whether the cause was her lingering disappointment that father had been denied both the presidential chair and the cabinet, or her unsettling distraction over Governor Sprague, or Mrs. Lincoln's greater sense of joy and triumph, she knew the president's wife had outshone her.

Even Father slept in past dawn the next day, but the household was bustling by midmorning. Over a late breakfast, Kate gave in to Nettie's pleas to describe the ball, although she did not divulge her conflicted feelings about Governor Sprague.

Soon thereafter, Father and Kate returned to the Capitol for his first full day as a senator for the Thirty-Seventh Congress. Nettie had been invited along too, but she had had quite enough of speeches the previous day and had begged to be allowed to stay home and draw. Once again within the Senate chamber, Father took his seat beside Senator Wade, Kate found a place in the gallery above, and after greeting other ladies and gentlemen she knew, she settled back to observe the machinery of government at work. She was proudly confident that with her father present, the people of Ohio would be well represented, and the peace and prosperity of the nation well served.

The first order of business was to appoint a committee to inform the president that the Senate was assembled and ready to receive any communication he would be pleased to make. The resolution passed, the committee was formed, and the Senate voted to recess for a half hour until the committee could report back from its errand to the Executive Mansion. Kate had to smile at the familiar back-and-forth and the often slow and tedious progress of the legislative body, but she conducted business of her own during the break, chatting with the wives of her father's colleagues and making introductions between people she thought ought to know one another. But even then, and after the proceedings resumed, she also kept careful watch over her father's rivals, in case she needed to alert him to a curious or clandestine pairing. Her observations were especially important on the few occasions when her father was obliged to leave the chamber and would not know what had occurred in his absence.

Father was away on an errand, she knew not what, when the Senate shifted from considering various resolutions to executive business, and the clerk prepared to read aloud messages from the president delivered by his private secretary, Mr. Nicolay. "To the Senate of the United States," the clerk began in a booming voice, "I nominate William H. Seward, of New York, to be secretary of state of the United States. Signed, Abraham Lincoln."

Kate glanced to the door through which her father had departed. It was probably just as well that he had missed that particular announcement, and the applause it had evoked.

"To the Senate of the United States," the clerk intoned, his eyes on the second message, "I nominate Salmon P. Chase, of Ohio, to be secretary of the treasury of the United States. Signed, Abraham Lincoln."

Someone behind her gasped. Stunned, Kate sat perfectly still, the words echoing in her thoughts. A gentleman murmured congratulations to her, and she nodded, eyes fixed on the clerk, then darting to the door, and to her father's empty chair. She must have misheard—but she knew she had not. Her heart thudded as the clerk read off the nominees for the Department of War, for the navy, for postmaster general, and on through the cabinet. Kate clasped her hands together in her lap, fixed her gaze on the doorway, and willed her father to return. She had no idea where he had gone, so she could not send a messenger running for him.

He was still away when the Senate, by unanimous consent, resolved to advise and approve Father's appointment and that of four other nominees. A few of the president's other choices were voted on and confirmed by a large majority, but with a few nays voiced by senators from North Carolina, Virginia, Arkansas, and Kentucky.

Other appointments, diplomats and assistant secretaries, were nominated and approved, and it was while Secretary Seward's son was being confirmed as the assistant secretary of state that Father returned to the chamber. Immediately, several of his colleagues approached to clap him on the back and shake his hand, and Kate's heart went out to him in that moment of confusion, for he had no idea why congratulations were in order. She watched, pained, as realization dawned on his face. Suddenly he gathered up his coat and satchel and strode from the room.

Murmuring apologies to those seated around her, Kate quickly rose and hurried from the gallery, expecting to meet her father in the rotunda, but although she waited, pacing back and forth and glancing down the corridors, he failed to appear long after he should have done.

She had been too slow and had missed him, and in his shock he had forgotten to wait for her.

Kate considered returning to the gallery, but the sudden bustle of senators and spectators in the corridors told her that executive business had been completed and the Senate had adjourned for the day. Thoughts racing, she began to walk home, wondering where Father had gone, hoping she would find him at his desk at the Rugby House writing a furious letter to Mr. Lincoln, and fearing that he had gone straight to the White House to voice his outrage and decline the appointment.

She wondered if any man had ever been offered a place in a president's cabinet in such an inexplicable, almost underhanded manner.

When Kate returned home, she found Nettie and Vina hanging red, white, and blue bunting around the parlor, and they had bought a cake to celebrate Father's first full day in the Senate. Kate laughed helplessly at the thought of a celebration, when she had no idea whether Father was at that moment elated or furious.

She waited, pacing until Nettie begged her to stop, and then she tried to distract herself with a novel, and then with letter writing to the many aunts, uncles, cousins, and distant friends who had asked her to send them her impressions of Inauguration Day. Shortly before suppertime, she heard the door open and Nettie greet their father delightedly. Setting her pen aside, Kate flew to meet him, and knew from the consternation in his expression that he had called on the president and was not altogether pleased with the words they had exchanged.

He had gone to the White House, Father reported as he sank into the room's best chair and Kate sent Vina to fetch some tea. "I expressed to him my anger, and my disappointment, and my shock at his neglect of the proper protocol and simple decency in his handling of this matter."

Kate tried not to wince as she imagined the scene, her father angry and hectoring, Mr. Lincoln somber and sympathetic. "And then?"

"And then, naturally, I declined the office."

Kate sank into the chair opposite him. "How did the president respond?"

Father sighed, ran a hand over his brow, and was silent for a moment. "He was very somber, and full of regret, and he noted quite correctly that, having been confirmed by the Senate, if I withdrew now, it would occasion him great embarrassment."

"It certainly would," said Kate carefully, "and you could suffer in the esteem of the people for it."

"It could weaken his administration before it could properly take hold, and it would damage the party," Father acknowledged. "He asked me to reconsider, and I told him that I would give it careful thought."

"I think that was the wise thing to do," said Kate, unable to keep a tremor of relief from her voice.

Father did reflect carefully that night, and prayed about it, and in the morning he told Kate that he had decided to accept the president's appointment. The Department of the Treasury and the second-most-powerful cabinet position were his.

It was not until later that Kate remembered Governor Sprague's prescient words at the Inaugural Ball. How had he known what was to come, when even Father had not?

Chapter Seven

$\mathcal{W}$hen Father sat down for the first time behind his polished walnut desk in his high-ceilinged office on the third floor of the southeast corner of the new Treasury Building, a magnificent marble structure at Fifteenth Street and Pennsylvania Avenue, tears of pride sprang into Kate's eyes, but she quickly blinked them away before Father or Nettie noticed. "You look quite at home here," she proclaimed. "These elegant rooms make the White House look shabby in comparison."

"The White House looks shabby compared to almost anything," said Nettie, quite correctly. "All that torn carpeting and worn-out furniture and cut-up draperies. I think if Mr. Lincoln could see your office, Father, he would want to trade jobs with you so that he could have this for himself."

"I rather think he would not," said Father wryly, and Kate hid a smile. "Besides, the White House might not remain an embarrassment much longer. Congress allots twenty thousand dollars to each administration to refurbish the White House, and from what I've heard, Mrs. Lincoln has begun spending the allowance with unrestrained delight."

"The Executive Mansion should be beautiful, elegant, and glorious," said Kate, stifling a twinge of envy as she imagined selecting draperies, carpeting, and furniture for the Executive Mansion, "as befits a distinguished nation." How wonderful it would be to have so much money to spend, and to put the mark of her own excellent taste on a building of such national and historic importance! She had enjoyed decorating their home in Columbus, and refurbishing the White House would have been an even more exhilarating task. It pained her to think what Mrs. Lincoln, fresh from the frontier, would consider tasteful and refined.

If her father could not reside at the White House, at least not yet, Kate was determined to see that he should have another home as befitting to his status and dignity as his handsome new offices were. And at last she found it: a three-story Greek Revival brick mansion at the corner of Sixth and E streets. It boasted a bracketed cornice, a pedimented entrance at the top of a stone staircase, and elaborate architraves around all the windows. The basement story was embellished with rusticated stone, and a low cupola atop the roof provided additional light and ventilation that would bring welcome relief from the humidity of summer. Inside were comfortable living quarters for the family and servants, a quiet study for Father, and spacious, elegant rooms for entertaining. It was a tolerable walk to the Treasury Building and not much farther to the White House, where Father expected often to be. Kate toured the residence on her own first, as she had done many times before at many other vacant homes, but after examining the building from cellar nearly to rooftop, she promptly scheduled a second viewing later that same day for the rest of the family. Father approved of the house, and Nettie adored it, and so Father leased the residence, agreeing to pay one hundred dollars a month in rent plus two additional dollars a week for wages for Mrs. Catherine Vaudry, the colored housekeeper in their landlord's employ. The expense was greater than Father had hoped to spend, considering that his salary was only eight thousand dollars a year, but it was quite reasonable for the size, location, and quality of the property. Father and Kate agreed that it was highly unlikely that they would find anything as suitable for less.

The residence was modestly but inadequately furnished, and while the foundation and structure were sound and the interior had been well kept, it was in desperate need of refurbishment. Kate was delighted when Father delegated this task to her. "You transformed our home in Columbus into an elegant, gracious residence where all visitors, from the most humble to the most illustrious, felt comfortable and welcome," he said. "I trust you will do the same here, where we can expect to entertain the most celebrated men of our age—senators, foreign dignitaries, and, of course, presidents."

She felt the warm glow that his praise always inspired when it came without qualification—so rare it had been, from the time of her earliest memories, that her father's praise was not preceded by twice again as much criticism. She knew how important a gracious home and a skillful hostess would be to her father in his new, exalted position, and she was gratified beyond measure that he entrusted that role to her.

She knew too that no one else could perform it half as well as herself, for no one else knew him as well as she, and no one was more devoted to him, and to his noble ambitions.

With his usual stern, anxious admonitions not to spend any more than she absolutely must, Father dispatched Kate to purchase wallpapers, carpets, furniture, china, anything that could not be sent or needed to be replaced from their home in Columbus. It was with great pleasure that she obeyed. She soon discovered that there was nothing suitable to be had in Washington City, so she made several trips to Philadelphia and New York to obtain what she needed, choosing one object here, another there, accumulating the perfect furnishings over time.

It was while she was on an excursion to Philadelphia that Governor Sprague finally called at the Rugby House. She learned about his visit only upon her return, and she was disappointed that she had missed him, disgruntled that he could not have come on one of the great many days she had been in Washington, annoyed with herself for caring either way, and quite unhappy that the purpose for his visit had been to bid the Chase family farewell, for the following day he was returning to Rhode Island, to his governor's chair and his bustling factories.

How fortunate it was that she did not care what William Sprague did, Kate reminded herself. She had hardly suffered from a dearth of interesting conversation in his absence; in fact, she had been only partly aware that he had remained in Washington after the Inaugural Ball. John Hay had called several times since that night, even though his work as the president's assistant private secretary kept him terrifically busy. Mr. Hay intrigued her with his stories of the White House, he was respectful to her father, and he never forgot to bring along a little gift for Nettie—new pencils, a cloth-bound sketchbook. Only two years older than herself in contrast to Governor Sprague's ten, he had been named

"Class Poet" in the year of his graduation from Brown, and he could enchant her with an evocative sonnet as easily as he could amuse her with a lighthearted joke. Nor was Mr. Hay her only admirer—and if Governor Sprague chose not to apply that title to himself, that was fine with her. She certainly did not admire *him*, she told herself firmly, banishing the Boy Governor from her thoughts.

Her thoughts were full enough with other, far more important matters. On the day after the inauguration, the first item placed upon the new president's desk had been a letter from Major Anderson at Fort Sumter, informing him that their provisions would be exhausted within a month, even though the men had already dropped to half rations. An addendum from General Scott acknowledged that he saw no alternative but surrender.

At the end of the month, President and Mrs. Lincoln hosted a state dinner, their first, for the cabinet members, their ladies, and a few other dignitaries. It should have been a delightful evening. The Blue Room looked splendid, a testament to Mrs. Lincoln's refurbishment scheme. The food was excellent, the company interesting and pleasant—with the exception of the hostess, who was in a particularly peculiar and demanding mood, at least when she was alone with Kate. Apparently she had been brooding over an imagined snub ever since the presidential train had passed through Columbus in February and Kate had not been there to welcome her. Kate tried to explain that the Chases had already left for Washington because Father had been appointed to the Peace Convention, but Mrs. Lincoln obstinately refused to accept that as a legitimate excuse. It was all very strange, and in parting, Kate spoke to her more imperiously than she should have done. She regretted her choice of words, but Mrs. Lincoln had been simply impossible and Kate had reached the limit of her tolerance. She was not some meek schoolgirl the First Lady could lord over, and Mrs. Lincoln might as well understand that from the beginning.

As they rode home from the dinner, Kate expected Father to rebuke her for not showing proper deference to the president's wife, but when he did not mention the exchange, she began to hope that its underlying tone had escaped him. "After the gentlemen withdrew to the Red Room," she said, to distract him, and also because she was curious, "I saw Mr.

Nicolay summon the cabinet into another chamber. I assume it was to discuss an important matter of state."

"Yes." Father inhaled deeply, weighed down by the cares of his office. "Mr. Lincoln read us a report from General Scott."

"Bad news, I gather."

"It could hardly be worse. The general believes it is now unlikely that the voluntary evacuation of Fort Sumter alone would have any effect upon the decision of those states now considering whether to remain with the Union or secede."

"How dreadful—but is that really a surprise? Have you not said all along that surrendering the fort would only embolden the secessionists?"

Father nodded. "I have said so, but few in the cabinet have agreed with me. General Scott also believes that in order to persuade these wavering slave states to remain in the Union, we would have to abandon Fort Pickens too, to prove that President Lincoln will keep the promises of his inaugural address and not interfere with slavery where it exists."

"The Union is meant to sacrifice two forts in order to keep eight states." Kate managed a bleak laugh. "Some would argue that what General Scott proposes is a fair trade, perhaps even advantageous."

"This is Seward's doing," Father said grimly. "He's had a temporizing influence on the president all along. He's long argued that if the president abandons Fort Sumter, the South would be appeased and would eventually return to the Union."

"That's wishful thinking with no basis in logic, in my opinion."

"Mr. Lincoln presented other arguments in his inaugural address that would be worthwhile to remember. He made a very convincing case for the illegality of any state to secede from the Union."

"I suppose it remains to be seen which promise Mr. Lincoln will keep," said Kate. "I cannot see how he can honor both."

"Nor do I. Surrendering the forts would embarrass the North and tear the country asunder, and sending relief to Major Anderson could provoke an attack that would lead to civil war." He fell silent for a moment. "The cabinet will meet again, tomorrow at noon, to discuss the latest intelligence from the South, and shortly thereafter, I expect Mr. Lincoln will make his decision."

"I hope he'll listen to your wise counsel," Kate said, taking her father's hand.

"Katie, dear," Father said solemnly, "hope first that my counsel *will* be wise, for at this moment I don't know how to advise him. From every direction I examine the problem, on the horizon, I invariably see war."

Kate's heart thumped, and she held his hand tighter.

They drove the rest of the way home in silence.

The following afternoon, Kate waited anxiously for her father to return home from the meeting at the White House. He brought stunning, though not altogether surprising news: After considering credible reports that Major Anderson's position was untenable and that loyalty to the Union was dead in South Carolina, President Lincoln had determined to supply and reinforce both Fort Sumter in Charleston and Fort Pickens on Santa Rosa Island near Pensacola, Florida. The majority opinion of the cabinet agreed, with only Mr. Seward and Secretary of the Interior Caleb Smith dissenting.

How and when these relief operations would be conducted remained to be seen.

Even as he advised the president on the crisis in the South, Father was obliged to devote most of his long hours to the financial and fiscal affairs of the nation. As the former counsel for the Cincinnati branch of the Bank of the United States and the director of several Ohio banks, he was as well suited for his new position as any of his predecessors had been, and better prepared than most. He was well versed in prevailing economic theories, and his sound, logical mind and industrious temperament would enable him to educate himself quickly in the unfamiliar field of government finance.

What Father discovered in his first examination of the country's ledgers was something just short of a disaster. The government was deeply in debt, with a mere three million dollars in its coffers against a total debt of almost sixty-five million. Corruption in the Buchanan administration, the Panic of 1857, and the rending of the Union had battered the nation's finances, and with Congress out of session and thereby unable to authorize new taxes and tariffs to raise revenue, Father was forced to seek loans to meet expenses. At first the banks resisted, demanding higher interest rates than the nation could afford, but Father appealed to the bankers' patriotism as well as their pragmatism and eventually managed to secure enough funding to keep the government solvent. "President Lincoln must hold the crumbling nation together," Father grumbled to Kate over an increasingly rare chess game. "Secretary Cameron must defeat the rebels, and I must figure out how to pay for it all."

But defeating the rebels was not entirely left up to Secretary Cameron, for Father soon took on numerous responsibilities that ordinarily belonged within the War Department. As a longtime resident of Cincinnati, just across the Ohio River from the crucial border state of Kentucky, Father naturally became the president's chief advisor on the region. Mr. Lincoln relied upon him to take principal charge of preventing not only Kentucky, but also Missouri and Tennessee, from succumbing to secessionist threats from within. Father authorized a loyal state senator to raise twenty Union companies from Kentucky, and he composed the orders that granted Andrew Johnson, the only United States senator from a Confederate state who had remained loyal to the Union, to muster regiments in Tennessee. All the while, the president was mindful that secessionist sympathizers lingered, often unknown, in every department, with the potential to substantially undermine the security of the Union. Since official agents could not be relied upon, President Lincoln, with the unanimous consent of the cabinet, instructed Father to dispense millions of dollars to a small group of trustworthy private individuals who would be authorized to negotiate contracts for the manufacturing of weapons and supplies required to mobilize the military.

Father's labors were many, and his daughters saw less of him as he toiled late into the night in his private office suite at the Treasury Building or rushed off to the White House for cabinet meetings at an unexpected summons from the president. With the house on Sixth and E streets not yet ready, Father encouraged Kate to undertake another shopping expedition to New York to purchase the last items they needed. Father's good friend Hiram Barney had invited the family to visit, and while Father's obligations made it impossible for him to leave Washington, the Chase sisters were happy to accept.

Mr. Barney had served as Father's commissioner of schools during his first term as governor of Ohio, and they had developed a strong friendship based upon mutual trust and commitment to abolition. Four years before, Mr. Barney had moved from Columbus to New York, where he had established a successful law firm. A handsome man of fifty years with a deep cleft in his square jaw, a thick dark mustache, and iron-gray hair swept back from a broad forehead, Mr. Barney possessed an air of strength, sincerity, and purpose, and he had worked tirelessly to help Father win the Republican nomination for the presidency in 1856 and 1860. Although the ventures failed, Father never forgot Mr. Barney's loyalty, and he was proud to have secured for his old friend one of the most prestigious and lucrative posts within the Department of the Treasury patronage, the collectorship of the custom house of New York. Mr. Barney stood to earn between twenty and thirty thousand dollars a year in salary and fees, more even than the president, and he controlled the posts of hundreds of subordinate employees. Mr. Seward, a native of New York State, had wanted to fill the post with one of his own loyal friends, but in this case Father had triumphed.

Kate and Nettie were met at the station by Mr. Barney; his wife, Susan; and the eldest of their six children, Will, a young man only a few months older than Kate. Slender and bespectacled, with a quiet, intellectual reserve, Will had graduated from Harvard College and had nearly completed his studies at Harvard Law School. Kate enjoyed his company, and she was also very much looking forward to reuniting with his younger sister, a lively, pretty girl of eighteen named Susan after her mother.

"My dear girls," Mrs. Barney exclaimed, spreading her arms for Kate and Nettie's embraces, which they happily gave. She was a slender, fair-haired, gentle woman, with long, graceful fingers that were almost always engaged in handwork of some sort, whether knitting or embroidery or playing sonatas on the family's piano, which was faithfully kept in perfect tune.

After resting from their journey for a day at the Barneys' lovely home in Spuyten Duyvil, Kate took care of her errands at the shops, and then spent a pleasant week reading, riding, calling on friends, and seeing the sights. She especially enjoyed Nettie's delight in her first experience of New York, which she took in with wide-eyed wonder.

One evening Mr. and Mrs. Barney escorted the Chase sisters and their own two eldest children to a performance of the New York Philharmonic at the Academy of Music. Afterward they were outside waiting for their carriage when shouts and commotion down the block drew their attention. "Extra! War begun!" one young newsboy bellowed. "Fire opened on Fort Sumter!"

"Anderson returning fire!" another newsboy shouted on the street corner close behind them. Startled, Kate whirled about and spotted the lad, barely visible within a crowd of anxious pedestrians, who snapped up his papers as quickly as he could take the coins from their hands.

Mr. Barney laid his hand on his wife's shoulder for a moment before striding off toward the nearest newsboy. Instinctively Kate hurried after him, and when he opened the *Tribune* she read over his shoulder, scarcely able to breathe, as the terrible news was delivered in a column of bold, abrupt bursts:

WAR BEGUN!
FIRE OPENED ON FORT SUMTER.
ANDERSON RETURNING THE FIRE.

Reported Breaches in the Fort.

Alleged Success of the Rebels.

Three War Vessels Outside the Bar.

Firing Ceased for the Night.

Hostilities to be Renewed at Daylight.

Several Rebels Wounded.

Major Anderson Stronger than Supposed.

Taking a deep, shaky breath, Kate rested her hand on Mr. Barney's arm and held on until her knees stopped trembling. Absently Mr. Barney patted her hand but kept his gaze fixed on the newspaper, his jaw clenched, the pages trembling slightly in his grip. Suddenly he folded the paper, tucked it beneath his arm, and murmured, "Come, Kate." Numbly she kept pace with him as he escorted her back to the family, who had settled into the carriage and were looking anxiously down the sidewalk after them through the windows.

None of them slept well that night.

The next day, newspaper correspondents in the South reported that Fort Sumter had sustained so much damage that it had been rendered utterly indefensible. When Major Anderson concluded that their position was untenable, he had accepted General Beauregard's terms of evacuation: He would be permitted to evacuate his command without surrendering his arms, and he and his men would be granted safe, unimpeded transport to the North.

As the exhausted, disappointed, and half-starved Union soldiers stood in formation on what remained of the parade grounds, the Stars and Stripes had been lowered, folded reverently, and presented to Major Anderson. Then, with the drum and fife corps playing "Yankee Doodle," the federal troops had marched from the crumbling stronghold they had defended faithfully since shortly before Christmas. The following morning, they had been transferred to the Union steamship *Baltic*, which soon departed for New York with Major Anderson's flag flying atop the mast.

In the aftermath of the shocking loss of Fort Sumter, a new patriotic fervor swept through New York City. For a moment, dissent fell silent and outrage replaced sympathy for the South as cries for a swift, forceful military response filled the air. Impromptu rallies and marches sprang up in parks and squares; the Stars and Stripes flew from nearly every mast and flagpole and balcony. "Sumter is lost but freedom is saved," the *New York Tribune* declared. Gone at last were thoughts of appeasement, of coaxing or bribing the traitor states in the South to return to the Union. "It seems but yesterday that at least two-thirds of the journals of this city were the virtual allies of the Secessionists, their apologists, their champions," another paper observed about the sudden shift in the temper of the city. "The roar of the great circle of batteries pouring their iron hail upon devoted Sumter has struck them all dumb."

On Monday, when President Lincoln issued a call for seventy-five thousand troops to suppress the uprising, with a certain quota required from each state, the men of New York rushed to form infantry regiments. Seized by military zeal, young men from upstate raced to the city, eager to enlist and to see a bit of action before the rebels were defeated and the excitement passed. Within two days of the president's call to arms, Colonel Ellsworth, Mr. Lincoln's friend from Chicago with whom Kate had danced at the Inaugural Ball, arrived in New York seeking to form a Zouave regiment of eight hundred choice men from among the city's firefighters. Kate had read about his plan in a brief notice in the afternoon paper on the day of his arrival, so she knew he was in the city, and she was pleased to see him across the room when they happened to attend the same levee at City Hall that evening.

"Colonel Ellsworth," she greeted him warmly after he had worked his way through the crowd to her side. "I cannot think of any other man I would rather see at this moment. Tell me, what is the news from Washington City? Have you seen my father recently?"

"I regret that I haven't had the pleasure of seeing Secretary Chase recently," the colonel replied. "I know that on the night Fort Sumter fell, the entire cabinet was closeted with President Lincoln until the small hours of the morning, but regrettably, I was not privy to their discussion."

"And what is the mood of the city?" Kate asked, hiding her disappointment.

"Much as it is here," he said. "Patriotism and loyalty for the Union have filled every heart, although there is greater worry there that the city will be threatened by rebel militia."

Kate nodded. For all that it was the capital of the Union, Washington was essentially a Southern city, surrounded by Maryland to the north and east, on the other side of the Chesapeake Bay, and Virginia to the west and south, with only the Potomac separating them. "If their hearts are equally patriotic and loyal, why do you come to New York to recruit for your Zouaves, instead of choosing among the men of Washington City?"

"I'm a native of New York State, and I want the New York firemen. There are no more effective men in the country and none with whom I can do so much." As he spoke, Colonel Ellsworth's voice became grave. "Miss Chase, I don't mean to alarm you, but our friends at Washington are sleeping on a volcano, and I want men who are ready at any moment to plunge into the thickest of the fight."

Her heart thumped with trepidation at his solemn certainty of coming danger. "When I'm home once again," Kate told him steadily, "it will be a great reassurance to know that you're commanding such courageous men in the defense of our city."

While New York and other states throughout the Union promptly organized volunteer troops in response to the president's call to arms, the governors of Kentucky, Missouri, North Carolina, and Virginia scornfully declared that they would furnish no regiments to go to war against their Southern brethren. Then, on April 17, two days after Mr. Lincoln issued his proclamation, Virginia seceded from the Union. It was a terrible blow to the North, but the rebellious states of the South rejoiced, knowing that it was only a matter of time before the new independent commonwealth of Virginia added its military and economic might to the Confederacy.

The next day, Major Anderson and his officers arrived in New York to a hero's welcome. It was a bright, breezy afternoon, so the Barneys and Chases went down to the Brooklyn wharves to witness the *Baltic* come in to the harbor. Thousands of citizens had gathered, and all the vessels in the bay and the houses along the shore had been decked with flags in honor of the heroes of Fort Sumter. As the ship approached with its escort, an artillery salute boomed from the guns at the forts and on the shore, and every nearby steeple bell rang, and everywhere the people cheered and waved flags. In reply, the *Baltic* waved her ensign and fired her cannon, to the delight of the crowd.

As the steamer came steadily and gracefully forward, Kate observed that a tattered flag of the United States flew from the foremast, and from the mizzenmast hung another, so badly damaged that it was nearly in rags. She was startled to see that the prow was shattered as if from a collision or the impact of a cannonball, and yet, thankfully, the ship was evidently seaworthy. Soldiers in ragged blue coats, dusty with what Kate imagined was the pulverized brick and mortar of the ruined fort, packed the deck, and although the men looked hungry and tired, they heartily returned the cheers from the shore, their voices hoarse but proud.

"That's Major Anderson," a man observing the scene from a ferryboat shouted. "On the wheelhouse. That's him right there!"

Excitement surged as word spread through the crowd. Shading her eyes with her hand, Kate spied a slight, clean-shaven man wrapped in a military overcoat standing atop the wheelhouse. The roar of approval that greeted Major Anderson and his men—so proud and patriotic and stirring—left Kate almost breathless, and tears came into her eyes as she too applauded the returning heroes.

Later, Mr. Barney informed them that Major Anderson had taken rooms at the Brevoort House, a fine hotel on the corner of Eighth Street and Fifth Avenue, where he had been reunited with his relieved and happy wife. Although he had traveled quietly there with friends who had met him on the landing, word of his arrival had spread swiftly, and soon a raucous crowd had gathered outside, cheering loudly and calling for the major to address them. "I confess I myself have imposed upon his rest," Mr. Barney admitted. "I've arranged for him to attend the bridal reception at William Aspinwall's home in two days' time so that we might meet him."

"I want to meet him too," said Nettie. "Oh, Kate, may we?"

Kate shook her head. "I thought we would leave for Washington that morning."

"Couldn't we stay just one day longer?" Nettie implored. "I miss home too, but it's just one day for the chance to meet the hero of Fort Sumter. Please, Kate?"

Kate wavered.

"Yes, please do stay," said Mr. Barney earnestly. "We would all enjoy another day of your company, and I think Mr. Chase would want you to learn the truth about Major Anderson's adventure from the man himself, so you can give him a better account than he would get from the newspapers or some dry official report."

That convinced her. The following morning, Kate, Nettie, and Susan strolled to the post office to mail a note to her father about their altered travel plans, chatting pleasantly about their gowns, offering suggestions for how to arrange one another's hair, and speculating about which gentlemen of their acquaintance might also attend. On their way back to the Barney residence, they heard newsboys' shouts and saw people racing to purchase their papers, fresh off the presses. "Massachusetts volunteers opposed in their passage through Baltimore," a boy shouted, waving a paper in the air. "Bloody fight between the soldiers and the mob!"

Susan stopped short and pressed a hand to her heart; Nettie gave a little gasp; but after a brief moment of stunned stillness, Kate took Nettie's hand and briskly led her to the corner with Susan trailing along behind. Quickly Kate dug into her reticule for a coin and bought the *Herald*, nearly tearing it in her haste to open it. As Susan and Nettie read along beside her, the dire headlines struck with chilling force.

THE WAR.

Highly Important News from Baltimore.

The Massachusetts Volunteers Opposed in Their Passage Through the City.

Bloody Fight Between the Soldiers and the Mob.

Two Soldiers and Seven Citizens Killed.

The Volunteers Succeed in Forcing their Way Through.

Total Destruction of the Arsenal at Harper's Ferry by the Federal Troops

Seizure of Northern Vessels in Virginia.

"But Maryland is in the Union," said Susan, looking faint. "How could such a dreadful thing happen there?"

"Southern sympathizers are everywhere," said Kate, folding up the paper and urging her companions on home as quickly as they could.

The nation was crumbling, but more than two hundred miles to the southwest, she knew that her father was fighting valiantly to hold it together. She longed to be there to support him, to lend him all the skills at her disposal, to do whatever she could to help him in that unprecedented crisis. Two days more, she told herself firmly. Two days more, and she and Nettie would be home.

But the next day, more news from Baltimore dashed her hopes. In the final study of the riot, it was determined that at least three soldiers and nine civilians had been killed and scores more injured. The damage to property had been even more devastating than originally known, for after the federal troops had escaped, frenzied Southern sympathizers had destroyed railroad tracks leading to the north, burned bridges, and severed telegraph lines, isolating Washington City from the rest of the Union.

Washington stood alone, stranded and imperiled, surrounded by enemies— and yet it was the only place Kate wished to be, and utterly impossible to reach.

The news that Washington was vulnerable sent a frisson of urgency racing through the North. While young men rushed to join regiments and engineers raced to repair the damaged bridges and railroad tracks, governors ordered their newly mustered regiments to Washington and military officers contrived other ways to transport them there, since Baltimore remained impassable.

In many ways, ordinary life continued much as it always had, though not unaffected by the escalating crisis. When the bridal party and guests gathered at the Aspinwall residence at the corner of University Place and Twelfth Street for the wedding reception, the Stars and Stripes was proudly displayed, and within, the elegant rooms were adorned with exquisite rare plants and shrubs and decorations of red, white, and blue, lending the celebration the air of a military ball.

The bride and groom were the guests of honor, of course, but second only to them came Major Anderson. When he and Kate were introduced shortly before dinner, he accepted her compliments with gracious humility, observing that he had endeavored to do his duty at Fort Sumter, as any other loyal officer would have done in his place. He looked to Kate to be in his midfifties and was of medium height but slender build, perhaps due to the deprivations of the siege. Clean-shaven, with a hawklike nose, elegant features bronzed by the sun, and brown hair that waved back from a high forehead, he had an air of quiet strength that even his evident fatigue did not diminish.

Kate listened, fascinated, as he politely responded to the many questions posed to him about his ordeal. He spoke plainly, without evident embellishment of his deeds, in a voice that carried the accents of his native Kentucky.

"Is it true," one wide-eyed matron asked, "that before you left Fort Moultrie for Sumter, you cut down the flagstaff there?"

"I did order it done," the major acknowledged. "I knew that as soon as we quit Fort Moultrie, the South Carolinians would seize the fort, and I didn't want any other flag but the Stars and Stripes to fly from that staff."

A murmur of admiration and respect went through the group, but the conversation was interrupted by the summons to dinner. Kate fell into step beside him as they went to take their places. "Forgive me, Major Anderson," she said, smiling. "If you have grown weary of the subject of Fort Sumter, say the word and I shall ask your opinion of the weather instead."

"Ask whatever you wish, Miss Chase," he said, returning her smile. "I will do my best to answer well."

"How did you keep your men's courage from faltering over so many months?" she asked. "It's a question of great importance to me, because I suspect we'll all need encouragement in the months ahead."

A thoughtful look came into his deep-set brown eyes, and when he halted in the corridor to consider his response, she paused too. "The men were brave, well trained and well disciplined," he told her. "It was not in their nature to panic or to surrender, despite the deprivations they endured."

"What will happen now?" Kate asked. "Some Northerners have argued that if Fort Sumter were surrendered to South Carolina, their rebellious people would be mollified, and they would willingly return to the Union."

"I truly doubt that will happen," Major Anderson said. "Or rather, Miss Chase, I am sadly confident that it will not. Our Southern brethren have done grievously wrong. They have rebelled and have attacked their father's house and their loyal brothers. They will not return to the Union unless forced to do so. They must be punished and brought back, but this necessity breaks my heart."

The days passed, and as the newspapers reported the progress of regiments from Rhode Island, Massachusetts, Ohio, and other loyal states to Washington, Kate impatiently waited for railroad service to be fully restored. At last word came that regiments had arrived in the capital and had immediately begun shoring up its defenses—but Kate's expectations that she and Nettie might finally go home were quickly dashed. Baltimore remained a dangerous nest of Southern collusion, and neither Father nor Mr. Barney wanted the sisters to attempt the journey unprotected.

"Mrs. Lincoln remains in Washington," Kate pointed out to Susan. "Is she braver than I? If the capital is safe enough for the president's wife, it is safe enough for me."

"Washington City may be safe enough," Susan acknowledged, "but getting there is another matter."

Near the end of April, Colonel Ellsworth and his Zouaves were sent off to Washington in grand style, with the presentation of numerous banners and guide flags in a splendid ceremony in front of the company's headquarters on Canal Street, stirring speeches by a representative from the New York Fire Department and Colonel Ellsworth, and a magnificent procession of soldiers and fire engines up Broadway, to the Astor House, past City Hall, and down Canal Street toward the North River. Massive crowds lined the parade route, especially around Collins's wharf, where the troops boarded the *Baltic* for transport to Washington. Once aboard, the Zouaves, gallantly attired in their red caps and shirts, with black pants and trim of gold braid, and each man shouldering a new Sharps rifle, were met on the upper deck by Mr. Cassius Clay, who offered rousing oration in their honor, evoking loud and prolonged cheers from the thousands of onlookers.

After the ceremony, Kate accompanied Mr. Barney down to the ship to bid Colonel Ellsworth one last farewell and to offer her heartfelt wishes for his success and safety. "If you happen to see my father," she added, "please tell him that I am determined to return to Washington as soon as I can find an escort who can assure our safety."

"I will certainly pass on your message," the colonel replied, "but Miss Chase, had I known you wished to join your father in the capital, I would have been honored to escort you and your sister. I would have given you my own stateroom aboard the *Baltic*."

"I confess it had not occurred to me to ask," said Kate, dismayed. "I wish with all my heart that I had."

"As do I," Colonel Ellsworth said. "When you do return to Washington City, I hope I may have the great pleasure of dancing with you again."

"I hope so too," she said. "Do be careful while you're out there defending the city so bravely, so that you will be fit for dancing afterward."

She should have been on that ship, Kate thought, her heart sinking as she watched it depart. She and Nettie could have been on their way home at that very moment.

She vowed not to let another opportunity slip through her fingers.

On the first day of May, Mr. Barney returned from dining out with Major Anderson with the news that the officer had been attached to the Department of the East and had been assigned the command of the division at Fort Hamilton, including the fortifications and garrisons in New York harbor and its vicinity. The day before, he had visited the fort on the southwestern tip of Brooklyn to muster and inspect troops stationed there, but he was expected to travel to Washington soon in order to present himself to Secretary of War Cameron.

"Soon?" Kate asked. "How soon?"

"Tomorrow or the next day," Mr. Barney replied.

"Perhaps he would allow Nettie and me to accompany him."

"Oh, yes, please," exclaimed Nettie. "I like him very much, and I miss Father."

Mr. and Mrs. Barney exchanged a look, and when Mrs. Barney gave a slight nod, Mr. Barney agreed that Kate could inquire.

She immediately wrote Major Anderson an earnest, charming letter describing their plight. A few hours dragged by, until a messenger brought Major Anderson's reply: He would be honored to escort the daughters of Secretary Chase home to Washington City, if they could be ready to depart two days hence.

Early in the morning two days later, after sharing tearful farewells and promises to write often, Mr. Barney accompanied Kate and Nettie in the carriage to the train station, where he entrusted them to the care of Major Anderson. "There's always a place for you in our home," Mr. Barney said in parting, but although he smiled, his brow was furrowed, his eyes anxious.

At noon their train pulled into Philadelphia, where a crowd had gathered in expectation of Major Anderson's arrival. Rest had revived the exhausted officer, so he willingly stepped out upon the platform to greet the well-wishers, although he modestly declined their calls for a speech. Kate and Nettie stepped off the train too, for a breath of fresh air and a chance to stretch their legs, and while they were waiting for the whistle to announce their imminent departure, Kate spied what looked to be an entire company of blue-clad Union soldiers boarding the train. Among their gear they carried eight large, locked boxes, which evidently were quite heavy and very important, for they were never left unguarded. Nettie cleared her throat softly and nudged Kate's arm gently with her own, so Kate knew her curiosity had been piqued too.

Two officers broke away from the company and approached Major Anderson, and after edging closer, Kate overheard enough to learn that the company was also en route to Washington, and that they carried with them half a million dollars in specie.

"What's specie?" Nettie murmured in Kate's ear.

"Coins," Kate said. "It must be contributions for the war—loans, perhaps, or funds raised from bonds."

"Will they be delivered to Father, do you suppose?"

Kate smiled, imagining the soldiers solemnly carrying the heavy boxes to Father's elegant office and dropping them with resounding thuds on the beautiful carpet. "I don't think so, but if the specie is for the government, it will be in Father's charge in a sense, even if it's locked away in a vault and he never sets eyes upon it."

Nettie seemed intrigued by the idea, but at that moment the whistle blew, and so they hurried back aboard the train and returned to their private car, where Major Anderson soon joined them. "The two officers informed me that Baltimore is still dangerously unsettled, and the train tracks may not yet be in adequate repair," he reported. "The company of soldiers you saw boarding the train will be taking a steamer from Perryville to Annapolis, and they have consented to let us travel with them."

"Thank you, Major," said Kate, smiling warmly, although she wondered what dangers had occasioned the change to their itinerary. "I'm sure the journey will be even more pleasant by steamer. The Chesapeake Bay should be lovely today."

Three hours after departing Philadelphia, their train arrived in Perryville, Maryland, where the Susquehanna River emptied into the northern end of the Chesapeake Bay. They disembarked at the station to loud cheers for Major Anderson from yet another crowd of eager admirers, many of whom pushed forward to shake his hand. While they made arrangements for their luggage to be carried to the steamer *William Whilden*, Kate observed the soldiers filing off the train, their arms and gear made ready, and the eight heavy boxes under watchful guard. Studying the crowd as Major Anderson escorted her and Nettie to the wharf, she hoped that the presence of the hero of Fort Sumter would distract the throng's attention away from the company's precious cargo. The boxes were unmarked, so their appearance would not give away their contents, but their weight could not be so easily disguised.

When they arrived at the wharf, they discovered that the soldiers had formed two lines flanking the route to the gangplank, and at Major Anderson's approach, they stood at attention and presented arms. Visibly moved by the spontaneous show of esteem, Major Anderson walked between the lines and boarded the ship, Kate and Nettie following close behind, proud to share in the honor given to their escort.

The *William Whilden* was not far off North Point, east of Baltimore, when a sailor shouted a warning that a ship had appeared in their wake. Kate, Nettie, and Major Anderson had been visiting the captain in the pilothouse, and they followed him as he strode out onto the deck and raised his spyglass to his eye. "I believe that's a privateer," he exclaimed, studying the unexpected vessel as it approached.

Nettie seized Kate's hand as the captain called for increased speed. "Does he mean pirates?" she asked, her blue eyes wide with alarm.

"We'll be fine," Kate murmured, although her heart quaked. She thought again of the crowds of onlookers who had seen the soldiers carrying the heavy, unmarked boxes aboard the ship under vigilant guard. Any observer could have surmised that they held something of great value, and certain factions would also consider Major Anderson a prize worth capturing.

"We're pulling away," someone cried out, and as Kate watched, clutching Nettie's sturdy hand in one of her own and the railing with the other, it did appear that they were gaining distance on the other ship. Then there was a commotion among the crew on the deck, shouts of alarm, and suddenly a cannonball came booming through the air above their heads. Nettie shrieked and dropped to the deck, pulling Kate down nearly upon her. As Kate regained her footing and helped her sister to stand, the brigand vessel fired another shot, even closer than before.

"They want to bring us to," Major Anderson said, his gaze narrowing upon the vessel.

"What will we do?" Kate asked. "Will they board us?"

"They'll never catch us," the major said firmly. "Look. Even now the captain is crowding on steam."

Even as he spoke, the *William Whilden* surged forward rapidly, and as the distance between the ships stretched almost imperceptibly, other crew members dragged into position the steamer's single cannon, a small howitzer, and prepared to defend their ship.

"Major Anderson," the captain called in between shouting orders to his crew, "I suggest you see your charges safely below."

With a brisk nod, the major took Nettie by the hand and offered Kate his arm. "Ladies, come with me now, if you would."

"Please let us stay and watch," Nettie begged, although her voice trembled and her face was white with fear. Kate wanted just as desperately to remain on the deck, knowing she would be even more frightened if she could not see what was happening, but Major Anderson was resolute and she knew it would be futile and embarrassing to protest. Just before they disappeared down the stairs, she threw one last look over her shoulder and saw that the pursuing ship had run up a black flag. No mercy would be asked, and none given.

Below, the minutes seemed to stretch on interminably, but just when Kate thought she couldn't bear another second, they heard footsteps descending and Major Anderson appeared. "Our pursuers changed course and moved out of sight," he told them. "The captain says you may return to the deck if you wish."

Nettie bounded to her feet and darted up the stairs, but Kate hung back to ask the major, quietly, "Do you know who they were?"

"Confederates, we assume," he replied. "Or privateers in their employ, or who share their sympathies. We're not far from Annapolis, and the captain doubts they'll dare approach us again."

Toward nightfall, when they landed at Annapolis, Colonel Benjamin F. Butler met Major Anderson on the dock, stocky and imposing in his blue uniform, entirely bald atop but with dark-brown hair grown long on the sides and back. His stern expression, bags beneath his eyes, and downturned mustache gave him the intimidating look of a belligerent bulldog, which Kate supposed was useful in his line of work.

Their train for Washington City would not leave for hours, so Colonel Butler invited Major Anderson and the Chase sisters to supper at a hotel near the Maryland State House. When Kate inquired about his regiments' journey from their home state to Annapolis, the colonel said that when they had arrived in Philadelphia, they discovered that the bridges were down and the Susquehanna ferry had been sunk. Marching his men on to Perryville, he commandeered the ferryboat *Maryland* and headed down the Chesapeake Bay, bypassing Baltimore as Major Anderson and the Chase sisters had done.

When Colonel Butler and the Massachusetts Eighth Regiment had arrived in Annapolis, they had found the rail lines torn up, the locomotives disassembled, the parts scattered, and all means of transportation to the capital destroyed. The enterprising men of the Massachusetts Eighth immediately set themselves to the work of laying the tracks, rebuilding the engines, and running the trains themselves. "When I saw the state of things," the colonel said, "I called out, 'Is there anyone here who can put together this locomotive?' One of our privates replied, 'Well, now, I guess so, Colonel, seeing as she was built in our shop.'"

"How lucky," Nettie exclaimed.

The regiment had been assigned to guard the road from Annapolis to Washington, and Kate felt greatly relieved to know that one important route into the city would be protected by such resourceful, industrious soldiers. It was thanks to their swift repair work that at long last Kate, Nettie, Major Anderson, and the company of soldiers boarded the train in Annapolis for the last stretch of their journey home.

On May 5, in the chill dawn of the early spring morning, Kate and Nettie arrived in Washington fatigued but happy, and very grateful to their kind escort. At the station, Major Anderson saw them and their luggage to a carriage, and then he left them to find both rest and breakfast before reporting to President Lincoln and Secretary Cameron.

As the carriage rumbled off to the Rugby House, Kate and Nettie peered out the windows at the transformed city, marveling at the changes that had been wrought in the weeks they had been away. Washington had become one vast military camp, the streets filled with soldiers in bright new uniforms, troops quartered in nearly every available space. The park across the street from their hotel, Franklin Square, had been converted into an encampment for the Twelfth New York Regiment, filled with rows upon rows of precisely arranged white tents, with the commanding officer's headquarters in the middle of the square, with an open space for marching and drilling.

But no sight was more welcome than Father's handsome face, his open smile, his expression of relief and joy, when he met their carriage outside the Rugby House and embraced them, welcoming them home at last.

In the days that followed, Kate and Nettie would often look out from the windows of their suite upon Franklin Square, especially when the Twelfth New York performed their afternoon dress parade, which provided a daily source of delight and entertainment. When the sisters next visited the Capitol, they discovered that it had taken on the appearance of a large military fortress, with soldiers bivouacked in the great rotunda and sentinels constantly on patrol. Even the vaults under the terrace had been converted into an enormous bakery, producing thousands upon thousands of loaves of bread every day for the vast multitude of hungry soldiers who had descended upon Washington City.

The immediate threat of invasion from the Confederates had passed, thanks to the swift response of the loyal Union states who had sent state militia and newly mustered troops to the capital to provide for its defense.

One of the first of these regiments to reach Washington, Kate learned on the day she returned home, was the First Rhode Island Detached Militia and Battery, under the command of Colonel Ambrose E. Burnside and led by the dashing Boy Governor, William Sprague.

Chapter Eight

$\mathcal{T}$he gallant Governor Sprague, who struck a daring, romantic figure astride a magnificent white stallion as he galloped about the city on regimental business, was the talk of Washington society. Father, Vina, Mrs. Douglas, and other acquaintances referred to his grand arrival so often that soon Kate was able to piece together the story without asking too many questions and raising suspicions that her interest in William Sprague was anything more than the ordinary curiosity of someone who had been out of town during a time of great excitement.

While Kate was stranded in New York, Governor Sprague had responded to President Lincoln's call for troops by immediately writing to him to offer the services of Rhode Island's light artillery as well as a regiment of infantry, a force of one thousand well disciplined, fully equipped, and completely trained men. It was said that he had given the state of Rhode Island one hundred thousand dollars of his own personal fortune to outfit the troops, and had himself purchased the ninety-six excellent horses that accompanied the artillery battery. One newspaper, noting that he was the only governor to lead his troops in defense of the capital, reported that he paid nearly all the personal expenses of his men, kept them supplied with clothing, and every month added ten dollars from his own purse to each man's pay.

With General Burnside in command, the governor had led the First

Rhode Island Regiment to the beleaguered capital so swiftly that they were the second to arrive, beaten by the Thirteenth Massachusetts by one day. At that time the citizens of Washington City had feared that invasion from the South was inevitable and imminent, and so Governor Sprague received a hero's welcome from a thankful, relieved populace. The ladies of the capital admired his debonair, dashing appearance, from his bold, decisive manner to the jaunty yellow plume he wore in his black felt hat. The men were impressed that a gentleman of his wealth and position bunked with his soldiers, making his bed beside theirs on the hard pine floorboards of the Patent Office, which had been assigned to them as quarters, and drinking water out of a tin cup like any humble private.

On May 1, the day that Kate had written to Major Anderson asking him to escort her and Nettie home, Governor Sprague's regiment had been sworn in before the president and a crowd of thousands of admiring spectators. After a dress parade from the regiment's headquarters at the Patent Office to the White House, fifteen hundred men had raised their hands as they took the oath, their voices resounding as one, and then had presented arms and marched before the president, who reviewed them from the portico with Father, the rest of the cabinet, General Scott, and a few other dignitaries. After the troops had passed, Governor Sprague and his principal officers had been introduced to President Lincoln and the cabinet. "The president was so impressed with Governor Sprague's regiment that he conferred with General Scott about summoning another regiment of Rhode Island men," Father told Kate over a game of chess on her second night back from New York. "General Scott said he was so much pleased with what he had seen that he gave his hearty approval, as did Secretary Cameron."

"Will this be another Millionaires' Regiment?" Kate asked lightly, citing the nickname the Rhode Island troops had acquired not only because Governor Sprague had outfitted them so richly, but because he was not the only man of wealth among the ranks.

"That remains to be seen," Father replied, allowing a smile. "I can say that since bringing his regiment to defend the capital, he has earned the admiration of the men, and apparently also won the adoration of the ladies. You would know more about that than I, Kate."

Kate froze in the midst of capturing her father's rook with her knight, but immediately recovered when she realized that her father was only referring to her greater awareness of the sentiments of the female population rather than any adoration of her own. "He is very well spoken of," she said indifferently. "He has certainly accomplished a great deal for a man of thirty-one. However, I think we should be grateful to all of our gallant protectors, not merely those who make a splendid appearance thanks to the wealth of a generous benefactor. Colonel Butler and the men of the Massachusetts Eighth, for example, impressed me very much at Annapolis, but few people here seem aware of their deeds, which were accomplished by sweat and toil."

Father looked surprised. "I thought you liked Governor Sprague. You seemed to enjoy dancing with him at the inauguration, and last year in Cleveland."

"I do like him," said Kate. "I simply wish that people appreciated actual deeds more than appearances. What has the First Rhode Island done other than arrive and parade, while the men of the Massachusetts Eighth have been rebuilding railroads and guarding the route from Annapolis to Washington?"

"You make a fair point," Father admitted, "but I hope you'll be more circumspect when you see Governor Sprague again."

"You should know me well enough not to worry about that. I shall be perfectly charming." She frowned as her father captured her bishop, which she had hoped to use to take his queen in two moves. "I don't expect to see him, in any case. He sounds terribly busy."

"Of course you'll see him," Father said. "He called on me the day before you returned and seemed very pleased to learn that you would soon be home from New York. It was my impression that he intended to call on you."

"Oh." Kate shrugged, laid her fingertips gracefully upon one pawn, pulled her hand away, and moved the one beside it instead. "I knew nothing of that."

"Do you not wish him to call? I could contrive a polite and credible excuse—"

"No, Father, that isn't necessary," Kate quickly interjected. "I don't object to seeing the governor again."

But Governor Sprague did not seem to be in any hurry to renew their acquaintance, and although she looked for him at the many parties and receptions organized to welcome the newly arrived officers to Washington, she always seemed to miss him by a few minutes or a few hours. She tried not to care. She had other matters on her mind—Arkansas seceded on May 6, Father seemed perpetually embattled with Mr. Seward for preeminence in the cabinet—and many other delightful, handsome gentlemen came to call, some with gifts of flowers, all with admiration in their eyes and respectful praise on their lips. It was from a few of these callers that Kate learned that not everyone was impressed by the warrior governor of Rhode Island.

"He is a small, insignificant youth who bought his place," John Hay complained when he and Kate went out riding one afternoon along the Potomac, enjoying the spring breezes and sunshine in a scenic spot away from the fetid smells of the city.

John sounded so uncharacteristically petulant that Kate laughed, astonished, and her horse tossed its head as if in agreement. "What do you mean?" she inquired lightly. "How can it be cause for complaint that he spends his own fortune to equip his regiment? Is that not better than taking money from the public coffers?"

"I'm not referring to his position at the head of his regiment, but at the head of his state," John replied. "Were you aware that he spent more than one hundred thousand dollars on his campaign for governor?"

The astronomical figure startled her, but she said, "I was not aware of that, but although that does seem excessive, I don't think there's anything inherently wrong with funding one's own campaign."

"It's not how much he spent but how he spent it. After the election, it came out that Mr. Sprague's partisans had escorted eligible voters to the polls, then paid them fifty dollars each after they cast their votes."

"That's a terrible accusation," Kate remarked. "Is there any proof?"

John nodded emphatically. "Witnesses swore to the fact afterward. It proved to be a sound investment on Sprague's part, for he won the election by little more than fifteen hundred votes. And thus the legend of the Boy Governor was born."

Kate had to laugh at his comically ironic tone. "This wild tale sounds like jealous hearsay from Governor Sprague's political rivals to me."

"You may be right," John admitted, and then, a bit sourly, added, "The Tycoon seems to like him quite a lot."

Kate hid a smile, for John had unwittingly divulged another source of

144 · JENNIFER CHIAVERINI

his discontent. "The Tycoon" was one of John's secret nicknames for the president, always spoken with sincere affection but never in his presence. "Shouldn't Mr. Lincoln's approval speak well of Governor Sprague?"

"Not always. Mr. Lincoln did marry the Hellcat, after all."

"Mr. Hay," Kate scolded, though she was secretly delighted. John heartily disliked Mrs. Lincoln, whom he described as demanding, irrational, and tempestuous. He and the president's private secretary, John Nicolay, referred to her as "the Enemy" between themselves, and John Hay often amused Kate with comical descriptions of how the two secretaries conspired to thwart Mrs. Lincoln's efforts to control her husband's schedule, dispense patronage, or influence his decisions. "You should not speak of a lady so."

"My apologies," he said, grinning, for he knew there was no love lost between the two women. But then his wicked mirth faded, and a worried frown took its place. "Mr. Lincoln might admire the Boy Governor's precocious achievements—"

"You speak of him as if he were a schoolboy who earned high marks for the term," Kate protested, laughing. "I happen to know he is eight years older than you, and his accomplishments are quite extraordinary."

"It is all surface," John insisted. "He has no education, he bought his governorship, and he plays at soldiering without any real experience in the field of war."

"Mr. Lincoln has no formal education," Kate countered.

"Fair enough, but he's endeavored all his life to make up for that with rigorous independent study. I wouldn't have admitted this a few weeks ago, but I've come to realize that Abraham Lincoln is one of the most well-read, wise, and learned men I've ever had the privilege to meet. I'm quite sure that Governor Sprague has never undertaken any program of intellectual self-improvement to compare to the Tycoon's."

With a sigh, Kate gazed heavenward, smiling and shaking her head. "Next you will say he did not earn his own millions."

John uttered a short, sharp laugh. "He earned them, all right, on the backs of the poor, suffering wretches who pick his cotton."

Kate was so shocked she brought her horse to an abrupt halt. "What on earth could you mean?" she asked, a frosty edge to her voice. It was one thing to tease and banter, quite another to speak slander. "Governor Sprague is from Rhode Island. He owns no slaves."

John brought his horse up short and turned to face her. "He doesn't own them per se, but he buys cotton for his mills from planters who do." His brow furrowed. "Miss Chase, where did you think he acquired the cotton for his mills? Who did you think picked it? Sprague has profited from slave labor as surely as any Southern plantation owner. Given your fervent and admirable abolitionism, I would think that you of all people would find that highly objectionable."

"I do," said Kate quietly, after a long moment. "I confess I never thought of it in quite that way. I should have, and I'm grateful to you for making me aware of it."

"Don't mention it," said John gruffly, looking aggrieved with himself, surely wishing he had never started in on Governor Sprague.

"Perhaps next time we should limit our gossip to the Hellcat," Kate suggested, smiling

John agreed that they probably should, and his expression told Kate more plainly than words that he was pleased and relieved to know that there would be a next time.

On a night in the second week of May, Kate was roused from her sleep by the pealing of alarm bells.

"Katie?" Nettie murmured drowsily beside her. "What is it?"

Instantly alert, Kate slipped from beneath the quilt and darted to the window. She heard the alarm more clearly there, but in the darkness up and down Fourteenth Street, she saw nothing amiss, and yet the bells rang on.

"What's wrong?" Nettie asked, sitting up in bed. "Are the rebels attacking?"

Kate felt a momentary stir of trepidation, but thinking quickly, she said, "I don't think so. I don't hear any artillery fire. Do you?"

They both fell silent and strained their ears to listen, but beneath the frantic tocsin they heard no low booms of cannon, no sharp crackle of rifle fire.

Nettie drew her knees up to her chest, anxious. "Should we wake Father just in case?"

Before Kate could reply, she heard floorboards creak in the other room as Father climbed out of bed. "Kate, what do you see at Franklin Square?"

Even with his spectacles on, in the dark of night at that distance, Father would not have been able to perceive more than the broadest of movements in the encampment across the street. "All seems quiet and still except for the sentries on patrol," she called. "Most of the campfires have burned down to embers, so it's difficult to say for certain."

"Very good. If the city were under attack"—a deep yawn interrupted him—"those soldiers would have been rousted from their tents and ordered to take up arms. If it were a government emergency, a messenger would have been dispatched to bring me the news. Go back to sleep, girls. Whatever has happened, we'll find out in the morning."

With a sigh, Nettie promptly fell back against the pillow and was soon asleep. Kate lingered by the window a while longer, studying the encampment of the New York Twelfth and listening for the ominous boom of cannon. She thought she smelled smoke, but the odor was faint, and probably her imagination. Eventually she slipped back beneath the quilt, put her arm around her sister, and drifted back to sleep.

In the morning, Will returned with the morning papers and the startling news that the Willard Hotel would have burned down the night before, if not for the swift and valiant actions of Colonel Elmer Ellsworth's Fire Zouaves.

With a gasp, Kate snatched up one of the papers—Father's least favorite, which he would not get to right away—and read that at three o'clock that morning, the building adjacent to the Willard, home to Mr. Owen's tailor shop and Mr. Field's restaurant, had been utterly engulfed by fire. As the flames had spread, hotel guests had fled the Willard, clumsily dragging their trunks and satchels down the stairs while the Willard brothers scrambled to rescue cash, ledgers, and essential documents from their offices. When the roaring blaze attacked the rear of the hotel, utter ruin seemed inexorable, but suddenly hundreds of Colonel Ellsworth's Zouaves had raced to the scene from their barracks in the Capitol. Having discovered the city's firehouses locked, they had broken in, taken the engines, and arrived at the Willard before the local firemen. In the absence of ladders, they had climbed upon one another's shoulders and scaled lightning rods to reach the higher floors, spraying water down from the smoking eaves. For two hours they had battled the conflagration, eventually reducing it to smoldering embers and saving the hotel.

Kate's heart welled up with pride as she thought of Colonel Ellsworth, how determined he had been to select the ablest, bravest men in New York City for the defense of the capital. Now they had saved an important part of it, and just as Colonel Ellsworth had believed, they had been ready and willing to plunge into the thickest of the fight.

"Can we go see it?" Nettie begged.

"The fire is out," said Father. "There will be nothing left to see but smoking ruins."

"That's fine. I don't mind. I still want to see it."

"I'll take her," Kate offered. "I confess I'm curious too."

Father agreed that they could go after morning scriptures and breakfast. Before long they were dressed and strolling down Fourteenth Street, where the smell of scorched wood and ash drifted on the air. A memory suddenly illuminated Kate's thoughts—Election Day the previous November, when the Neil House in Columbus had burned to the ground. But the Willard Hotel had not suffered such a calamitous fate, she observed from a few blocks away. As best as she could see through the crowd that had gathered all around the block, although the adjacent building was a total ruin, the Willard Hotel had sustained relatively minor damage to its rear. As a small token of their immense gratitude, Kate overheard, after the fire had been extinguished, the proprietors had invited all of the New York firemen, as well as members of the Massachusetts Fifth Regiment and the New Jersey First who had also rendered service, into the hotel for a well-deserved breakfast. At that moment, the Zouaves, looking remarkably cheerful and energetic though streaked with soot and sweat, were busily engaged in tearing down the burned walls of the ruined structure, basking in the admiration of the gathered throng.

When the sisters returned to the Rugby House, Kate wrote Colonel Ellsworth a letter of congratulations, and when she saw him a few days later at a review of the district militia on the White House grounds, she said, "Back in New York, I told you that it would greatly reassure me to know that such courageous men were defending our city, and now you have justified every bit of my faith in them, and in you."

He accepted the praise with a gallant bow. "Thank you, Miss Chase. I'm exceedingly proud of my men. They performed with exemplary courage and skill that night."

"They did indeed, and it is a testament to your leadership." She gave him a teasing smile. "I know of someone else who will be exceedingly proud. Since I know you are too modest to do so, I'm going to collect every newspaper report I can find about your Zouaves' adventure and send them to Miss Carrie Spafford of Rockford, Illinois. She should know what a brave, ingenious man she is going to marry."

Colonel Ellsworth smiled broadly, but not without a small measure of pleased embarrassment. "If you insist, Miss Chase, I won't object."

With the threat to the Willard Hotel and the narrow escape of its occupants fresh in their minds, the Chase family was relieved and thankful to move at long last into the mansion on the corner of Sixth and E streets. Kate, Nettie, Vina, and their new housekeeper, Mrs. Vaudry, took charge of moving in, unpacking, and arranging Kate's lovely purchases from New York and Philadelphia in place among the cherished items shipped from their home in Columbus, which Father's agent still had been unable to sell. Father had been counting on the funds from that sale to pay for the furnishings for their Washington home, but the real estate market in Ohio lingered in its slump, and Father found himself deeper in worrisome debt. Reluctantly, he resorted to asking Mr. Barney for a loan of ten thousand dollars.

As soon as they were settled in their new residence, Father held a reception in the splendidly furnished rooms to mark the occasion, but it was Kate who planned every detail from the invitations to the refreshments to the musical entertainment and the flowers. Kate had invited Mrs. Lincoln as a matter of form, knowing that she would not come, for by custom the First Lady could not accept any invitations to private homes. The Lincolns were absent, but all of the members of the cabinet attended with their wives, if they were in the city, as did Major Anderson, who had not yet returned to New York.

Their most reluctant guest was unquestionably Mr. Nathaniel Hawthorne, who Kate surmised attended out of a sense of duty rather than any expectation of pleasure. Upon his arrival, he spoke haltingly as he offered Kate the perfunctory compliments on her new home, and he seemed thoroughly wretched in the crowd. He brightened considerably when he spied Nettie across the room, and he made his way to her, speaking as little as possible to those who addressed him. As Kate watched, he sat and spoke with Nettie for a few minutes but departed soon thereafter, his expression conveying a devout thankfulness that the ordeal was over.

British ambassador Lord Lyons was the most illustrious of the foreign dignitaries who attended, and Kate took special care to welcome him warmly and provide all the attention and flattery that he seemed to desire, for relations between their two countries were in a fragile state. With the possibility that Great Britain might recognize the Confederacy as a sovereign nation in order to ensure a steady supply of Southern cotton for British mills, no amount of goodwill cultivated for the Union would be wasted.

Colonel Ellsworth was among the many military officers who visited, and he was justly praised for the courageous actions of his Fire Zouaves, who had become quite the favorites of the people of Washington despite their reputation for occasional raucous behavior. Another notable guest—arriving late, unaccompanied, and not entirely expected—was Governor William Sprague.

He came to Kate first, even before shaking hands with her father, perhaps because Father was engrossed in conversation with Secretary Cameron in another room. "Miss Chase," Governor Sprague greeted her, taking the hand she offered him. "What a pleasure it is to see you again. Washington City is at its most beautiful in springtime, and it is all the lovelier for your presence."

"Why, thank you, Governor." She did not know quite what to think. "I understand the city is all the safer for yours."

He smiled, pleased, but offered a self-deprecating shrug. "Well, we don't fight fires as efficiently as Ellsworth's Zouaves, but if the enemy should approach, we will not fail to rebuff them."

He spoke for a while, proudly and earnestly, about the organizing of his regiment, the men's training at arms, and their fierce loyalty to their country. Kate felt her wariness ebbing away, and gradually a sensation of warmth and admiration filled her. He spoke so well of his men, as if he were their devoted elder brother as well as their military leader, that she could almost forget the doubts John Hay had sown.

Her duties as hostess left her less time to chat with the governor than she wished, but later, when he bade her good-bye, he asked if he might visit again soon. She agreed, and when he called two days later, Father asked him to come for supper the following night, and the evening passed so pleasantly that Governor Sprague invited her to go riding the following afternoon. They were seeing too much of each other, Kate thought, and people were sure to gossip. But she had come to enjoy his company and conversation more than she had imagined she would, so she banished her concerns and accepted.

Governor Sprague's white stallion was a creature of magnificent grace, power, and beauty, and he rode with a natural confidence and masterful skill that Kate, an accomplished horsewoman, found impressive and appealing. And yet, as they followed the same shaded path along the Potomac she had last traveled with John Hay, she could not help mulling over his warnings that the Boy Governor was less than what he seemed.

Delicately, weaving her questions into the conversation so deftly that the governor would not feel subjected to an inquisition, Kate tested his responses against John Hay's incriminations. The question of whether he had won the gubernatorial election by bribing voters was too ridiculous to address, but when she inquired in a circumspect fashion about his opinions regarding electioneering and ethics, his responses were morally sound. When she mentioned her father's devotion to the abolitionist cause, the governor himself admitted, without any prompting, that it aggrieved him that the cotton for his mills relied upon slave labor. In fact, it was a trip to the South to consult with plantation owners that had made him fully aware of the horrors of slavery and had compelled him to become an abolitionist and to give generously to abolitionist causes.

It was more difficult to broach the subject of education. When she mentioned her favorite books and authors, he remarked approvingly of her choices but acknowledged that he had little time for reading other than government documents and pending legislation. When she shared amusing anecdotes from her years at boarding school, he laughed but told no stories of his own. Finally, thwarted at every turn, she abandoned subtlety and said, "I suppose, Governor, you were too eager to make your mark in the business world to idle away the years in school."

"Though I'm not much of a scholar myself, I've never equated hours spent in study with idleness," he replied easily. "Do you, Miss Chase?"

"No," she said. "No, I do not."

His stallion had cantered a few paces ahead, eager to run, but the governor settled him with a firm word and a pat on the neck. Waiting for

Kate to catch up, he fixed her with an evaluative look over his shoulder, the long yellow plume in his hat waving in the breeze. "Would you care to hear a very sad story, Miss Chase?"

"If you wish to tell one."

"I was a good student as a youth. Not brilliant like your father, but diligent and quick to learn, when I wasn't distracted by the usual preoccupations of an active boy." His gaze turned inward for a moment, but then he smiled at her, rueful. "My father's ambition was that I would attend college, probably Brown, and become a lawyer or a man of business like himself, but my dream was to attend West Point and become a valiant general."

Kate smiled sympathetically, knowing that neither ambition had been achieved.

"On New Year's Eve of 1843—which was my mother's birthday, as well as my parents' wedding anniversary—my father completed his usual Sunday-night ritual of a hearty family dinner followed by a vigorous walk of several miles out to our farm." His eyes were on the road ahead, but he brought his stallion close alongside Kate's mare. "On the way home, someone attacked him, shooting him first in the arm and then cracking his head open with the stock of the gun."

Kate gasped. "How dreadful!"

"The assailant flung the weapon in a ditch, where it was later found and identified as the murder weapon."

"Murder," Kate breathed. Until that moment, she had hoped Mr. Sprague had survived the terrible attack.

"My father was a good man, generous to his workers, and his mill was the largest employer in the region." The governor's voice was steady, as if the events had lost their power to pain him. "And yet even such a man makes enemies. He had prevailed upon the city council to deny a liquor license to a group of brothers who ran a nearby gin mill, where too many of my father's employees spent too much of their time, rendering them too often unfit for work. One brother had been spotted skulking about one of my father's mills, and another was proved to be the owner of the murder weapon. That brother was eventually convicted of the crime and executed."

"Oh, Governor Sprague." He was close enough that she could reach out and touch his arm. "I am so terribly sorry."

"I was thirteen." He fell silent for a moment. "I was permitted to remain in school for another two years, but then my uncle, who had taken over my father's mills, pulled me out of school and put me to work in the family business." When he turned to her and held her gaze, she was suddenly conscious of her hand lingering on his arm and quickly withdrew it. "At the time, my uncle was a United States senator, and before that he had served as the governor of Rhode Island. Did you know that?"

"I had heard that you came from a political family," Kate acknowledged, "but I assumed that your father was the politician."

"No." He seemed amused by the thought. "So, at fifteen, I began learning the business of cotton milling and calico printing from the lowest drudgeries upward. When I wasn't toiling in the counting rooms, I drilled with the Providence Marine Artillery Company. It wasn't West Point, but joining the militia satisfied my martial ardor, and eventually I was promoted to colonel."

They had come to a secluded spot on the path, where a stand of willows trailed their long branches into the river. "Shall we walk for a while?"

Kate nodded, unwilling to interrupt his story. He halted his horse, climbed down, and tied the reins to a tree before assisting Kate to the ground. He offered her his arm, and they strolled in the shade of the trees. "I passed thirteen years in this fashion, advancing in the business and in the militia. And then, in 1856, my uncle died of typhoid fever. With our patriarch gone, the company passed to the next generation—my elder brother, my cousin, and myself. We formed a new business called the A. & W. Sprague Company, but my brother preferred horse raising and racing to calico, and my cousin was weak-willed when it came to liquor, and so almost every responsibility fell to me."

"I imagine you were well prepared for the role."

"Indeed, yes. My uncle's insistence that I begin at the very lowest place and work my way up made sure of that." He turned to her and took both of her hands in his. "And that, Miss Chase, is the story of my curtailed education and thwarted ambitions."

"Thwarted ambitions," Kate echoed, incredulous. "I strongly disagree. You are governor of Rhode Island, and the commander of the First Rhode Island Regiment. You didn't attend Brown or West Point, but your achievements are all the more impressive for that, and for the other hardships you have overcome."

He held her gaze again, and she felt a strange, warm trembling in the pit of her stomach. "Are they, Miss Chase?" he asked, in a voice that was quiet and gently mocking. "Are you impressed?"

"Perhaps," she said, her voice faint. "A little. Not very much at all, now that I reconsider."

His eyes lit up with mirth, and she thought he might burst out laughing, but instead he cupped her cheek with his hand, and before she could think, he pressed his lips against hers, soft and warm but insistent, the silky hairs of his mustache brushing against her cheeks and mouth.

She forgot to pull away. She was supposed to pull away, she remembered somewhat vaguely as his mouth gently explored hers, and perhaps she should slap him, or shriek, but instead she found herself melting into him, and kissing him back, until she finally had to pull away, gasping, not because she wanted to but because her head was spinning and she needed to breathe.

"We should go back," she managed to say, taking one hesitant step away, but he held her hands and did not let her go far. "We should, Governor. At once."

"We should not," he said lightly, brushing her cheek with the back of his fingers. Her skin grew warm where he touched her. "We should stay here, and you should kiss me again."

"Governor—"

"And you should call me William."

"Governor Sprague," she said firmly, forcing strength into her voice, "we are unchaperoned. This will not do. If we are observed like this, it could ruin me, and you know it. It could destroy my father."

He stopped caressing her cheek and let his hand fall to his side, but his other still held hers. "Sadly, you are probably right." He offered her his arm, and inclined his head to indicate that he meant only to escort her away from the seclusion of the willow grove. "I would not have harm of any sort come to you, Miss Chase."

She managed a tight smile, took his arm, and they walked back to where the picketed horses grazed. They passed no one else, but as the governor helped her back into the saddle, an older gentleman on a tired brown horse clopped slowly by and lifted his hat. The governor replied in the same fashion, and Kate nodded politely, which was more than etiquette required her to do. Had he recognized them? It would not matter if he had—they were no longer in a compromising position. But if Kate had not insisted they leave when they had—

She took a deep, shaky breath as Governor Sprague mounted his stallion. "Shall we go?" he asked, smiling as if nothing were amiss. She managed a nod.

They rode side by side in silence except when the governor pointed out interesting sights along the way. Kate's thoughts were in a whirl. She had let him kiss her, and they had no understanding of any sort—it was fair to say that they hardly knew each other. What did he think of her? What stories would he spread?

She was close to tears as they reached Fourteenth Street, but she inhaled deeply and blinked her eyes, determined to regain her composure by the time she reached home, or there would be too many questions from Nettie and perhaps even Vina and Mrs. Vaudry. She could not bear that.

The governor accompanied her to the stables, where she left her horse in the care of the groom and the governor left his only long enough to walk her to the front door. There he thanked her for the ride and asked, "May I call on you again?"

The question was so oddly unexpected that she had no time to think. "Yes," she blurted, "but no more riding unless we take Nettie with us."

"Ah." A slow smile spread across his face. "I suppose that would be prudent. Perhaps we could stay here and play chess instead, while Nettie looks on from the sofa, drawing her little pictures. Or we could take a carriage ride, and the driver will be the third to our party."

She could not tell if he was amused or annoyed. "If that sounds too dull, you needn't visit at all."

His smile deepened, and without another word, he lifted his hat to her, turned, and strolled back to the stable.

When he was gone, Kate pressed the back of her hand to her forehead to calm her scattered thoughts, and took a slow, deep breath—and then forced a smile and waved when a neighbor lady passing by called out a greeting. Such public displays of distress would not do. She lifted her chin, assumed a serene expression for the benefit of anyone who might be watching, and went inside, feigning the lighthearted innocence she feared she could no longer claim.

Nearly every move Mrs. Lincoln made attracted the attention of gossips and the press—two groups that often overlapped considerably—so when she and her cousin Mrs. Grimsley embarked upon an extensive shopping expedition in New York, newspaper correspondents hounded their every step, setting telegraph lines buzzing with stories of their whereabouts and pastimes. The papers filled columns with reports of Mrs. Lincoln and her entourage attending the theater, inspecting carriages at a manufacturer, dining out, enjoying soirees, and visiting local luminaries, but with soldiers sleeping on the floor of the Senate or in encampments about the city, her frivolous activities invited spiteful commentary. When Kate read of Mrs. Lincoln's lavish expenditures upon carpets, china, mantel ornaments, and other furnishings for the White House, she shared the newspapers' opinion that the First Lady was indulging herself to the point of embarrassment. While it was true that Kate too had enjoyed decorating her new home, she had not spent the people's money, nor had she been wasteful and extravagant. She could not imagine how Mrs. Lincoln could afford such luxuries on the congressional allowance of twenty thousand dollars. Either she had acquired the money through other, perhaps questionable, means, or she was plunging into debt. Either way, Kate was not alone in finding her behavior irresponsible and unbecoming her status as the First Lady of the land.

Mrs. Lincoln's heedless extravagance made her seem blissfully unaware of the crisis facing the nation, but no one else in Washington City could ignore the Confederate threat looming ever nearer. On the day Virginia had seceded, the secessionist proprietor of a hotel across the river in Alexandria had raised a Confederate flag high above the city, where it waved and snapped in the breeze, taunting the residents of the capital with the threat of invasion. The flag was a constant source of vexation to Mr. Lincoln too, Kate knew, for John Hay reported that he would often study it in silence through a spyglass from his office in the White House, and Colonel Ellsworth had vowed to tear it down for him at the earliest possible opportunity. The colonel hinted that a suitable occasion might not be far off, which told Kate that an invasion of Virginia, and all the dangers that implied, was imminent.

But other officers acted sooner. On May 12, as the newly appointed commander of the Department of Annapolis, Colonel Butler led one thousand of his Massachusetts men through a driving rainstorm into Baltimore, where they occupied Monument Square and set cannon atop Federal Hill, a strategic point above the downtown and the inner harbor. As if to exact a certain measure of revenge, he allowed the Sixth Massachusetts, the regiment that had been attacked as it had passed through the city two months before, to bivouac in City Hall along with the Eighth New York. He then issued a proclamation forbidding all unofficial assembly, banning the shipment of arms to the South, and declaring that any display of Confederate flags or symbols would be regarded as giving aid and comfort to the enemy. His imposition of martial law brought order to the mutinous city and proud delight to the people of the North, but Father told Kate that Colonel Butler's unauthorized actions had angered his superiors. They would soon bestow upon him the mixed honor of a promotion to major general and a transfer out of Maryland to Fort Monroe in Hampton, Virginia, where he could be more easily constrained.

The day after Colonel Butler occupied Baltimore, Great Britain declared neutrality in the American conflict, inspiring triumphant joy throughout the South, for under international law, their position gave the Confederacy the right to acquire loans and buy weapons from them. Less than a week later, the Confederate Congress voted to establish their capital in Richmond, Virginia, one hundred miles south of Washington, and the day after that, North Carolina seceded from the Union.

The ongoing disintegration of the nation heightened worry and alarm in the capital, where military regiments drilled and paraded and prepared for war. Governor Sprague's regiment moved from its headquarters in the Patent Office to a camp on a high ridge north of the Capitol, and when he next called at the Chase residence, he cordially invited Kate and Nettie to visit his troops. The governor escorted them as they rode out on horseback to tour the encampment and meet the officers and men, who were splendidly attired in their uniforms of gray pants, dark-blue flannel shirts, scarlet blanket rolls slung over the shoulder, and black felt hats rakishly rolled up on one side. Kate and Nettie distributed delicacies from their kitchen and garden to the soldiers, thanking them for their protection—Nettie in her sweet, amusing way, Kate with a more gracious but impressive manner, judging by the men's blushes and stammers. All the while, Kate was mindful of Governor Sprague's presence close by her side, and she could almost feel the warmth of his mouth on hers again, until she found herself quite distracted and agitated, wishing with only the barest hint of shame that they could be alone again in the willow grove by the river.

Afterward Kate often rode out to visit the First Rhode Island Regiment, sometimes with Nettie, sometimes alone, always bearing gifts of food or flowers or books. Although her contributions were not necessary, for Governor Sprague provided for his men's every need, they were well appreciated, and it was soon apparent that the men regarded the special attention the Belle of Washington bestowed upon them as a particular source of pride.

Governor Sprague never failed to escort Kate safely home again, and whenever he called on her there, or saw her at a reception or dinner or levee, he treated her with utmost respect and courtesy. While he admittedly possessed a few rough edges, which always reminded her, and probably everyone else, of the sharp distinction between his background and that of most gentlemen of the Washington elite, they somehow rendered him more endearing.

How could she not excuse his occasional lack of polish, considering that he had lost his father to terrible violence just as he was becoming a man?

One morning in late May, Kate woke to the mournful tolling of firehouse bells and knew immediately that something dreadful had happened.

When she went down to breakfast, she found Father at the table, his Bible in hand, his expression full of pain and sorrow. "What's wrong?" she asked, her heart plummeting.

He set his Bible aside, rose, and came to the doorway to take her hands in his. "My dear Katie," he said tenderly. "Perhaps you should sit down."

"I prefer to stand," she said, but her grip on his hands tightened. "Tell me what happened, please."

"A messenger came from the White House this morning with grievous news," he began gently, as if he feared too loud a voice would shatter her. "Last night, a squadron of Union cavalry and ten Union regiments of regulars and volunteers quietly crossed the Potomac by bridge and steamboat. Some of the troops occupied Arlington Plantation, General Lee's estate, and the hills overlooking Washington City. Other troops moved on to Arlington."

Kate felt her heart thudding in her chest. "Was the First Rhode Island among them?"

"No," he said, "but Colonel Ellsworth's Fire Zouaves were."

Kate took a deep, shaky breath. The colonel had called on her the previous evening, strangely energized and hinting that his troops would have a taste of war soon. He had brought her a pretty bouquet of jasmine and white roses, which she had placed in a crystal vase in the best parlor. "What happened?" she asked again, although she dreaded her father's reply.

"One of the transport ships, the *Pawnee*, arrived at Alexandria ahead of the others. Without authorization, the commander sent a lieutenant into Alexandria under a flag of truce, to warn the Confederate commander that they faced an overwhelming force, and that he had until nine o'clock to evacuate or surrender."

Evidently the commander had chosen one or the other rather than to defend the city, for Alexandria was so close to Washington that if the rebels had resisted, the distant sounds of battle would have woken the citizens from their sleep. "What did they do?"

"They chose to retreat. Colonel Ellsworth's transport had arrived by then, and not knowing about the flag of truce, it had exchanged fire with rebel guns on the shore. Before long the lieutenant reported to Colonel Ellsworth that the rebels declined to fight because the town was full of women and children. Most of the rebel troops left Alexandria by train well before the nine o'clock deadline, but about thirty-five cavalry rear guard remained behind. They were immediately taken prisoner when Colonel Ellsworth's Zouaves and the other Union troops entered the city. While other officers captured the customs house and the railroad depot, Colonel Ellsworth set out to seize the telegraph office."

When he fell silent, Kate steeled herself. "Pray go on, Father."

"On his way there, the colonel passed the Marshall House at King and Pitt streets—you know the place, if only from a distance. It's the hotel where that flag of the Confederacy has been flying so brashly for more than two months."

Kate felt faint. "Colonel Ellsworth told me once that he had promised President Lincoln to tear it down at the earliest possible opportunity. The sight of it vexed the president so."

"It vexed everyone in Washington City," said Father. "A gaudy symbol of treason, obnoxiously defiant. Perhaps the colonel thought the president might be watching the hotel at that very moment, and perhaps he wanted to signal that the town had been captured. He cannot tell us now."

Tears welled up in Kate's eyes, and she braced herself for the worst.

"Colonel Ellsworth, that poor, bold young man, strode into the hotel and up to the roof, where he took hold of that flag and ripped it down. As he carried the notorious banner downstairs, where some of his men waited, the proprietor suddenly appeared carrying a double-barreled shotgun. He fired upon Colonel Ellsworth from point-blank range and struck him full in the chest."

Kate pulled her hands free from Father's and sank into a chair. "Oh, Dear Lord, let it not be so."

"I am so sorry, my darling child." Father lay his large, warm hand upon her bowed head. "One of his Zouaves immediately avenged him, killing his assailant with a single musket round to the head."

"What good did that do?" Kate choked out bitterly. "What does that matter? Did it bring Colonel Ellsworth back?"

"Of course not, Katie. It couldn't. But we must take some consolation in knowing that the colonel died in the valiant service of his country, and that he was the only casualty of the mission."

It was very small consolation—and Kate suspected it would bring no comfort at all to his fiancée, whom she imagined peacefully asleep in Rockford, Illinois, or sitting at the breakfast table with her family, unaware that she was enjoying the last few contented hours she would know for many a day.

Later that morning, Father learned from Mr. McManus, the elderly White House doorman, that Mr. Lincoln had been in his library with visitors when word came of the colonel's death, and that he had been so overcome by emotion that he had been rendered speechless. The household had plunged into mourning. Colonel Ellsworth was only a few years older than Mr. and Mrs. Lincoln's eldest son, Robert, and he was like another son to the president. He had taken up the study of the law at Mr. Lincoln's urging, and he had been part of the honor guard that had accompanied the president-elect on the train from Springfield to Washington. Kate knew that Mrs. Lincoln was nearly as fond of Colonel Ellsworth as her husband was. She would be heartbroken.

The colonel's remains were brought to the Navy Yard, where throughout that long, sad day, thousands came to pay their respects. Kate was not among them; her grief was too raw, and she could not bear such a public display of it.

Later that evening, Colonel Ellsworth's body, clothed in the uniform in which he had perished, was placed in an elegant paneled rosewood coffin with a glass top, his sword and cap arranged at his head. The coffin was covered with bouquets of rare and beautiful flowers and draped with the Stars and Stripes, and with a detachment of the New York Seventy-First as a guard of honor, he was escorted to the White House, where he lay in state in the East Room.

At eleven o'clock the next morning, Kate, clutching the bouquet Colonel Ellsworth had given her two nights before, clung to her father's arm as Reverend J. Smith Pyne and several assistant ministers performed the services of the Episcopal Church. After Reverend Pyne spoke his concluding prayer for peace, the grand procession to the train station formed in the circular drive in front of the White House. Kate wept silently into her handkerchief as her father escorted her to their places in it, finding no comfort in the solemn splendor of the military regiments, the delegations from fire companies, the hearse drawn by four white horses, or the groom on foot leading Colonel Ellsworth's horse, which bore an empty saddle.

As the dignitaries climbed into their carriages, Corporal Brownell, the Zouave who had shot Colonel Ellsworth's murderer, presented the bloodstained secession flag to Mr. and Mrs. Lincoln. They were moved to tears, but as soon as the corporal turned to go, Mrs. Lincoln snatched her hands away and left the flag to her husband alone, as if it were an object of horror rather than a cherished relic.

For the first time in their brief acquaintance, Kate thought she understood exactly how Mrs. Lincoln felt, and she did not fault her for shuddering and pulling away. She too could not bear to look upon the terrible banner for which her friend had sacrificed his life.

The procession set out, making its way from the White House down Pennsylvania and New Jersey Avenues to the depot. Immense crowds had gathered to witness the brave young soldier's last journey, many weeping openly, although they could not have known him. All along the Avenue flags were lowered to half-staff, shops were closed, and bells tolled a solemn requiem.

The coffin was placed with much ceremony into a railcar, but just before the doors were closed, Kate tore herself away from her father and hurried across the platform to one of the officers belonging to the honor guard that would accompany Colonel Ellsworth home.

"If you please, sir," she said, her voice rough from grief as she divided her bouquet in two. "Colonel Ellsworth brought me these flowers only two nights ago, when he was still so full of life. Would you please see that they are given to his parents?"

Startled but sympathetic, the officer promised he would.

Kate thanked him and turned away, and as the doors to the railcar closed, she returned to her father and took his arm again, pressing the rest of her bouquet to her heart.

Slowly the train chugged away from the station. No one on the platform moved until it had disappeared from sight.

Chapter Nine

*T*he day after Colonel Ellsworth's funeral, Kate wrote to Miss Carrie Spafford to express her condolences for the young woman's loss. She did not dwell on how he had died, for she had only secondhand accounts and Miss Spafford had surely suffered through enough reports of his fall already. "He spoke of you often, and with great affection," Kate wrote instead. "Although our acquaintance was brief, I can tell you sincerely that I believe his love for his country was outshone only by his love for you." She enclosed a lengthy account of the funeral from the *National Republican* so Miss Spafford could see how beloved Colonel Ellsworth had been to his men, his friends, and the people of Washington.

In early June, another death rocked Washington and the nation. After a severe attack of acute rheumatism followed by a brief, painful decline, Senator Stephen A. Douglas perished in Chicago, where he had traveled on a speaking tour to rally the people of his native state to the Union cause. It was in that city where he was laid to rest, and Kate read sadly of the tremendous outpouring of grief at his funeral, the tolling of bells, the artillery salutes, the wailing dirges of the bands. Nearly eight thousand mourners comprised the funeral cortege, which stretched for two miles and took an hour to pass. Thousands of people from throughout the city and state and regions beyond lined Lake Street and Michigan Avenue to pay their respects as the celebrated "Little Giant" journeyed to a peaceful resting place in Cottage Grove near the lake-shore. He was only forty-eight.

In Washington, the papers and the people celebrated his life and accomplishments, and in tribute to his former rival turned steadfast friend, President Lincoln ordered flags lowered to half-staff and the prominent buildings of the capital draped in mourning. Kate knew that Adele Douglas, a native of Washington City, had wanted her husband buried in the nation's capital, but a committee of various state and municipal authorities had prevailed upon her to inter his remains in Illinois. She acquiesced to their wishes, not with reluctance but with pain.

When her widowed friend returned to Washington after the funeral, Kate called on her to express her sorrow and sympathy. Mrs. Douglas was clad in black from head to foot, her skin pale, her eyes dry but red-rimmed, her manner quiet but composed. She and Mr. Douglas had no living children—their only child, a daughter, had perished in infancy—but she had raised two sons from his first marriage, and she had a great many friends, so she would not mourn alone.

"What will you do now?" Kate asked her gently, after Mrs. Douglas had described in a calm, unwavering voice the funeral and the Masonic ceremonies that had followed. "Will you move to Chicago?"

Mrs. Douglas uttered a sad, small laugh. "Oh, no," she said, shaking her head. "Chicago was my husband's home, but this city is mine. I intend to remain here, where we were happy together." She managed a wan smile. "You and I are both political creatures, Miss Chase. Neither of us would be happy so far from the center of things."

"I am glad for my own sake you will not be leaving us too," Kate told her, clasping her hand. She wondered how many more friends would lose their lives, and how many more would be widowed, before the terrible rebellion could be quelled.

Five days after Senator Douglas's death, Tennessee seceded from the Union. Soon thereafter, Governor Sprague called at the Chase residence and invited Kate to go riding, and something in his guarded expression told her not to invite Nettie along. The governor led her on another route rather than the river path that led to the secluded willow grove, which rendered her both relieved and disappointed. Instead they rode out to the encampment of the Rhode Island First, where they watched the regiment drill on the grass before riding on to admire the view of the city from above.

She knew he had something unpleasant to tell her, and when he finally began, reluctance made him terse and abrupt. "Tomorrow I return to Rhode Island."

"So soon?" she asked, although it was not really soon at all. He had lingered in Washington much longer than he had intended, and she had always known that day would come.

"I can't leave the legislature unsupervised for too long," he said, managing a pained smile. "My brother needs me back at the mills, and the people of Rhode Island need me back at the State House."

"Of course they do. I understand."

"I also hope to organize another regiment there," he added, almost as an afterthought. "President Lincoln and General Scott have been so pleased with the First that they're eager to receive more Rhode Island men into the service."

"Yes, I've heard," said Kate, remembering her father's description of the ceremonies on the White House grounds the day the regiment was sworn in.

"May I write to you while I'm away?"

She arched her eyebrows at him. "I'd be rather unhappy with you if you didn't."

"Then I promise to write often. I could not bear to make you unhappy."

Then he should stay another week, Kate was tempted to suggest. Or another month. Surely Rhode Island and the A. & W. Sprague Company could do without him for that long. "I'll look forward to your letters."

"Kate—" He broke off as two officers walked past, and salutes were exchanged. "Miss Chase," he began again. "I hate to part with so much left unsaid. If we were alone—" He frowned over his shoulder at the encampment full of soldiers, but when he turned back to her, his gaze was intense, slightly mocking, and yet imploring. "If we were alone, I would kiss you."

"If we were alone, I would let you."

She fell silent, confounded by her own boldness. She had not intended to say anything of the sort. He was leaving and she had no idea when he might return. He had acquired many female admirers during his time in Washington, and almost certainly had another girl back in Providence, or two or three to choose between. She had meant to let him go on believing her to be only vaguely interested in him so that he would not take her feelings for granted. Instead she had all but admitted that he had captured her heart and imagination the way no other gentleman of her acquaintance ever had.

She tried to think of a clever phrase to undo the confession, but she could think of nothing, so instead she made a hopeless little shrug, and smiled, and turned her horse toward home. His white stallion fell into step beside her, and they rode on without speaking until they reached the Chase residence. There William helped her down from her horse, his hands lingering on her waist for a moment before he released her. "Good-bye, Miss Chase," he said gruffly.

"Good-bye, Governor. I hope you have safe travels."

He nodded, swung himself up into the saddle, lifted his hat to her, and rode away.

Governor Sprague wrote to her as he had promised to do, but his letters were infrequent and somehow both cordial and distant, as if she were a constituent whose vote he sought but whose friendship he did not crave. Puzzled and disappointed, she nonetheless responded with pleasant good cheer, hoping his former frankness would return. Perhaps he feared that her father read her mail. Perhaps he had an understanding with a beautiful young belle in Providence, and regretted indulging in a flirtation while traveling out of town. Perhaps he simply did not write well. Whatever the reason, in his absence Kate began to look upon his inexplicable fluctuations between hot ardor and cool indifference with a more critical eye, and she gradually became annoyed with him, and with herself for tolerating his peculiar temperament. She had many other, more constant, suitors vying for her attention, and she resolved to enjoy the company of other gentlemen without feeling obliged by any particular attachment to Governor Sprague.

And yet, when his letters arrived, her heart leapt with joy, she savored every dispassionate line, and she invariably wrote back without delay. Sometimes she forced herself to wait, so as not to seem too eager or too idle, for she was certainly neither. Her days were full from dawn until well after twilight. As spring bloomed into summer, many of the Washington social elite fled the heat and the stench and the sickliness of the capital for cooler climes, but Kate remained to establish her father's social calendar, as well as her own, to his best advantage.

Every morning began with the household gathering together for a scripture reading and prayer, but immediately afterward, they all set themselves to her father's business. Kate continued the custom they had established in Columbus of hosting breakfasts for visiting dignitaries and government officials who sought an unhurried, uninterrupted audience with him. After the meal, when Father was obliged to hurry off to the Treasury Building or the White House, Kate would preside at the table, encouraging frank criticism of the administration, forging agreements, making arrangements, granting favors, and taking careful note of significant details the gentlemen unwittingly let fall, valuable information she would either pass on to her father or employ on his behalf. After the guests departed, she would attend to her correspondence and fend off the occasional patronage seeker who had been turned away at her father's office but hoped that her recommendation would encourage him to change his mind.

With the day well begun, she would embark upon her morning calls to the social and political elite—enjoying companionship and gossip, shoring up support for her father, seeking information, advancing his causes, and most often a combination of all four—or she might receive callers at home. Mondays, in particular, were reserved for what was known as "cabinet calling," a weekly occurrence in which the cabinet secretaries' wives—or daughter, in Father's case, or daughter-in-law, in the case of Mr. Seward—would all receive callers at their homes, and so on Monday mornings, the ladies of Washington would make the rounds, visiting each cabinet member's residence in turn. Afternoons were for attending receptions; visiting Congress to observe an important debate; riding out into the countryside to call on a general at his headquarters or offer gifts of her kitchen, gardens, and knitting basket to the troops; tutoring Nettie; taking care of various household appointments; or, on a particularly lovely day, setting out on a long horseback ride through Rock Creek Park, as often alone as with a gentleman admirer or a company of friends.

Every Wednesday evening, Kate hosted elegant candlelight dinners that soon became the most celebrated and anticipated events of the capital's weekly social calendar. With meticulous attention to the finer points of etiquette, Kate composed the guest lists, planned the menus, and devised seating arrangements, often recalling her friend Miss Harriet Lane's laments about her struggles to safely arrange places for feuding guests throughout the tense secession winter. Father presided at the head of the table, and Kate encouraged lively, entertaining conversation from her place at the foot. Music, dancing, and more conversation followed the meal. Kate was proud that diplomats and statesmen considered it a true honor to be her guests, and even the most prominent men of letters found that they needed their wits about them to match her in conversation.

On the other nights, more often than not Kate would dress with care in one of her best gowns, take her father's arm, and set out for a dinner, levee, ball, or reception. Wherever they went, she felt vivacious and lovely, admired and happy. It was easy to charm everyone she met, because she so thoroughly enjoyed herself, and her warmth and pleasure were contagious. If there were times when she regretted the simplicity of her wardrobe, her lack of jewels, her abundance of white linen and scarcity of silk, she refused to let it show. For the time being, her simplicity and minimal adornment evoked admiration and even imitation from the other ladies, for her style of choice, or so they all believed it to be, emphasized her youth, natural grace, and loveliness. Kate knew that eventually the novelty would fade, and her admirers would judge her lack of jewels and silk more critically, but she hoped that by then, somehow, she would be able to afford more expensive adornments.

Comparisons to Mrs. Lincoln, the only lady in Washington society ahead of her in rank, were inevitable. Kate overheard enough gossip to know that while her artful simplicity of attire won praise, Mrs. Lincoln was considered plain despite her diamonds and pearls and exquisite silk dresses, whose beauty she diminished with too many embellishments, unsuitably low necklines, and an overabundance of flowers in her hair. Both ladies were considered well versed in politics and excellent conversationalists, but Mrs. Lincoln often seemed tense and anxious, tired and overwrought, while Kate's fresh, spirited discourse evoked delight in her listeners. Mrs. Lincoln was often snubbed by Washington's social elite, while Kate was invited everywhere, sought out by everyone. Although it was true that Mrs. Lincoln did on occasion prove that she could charm and impress as well as any other cultured, well-educated woman, more often than not, she seemed tempestuous, flighty, strident, jealous, and uncertain, as if she wanted too badly to win approval. In striking contrast, Kate conveyed self-assurance, confidence, poise, and intelligence beyond her years, with a regal grace and vivacity that made her the center of attention at every gathering, although, unlike the First Lady, she never seemed to seek it.

It was little wonder that Mrs. Lincoln despised her, Kate considered, with a hint of annoyed exasperation. She had not sought a rivalry with Mrs. Lincoln, but from the moment Mrs. Lincoln had made it her ambition to put Kate in her place, their roles had been cast, their course set. Now Kate would never defer to Mrs. Lincoln, never acknowledge her as her social superior. Kate did not have the White House—at least, not yet—but she did have her pride. In lieu of the title First Lady, for the moment she would accept Belle of Washington—and let Mrs. Lincoln try to claim that for herself if she could.

One sultry Monday afternoon near the end of June, Kate sought a breath of fresh air in the cool shade of the garden with a cup of apple cider still cold from the cellar and the morning papers, which she had been unable to read at breakfast because her father had been entertaining guests. Seated gracefully on a quilt spread on the grass, she was perusing the "Local Matters" column of the *Daily National Intelligencer* when the name of a particular state caught her eye, and she eagerly skipped ahead to see if it contained a particular name.

> THE SECOND RHODE ISLAND REGIMENT, accompanied by the Providence Marine Artillery with a full battery of six pieces (James's rifled cannon), arrived here Saturday morning. They bring with them upwards of one hundred horses and eighteen wagons, including ambulances, besides tents and conveniences of every kind. They are thus ready to take the field at any moment. Their uniform is neat and comfortable. The coat of blue is loose fitting, and the pantaloons of gray, with a narrow stripe; hats resembling the army pattern are worn by all. They have gone to their encampment north of the city. Governor Sprague and

a portion of his staff, including Cols. Goddard and Gard-
ner, accompanied the regiment.

Kate set the newspaper down on her lap, stunned. Governor Sprague
had returned to Washington. Not only had he failed to write to tell her
he was coming, he had not called on her even once in the three days
since his arrival.

She was tempted to ride out to the Rhode Island encampment with
the usual gifts for the troops, then feign mild surprise and unmistakable
disinterest when she happened to cross paths with the governor. Or perhaps instead she should send one of the servants out with a basket of
delicacies from her garden, with a note welcoming the governor back to
the capital and congratulating him on organizing another regiment so
quickly that he had not had time to inform his friends of his impending
arrival.

But, no, that would not do either. She would not pursue him. She
shouldn't even want him. He was ten years older than she, although admittedly that wasn't an insurmountable obstacle. His lack of education,
however understandable, would render their conversations dull over
time, although it hadn't yet. His use of tobacco and whiskey troubled her,
and her father, who eschewed both, thought less of him for indulging.
She had no intention of leaving Washington City for Rhode Island, not
before seeing her father in the White House and serving as his First Lady
there. The longer she sat, with the edges of the newspaper curling limply
in the humid air and her cup of cider becoming a tepid bath for gnats
and wasps, the more reasons she could name for why she and the Boy
Governor of Rhode Island would be a bad match.

But she wanted him even so, and it hurt that he apparently did not
want her.

"And that is the best reason of all to dismiss him from my thoughts,"
she declared to the flowers and the birds and the buzzing insects. She
lifted her chin, poured her cider onto the grass, set the cup on the quilt,
and resumed her study of the news of the day, determined to find some
interesting, useful item to mention to Father at supper that evening.

From John Hay, Kate learned that President Lincoln was spending the
stiflingly hot summer days drafting the report he would deliver to Con-

gress when it assembled for the special session on July 4. Kate was in the gallery on Friday, July 5, when John Nicolay brought the president's message to the Senate chamber, where the clerk read it aloud. The address began with a summary of the secession crisis and the effort to relieve Fort Sumter, which had been thwarted before it truly began by the assault from the South Carolina militia at Charleston. No choice had been left to Mr. Lincoln but to invoke the war powers of the government, he claimed, so as to resist the force arrayed for the nation's destruction with forces committed to its preservation. It had been necessary to call for troops, and also to suspend the writ of habeas corpus, a privilege that had been exercised sparingly and always in accordance with the provisions established by the Constitution. "It is now recommended that you give the legal means for making this contest a short and a decisive one," the president had declared, "that you place at the control of the government, for the work, at least four hundred thousand men, and four hundred millions of dollars."

As the proposal met with irrepressible applause, Kate drew in a sharp breath, knowing that if Congress did approve such an enormous sum, it would be up to her father to find it.

The president went on to make a convincing case for why the money and men were utterly essential to the survival of the nation and its liberties, and also to argue why the Constitution did not allow any state to withdraw from the Union without the consent of the Union and the other states. "This is essentially a People's contest," the president asserted. "On the side of the Union, it is a struggle for maintaining in the world, that form, and substance of government, whose leading object is, to elevate the condition of men—to lift artificial weights from all shoulders—to clear the path of laudable pursuit for all—to afford all, an unfettered start, and a fair chance, in the race of life."

They were stirring words about a noble ideal, but Kate wished she could ask the president to explain precisely whom he meant by "men" and "all." Did he include the millions of enslaved persons in the rebellious South and the tenuously held border states? Would he lift his metaphoric burdens from the bent, encumbered shoulders of the people who were forced to carry all-too-real burdens? Kate leaned forward in her chair, listening intently, but not only did the address conclude without clarifying that particular matter, the president also failed to mention slavery at all, except once in passing, when he referred to "the States commonly called Slave states."

Kate was thoroughly disappointed and indignant. "If a foreigner newly arrived on our shores with little foreknowledge of our country read that address," she complained to her father afterward, "he would have absolutely no idea that the South wages war upon the government in order to preserve slavery, although every single American—man, woman, and innocent child—knows that to be the cause."

"This is Seward's influence, I'm certain," her father replied. "The president listens overmuch to his cautions and criticisms instead of trusting in the strength of his own popularity with the people." Then he sighed, and reluctantly added, "But perhaps he took the wiser, more prudent path on this occasion by not emphasizing slavery."

"Father," protested Kate, "you can't mean that. You're the most ardent and devoted abolitionist in his cabinet."

"A title I bear proudly, but nevertheless, it is perhaps better to leave the sword of emancipation in the sheath at this time. The majority of the Northern people, as well as the Congress, seem to prefer to consider the purpose of the war to be the preservation of the Union rather than the elimination of slavery."

Kate shook her head, exasperated. "I fail to see how we can accomplish one without the other."

"It may very well be that we cannot." Father smiled, a little worriedly, and took her hand. "I agree with the president that we must take care not to lose support in the North or to drive any more states from the Union, but make no mistake, daughter. If the issue is distinctly presented—death to the American Republic or death to slavery—slavery must die."

Although Kate's opinion of the address remained decidedly lukewarm, Congress was evidently persuaded, for they responded to the president's call for more money and troops with swift resolve. Instead of the four hundred thousand men Mr. Lincoln had requested, they ordered half a million men recruited, and authorized the appropriation of even more funds than he had sought. The House and Senate also passed a joint resolution legalizing several measures the president had taken to defend the Union while Congress was at recess—calling up three-month troops, instituting blockades—but they did not approve his suspension of habeas corpus, a rare point on which Republicans and Democrats agreed.

Nettie was astounded by the immense sum Congress had granted for the war effort. One morning over breakfast, she speculated about all the many things that money could buy if it did not have to go to rifles and cannons and food for the troops. Kate hid a smile as Nettie chattered on, for she suspected that her younger sister imagined railcars full of bags of gold coins being delivered to General Scott's headquarters. "That's a lot of money," Nettie eventually concluded, breaking a crust off her toast for emphasis.

"That's an understatement," said Father dryly. "The question remains, where is it all to come from?"

"From the vault at the Treasury Building?" Nettie suggested helpfully. "From the bank?"

"Exactly, Nettie, from the bank." Father folded his napkin, pushed back his chair, and rose. "It may require some arm twisting of bankers, but I will contrive to get money from the banks and into the nation's vault."

He departed then for his offices at the Treasury Building, and after he was gone, his daughters fell silent as they lingered at the table.

Eventually Nettie said, "It's Father who has to figure out how to pay for everything."

"That's right," said Kate. "Without Father, the bills wouldn't be paid. That would mean no soldiers, no army, no guns, no cannons, no tents or uniforms or provisions."

"Do you suppose the people understand that Father is just as important as General Scott when it comes to fighting the war," Nettie wondered, "maybe even as important as President Lincoln?"

For a moment Kate could only stare at her younger sister, surprised by her unexpected, precocious insight. "The wiser ones surely do," she replied. "As for the rest, we must do all we can to enlighten them by November of eighteen sixty-four."

As the sultry July days passed, the loyal citizens of the North clamored ever more insistently for the army to take firm and decisive action against the rebels. The battle cry "Forward to Richmond!" echoed in newspapers and speeches throughout the Union, but except for a few minor expeditions and skirmishes, the army commanders seemed content to drill and parade and amass greater numbers rather than confront the enemy. Giving voice to the people's impatience, Senator Lyman Trumbull of Illinois introduced a measure demanding the "immediate movement of the troops, and the occupation of Richmond before the 20th July," the date the Confederate Congress intended to reconvene in their new capital city. With more than fifty thousand Union soldiers in Washington, the fear of invasion from the South had greatly diminished, and when the residents of the Northern capital observed the great numbers of smartly uniformed and outfitted soldiers camped in public buildings and filling their streets and parks and taverns, most Washingtonians could not understand why they were not being sent out into the field immediately. The consensus was that time was of the essence, that it was crucial to get the war over with as soon as possible, before the three-month men's enlistments expired and they went home.

Kate knew, but could divulge to no one, that President Lincoln and his cabinet had already approved a plan to move on the rebels within weeks, if not days. At first General Scott had resisted, for he believed his army, though well dressed and determined, was unprepared for a major offensive. President Lincoln prevailed upon him, noting that if the army did not advance soon, the morale of both the troops and the people of the North would suffer. European heads of state might interpret their inertia as reluctance or a lack of resolve, and perhaps decide to recognize the Confederacy.

Eventually General Scott acquiesced to the wishes of the president and his cabinet, and he approved the plan General Irvin McDowell had devised to engage Confederate general P. G. T. Beauregard's forces at Manassas, a town about thirty miles southwest of Washington City. General McDowell—a graduate of the United States Military Academy, a veteran of the Mexican War, and a fellow Ohioan who looked upon Father as a mentor—intended to take thirty thousand troops to Manassas, where he would outflank and overrun General Beauregard's forces, roughly twenty thousand strong. In the meantime, Union general Robert Patterson would engage General Joseph Johnston's nine thousand rebels at Winchester, Virginia, to prevent them from reinforcing General Beauregard. Father told Kate that the plan was intelligent and ought to succeed. The only question was when and how it would be undertaken.

Not long after President Lincoln's address was read in the Senate, Kate and Nettie were invited to accompany Secretary of War Simon Cameron, adjutant general of the army Lorenzo Thomas, their wives and daughters, and several friends and assistants on an excursion to Fort Monroe at Hampton Roads, Virginia, where the James and York rivers emptied into Chesapeake Bay. The purpose for the trip was to assess the fort's preparedness to act as a base for an offensive campaign, but Secretary Cameron decided it could also serve as a sightseeing trip. While Norfolk, just across the water, had fallen to the Confederates when Virginia seceded, Fort Monroe had always remained under Union control, so the trip along the Chesapeake would be perfectly safe. Kate and Nettie exchanged a skeptical look at that pronouncement, but they did not mention their confrontation with the privateer the previous May lest they compel Secretary Cameron to revoke his invitation.

It was a thoroughly enjoyable and at times exciting outing, with the preparations for war both thrilling and ominous. A grand review was held in their honor at the fortress, and later in the day, the party reviewed the troops at Newport News and Camp Hamilton as well. Kate and Nettie were especially pleased to pay their compliments to General Butler, whom they had come to regard, along with Major Anderson, as their own special protector. Kate also took note of the "contrabands" working at the fort, former slaves who had escaped to Union lines and had been hired to work for the army.

Their employment at Fort Monroe, like most of General Butler's unauthorized schemes, was not without controversy. In May, three fugitive slaves had come to the fort after escaping from a Confederate battery they had been ordered by their master to help construct. When their master demanded that they be returned, General Butler had refused, arguing that the Fugitive Slave Law did not oblige him to return the runaways because their labors had supported Confederate troops and they had fled a state in rebellion. Instead General Butler declared the three fugitives "contraband of war" and paid them to work for the Union instead, an offer he had extended ever since to other slaves who managed to reach Fort Monroe. Kate had been curious to see how his policy worked in practice, since Father believed colored men ought to be allowed to enlist in the army, not only as laborers but as soldiers. She knew he would be eager to hear her observations.

When she and Nettie returned home at the end of a long, fascinating day, they found Father in the garden, but he was not alone. "Governor Sprague," Nettie cried out, hurrying down the cobblestone path to the shade of the trees where the men sat talking earnestly. At the sound of Nettie's voice, they glanced her way, spotted the sisters, and rose from their chairs to welcome them. While Nettie darted ahead eagerly, Kate followed behind at a more leisurely, deliberately indifferent pace.

"Why, Governor Sprague," she said when she reached them, offering him her hand. "I do seem to recall reading that you had returned to the capital."

He smiled disarmingly. "Yes, about two weeks ago."

"I see." Kate nodded politely, but inside she was seething. To acknowledge that he had been back a fortnight without calling on her, as if there were no reason why she should have expected to hear from him sooner, without even the slightest hint of an apology—did he think his company so desirable that she would tolerate the slight without taking affront?

"I did call earlier," he said, still smiling away as if he noticed nothing amiss. "You were out."

"Did you indeed?" said Kate, concealing her surprise. Vina would have told her, surely. "When was this?"

"Earlier this morning."

"Ah." At least a week too late to redeem him. "Well, I'm sure you and Father have a lot of catching up to do. Nettie, should we go inside?"

"I think I'll stay." Nettie seated herself on a stone bench in a rather good imitation of her sister's grace.

Kate felt betrayed, but she knew that was unreasonable, so she smiled warmly and said, "As for myself, I have letters to write, so if you'll please excuse me—" She nodded to each of them, the governor last of all, and turned back toward the house.

She was nearly halfway there when she heard quick footsteps on the path behind her. "Miss Chase, if you please."

Muffling a sigh, Kate turned and fixed the governor with a vaguely inquisitive smile. "Is there something you need? More refreshments, perhaps?"

"No, thank you." He peered at her with a rueful grin like a schoolboy who knew he deserved a scolding. "I came by this morning to invite you to accompany me to an exhibition on the Washington Monument grounds this afternoon. The Second Rhode Island Regiment demonstrated the James rifled cannon."

"How interesting."

"President Lincoln certainly thought so. He and several military engineers offered their warmest commendations. Do you know, the cannon's range is between three and four miles?"

"My goodness," she replied with polite coolness. "That is quite far. I hope the accuracy is equally sound."

"It is, I assure you," he said proudly. "I'm sorry you weren't able to see the test. Perhaps tomorrow we could go riding together, and I could tell you more about it."

"Oh, I'm so sorry, but I've already agreed to go riding with Mr. Hay tomorrow."

The governor's smile faltered. "The day after, then?"

She shook her head. "Mrs. McLean is having a reception, and I offered to help her prepare."

"I see." His smile had become a grimace. "You're a very busy young lady."

"And you, I'm sure, have been very busy yourself." She inclined her head in a parting bow. "Congratulations for the successful exhibition. Good day, Governor."

He nodded glumly as she turned her back to him and went inside. She would have felt sorry for him had he not been so unkind to her before.

She made sure to be in her father's study busily engaged with her correspondence when the governor departed so she would not be obliged to bid him a second farewell. Only when she knew he was gone did she emerge and seek out her father, who was displeased with her. "You could have remained to talk with us a little while," he protested.

"Nettie stayed to play hostess," Kate pointed out, feigning innocence, "and it was you he came to see."

"Perhaps, but I think the governor would have enjoyed hearing your observations about Fort Monroe."

"Another time, perhaps."

"Another time, *certainly*," Father corrected. "When will you be home from your ride tomorrow?"

"I'm not sure. It depends on the weather and the horses. By late afternoon, in any case."

"Good," said Father, "because Governor Sprague is coming to dine with us."

Kate had no time to spare, so rather than squander any of it in protest, she sighed inwardly and assured her father that she would see to everything, as she always did. She quickly devised a menu, instructed Mrs. Vaudry, the housekeeper, and Addie, the cook, and invited two other couples and Mrs. Douglas so that Governor Sprague's attentions would be diluted among a larger party. Father seemed especially pleased that she had included Mrs. Douglas, and something in his bashful eagerness made Kate suspect that the lovely widow's charms were not lost on him. Ordinarily a widow would not accept a social engagement so soon after her husband's death, but Kate had wanted to invite her and so she did. If Mrs. Douglas cared what prying gossips thought, she could have declined. Kate thought she at least ought to be given the choice.

Kate put the dinner preparations out of her thoughts while she went riding with John Hay, determined to enjoy his company and not anticipate anyone else's. The ride was exhilarating, the scenery charming, and John was, as always, amusing and clever. He intrigued her with stories of President Lincoln's late-night debates with his staff, and had her laughing with shocked amusement when he revealed the new nickname he and John Nicolay had devised for Mrs. Lincoln: Her Satanic Majesty. "That is too cruel," she protested, fighting to contain her laughter, but John merely grinned wickedly and worked the unkind sobriquet into the conversation at every possible opportunity.

She returned home in plenty of time to wash and dress and supervise the last-minute preparations, and to greet her guests at the door when they arrived. Mrs. Douglas was as gracious and beautiful as ever, and although she was draped from head to foot in black crepe, her attire was so exquisitely fashioned that Kate wished, not for the first time, that she could afford Mrs. Douglas's exceptionally gifted dressmaker. The two couples were longtime friends of her father from Cincinnati and Columbus, as dear and well-known to Kate and Nettie as their own aunts and uncles, and always pleasant company. Governor Sprague arrived, handsomely attired in his dress uniform, bearing gifts of flowers for her and Nettie, which had the younger girl blushing sweetly.

Although it was pulled together at the last minute, the dinner party was a complete success, in part because Kate deftly arranged never to be left alone with the governor, so he was powerless to play upon her sympathies and persuade her to forgive him. She would have considered the entire evening a triumph if only he had not returned to the house after the other guests had departed, claiming to have mislaid a glove.

"I'll look for it," Nettie promised, darting off to the dining room.

"Miss Chase," the governor said quietly when they were alone, "I think we should always be honest with each other."

She furrowed her brow, feigning confusion. "By this declaration, do you mean to say that you haven't been honest with me in the past, or that you're not usually honest with people as a matter of course?"

"Neither." He regarded her with dark, contrite eyes. "You feel that I've neglected you."

"Why should I?"

"Because I have."

She regarded him steadily. "You could neglect me only if we had an understanding, which we don't. You haven't neglected me, because you had no obligation to me. Rest assured, your conscience is clear."

"Then why doesn't it feel clear?" Without waiting for an answer, he said, "Miss Chase, I would like us to have the sort of friendship where you would feel neglected if you didn't hear from me often, if I forgot to write or failed to visit."

Kate laughed, astonished. "I don't consider that a proper friendship at all, burdened as it is with expectations of neglect."

"Don't pretend you don't understand me." His voice was low and impassioned. "I don't want to feel like you have to go riding with John Hay, or any other man, because you fear I am inconstant."

"I go riding with John Hay because I like him," she said sharply. "He's my friend, and he is always pleasant company."

Pained, the governor put on his hat, the famous black felt hat with the long yellow plume and the rakishly rolled brim, and stepped toward the door. "Miss Chase," he said resignedly, "I would like very much for the . . . the feeling between us to go back to the way it was."

"I *don't* want that," Kate said. "I've been unhappy. You made me so. I have no claim to your affections, but I think you trifled with me, and I will not endure it."

"You will not have to," he said. "But understand, Kate, I have responsibilities. An entire state looks to me to guide them through this time of crisis. If I forget to write love letters because I'm busy leading a state and mustering a regiment to fight the rebels, I think that is forgivable. Even so, I won't neglect you again, if neglect is what it was."

"I found it," said Nettie. Kate whirled about and discovered her sister standing on the far side of the foyer, holding a man's leather glove and watching them uncertainly.

"Very well done, Miss Nettie," said the governor, smiling kindly as he held out his palm. Nettie beamed and brought the glove to him, and blushed a deep pink when he thanked her and bent to kiss her on the forehead. When he straightened, he regarded Kate seriously, his eyes deep, soulful, and almost level with her own. "As for you, Miss Chase, are you free to go riding with me tomorrow afternoon?"

She shook her head, wondering whether he had forgotten or thought she had lied. "Mrs. McLean's reception."

"Of course." He considered. "The day after?"

Kate knew that if she refused him, he would not ask her again for a very long time, if ever—and suddenly the very thought was unbearable.

"Yes," she said, for it was what she had wanted to say all along. "I will go riding with you, Governor Sprague."

Chapter Ten

$\mathcal{I}$n the days that followed, Governor Sprague was true to his word. He called on Kate often and was so attentive that she could almost forget how lonely he had made her feel in the weeks before.

He confided in her his ambitions, his disappointments, his hopes, his fears—but, still wary, she guarded her heart more carefully than before, and listened to his confidences more often than she shared her own. When they rode out together one morning to visit the Rhode Island encampment on the shady ridges above the city, he revealed that in May, he had written to Secretary Cameron suggesting that he be granted a commission with the rank of major general. When the secretary of war offered him a mere brigadier generalship instead, Governor Sprague had declined. "I told him that the people of Rhode Island could not accept a position of less rank for their governor," he told her.

"That was probably wise," she remarked. "You wouldn't want an empty title. The wags and wits claim that one cannot throw a stick in Washington City these days without striking six brigadier generals."

The governor laughed and seemed much reassured, and all the more endearing for the way he responded to her confidence in him. Although he was bold and daring, she detected a note of uncertainty intermingled with his courage and pride. It came, she surmised, of having no father in the home from the time he was quite a young man. Father too had lost his father at a young age, and it had thrown his family into financial difficulties, but Father had always found other men to serve as guides and mentors, from his brilliant but stern uncle Philander Chase, the Episcopal bishop of Ohio and school headmaster, to William Wirt, attorney general to President Adams and Father's instructor as he studied the law, as well as numerous others throughout his life. If Governor Sprague had benefited from the guidance of great men as Father had done, he would not be afflicted by self-doubt, which he sometimes, to Kate's chagrin, attempted to silence with whiskey. When Kate reflected upon all that William had accomplished on his own without such guidance, she considered it a testament to his perseverance, strength of character, and extraordinary abilities. It was entirely possible that he would earn the rank of general in the field with his Rhode Island regiments before long. It was even conceivable that he could someday become president.

Sometimes Kate imagined what it would be like to be First Lady not once but twice—first in her father's administration, and later, as William's wife. But she only rarely indulged in such silly daydreams, and she never divulged them to William.

In the middle of July, General McDowell at long last began to advance his command from Washington and Alexandria deeper into Virginia. Kate and Nettie were out walking one morning with Bishop Charles McIlvaine from Ohio, who was visiting their family, when they observed the lengthy procession of soldiers, army wagons, and accoutrements filing across Long Bridge over the Potomac. "What are those curious carriages there?" asked Nettie. "The oddly shaped ones, with the black curtains."

Bishop McIlvaine studied the long, dark vehicles as they rolled slowly over the bridge. "Those are ambulances."

"So many!"

"Let us pray they will need no more than this," the bishop replied solemnly. He was tall and slender, with snow-white hair, bright-blue eyes, and noble features that usually offered a gentle and compassionate expression but at that moment had settled into sad resignation.

Kate's heart sank as the sunlight gleamed off the polished metal and fresh paint and the breeze stirred the curtains. The ambulances would never again be as bright and shining as they were at that moment, not after they had been splattered with battlefield mud and gore, and had borne their ghastly burdens of suffering and death.

Two days later, on July 18, General McDowell and his thirty-two thousand troops approached Centreville, where General Beauregard waited with about twenty-two thousand Confederates stretched out along an eight-mile front on the other side of a creek called Bull Run. General McDowell's movements had been anything but a secret. For weeks, newspapers throughout the North had eagerly reported the names and positions of regiments, information they easily collected from casual, careless talk in encampments and taverns—and Northern papers were smuggled into Richmond within a day or two of publication, just as Confederate papers were brought into the North.

On the same day General McDowell reached Bull Run, William accompanied Major John Barnard of the US Corps of Engineers on a reconnaissance mission to Blackburn's Ford, a crossing between Manassas and Centreville in Virginia. He had promised Kate that he would return safely, but a heavy sense of dread hung over her the entire time he was away. When he returned, exhilarated and proud, to report that the sortie had succeeded, he cheerfully described how they had been fired upon by the Confederates but had escaped unharmed. The mission had satisfied William's long-held desire to "feel the enemy," as he put it, and he was eager to return to the field to test his regiments' mettle against that of the swaggering, boastful rebels, who claimed that one Southern man could whip a dozen Yankees.

By Sunday morning, word had spread throughout Washington that an exciting battle was imminent, and thousands of citizens eager for diversion packed picnic hampers and hired carriages to take them out to watch the spectacle. Politicians determined to witness history, reporters chasing the story, curious workmen, ladies with parasols thrilled by the prospect of danger and heroism—all wanted to watch Brigadier General Irvin McDowell and his mighty Army of Northeastern Virginia soundly defeat the rebels before marching on to take Richmond and bring a quick and decisive end to the conflict.

"May we go and watch too, Father?" Nettie implored, watching from the window as carriages and wagons packed with sightseers rumbled past their home. "Bishop McIlvaine can escort us."

Bishop McIlvaine's eyebrows rose as if the proposal had caught him entirely by surprise and was not particularly agreeable. Fortunately for him, Father promptly shook his head. "Even escorted by a clergyman, a battlefield is no place for young ladies," he replied. "Nor are the hills above a battlefield. The lines could shift, a cannon could misfire, a stray bullet could find an innocent mark—no, absolutely not."

Nettie was desperately disappointed, but Kate was relieved. William was out there leading the Rhode Island artillery battery, and if he should fall, she could not bear to witness it.

The Chase family attended church together that morning as if it were any ordinary Sunday, but the battle was never far from their thoughts. At midday, Father joined President Lincoln and the rest of the cabinet in the telegraph office in the War Department to await news from the field. Kate lingered at home until her curiosity and apprehension became intolerable, and then she invited Nettie to go for a walk, to see what they could learn. Nettie eagerly accepted, and they both kept their eyes and ears open as they strolled down Fourteenth Street toward Lafayette Square. As they approached the Willard Hotel, they spotted a jubilant crowd hundreds strong gathered around the entrance. Suddenly a young man with his hat and coat askew pushed his way to the front, climbed atop a low stone wall, and read aloud a dispatch from the field. The Union troops had driven the rebels south into the woods, he announced, and a complete victory seemed assured. As the throng burst into vehement cheers, fairly intoxicated with joy, Kate felt a tremulous wave of relief wash through her, although she knew that even a decisive Union victory could not guarantee that William would survive the day.

The sisters walked home to the sounds of rejoicing in the streets and the distant rumble of artillery to the west. Their hopes rose as the afternoon passed, and shortly before five o'clock Father returned, fairly bursting with relief and elation. Every fifteen minutes, bulletins had arrived from the telegraph office at Fairfax Station about three or four miles from the battlefield, and throughout the long day, they had brought increasingly good news. "At half past four, we received the news we had long awaited but could not have taken for granted," Father told them. "The Union army has achieved a glorious victory."

"Oh, thank heavens," Kate said, pressing a hand to her stomach, where a knot of worry at last began to unravel.

"Praise God," said Bishop McIlvaine. "May this be the first and last great battle of the rebellion."

"It is expected that General McDowell will reach Richmond within the week," said Father. "This insurrection will be over soon."

Victory was so certain that the cabinet was no longer required at the War Department, and Mr. Lincoln had gone out for his usual Sunday carriage ride, accompanied by his two youngest sons and Secretary Bates. It was the best possible news they could have hoped for, and yet Kate's joy was incomplete, and would remain so until she heard from William.

Shortly after seven o'clock, a messenger arrived from the White House, and as Father read the dispatch, he grew pale and still. "What is it?" Kate asked.

"The cabinet has been summoned back to the War Department," he said grimly, reaching for his hat. "General McDowell's army is in full retreat. The day is lost."

"How can this be?" the bishop asked, astounded. "The battle was declared a total Union victory."

"Apparently that declaration was premature." Father patted Kate's shoulder and kissed Nettie swiftly on the cheek. "I'll send word when I know more."

Kate waited in vain for a message from her father, concealing her anxiety for Nettie's sake, eventually sending her off to bed with a kiss and reassurances that all would be well. Bishop McIlvaine sat up with her, his head bent in prayer over his Bible, often stealing pensive glances to the window.

Around midnight, Father returned home, utterly exhausted. "McDowell verified the loss," he said. "The army is in full retreat, and now our only hope is that they will reach safety before they are slaughtered. Immediate reinforcements have been called to defend Washington."

Kate took a deep, shaky breath. "Are the rebels in pursuit? Do you expect them to try to invade the city?"

"They should try to press their advantage," said Father shortly. "It is what I would do." Then he caught himself. "Katie, dear, don't worry. No harm will come to you and your sister."

He could not possibly know that for certain, but Kate nodded to show him she trusted him and was unafraid.

They all went off to bed, but Kate tossed and turned, drifting in and out of sleep. In the gray dawn, she awoke to the rumbling of heavy wagons on the street below. An apprehensive impulse compelled her to go to the window, where beneath a dark and murky sky, long carriages were passing in the midst of a heavy rain. Suddenly, with a rush of sickening dread, she recognized the ambulances she and Nettie had watched crossing Long Bridge only days before.

Quickly she washed and dressed. Although she had tried to be quiet, she inadvertently woke Nettie, who stumbled out of bed and went to the window, where she was quickly shocked into full wakefulness. "Sister, come see."

Kate hurried to her side, and together the sisters watched in stunned amazement as carriages and wagons and horses carried stricken, terrified men and women past as quickly as their tired horses could go. It took Kate a moment to recognize them as the same cheerful, excited spectators who had so enthusiastically set out for the hills above Centreville to observe the battlefield the previous day. Soon thereafter soldiers began to straggle down the street in front of the Chase residence, their expressions stunned and haggard, their uniforms torn and disheveled, their ranks diminished. Too famished and exhausted to press on, many of the soldiers dropped their kits in doorways, on sidewalks, on empty lots, and lay down to sleep where they were.

Before the family sat down to a hasty breakfast, Father, his eyes shadowed and red as if he had not slept, instructed Addie, the cook, to prepare gallons of strong, hot coffee to serve to the woeful, stunned soldiers from a basement door of the kitchen that opened out upon the street. When the coffee ran out, Addie made more, and throughout the day, Kate, Nettie, Vina, and Mrs. Vaudry poured coffee and murmured encouragement, and glad enough the ragged soldiers seemed to receive both.

More wounded came in from the battlefield too, brought into the city by the wagonload. When word went out that there were not enough beds for all the soldiers who needed them, nor enough bandages, nurses, food, or hospitals for that matter, Father offered to accommodate as many of the wounded as their house could hold. Soon one of the long black carriages stopped at their front door to discharge a battered and bloodied soldier, and after that, more suffering men were brought into the house until nearly a dozen filled the beds and sofas, groaning and coughing and calling deliriously for mothers and sweethearts.

Kate and Bishop McIlvaine flew into action, nursing the men and tending their wounds, while Nettie, who had refused to be sent to her room away from the horrible sights and sounds and odors, hurried from room to room with a pitcher of cool water and a cup, which she bravely offered to the men who were able to accept. Her eyes widened and her cheeks flushed whenever she came to the front parlor, where a soldier, a boy no more than twenty, swore profusely from the pain, almost without pausing to take a breath.

For hours the people of Washington waited in dread for the Confederate army to press their advantage and take the city, but the invasion never came. Many also waited anxiously for word from loved ones who had been engaged in the battle or had gone to watch it. Kate had heard nothing of William, but worrisome rumors claimed that the Rhode Island regiments had been in the thick of the fight, until they had broken ranks after General Johnston brought nine thousand fresh Confederate troops to reinforce General Beauregard. Rebel cavalry and infantry had swept from the forests and crashed down upon the Union columns, which had broken apart and fallen into an uncontrolled retreat. Many prisoners had been taken, but William, who despite his uniform and title held no commission, would not be protected by the usual rules of war.

All that day and the next Kate waited pensively as she tended the wounded soldiers left in her care, looked after Nettie, and, whenever she had a moment to herself, skimmed the disheartening reports in the press and carefully examined the casualty lists. Finally, shortly after breakfast on Wednesday morning, William appeared on their doorstep.

"I should have sent my card two days ago," he said to Kate by way of greeting. "After I promised not to neglect you—"

"That's quite all right," said Kate quickly, too relieved to care about the delay. "I'm very glad to see that you're alive and unharmed—very, very glad."

She invited him in, introduced him to Bishop McIlvaine, and sent word to the kitchen for coffee and biscuits and preserves to be brought out, in case William had not had breakfast. He devoured the food as if he had not eaten for weeks, but in a distracted, impatient fashion as if his thoughts were elsewhere and he wanted to rush off and join them. "I was in charge of a battery of artillery," he began without preamble. "One of our guns was the first cannon discharged at the enemy's line of battle of the war. I furnished the first ammunition myself."

"I'm sure that will long serve as a point of honor for your men," Kate said.

"Honor," he said bitterly. "If they ever had any."

Kate was shocked. The Rhode Island regiments were William's pride and joy. She had never heard him disparage them before.

"When the battle commenced, the men were detached and separated. Some of the men stood firm, but others"—he shook his head, frowning—"others were confused."

"How close were you to the enemy?"

"Only half a pistol shot distance away. Men were struck and died where they fell. Horses too. I continued to supply ammunition from horseback, and did my utmost to give confidence to the line. The bullets were so thick and close that my loose blouse bears their holes."

"My goodness, Governor!" Kate exclaimed, pressing her hand to her heart, which thumped almost painfully.

"The Union lines held, but it was a grueling struggle, and the men seemed disinclined to charge." He stood suddenly and paced the length of the dining room, pausing to glance out the window before fixing her with a look that seemed almost defiant. "The men will remember when I rode in front of them, the only officer they could see, and struck their muskets to a level with the enemy. And I shall never forget the blast of enthusiasm with which these twelve hundred men received me. Then, Kate, then we were ripe for a charge. I led." He fell silent, and grief swept over his face. "My horse was shot."

"No!" Kate cried out. "Not your white stallion. Not that magnificent creature."

William nodded. "He perished, and there was nothing I could do to comfort him as he died. I took off his saddle in front of the line—and the men fell back, without orders to do so."

So the rumors were true. "Perhaps in the confusion—"

William cut her off with a quick gesture. "No. They did not misunderstand me. Their courage deserted them, and they deserted me." He barked out a laugh, short and bitter. "The officers led the way."

"Oh, William," she said. "That's inexcusable. It's reprehensible."

"It was utter chaos," he continued. "Wagons carrying men and arms toward the battle were blocked by ammunition carts in full retreat. The heat, the dust, the uproar—all defy description. Men were running past me, their faces streaming perspiration, and many must have lost or discarded their weapons in flight, for they carried none." He inhaled deeply and let out a long, slow breath as if barely containing his rage. "They told me their three months' enlistments had expired, and that they were determined to go home. And so they did."

Kate had been too preoccupied with the wounded soldiers in her care to ride out to the Rhode Island encampment above the city, not even to seek news of William. "They went home to their camp," she asked, "or home to Rhode Island?"

"The latter, to my everlasting shame, and theirs. They didn't even pause long enough to answer the call for reinforcements to protect the capital. Thus the regiment was led off by the so-called million-dollar men who would not stay to fight, but the artillery remained and I with it." He shook his head, his jaw clenched in anger. "If Burnside's men had held, they would have carried the day, but instead, they neglected to guard the rear of the army."

They were not the only regiment to fail in that regard, Kate knew.

"I remained on the field," said William, weariness overtaking the anger in his voice. "As twilight fell, I wrapped myself up in my greatcoat and fell asleep, awaiting reinforcements."

"Alone and undefended? What if a rebel had come by and shot you?"

"Then I'd be dead, and I'd be spared the embarrassment of my regiment's cowardice," he snapped, but he immediately amended his words. "My apologies. It is wrong to mock death when so many men lost their lives today, and it is always wrong to speak harshly to you."

"I understand," she replied, regarding him with fond amusement. "You've had a very difficult day, so I've resolved to be more forgiving than usual."

He managed a wan smile. "You are an angel."

"Yes, so I've been told."

He frowned briefly as if wondering who might have told her that, but then his thoughts turned back to his own story. "When I woke, it was about two o'clock in the morning, the field was dark and quiet, and I was alone. I mounted a horse I found wandering without its rider, jumped the fences, and made for Washington. Along the way I passed a trail of disgrace—the ground strewn with abandoned coats, blankets, firelocks, cooking tins, caps, belts, bayonets—the detritus of cowardly flight."

Kate could only shake her head in sympathy. She was not convinced that it was fair to label all the men who had retreated cowards, but it was not the time for that debate.

"I reported at once to President Lincoln, finding him awake in his office, as I had expected. I prevailed upon him to send forward new troops to stop the disorder, but he refused."

From what Father had told Kate of General Scott's and Secretary Cameron's reports, Mr. Lincoln had made the only reasonable decision, but again she kept her own counsel. "What will you do now?" she asked instead.

"Now?" He shrugged and shook his head. "Gather up whatever stragglers from the Rhode Island regiments I can. Organize them into a company if enough remain, a squadron if that is all I have enough for. I'll return home and recruit more troops."

"How soon?"

He glanced her way, and his chagrin told her he had not considered how that news might grieve her. "I have not decided," he said. "But I will return, with braver men than before."

"I have every confidence that you will," she told him, but her heart sank a little all the same.

Chapter Eleven

AUGUST 1861–JANUARY 1862

In the aftermath of the shocking defeat at Bull Run, Washingtonians nursed the wounded and mourned their dead and wondered how the terrible reversal had come about. The press took to calling the Union's disorderly retreat from the battlefield "the Great Skedaddle," bringing shame upon the federal soldiers and heartening their enemies throughout the South. The longer the people's bewilderment remained unsatisfied, the hotter their anger burned, until the newspapers demanded answers in ever more belligerent tones and recruiting offices overflowed with angry volunteers eager for revenge.

Although Mr. Lincoln maintained a calm, stoic front for the public, Father observed that he was in fact quite melancholy. Newspapers throughout the North castigated him for his army's embarrassing performance, but rather than firing back acerbic retorts, the president listened patiently and attentively to their criticisms, and more important, to reports from the field explaining what had gone wrong. He sequestered himself with his cabinet and his most trusted generals, using the bitter lessons learned to shape a new military strategy and to ensure that the Union never again experienced such a debacle.

Soon President Lincoln issued orders for the troops to be "constantly drilled, disciplined, and instructed," so that the confusion and disorder of the battlefield never again led to widespread panic. When he learned that the three-month men had initiated the retreat, he proposed to discharge any of them who did not wish to commit to a lengthier term of service. He ordered blockades set up before the Confederacy could make the most of their victory by strengthening ties with opportunistic, professedly neutral European nations. Last, he sent a telegram to General George McClellan, presently serving in western Virginia, with orders to report to Washington and take command of the Army of the Potomac. Although General McDowell and his wife were dear friends of the Chases, and they were sorry to see General McDowell replaced, Mr. Lincoln's choice nevertheless gratified Father's pride, for General McClellan was another fellow Ohioan whom he had recommended to the president.

Kate observed that Mr. Lincoln also wisely endeavored to regain the confidence of his army and his people. He visited regiments—often with Mr. Seward by his side, Father noted sourly—and raised the soldiers' spirits with encouraging, inspiring speeches, marked by his characteristic humor. He pledged to provide the troops with everything they needed and encouraged them to appeal to him directly if they were wronged. As the summer passed, the Northern press again turned in the president's favor, commending his firm resolve and applauding a renewed patriotism throughout the Union, which was most readily apparent in the thousands of volunteers who signed up for three-year enlistments.

Pride and confidence and favorable public opinion could be restored, Kate knew, but the people of the North would never regain their certainty that the war would be swiftly and easily won. The stunning defeat at Bull Run had dispelled those vain illusions forever.

The first days of August were oppressively hot and humid, with no relief on the horizon. After hosting a state dinner for Prince Napoléon III—to which Father, but not Kate, was invited—Mrs. Lincoln took her sons Willie and Tad and her cousin Mrs. Grimsley on a vacation to Manhattan and upstate New York. They were among many residents of Washington to flee the torrid, muggy weather for the cool breezes of the North, and in their absence, the social whirlwind of the capital subsided.

William was among the exodus, although he left for Rhode Island for entirely different reasons. When he arrived home, he was given a hero's welcome, and in a letter to Kate he confided that the people's joy and pride compelled him to remain silent about the Rhode Island regiments' dismal performance at the Battle of Bull Run. "It is not because I wish to preserve their reputations," he admitted, "but because if the truth were made known, it would hurt recruitment efforts."

That was the last thing Kate wanted, because the sooner William recruited a new regiment, the sooner he could return to Washington. On their last day together, they had gone sailing on the Potomac, and in the privacy of the boat she had allowed him liberties she had never granted another man, and could not quite believe she had granted him. She longed to feel his touch again, and yet she knew that it was perhaps best that she could not. She came dangerously close to allowing desire to overcome reason whenever she was alone with him, and she knew enough about men to understand that the more a lady consented to, the more would be expected. She would be ruined if she permitted too much.

Not everyone fled Washington in the heat of August. Soldiers, opportunists, politicians, aspiring nurses, newspaper correspondents, and ambitious folk of all kinds continued to make their way to the capital. Some came to settle and stay, at least for the duration of the war; others were merely visiting, and among these, many were eager to see Father. A seat at the table at one of Father's breakfast parties was highly coveted, for in addition to a better meal than one could find at a crowded hotel or boardinghouse, guests would enjoy Kate's enchanting company and an almost private audience with the secretary of the treasury. One guest, Mr. John Garrett, the president of the Baltimore & Ohio Railroad and a longtime acquaintance of Father's, appreciated their hospitality so much that afterward he sent both the Chase family and the Lincolns a consignment of live terrapin to grace their dinner tables.

Nettie shrieked when Father pried open the crate with a crowbar and they discovered the reptiles within, some crawling over one another, others hiding within their shells. "I would rather Mr. Garrett had sent us a puppy," she said, summoning up her courage and peering into the crate. "But I suppose I'll get used to them."

Father let out a rare laugh, but Kate only smiled as she said, "Nettie, darling, these aren't meant to be pets. We're expected to eat them."

"What?"

"They're considered quite a delicacy here in the East."

"Come, now, daughter," said Father. "You know people eat turtles. You've eaten turtle soup on several occasions."

"I didn't know they were these kind of turtles."

"What kind of turtles did you think they were?" Kate asked, laughing. "The kind that grow on turtle trees?"

"No, but"—Nettie winced as she watched the terrapin crawling awkwardly around the bottom of the crate, some trying to scale the wooden wall and topple over the edge to freedom—"in soup they don't have legs and shells and faces."

Kate and Father exchanged a look, and they knew that Mr. Garrett's gifts would never be served in their dining room. "What shall we do with them?" Kate asked her father.

He thought for a moment. "Perhaps they would find the basement comfortable."

Nettie was very pleased by this suggestion, as the basement was a far better destination than the cookstove, so Father and Will hauled the crate to the basement and left the top off. It was only a matter of hours before the reptiles deserted the crate and scuttled off into the nooks and crannies of the dimly lit room, and within a few days, all had contrived to flee the house, if terrapin can be said to flee, through a hatch Kate had deliberately propped open. Most were never seen again, but occasionally the sisters spotted one or two ambling unconcernedly in the garden as if unaware of how narrowly they had escaped their doom.

With her own captives liberated, Nettie became quite concerned about their brethren that had been shipped to the White House. The next time both sisters accompanied Father to an event where the president was in attendance, Nettie, her brows drawn together in worry, asked him what had become of his terrapin. Mr. Lincoln, who Kate had observed was always kind and solicitous to children, smiled upon Nettie and confessed, "I felt so sorry for the poor little fellows that I took mine all out into the garden and let them run away."

Nettie nodded seriously and told him she thought he had made the right decision.

Another new arrival to the capital—and one who received a far grander and more widespread welcome than the terrapin—was General George McClellan. Handsome, athletic, and at thirty-four one of the

Union's youngest generals, General McClellan was celebrated and cheered by a relieved populace who believed he was the man to create a strong, disciplined army out of the scattered, inexperienced troops still shaken by the terrible rout at Manassas. Descended from a distinguished, well-educated Philadelphia family, he had attended excellent schools, including the military academy at West Point. Reassuringly, he had recently defeated a band of Confederate partisans in western Virginia, the Union's only victory in the war thus far. Under his direction, the capital soon took on a more martial appearance; no longer did hotel bars spill drunken soldiers into the streets, nor did troops wander the city late at night pounding on doors in search of lodgings. General McClellan seemed to infuse the demoralized army with his own abundant confidence, and their renewed courage and pride was soon evident in their marching, their carriage, and their words.

Father said that President Lincoln hoped the young general's spirited strength would complement the mature General Scott's experience and wisdom, and that together they would form a powerful, effective team. Privately, Father was somewhat concerned that General McClellan seemed to view General Scott as more of an obstacle than a partner. He infuriated the old soldier by questioning his judgment—even putting his concerns in a letter that he copied to the president—and by arguing that the Army of the Potomac was entirely insufficient compared to the vast numbers of Confederate troops arrayed against them. "Mr. Lincoln mollified the generals by asking McClellan to withdraw his letter," Father told Kate, "but I fear they've achieved a temporary peace at best."

The rival generals were not the only officers to create additional difficulties for an already overburdened commander in chief. At the end of August, Major General John C. Frémont, commander of the Department of the West, issued a proclamation freeing the slaves of Confederates within the state of Missouri. Not only had he not received any authorization from the president beforehand, but Mr. Lincoln first learned of Frémont's proclamation on the same day and by the same method Father, Kate, and most of the nation did—from the newspapers. Acting entirely on his own, General Frémont had defined the war as what Kate had always thought it to be: a war against slavery. Furious, Mr. Lincoln commanded General Frémont to rescind the proclamation, and when the general refused, the president revoked it himself, angering Northern abolitionists and provoking a storm of criticism from Radical Republicans in the Congress and the press.

"Slaves were freed, and now your Mr. Lincoln has put them back into bondage," Kate lamented one afternoon as she and John Hay went riding along the Potomac. She usually refrained from criticizing Mr. Lincoln in his company, for he had become more loyal and admiring of the Tycoon with each passing day in his employment. In unspoken agreement, John held back his criticism of William Sprague, which Kate knew was inspired mostly by envy.

"Mr. Lincoln was convinced that making this conflict a war against slavery instead of a war to preserve the Union would drive Kentucky right out of it," John explained. "If you had seen the alarmed and panicked letters the president received from Unionists in Kentucky after Frémont's reckless act, you'd understand why he had no choice but to do exactly as he did."

"Perhaps I would," said Kate, more icily than she intended. She would like John much better if he did not believe Mr. Lincoln to be so superior to every other man in the cabinet, including her father.

"Now, Kate," he cajoled. "Don't be cross just because on this one matter I've taken the Tycoon's side instead of yours."

"Who says I'm cross?" said Kate airily. And how could he suggest it was only that one time? John rarely disagreed with anything the president did or said anymore, and his conversations had become much less entertaining for it. "I'm merely regretful that you embrace willful ignorance out of blind, misguided loyalty to your boss."

John whooped with laughter, causing his horse to toss its head and whinny in annoyance. "My loyalty is neither blind nor misguided," he said, patting the horse reassuringly on the withers. "I came to it gradually, as I realized how much Mr. Lincoln deserves it."

Kate sighed with exaggerated sorrow, although in truth, she did feel a pang of regret. Already John's ever-increasing admiration for the president was creating friction in their friendship. She dreaded to think how badly they would get along three years hence when her father competed with Mr. Lincoln for the Republican nomination.

"If it makes you feel any better," John confided, "Mrs. Seward feels as you do. She's furious with Mr. Lincoln for revoking the proclamation and with her husband for allowing it, and since she can't scold the president, her husband bears the brunt of her fury."

"I always did like Frances Seward," Kate remarked, her temper much improved. John grinned, and she smiled back at him, their harmony restored for the moment.

September brought blessed relief from the heat and humidity, but Nettie did not welcome the end of summer, for Father had arranged for her to attend boarding school at the Brook Hall Female Seminary in Media, Pennsylvania, west of Philadelphia. She was a bright student, but the coursework was rigorous and she was often homesick. Nettie turned fourteen that month, and she spent part of that day composing a letter to her sister. "Today is my birthday, I ought to have some proper thoughts for the *great?* occasion, and I fully intended to have them, but I can not for the life of me think what they were"—Kate laughed aloud—"except that I want to see you and Father ever so much but I think of that often or rather always."

Kate felt a wrench of sympathy for her sweet, lonely little sister, but the sentiment was startled out of her by the paragraph that followed. "Is Gov Sprague back yet?" Nettie inquired. "I wish (if you do not think me impertinent) that you would marry him. I like him very much wont you? But of course not until I grow up I shant give my consent before that, perhaps though he may get tired of waiting."

Kate needed a moment to collect her thoughts before she read on. Such a bold suggestion from a young girl, who Kate suspected was more than half in love with William herself! Kate had tried to conceal her increasing admiration for him, but Nettie's query proved she had not done so particularly well. William had never spoken of marriage. Perhaps he had been called the Boy Governor so often that he had forgotten he was a gentleman of thirty-one and was still waiting until he came of age to marry. Kate desired him very much, and her feelings of affection were powerful and enduring, but she was not sure how she would respond if he proposed. He possessed many attributes that would make him an excellent husband, but Kate could not imagine leaving her father's house, certainly not before the 1864 election.

But William did write to her, warm and frequent letters. At the end of September, when he returned to Washington with fresh troops and engaged in a brief skirmish in Virginia, she worried terribly for him, and when he called on her at home afterward, she was so relieved and grateful to see him unharmed that she pulled him into the butler's pantry and kissed him full on the lips, allowing him to explore her mouth with his tongue as he seemed to like to do before quickly breaking free at the sound of Mrs. Vaudry's footsteps in the hall.

William's visit to Washington was all too brief, and when he returned to Rhode Island Kate missed him very much, but she was never at a loss for ways to occupy her time and thoughts. Throughout late summer and early autumn, she traveled to New York and Philadelphia and elsewhere, sometimes with Father, sometimes with one or more of her many cousins. Father had never been more preoccupied with his work—prevailing upon bankers to offer enormous loans to the government at reasonable rates, organizing the sale of bonds, proposing new tariffs and taxes. By October, Mrs. Lincoln and the ladies of the elite had returned to Washington, and the social season resumed, defiantly merry as the war hung foreboding above their receptions and balls and levees.

The battlefront had moved away from the outskirts of Washington, but every day brought new reports of intense fighting and grisly descriptions of death and destruction. War raged in several states, and the Union army endured one demoralizing defeat after another. In the middle of October, the Lincolns lost another dear friend from Illinois, Colonel Edward Baker, who was killed along with forty-eight of his men on a riverbank at Ball's Bluff. So many others were seriously wounded that the hospitals again could not accommodate them all, and the Chases once more welcomed sick and injured soldiers into their home, among them Oliver Wendell Holmes Jr., a son of the renowned poet.

Colonel Baker's death was as devastating to the Lincoln family as Colonel Ellsworth's had been. From John Hay, Kate learned that Mary Lincoln was utterly distraught. Edward Baker had been the namesake of her second-born son, who had died years before as a very young child. Willie and Tad also adored the colonel, and the tenderhearted, introspective Willie composed a touching poem in his honor, which was printed in the *National Republican* and was actually quite good for a boy's composition. Kate sent flowers to the Lincolns on behalf of the Chase family along with a sincere letter expressing her condolences. She did not know whether Mrs. Lincoln would appreciate a letter from a young woman she despised or furiously tear up the page and throw it upon the fire, but sending a letter was the proper thing to do in such circumstances, and she would rather Mrs. Lincoln be angry at her for extending a courtesy than for withholding it.

By that time, General McClellan's image had lost much of its luster and murmurs of puzzlement had swelled into a chorus of discontent. The people of Washington City gloried in the magnificent performance of General McClellan's army, more than fifty thousand strong, as they marched in perfectly straight columns in perfect unison through the streets and on the well-trampled parade grounds, but they were frustrated and bewildered by the general's apparent reluctance to lead such well-trained men onto the field of battle. General McClellan insisted that they were not yet prepared, nor were their numbers great enough to confront the vastly more numerous enemy. The defeat at Ball's Bluff—which he blamed on everyone but himself, including Colonel Baker—only increased the people's impatience, and both Father and John Hay observed that the president was becoming increasingly exasperated with him.

General Scott had grown weary of grappling with the young upstart, who insulted him regularly, ignored his orders, and defied the chain of command by failing to keep General Scott informed about his position and the size of his forces. Unwilling to contend with his junior officer for control of the military, General Scott informed the president that he would willingly retire as soon as appropriate arrangements could be made. He had served long and honorably, but he suffered from dropsy in his feet and legs and paralysis in the small of his back, so he could not walk or sit on a horse. He might have stuck it out for the sake of the Union if Mr. Lincoln's attempts to mediate a truce between the two generals had brought about any improvement in their relations, but all his efforts had been in vain. Finally, on November 1, President Lincoln reluctantly accepted General Scott's resignation letter, which was published in all the papers alongside Mr. Lincoln's sincere and gracious reply.

At five o'clock in the morning two days later, a large crowd assembled at the train station to bid General Scott farewell—loyal admirers and numerous aging veterans who were determined to pay their respects to the old soldier despite the driving rain and the early hour. General

McClellan, General Scott's entire staff, and a cavalry escort saw him off, and Father and Secretary Cameron accompanied him on his journey home to Harrisburg. "All were grieved to see General Scott go," Father told Kate upon his return. "With the exception of General McClellan, I suppose. We shall see what he can accomplish now that he no longer has Scott to blame for his difficulties."

General McClellan was Father's man, so Father keenly wanted him to succeed, but McClellan's disrespect for his venerable superior officer had left Father disillusioned and disappointed. He hoped for the best as President Lincoln appointed General McClellan to succeed General Scott as general in chief of the Union army. Kate did not care for the new general in chief—he had tumbled out of her favor the moment she heard him declare that since the institution of slavery was recognized in the Constitution, it was entitled to federal protection—but she prayed he would be a good leader and bring about a swift victory for the Union.

Two weeks after General Scott's departure, Kate learned that General McClellan's promotion had not taught him humility and likely would not inspire a new, respectful sense of cooperation with his commander in chief. One afternoon, when plans to go riding were thwarted by a heavy, cold drizzle, John Hay sat with Kate in the Chases' parlor fuming about General McClellan's arrogance and disrespect. "Yesterday, Mr. Seward and I accompanied President Lincoln to call on McClellan at his home," John told her, his voice taut with anger. "We were told that the general was at a wedding, and we were shown to his parlor, where we waited for an hour. When McClellan arrived home, his servant told him that the president was waiting, but he quietly crept past the parlor and up the stairs to his bedchamber. A minute passed, and then another, and with every tick of the mantel clock my blood grew nearer its boiling point."

"And Mr. Lincoln?" Kate asked.

"He sat patiently all the while, dignified and unflustered, which I must confess shamed me into trying harder to master my angry restlessness," said John. "After another half hour dragged by, Mr. Lincoln reminded the servant that he was waiting, only to be informed that the general had retired for the night and could not see him."

"Such impudence," said Kate, astounded. "How unbecoming an officer."

"It is the arrogance of epaulettes," said John scathingly. "Mr. Lincoln accepted the rebuff with good grace, and seemed not altogether troubled by McClellan's insolence. As we returned to the White House, the president said that he preferred not to score points of etiquette and personal dignity." He frowned and shook his head, indignant. "He even said, and I am not altogether sure he was joking, that he would hold McClellan's horse for him if it would help him achieve victory."

"Mr. Lincoln seems as humble as General McClellan is arrogant."

"There are days I wish President Lincoln had less humility," John admitted. "This is not the first occasion McClellan has kept him waiting, and I doubt it will be the last."

"Perhaps Mr. Lincoln should visit him less frequently," Kate suggested. "If he wishes to speak with his general, he should summon him to the White House instead. The grand setting will impress upon the general the dignity of Mr. Lincoln's high office and their relative rank, and less of the president's time will be wasted."

"That's an excellent idea, and I'll do my best to put it forward," said John, with an admiring smile. "Really, Kate, you should be working in the White House."

"Perhaps someday I shall," she said. "I can only imagine the cruel nicknames you would invent for me if I did."

John laughed aloud, and she silently congratulated herself for cheering him out of his indignant anger. If her advice helped the president too, John would remember, and would appreciate her all the more.

Although Kate took exception to General McClellan's disrespect for the office of the president, she did not share John Hay's boundless veneration for Mr. Lincoln. He had not done as badly in his high office as she had feared he would, but he had not done as well as her father would have in his place either.

As the autumn leaves fell and the winds took on the chilly bite of early winter, she kept up her usual schedule of entertainments with alacrity and great enjoyment, welcoming important politicians and dignitaries to breakfast parties, receptions, and dinners every day of the week. Radical Republicans and other sympathetic guests knew that within the Chase residence, they could freely criticize the Lincoln administration without fear of repercussions. Kate took particular pleasure in sharing gossip about Mrs. Lincoln, who was perpetually embroiled in one scandal or another, from her shockingly excessive expenditures for her White House renovations to the coterie of questionable characters who populated her evening salons. A matter with greater relevance to the nation was her uncertain loyalties. Mrs. Lincoln was from Kentucky, and her family had owned slaves, and she had one brother, three half brothers, and three brothers-in-law in the Confederate army. Privately, Kate believed that Mrs. Lincoln was a stronger abolitionist than Mr. Lincoln, and that she was fiercely loyal to her husband and thus would never intentionally undermine his administration, but if others wanted to speculate and doubt, Kate would not insist upon changing the subject.

At the end of November, Kate alleviated her sister's homesickness somewhat by visiting her at Brook Hall, and a month later, the school holidays began and Nettie came happily home. Despite the gloom of wartime, the Chase family enjoyed a merry Christmas—with the possible exception of four hours on Christmas Day, when Father was summoned to the White House for an extraordinary cabinet meeting to discuss the Trent Affair.

In early November, a Union warship, acting without orders from Washington, had intercepted the British mail steamer *Trent* after it ran the blockade of Havana. Boarding the ship, Union sailors arrested two of its passengers, the former United States senators turned rebels James M. Mason and John Slidell, who were en route to Great Britain and France to petition for formal recognition of the Confederate government. After they were courteously escorted off the ship, Mr. Mason and Mr. Slidell were imprisoned at Fort Warren in Boston, and the *Trent* was allowed to resume its journey. At the time, Father had told Kate that his only regret was that the Union captain had not seized the *Trent* too.

Although the people of the North, desperate for good news, rejoiced to see the Confederate agents thwarted, the British were outraged by the affront to their declared neutrality. For weeks, furious diplomatic exchanges had flown back and forth across the Atlantic, with British minister to Washington Lord Lyons striving tirelessly to mediate between them and President Lincoln, and his cabinet gravely concerned that the incident would escalate into a war the Union simply could not afford. On December 19, the British government declared that the arrests were an affront to their national honor, which could be restored only if Mr.

Mason and Mr. Slidell were released to British protection and if the United States offered a formal apology for its aggression. If the United States did not comply, Lord Lyons and his entire delegation were ordered to return to Great Britain.

When Lord Lyons brought the official dispatch to Mr. Seward, he generously agreed to leave it for the secretary of state and president to read and consider before he presented it to them formally. Mr. Seward immediately sequestered himself at home to draft a reply that would allow the United States to release the prisoners, and thereby avoid war, without upsetting their own citizenry, who would not bear the humiliation of meekly submitting to British demands. On Christmas Day, the cabinet met at the White House at ten o'clock so Mr. Seward could present his complicated argument for why releasing the Confederate agents would actually follow established American legal precedent, allowing them to acquiesce to the British demands without shame. For four hours they debated, and when they adjourned at two o'clock, Mr. Lincoln said that Mr. Seward should continue drafting his reply explaining why the prisoners should be released, and in the meantime, he would prepare arguments to the contrary. The cabinet would reconvene the next day to compare their separate cases and try to reach accord.

Throughout the holidays, the mansion on the corner of Sixth and E streets had been full of guests, cherished family and friends, many of whom had traveled all the way from Ohio. Kate had kept everyone merrily entertained during Father's absence Christmas morning, but as soon as he came home, she propelled him off to his study so he could tell her what Mr. Seward had proposed and what had been decided. "The prospect of returning the prisoners is gall and wormwood to me," Father declared after he had told her everything. "Rather than consent to the liberation of these men, I would sacrifice everything I possess."

"Father, you of all people know that we can't afford two wars."

"Of course we can't, but Great Britain doesn't want war any more than we do. If we call their bluff, they will not attack us."

"Can we be certain of that?"

"We've received confidential assurances from respected officials in London that if the present dispute is resolved amicably, Great Britain will not interfere further in our American conflict. That suggests to me that they are not eager for war."

"By not interfering further," Kate queried, "do they mean that they will not recognize the Confederacy?"

Father spread his hands and sighed. "That's how I understand it."

"Then this dispute *must* be resolved amicably," Kate said, "even if that means appeasing the British at the expense of our pride. At this moment, nothing could help the Union cause more than avoiding a new war with Great Britain and keeping them out of our current one."

Father mulled over her words, and nodded. "Of course you're right, but I resent the necessity of releasing the men, and it's disingenuous of the British to pontificate about their neutrality while advocating for two would-be rebel diplomats."

"You make a fair point, but I don't see any other way." Kate sighed, sat down beside him on the sofa, and rested her head on his shoulder. "Perhaps inspiration will strike Mr. Lincoln and Mr. Seward while they sleep tonight, and they'll contrive some other, more tolerable option you and I haven't thought of."

Father uttered a short, dry laugh. "That would be a Christmas miracle indeed."

They rejoined their guests, and later, restored by a delicious Christmas feast and the company and laughter of loved ones, Father appeared less haggard and plagued by worry. Even so, after everyone went off to bed and the house grew dark and still, Kate thought she heard Father pacing in his bedchamber, and she imagined him brooding.

The family and guests were at breakfast the next morning when Mr. Seward showed up unexpectedly at the door. Father invited him in to dine with them, but Mr. Seward accepted only a cup of coffee and asked if he could read to Father the revised draft of his dispatch. Father readily agreed, and having finished his breakfast, he escorted the secretary of state to his study. Although she had not been invited to accompany them, Kate quickly excused herself from the table and hurried after, and when she shut the study door behind them, the two men gave no indication whatsoever that her presence was unexpected or unwanted.

Mr. Seward read the document aloud, all twenty-six pages of it. Although the legal argument seemed somewhat convoluted to Kate, Father listened intently, nodding from time to time. "I think it is well done," he said when Mr. Seward had finished. "And I think you are right."

Looking greatly relieved, Mr. Seward thanked him, offered his regards to Kate, and departed with assurances that he would see Father soon at the White House. "His reply offers no apology," Kate pointed out when they were alone.

"Yes. The British won't like that, but our people will, including the president and his cabinet."

Sure enough, when the president and his cabinet met later that day, all admitted to regretting the necessity of releasing the prisoners, but they were satisfied that no apology would be rendered. The dispatch was unanimously approved, and Father returned home soon thereafter, smiling and humming a Bach Christmas cantata.

In the days to come, the British would accept the decision and the people of the North would meet the fragile accord with relief, not outrage. The crisis averted, the Chase family resumed their holiday observances with thankful hearts. Kate's only disappointment was that William did not visit. He had said that he would try, but on the day before he had been expected, Kate had received a letter expressing his regrets instead. She tried not to dwell upon his absence, and indeed she was never truly lonely, surrounded as she was by affectionate friends, aunts, uncles, and cousins. She understood that the demands of William's offices, both official in Providence and unofficial in the field of war, left him little time for travel.

On New Year's Day, Father escorted Kate and Nettie to a grand reception at the White House. The cabinet, the diplomatic corps, the Supreme Court, and military officers arrived at eleven o'clock, but after them, the public were invited to pour through the receiving line and pay their respects to the president and his wife.

It was an unusually beautiful day, the sky clear and bright, the air soft and balmy, more reminiscent of May than January. The grounds of the Executive Mansion were already packed when the Chases arrived, but they managed to squeeze their way inside, offer New Year's greetings to Mr. and Mrs. Lincoln, and make their way outside again before the crush of people swelled to even greater proportions.

"I can only imagine how many hands Mr. Lincoln will shake today," Nettie remarked when they reached the front portico. The unseasonable temperate breeze offered a welcome respite from the packed, overheated public chambers of the mansion. Although the rooms had become uncomfortable after the public had poured in, Kate had to admit that Mrs.

Lincoln had refurbished them magnificently. Gone were the tattered drapes and worn furniture, the stained carpets and ripped wallpaper. Now exquisite Parisian paper adorned the walls, gleaming new china graced the tables, and fine, lush rugs felt soft and restful underfoot. The refurbished Executive Mansion was as tastefully and elegantly appointed as any home or public edifice Kate had every visited, as befit a glorious nation. She was proud and pleased to think of the fine impression it would make upon visiting foreign dignitaries—but she wished that she had been the First Lady to arrange it.

The Chases had just climbed into the carriage and were setting out for home when Father suddenly bolted upright in his seat and began patting his greatcoat, and then searching all of his pockets with increasing alarm.

"What's wrong?" Kate asked.

His brow furrowed in utter disbelief. "My pocket was picked at the reception."

"What?" she cried. "Are you certain?"

"I've checked every pocket, and my purse is gone."

Kate steeled herself. "How much did it carry?"

"Sixty dollars in gold."

Nettie gasped. "Should we go back and look for it?"

"It would be no use. The thief will be long gone by now." Father shook his head. "I cannot believe it. I was robbed in the White House."

He had been robbed *of* the White House, Kate thought, although she refrained from saying so aloud. They had both been betrayed out of what should have been theirs, and every visit made her feel the sting of disappointment anew.

At home, Father summoned the authorities and reported the theft, although he had little hope that the money would be restored to him. The Chases had no time to mourn the loss, however, for they were hosting their own New Year's Day reception, which promised to be a far more enjoyable occasion than the unexpectedly expensive visit to the White House had been.

Later that afternoon, Father and Kate received guests in their grand, spacious drawing room, with the kind assistance of Mrs. McDowell, the general's wife. The most brilliant and distinguished military officers, diplomats, elected officials, men of business, and their ladies were in attendance, the gentlemen elegant in their uniforms or formal suits, the ladies beautiful in their fine gowns. Kate was sure to make all and sundry feel welcome and merry, but she paid special attention to Lord Lyons, to help ease the lingering tensions between their two nations, and to thank him for his fair and frank negotiations with his American counterparts.

"*Pax esto perpetua*," Father greeted him when he arrived, a smile softening the formality of his bow.

Lord Lyons inclined his head in return. "I hope that my conduct will ever be that of a peacemaker."

"I am certain it will," said Kate, smiling warmly, taking his arm, and offering to show him a particular rare volume in her father's library that she had mentioned to him the last time they had met. He went with her gladly, and as they conversed, she deliberately kept the mood light and pleasant, with no mention of the Trent Affair, which both of their countries undoubtedly hoped the other would soon forgive and forget.

Chapter Twelve

On the second day of the New Year, the Chase family marked the occasion with a more intimate gathering than those they had previously enjoyed during the holidays—a delicious turkey feast with their houseguests and a few dear friends, including General McDowell, Mrs. McDowell, and Massachusetts senator Charles Sumner. Father and Kate saw Senator Sumner the following evening too, for all had been invited to attend a lecture at the Smithsonian Institution offered by Horace Greeley, the editor of the *New York Tribune* and arguably the most prominent abolitionist orator in the nation.

More than a thousand people filled the auditorium to hear the bald, bespectacled abolitionist speak, and while Kate found a seat in the house, Father was escorted to a chair on the stage behind Mr. Greeley's podium alongside Mr. Lincoln and ten congressmen. Kate wondered who had arranged for the twelve to be seated onstage, which was probably intended as an honor but strongly implied that they endorsed Mr. Greeley's positions. Perhaps most of the men did, but as Mr. Greeley launched into his fiery oration, Kate understood well that the president certainly did not. Mr. Lincoln sat stoically as Mr. Greeley declared that General Frémont had been absolutely correct to attempt to grant freedom to the slaves of Confederates in Missouri, and every time he mentioned the general's name, certain factions in the crowd shouted and jeered at President Lincoln. At one point, Mr. Greeley fixed his gaze squarely on the president and proclaimed that the war's sole purpose should be the demise of slavery. Most of the audience cheered and applauded in agreement, but Mr. Lincoln merely sat straight in his chair, silent and patient, his expression impassive. Kate marveled at how well he endured it, and although she did feel some sympathy for him, she reminded herself that he could have spared himself the embarrassment if he had been a stronger advocate for emancipation.

The following day, most of the Chases' friends and family departed, and soon Nettie reluctantly did as well, for her school holidays had come to a close. She left for Brook Hall escorted by her cousin Ralston Skinner, but midway through the journey she fell terribly ill with scarlet fever. Father was as frantic as Kate had ever seen him, for he had lost his first-born child to an epidemic of the same terrible disease the year Kate was born—Kate was, in fact, the namesake of this poor, lost, much-beloved little girl, as well as the woman who had died giving birth to her.

Kate immediately hurried off to her ailing sister's bedside, departing on the evening train with her father's good friend, the wealthy Philadelphia banker Jay Cooke. Under a doctor's care, and with the tender, watchful ministrations of Kate and Mr. and Mrs. Cooke, Nettie made a fine and steady recovery, but not before Kate fell ill with a less severe case of the same fearsome disease. Within a fortnight both sisters recuperated enough to move on from Philadelphia, Nettie to school and Kate home to Washington, but it was an anxious time for them all, especially for Father, who was so fearful for their lives that in a sense he suffered more than they.

Because of her time away from the capital, Kate missed much of the upheaval that rocked the president's cabinet that January. President Lincoln had become so frustrated with corruption and malfeasance in the Department of War that he finally ousted Secretary Cameron. When the scandal-ridden general received Mr. Lincoln's terse letter of dismissal, he wept, declared it a personal degradation, and called on Father that evening after dinner to enlist his help. With the aid of Secretary Seward, Father persuaded Mr. Lincoln to withdraw the brusque letter in lieu of a cordial note indicating that General Cameron had requested to be released from his duties. Kate had always rather liked the general and was sorry to see him go, but of course she was sorrier still that he had engaged in the unethical behavior that had led to his removal.

Like Father, Kate was delighted with Mr. Lincoln's choice to succeed General Cameron as secretary of war: Edwin Stanton, a lawyer from Cincinnati, a fellow staunch abolitionist, and a longtime intimate friend of Father's. The sudden announcement of General Cameron's resignation and Mr. Stanton's appointment took most of the cabinet by surprise, but on the whole they found the arrangement satisfactory, as did the Senate, which promptly confirmed the nomination.

President Lincoln had also become increasingly impatient with his young, arrogant general in chief, who had assembled and trained a powerful army and yet still insisted he dared not lead them into the field because his forces were overwhelmingly outnumbered by the Confederacy's. To Kate, General McClellan sometimes seemed like a fastidious housewife who labored for years to stitch a masterpiece quilt, only to hide it away in a trunk for safekeeping rather than use it. The quilt remained unstained, unworn, and unfaded, but the bedchamber was not as lovely as it could have been and its occupants shivered from the cold.

The president's urgent calls for forward movement upon the rebels did little to prod General McClellan away from his headquarters on Fifteenth Street, where he had arranged for a telegraph office to be established and had ordered that every message from the field had to pass through him. He seemed even more loath to depart his residence on H Street, where he hosted sumptuous dinners every evening for nearly two dozen guests, many of whom were members of the Southern-born and sympathetic elite. Most people of the North chafed at General McClellan's interminable, inexplicable delays, but Kate's father had another cause for concern: The Treasury was nearly bankrupt from the enormous expense of providing for hundreds of thousands of stationary soldiers, but Father could not replenish the coffers because the army's lack of forward progress had rendered bankers and the public too disgruntled to offer the immobile government any more of their hard-earned money.

Since late December, General McClellan had been bedridden from typhoid, but the newly formed Congressional Joint Committee on the Conduct of the War suspected that he was feigning illness to justify his inaction. Soon after Kate had left to join Nettie in Philadelphia, the committee met with President Lincoln and his cabinet to vehemently denounce the general and to urge the president to take greater control of the army. Perhaps because his ofttimes rival, Ohio senator Benjamin Wade, led the committee, Father vigorously defended the embattled general. Four days later, after attempting to visit General McClellan but being turned away, President Lincoln summoned Father, most of the other cabinet members, and two generals to a "Council of War" at the White House, where they discussed the problems facing the administration and began devising a strategy for an advance upon the Confederates. The Council of War met again the following day, and the cabinet in special session the next. General McClellan must have realized that the planning of the war was going to go on with or without him, for he experienced a miraculous recovery and was able to attend a council of generals the president convened on January 13. Whether General McClellan would finally commence the forward movement the president and the public so desired remained to be seen, but President Lincoln apparently wanted to permit no room for misunderstanding. Shortly after Kate returned to Washington, he issued General War Order No. 1, which named February 22 as "the day for a general movement of the Land and Naval forces of the United States against the insurgent forces."

Kate's absence from Washington was also marked by a modest stack of letters from William that she discovered, thankfully unopened, in her bedroom upon her return. "I was surprised to see so many letters from Providence," said Father somewhat peevishly when he discovered her reading them. "I had supposed Governor Sprague was nothing to you except a friend. If any other relation is desired by him toward you I ought to know about it."

"Of course you should," said Kate, keeping her voice reasonable and steady. "I am sure if he ever has other intentions, he will speak with you. Until then, we both must assume that he desires nothing more than my friendship."

Father seemed satisfied by her reply, but she began to wonder if gossips were circulating stories about her and William, a concern that seemed justified by one of Nettie's letters from school. "Dear Sister," she began, "I am going to ask you a question, which you may think I have no right; but I do love you so dearly, that all that concerns you, *seems* to concern me also. Are you really engaged to Gov Sprague? If you think it is not my business and I have no right to ask you Please say so and I will never ask you again."

Startled by her sister's question, Kate nevertheless adopted an air of reassuring calm and wrote back that Nettie was welcome to ask her any question she wished—a sister's privilege Kate intended to invoke from time to time—but in this case, whatever rumors Nettie apparently had heard were false. "I am not engaged to anyone," Kate wrote. "If that day should ever come, I will share the happy news with my only dear sister myself, and I promise you shall know about it long before the papers do."

Kate was tempted to write a breezy, cheerful letter to William telling him of Father's concerns and Nettie's questions, more to see how he would respond than to prompt him into action. Fortunately she thought better of it before putting pen to paper. The truth of the matter was that William's letters alternately charmed and distressed her. For weeks at a time, he would seem interested, ambitious, eager, and confident—not only about Kate but about his work and his soldiery too—but then weeks would follow in which his letters were melancholy, terse, discouraged, and discouraging, if he bothered to write at all. William's sudden and dramatic shifts in temper upset and confused Kate until she became more accustomed to them. She crafted her letters with care, uncertain whether something she wrote was the catalyst that shifted his mood in one direction or the other. Ever mindful of his tragic childhood, she was certain that if only they could be together, in the same city, she could help him learn to master his temper. The distance between them was the cause of their occasional discord, and if that could be remedied, all would be well.

Soon after Kate's return to Washington, she learned that Mrs. Lincoln was planning an extravagant evening ball to be held at the White House in the first week of February. Kate learned from Mrs. Douglas, who employed the same dressmaker, that Mrs. Lincoln had commissioned an off-the-shoulder, white satin gown with a low neckline, flounces of black lace, black and white bows, and a long, elegant train. From John Hay, Kate heard that Mrs. Lincoln was planning an elaborate menu of roast turkey, foie gras, oysters, beef, duck, quail, partridge, and aspic, complemented by an assortment of fruits, cakes, and ices, and fanciful creations of spun sugar. The First Lady sent out more than five hundred invitations to prominent men in government and their wives, as well as to certain favorite friends, important Washington personages, and visiting dignitaries.

As word of Mrs. Lincoln's lavish plans spread, she yet again provoked criticism from her usual detractors, who expressed astonishment and disgust for the vain spectacle of the ball and its hostess. But in spite of such denunciations, since the event was not open to the public, invitations remained highly coveted items. "Half the city is jubilant at being invited," John told Kate, "while the other half is furious at being left out in the cold."

"Not everyone fits into the two halves you describe," Kate noted. "What about Senator Wade?"

"Ah, yes." John grinned impishly. "Your fellow Ohioan did greatly displease Her Satanic Majesty with his reply."

Rumors of Benjamin Wade's acerbic rejection had come from other sources, but John had confirmed them. "Are the President and Mrs. Lincoln aware that there is a civil war?" Senator Wade had written acidly as he spurned the invitation. "If they are not, Mr. and Mrs. Wade are, and for that reason decline to participate in dancing and feasting." Imagining the red flush of mortification that must have come to Mrs. Lincoln's pale cheeks as she read the note, Kate could almost forgive Senator Wade for the cold, discourteous manner in which he had treated Father in the months leading up to the Republican Convention two years before.

Senator Wade was not alone in his opinion. A great many of Mrs. Lincoln's invitations had been brusquely declined, or so John reported, and nearly one hundred were returned with indignant notes protesting her excessive frivolity when the nation was distracted, mournful, and impoverished by the war. And yet Mrs. Lincoln did not moderate her plans even a trifle in response to her critics. Kate supposed she would have done the same in the First Lady's place.

Kate was astonished, then, a few days before the ball when John soberly confided that Mrs. Lincoln wanted to cancel the entire spectacle. "Why?" protested Kate, who had been invited along with Father and had been looking forward to it, and not only to see whether it measured up to expectations, which had soared after the *New York Herald* predicted that the ball would be "the most magnificent affair ever witnessed in America." Father had permitted her to buy a new silk gown for the occasion, and although she had entertained wistful daydreams of donning it for the first time on a night when she would dance in William's arms, Mrs. Lincoln's party would have been an ideal time too.

"Not long ago, young Master Willie caught a severe cold while riding his pony in foul weather," John said. "A few days ago, it turned into a bad fever. Mrs. Lincoln said that it was ridiculous to think of hosting a grand ball with Willie on his sickbed, but the Tycoon said that she had gone to too much trouble and expense to call back the invitations now. Their doctor examined the boy, declared that he was on the mend, and said there was no reason why the ball should not go on as planned. The Hellcat acquiesced, but now she frets and worries incessantly, as she always does when the boys fall ill."

"Not without reason. She lost a child to sickness before. She must live in terror of losing another."

"I suppose." John tugged at his ear and regarded her appraisingly. "It is strange to hear you defending Mrs. Lincoln."

"Why, John," she said airily, "I'm not entirely heartless."

"You are not heartless at all," said John levelly. "You have the strongest, most honest, and most loyal heart of any woman I know."

For a moment he looked as if he might say more, but instead he rose, bade her farewell, and gruffly asked her to save a dance for him, if the ball was not canceled.

Days passed, and Mrs. Lincoln did not recall her invitations, so at nine o'clock on the evening of February 5, Kate put on her simple gown of mauve silk and arranged her hair in a Grecian knot adorned with a wreath of tiny white flowers. When she was ready, Father escorted her to the carriage that whisked them off to the White House, where they presented their cards and were granted entrance. The Marine Band played operatic airs in the vestibule, and the Green, Blue, and Red parlors, where guests mingled and chatted, were decorated abundantly with flowers. Mr. and Mrs. Lincoln received their guests in the East Room, a chamber so large and bright and opulent that it was almost impossible to believe that Union troops had been quartered there in the early months of the war.

When Kate and her father joined the receiving line, she noted that Mrs. Lincoln's gown was even more sumptuous than Mrs. Douglas had described; the deep train was swathed in black Chantilly lace, the décolletage was as low as it could modestly be, and a garland of myrtle trailed down the skirt, echoing the wreath of black-and-white crepe myrtle Mrs. Lincoln wore on her head. She wore myrtle and the colors of half mourning, a lady ahead of Kate in the receiving line whispered to a companion, in honor of the late Prince Albert as a gesture of goodwill to Lord Lyons, who was also in attendance.

It was quite some time before Kate and her father reached the front of the receiving line, but once there, Kate exchanged a few pleasant words with the president before turning to Mrs. Lincoln and asking gently, "How is young Willie? I heard that he is ill."

For a moment Mrs. Lincoln looked as if she might weep. "He is quite unwell, it grieves me to say, quite unwell. But Doctor Stone assures us that he has passed through the worst of it, and he will soon be all right."

"I am very glad to hear that," Kate said sincerely, reaching for her hand. Mrs. Lincoln looked half-stunned as Kate held her hand for a moment, patting it reassuringly, and offered her a sympathetic smile before moving on to let the next guest enjoy a moment with the president and his wife.

Except for a few self-righteous folk like Senator Wade, all the elite of Washington society were present—the members of the cabinet and their ladies, generals and their senior staff, diplomats, senators, congressmen, and even prominent lawyers and men of business. General McClellan, clad in his dashing dress uniform and looking much recovered from his lengthy illness, escorted his blond, blue-eyed wife, Ellen, nine years younger than he and at least two inches taller, lovely though reserved in a white tunic dress with bands of cherry velvet and a headdress of white illusion. General Frémont's most notable adornment was a scowl, but his wife, Jessie, was in excellent spirits, laughing and chatting merrily. Kate spoke at length with Senator Sumner, but she could not grant John Hay's request for a dance, as Mrs. Lincoln had canceled the dancing out of deference to Willie's condition. The Comte de Paris and the Duc de Chartres, the two young princes of the House of Orleans exiled from France, were handsomely attired in the blue uniforms of officers of the Union army, and they commanded much of her time, pleased to converse with someone so gracefully fluent in their native tongue. Kate liked them both, especially the intelligent, elegantly featured Comte de Paris, but for conversation she secretly preferred their uncle, the Prince de Joinville, for he was fascinated by life in America and was endearingly eager to learn all he could about it.

On several occasions, Kate noticed that Mr. or Mrs. Lincoln would slip from the room and return minutes later with downcast expressions they quickly tried, unconvincingly, to conceal. She could only assume that they were taking turns hurrying upstairs to check on Willie, who was being attended by Mrs. Lincoln's apparently rather versatile dressmaker, Elizabeth Keckley. Each time one of the anxious parents returned to the party, Kate hoped to see in their faces a look of relief, a thankful smile, but evidently whatever they beheld in the sickroom evoked only worry.

Shortly before midnight, President Lincoln, with Miss Browning of Illinois on his arm, and the First Lady, escorted by the young lady's father, Senator Browning, led the promenade around the East Room to the dining room entrance—where their procession abruptly halted at the locked doors because the steward had misplaced the key. "I am in favor of forward movement," a man declared within the crowd gathered around the doors, and everyone laughed, even General McClellan.

Once the key was located and the guests given entry, Kate beheld a feast that surpassed all her imaginings. Near the entrance, an elegant table held plates of tiny sandwiches and a Japanese bowl filled with champagne punch; but although servants clad in spotless new mulberry-colored uniforms filled delicate china cups with a silver dipper and offered plates, most guests declined in favor of the abundance of the dining room just beyond. Kate had heard that the exclusive caterers, Maillard's of New York, had ordered a ton of game, and as she eyed the platters of turkeys, hams, venison, pheasant, ducks, and partridge, she could well believe it. In the center of the table lay a looking glass, and around it were arranged the fancy pieces of confectionary. At the head of the table was a large helmet crafted of sugar, signifying war. Nearby, the frigate *Union* was in full sail in spun sugar on a flag-draped stand. On the opposite side, water nymphs of nougat supported a fountain, and all around, beehives of sugar cradled generous portions of charlotte russe. Artfully scattered between the larger pieces were Chinese pagodas, Swiss cottages, Greek temples, and baskets and cornucopias, all of sugar, all bearing sugared fruits. An impressively large model of Fort

Pickens constructed of cake commanded pride of place on a side table, evoking murmurs of admiration from all who beheld it.

Suddenly Kate's appetite fled. She had been enjoying herself tremendously all evening, except for her worries about the poor, sick child upstairs, but at that moment she felt weighed down by an overwhelming sensation of defeat. Although Mrs. Lincoln had rarely looked more miserable than she had that evening, the lavish gala would surely mark her triumph in Washington society. No one had complained about excessive expense as they marveled at the magnificently refurbished rooms, and no one would leave that enticing dinner table disappointed. Kate might be more beautiful, more engaging, more poised, but her gracious, comfortable, happy home could not compare to the White House, and she could not command the Marine Band to entertain her guests, and although Addie was an excellent cook, she did not possess the genius of excess that marked Maillard's of New York. Kate never could have put on a gathering as lavish and wonderful as Mrs. Lincoln's glorious party, and not only because it would cost more than her father's annual salary. As long as she held the White House, Mrs. Lincoln would have an advantage over Kate, and there was little she could do about it.

As she took her seat at the table among the other guests, Kate firmly banished her sad, self-pitying, awestruck thoughts. She had much to offer that Mrs. Lincoln lacked, qualities that could not be purchased in a shop on Fifth Avenue or ordered from Paris. She would put her faith in her own mind and her own heart, because clothes could be torn and furniture broken and elaborate confections turn stale, but nothing could rob Kate of herself.

She ate sparingly, her appetite returning as the conversation drew her in and her natural confidence reasserted itself. All would be well, if she did not lose faith.

After supper, the Marine Band played on, and the contented guests promenaded through the resplendent rooms, and talked, and laughed, and forgot the war for a little while. At three o'clock the party drew to a close, and Father escorted Kate to their carriage.

"Mrs. Lincoln put on a magnificent gala," Father remarked as they rode home, stifling a yawn. "I cannot imagine anyone could have done better."

"No," said Kate, suddenly exhausted, and feeling bruised. "I don't suppose you can."

In the days that followed Mrs. Lincoln's glorious ball, the newspapers and the public gave the evening overwhelmingly positive reviews. The *Washington Evening Star* complimented the "beauty and quiet good taste of the floral decorations" and declared that "The supper was, in many respects, the most superb affair of the kind ever seen here." Mrs. Lincoln, they noted approvingly, had been "tastefully, elegantly dressed," and *Leslie's Illustrated Newspaper* described her as "our fair Republican Queen," attired "in perfect keeping with her regal style of beauty." Although a few curmudgeons who had not attended still grumbled about the excess, most people concurred with the *Evening Star* that "In the completeness of its arrangements, the distinguished character of the guests assembled, and the enjoyment afforded to those present," Mrs. Lincoln's party would rank as "by far the most brilliant and successful affair of the kind ever experienced here." Kate granted that the praise was well deserved, but it stung to see that although numerous guests were mentioned by name, their attire and comportment described in fine detail, Kate and her father were not.

Kate wished that the magnificent evening had been hers, and that the reporter had singled her out as being a particularly brilliant guest, and that he would have had cause to rave about her elaborate gown and sparkling diamonds, but she did not have the heart to envy Mrs. Lincoln, for she knew the worried mother was not savoring her triumph. Alongside the glowing descriptions of the ball were terse reports of troop movements and naval maneuvers—and sympathetic briefs that Willie's condition had not improved, and that his younger brother Tad had become afflicted by the same malady.

Aside from the success of the ball, the only good news the Lincoln family received in those first weeks of February came from Tennessee, where the unkempt, reputedly drunken, and unreliable General Ulysses S. Grant captured Fort Henry on the Tennessee River, and, ten days later, Fort Donelson on the Cumberland. The assault on Fort Donelson had been particularly bloody. The papers breathlessly reported that when the battered Confederate commander proposed a cease-fire so that they could negotiate terms, General Grant telegraphed back the terse phrase that would soon evoke a roar of approval across the North: "No terms except unconditional and immediate surrender can be accepted." The commander capitulated, the Union troops took fifteen thousand Confederate prisoners, and General Grant became a hero. Jubilation filled every Northern city and town, and hundred-gun salutes were fired in celebration of the first significant Union victories of the war. In the capital, President Lincoln signed papers promoting Grant to major general, and city officials quickly made plans to celebrate the two victories, as well as the 130th anniversary of George Washington's birth, with an elaborate illumination of the city's public buildings. Reports that General Grant was a humble man of the people who had taken the field with only a spare shirt, a hairbrush, and a toothbrush invited inevitable comparisons to General McClellan, whom everyone knew had needed six wagons, each pulled by a team of four horses, to carry his attire and personal belongings to the front.

But the national rejoicing did not touch the White House, where young Willie and Tad languished in their sickbeds, tended by their devoted mother and the reassuring, eminently capable Mrs. Keckley. John Hay had tears in his eyes when he told Kate that Willie suffered the worst, and that with each passing day he declined, steadily and inexorably, while his parents watched and waited and prayed. The president canceled a cabinet meeting and Mrs. Lincoln a levee rather than venture too far from their son's side, and when Willie's best friend visited, he refused to go when evening came but curled up on the floor next to the ailing child's bed and fell asleep. As word of Willie's desperate condition spread through the capital, the celebratory illuminations were canceled out of respect, and the newspapers, even those most critical of President Lincoln and the First Lady, expressed their heartfelt concern and hopes for both children's swift recoveries.

On February 20, a mild, sunny day, Willie died, his two weeks of suffering ended by the eternal peace that all who loved him had prayed would be long deferred.

Soon word came to the Chase residence that Tad was expected to survive, though he was terrified that he would die like his brother. Mr. Lincoln was utterly devastated, and his wife so staggered by anguish that she had taken to her bed, inconsolable and keening. Kate absorbed the terrible news in a state of numb, shocked disbelief, while Father, pale and shaken, sank heavily into a chair, groped for his Bible on the side table, and held it on his lap, unopened and unseen. "There is no pain like the grief provoked by the loss of a child," he said in a strangled voice. "Mr. Lincoln knows this already, but this, to lose his most precious, beloved child—" Tears in his eyes, Father cleared his throat and shook his head. "There are no words for it. May God comfort him."

Kate ran to her father, sank to the floor beside his chair, and buried her head in her arms on his lap. Distractedly, Father stroked her hair as she wept.

Having received no orders to the contrary, Father reported to the White House at eleven o'clock the next morning for the usual Friday cabinet meeting, but when he returned home, he somberly reported that Mr. Lincoln had not attended, and that in the family's private rooms, Mrs. Lincoln had collapsed in paroxysms of grief, shrieking and wailing in anguish until a physician dosed her with laudanum. The White House had been draped in the black crepe of mourning, the curtains drawn, the mirrors covered. Mr. Lincoln had arranged for a capable nurse from one of the military hospitals to care for Tad, while Mrs. Keckley and a few other close friends watched over Mrs. Lincoln, who, whenever she drifted out of her drugged stupor, became delirious and wild with newly felt despair.

Later that day, the cabinet members and their wives, and Kate, called at the White House to express their condolences as a group to President and Mrs. Lincoln. The First Lady was too unwell to leave her bedchamber, but Mr. Lincoln, haggard and bowed with grief, accepted their respectful sympathies with quiet thanks, his face ashen, his eyes red and tormented.

"I pray you will never know the pain he and Mrs. Lincoln suffer today, my darling Kate," Father said as they made their slow and sorrowful way home.

Kate knew that her father knew that pain all too well, and that his powerful empathy for the grieving parents made him feel his own bitter losses anew. She wanted more than anything to offer him words of comfort, but she knew none would suffice, and that it was better to be silently sympathetic than to offer feeble platitudes that would do nothing to ease his pain.

Attired in deepest black, Father and Kate joined the scores of mourners at Willie Lincoln's funeral in the East Room on the Monday following his death. Congress had adjourned so that its members might attend, and as Kate glanced around the room from behind her veil and recognized Vice-President Hamlin, the members of the cabinet, the diplomatic corps, the generals, the dignitaries, and many of their ladies, she shuddered, struck by the chilling realization that most of the mourners had been feasting and laughing and chatting happily in that very room at the ball less than three weeks before. On that night, despite all her maternal cares, Mrs. Lincoln had presided with elegance and pride, but now she was too prostrate with grief to leave her bed and attend her beloved child's funeral. How quickly joy turned to sorrow, Kate thought, pressing her handkerchief to her lips and closing her eyes to hold back tears as the minister read aloud from the scriptures, words of resurrection and eternal life. How swiftly one could plummet from the heights of triumph into the unfathomable depths of loss.

The remains of young William Wallace Lincoln were interred in a vault at Oak Hill Cemetery in Georgetown, where they would lie until they could be buried in the family plot in Springfield.

In the weeks that followed, John Hay, looking as if he had absorbed no small portion of the haggard grief of the man he so admired, confided in Kate as if unburdening his sympathetic heart was the only salve for his pain. Mr. Lincoln carried on with the duties of his office with stoic surety, but on the one-week anniversary of his son's death, he had locked himself in the Green Room, where Willie had lain in repose before his funeral—to be alone with his thoughts, to remember his beloved son, to pray—John could only wonder. Mr. Lincoln observed the private mourning ritual every Thursday for several weeks thereafter, and it seemed to offer him solace. Tad improved day by day under the watchful eye of Nurse Pomroy, but as he would take his medicine from no one but his father, the president was frequently called out of meetings to administer the dose, and he readily went. Robert, called home from Harvard by the tragedy, grieved the loss of his young brother, but he endeavored to maintain a brave, manly front, and was tenderly solicitous of his grieving mother. Mrs. Lincoln alone found no lessening of her grief. She was alternately paralyzed by sorrow or frantic with despair, and her sudden bouts of keening frightened Tad and alarmed the entire household. Mrs. Keckley was by her side almost constantly, and at Robert's request, one of

Mrs. Lincoln's elder sisters came for an extended stay to look after her, but Mrs. Lincoln would admit almost no one else, as Kate learned when she called at the White House in early March only to be turned away after leaving her card. It was an odd consolation to know that she was not the only lady Mrs. Lincoln refused to see.

For months thereafter, Mrs. Lincoln withdrew from the world, shrouding herself in black, canceling her receptions and levees and, as spring turned to summer, forbidding the traditional concerts on the White House lawn. Unlike his wife, President Lincoln could not shut himself away from the world, not with the fate of a nation depending upon him, nor could Father and the rest of his cabinet and all his generals set aside the work of preserving the Union to allow the president time to mourn.

But Mrs. Lincoln could shut herself away in the White House, and so she did, and the First Lady's self-imposed exile elevated Kate to the rank of the highest lady in the capital.

At last Kate reigned as the undisputed queen of Washington society, but she took no pleasure in her triumph, knowing that it came at the expense of her rival's unfathomable grief.

Chapter Thirteen

*T*he date Mr. Lincoln had established for the Union army's advance upon the rebels, February 22, came and went, with the president too deeply preoccupied with Willie's death and Tad's lingering illness to condemn his general in chief for his perpetual immobility. Discouraged and indignant, Secretary of War Stanton called on Father at home to vent his frustration. "There is no more sign of movement on the Potomac today than there has been for the past three months," he complained, pacing in Father's study.

"Perhaps General McClellan is waiting for fair weather," Father suggested wearily. He had grown tired of defending the general, who, as far as Kate could see, had done little to earn her father's faith and loyalty in the first place and had squandered all his goodwill.

"The army has to fight or run away," Stanton declared, "and while men are striving nobly in the West, McClellan's champagne-and-oyster suppers on the Potomac must be stopped."

Father and Kate agreed, and she trusted that Secretary Stanton, who had scoured the Department of War free of corruption, possessed both the moral and political authority to reform General McClellan. Before long he made significant progress by moving the telegraph office from General McClellan's headquarters on Fifteenth Street to an old library room adjoining his own office on the second floor of the War Department. General McClellan was reportedly furious at the change, for not only had Secretary Stanton seized control over military communications, but he had also ensured that President Lincoln would thereafter spend many hours every day with his secretary of war rather than his general in chief.

Three days after General McClellan disregarded his deadline, President Lincoln signed the Legal Tender Act, which provided for the issuing of United States notes as legal tender. Father, an inveterate hard-money man, had accepted the necessity of legal tender only reluctantly, but once he had, he had worked vigorously to ensure that a legal tender clause would be included in the pending finance bill. Debate had raged for weeks as opponents argued that printing the so-called greenbacks would be an unconstitutional exercise of power that would lead to the collapse of the economy and the mass defrauding of the people. Father had labored incessantly to push the bill through, wheedling recalcitrant congressmen and arranging for meetings between concerned bankers and members of the House and Senate finance committees. It was only after the legal tender clause was separated from the overall finance bill that it passed both houses, and the day it was signed into law marked a personal and political victory for Father. The notes were swiftly engraved, printed, and put into circulation, and the troops, who had gone without pay for months while the debate wore on and the value of old Demand Notes deteriorated, at last received what was owed them.

Less than two weeks later, General McClellan finally ordered his massive Army of the Potomac to break camp. Kate and Father speculated whether pressure from Secretary Stanton, jealousy of General Grant's victories in the West, or something else entirely had been the catalyst, but whatever it was, they joined most people of the North in relief that at last the wait was over. The rebels learned the Union troops were on the way—with the newspapers covering the story, it was hardly a state secret—and they pulled back from Manassas to the shores of the Rappahannock. When General McClellan's scouts reported the withdrawal, he led his troops into the rebel encampment to capture rebel stragglers, only to discover that the area was entirely empty of men and material—and that the heavy artillery that had rendered him immobile for so many months were nothing more than "Quaker guns," wooden logs painted to resemble cannons. When word of the ruse hit the papers, the general's critics roared in outrage and demanded his ouster. Three days later, President Lincoln responded by relieving him from his duties as general in chief, but retaining him as commander of the Army of the Potomac.

"That does not go far enough," grumbled Father, who had become one of the general's strongest detractors, in no small part because President Lincoln and the cabinet had put their trust in General McClellan based upon Father's recommendation, and he felt his trust in his fellow Ohioan had been betrayed.

"He may prove his courage and brilliance yet," Kate said, although she had little hope of it.

Acting on direct, emphatic orders from President Lincoln himself, General McClellan led the Army of the Potomac—nearly a quarter million strong, proud, disciplined, and well trained—away from their base camps around Washington City and down the Potomac, carried by a fleet of more than four hundred ships to Fort Monroe. Over breakfast at the Chase residence one morning not long after the troops departed, an outraged Secretary Stanton told Father that friends in the field had warned him that insufficient forces had been left behind to defend the capital, despite President Lincoln's explicit commands that Washington must be left, in the judgment of all the commanders of army corps, entirely secure. "I referred the matter to the adjutant general," Secretary Stanton said, fuming, "and he concluded that the president's orders had been completely disregarded."

"What defenses remain to us?" asked Kate, keeping her voice steady as she poured the secretary another cup of coffee.

"I don't want to alarm you, Miss Chase," he replied, looking as if he wished he had not spoken so freely in front of her. "But if I am to be frank, we have fewer than twenty thousand raw recruits, with not a single organized brigade among them."

He did not need to explain that a sudden attack would break that fragile line of defense into pieces.

"You must tell the president," Father urged, and Stanton assured him that he already had, that he had gone to the White House shortly before midnight, as soon as he had read the adjutant general's report. Mr. Lincoln, gaunt and melancholy, had assured him he would take immediate action.

True to his word, President Lincoln promptly recalled General McDowell's First Corps back to Washington, provoking General McClellan's ire but rendering the capital and its people safe once more—or at least safer than they otherwise would have been. In the days that followed, the president continued to urge his stubborn general forward, and the general continued to insist that his forces were vastly outnumbered by the enemy, and Kate continued to wonder why the president simply did not strip General McClellan of his command, if he was so unwilling to use it properly.

In the meantime, while General McClellan massed his army on the outskirts of Yorktown about fifty miles southeast of Richmond, General Grant defeated the rebel forces at Shiloh in Tennessee, but it had been a costly battle, the bloodiest of the war so far, with more than thirteen thousand killed, wounded, or missing on the Union side and nearly eleven thousand for the South. Among those killed was Mrs. Lincoln's half brother Samuel B. Todd, an officer serving with the Twenty-Fourth Louisiana. His death reminded Mrs. Lincoln's critics of her family's ties to secessionists and stirred up the old, tired questions about her loyalties—an appalling, unnecessary thing to do when the White House remained draped in mourning black, Kate thought, showing callous disregard for Mrs. Lincoln's unrelenting grief. So recently celebrated throughout the North, General Grant suddenly found himself vilified in the press. Many called for his removal, but President Lincoln replied, "I can't spare this man; he fights." Kate wondered if General McClellan heard the rebuke in the president's words, and whether it would make any difference.

While war raged in the West and seemed perpetually deferred in Virginia, other battles were fought and won in the long struggle to end slavery. On April 16, a beautiful spring day, President Lincoln signed an act of Congress abolishing slavery forever in Washington City. The measure had been hotly contested in Congress and in the press, and through letters and petitions to congressmen, editors, and anyone else with any degree of influence, a great many white citizens of the capital demanded that the bill be voted down. In the end their complaints and protests went unheeded, the measure became law, and the colored residents of Washington responded with unrestrained jubilation. Voices rose in joyful cheers and reverent hymns throughout colored neighborhoods, where community leaders, well aware that their every action was being watched and judged, urged them to respond with quiet dignity. Their faith in the president had been renewed, as was their resolve to see slavery abolished everywhere, for everyone, for all time.

As thankful and happy as Kate was that the enslaved people of Washington City had been granted their freedom, she still felt a stirring of apprehension to see Mr. Lincoln, a relative latecomer to the abolitionist cause, suddenly celebrated as its great champion. For decades Father had been known as the true friend of the Negro people, a standard bearer for their rights and liberties—as opposed to Mr. Lincoln, who had often said he had no intention of interfering with slavery where it already existed. If he were suddenly to embrace abolitionism, his transformation would be good for the cause and for his immortal soul but potentially disastrous for Father, who would have a more difficult time drawing ethical distinctions between himself and the incumbent in the race to win the Republican presidential nomination in 1864.

If Father shared Kate's worries, he did not let them interfere with the performance of his duties. On May 5, he accepted President Lincoln's invitation to accompany him on a trip to Fort Monroe, in hopes that a personal visit to General McClellan would galvanize him into forward movement. Secretary Stanton and General Egbert Viele joined them aboard the *Miami*, a five-gun ship in the revenue cutter service, for the twenty-seven-hour journey to Hampton Roads. When Father returned a week later, elated and triumphant, he shared an enthralling tale with his daughters—of hours spent on deck entertained by Mr. Lincoln's jokes and stories; hours more poring over maps of Virginia and studying troop positions; their intense discussions leading them to the conclusion that the crucial port city of Norfolk ought to be attacked immediately; a dangerous nighttime climb from the *Miami* to the flagship *Minnesota*, from which Commodore Goldsborough led the attack; of driving off the fearsome Confederate ship the *Merrimac* with the help of the Union ironclad the *Monitor*; and ultimately, of compelling the rebels to evacuate Norfolk and scuttle the fearsome *Merrimac*.

"I thought this trip was only meant to goad General McClellan into action," said Kate, astounded by his adventure. "You didn't tell us you were embarking on a military campaign."

"We didn't know until we were in the midst of it," Father explained, beaming. Kate could not recall the last time she had seen him so exultant. "I tell you, my darling girls, I have never admired the president more."

Kate and Nettie exchanged a look. They had never known him to admire the president at all.

"It was a brilliant week for Mr. Lincoln," Father declared, oblivious to their skepticism and surprise. "I think it quite certain that if he had not come down to Fort Monroe, the enemy would still possess both Norfolk and the *Merrimac*, as grim and defiant and as much of a terror as ever. Now nearly the entire coast is ours."

"I'm sure he couldn't have done it without you, Father," said Nettie loyally.

Father pondered that for a moment. "No, I suppose not, nor without Stanton. We owe our victory to a serendipitous meeting of the minds."

Nettie nodded thoughtfully, but Kate had heard quite enough praise of Mr. Lincoln for one day. "Well," she said brightly, tucking her arm through her father's, "let us hope this newfound spirit of collaboration persists, and leads to many more joint victories for you and the president."

Surely it would not be all bad, she reflected, if a stronger friendship and mutual respect grew between the two rivals.

But Father's admiration of Mr. Lincoln proved to be short-lived.

While the men had been off on their excursion, far to the south at Hilton Head, Union major general and commander of the Department of the South David Hunter had ordered the emancipation of all slaves in South Carolina, Georgia, and Florida—without authorization from his commander in chief. The sixty-year-old general, who had accompanied Mr. Lincoln on the inaugural train and had suffered a dislocated collarbone fending off overeager crowds in Buffalo, had then begun to enlist able-bodied men of color from the states within his jurisdiction, arming them and forming the First South Carolina African Descent Regiment.

Father, Kate, and all within their circle of abolitionists and Radical Republicans rejoiced, for General Hunter's General Order No. 11 surpassed even what General Frémont had attempted in Missouri the previous August. They were mindful, however, that the president's recent emancipation of the enslaved people of Washington City did not mean that he had become such a staunch abolitionist that he would tolerate his old friends enacting radical measures without first obtaining approval from the White House.

Hoping to forestall a perfunctory rejection of General Hunter's order, Father promptly wrote to the president to urge him to keep it in force. "It seems to me of the highest importance that this order be not revoked," Father wrote. "It will be cordially approved, I am sure, by more than nine tenths of the people on whom you must rely for support of your administration."

Mr. Lincoln's reply was quick, curt, and impossible to misunderstand. "No commanding general shall do such a thing, upon *my* responsibility, without consulting me."

Ten days after General Hunter issued his General Order No. 11, President Lincoln officially revoked it, acknowledging that in so doing, he knew he was likely to displease, if not offend, many people whose support he could not afford to lose.

Secretaries Seward and Stanton endorsed the president's ruling, but Father adamantly disagreed and made no secret of it. He publicly denounced the rescinding of the order, earning him praise from Horace Greeley, the abolitionist editor of the *New York Tribune*, a long-time critic of President Lincoln who had not been especially enamored with Father either before then. To Mr. Greeley Father confided that the nullification of General Hunter's order had "sorely tried" him more than anything else he had witnessed in Washington, "though I have seen a great deal in the shape of irregularity, assumptions beyond law, extravagance, & deference to generals and reactionists which I could not approve."

Father persisted in criticizing Mr. Lincoln so boldly and so often that Kate carefully encouraged him to adopt a more moderate tone, but he had already provided enough grist for the rumor mill to keep it grinding away long after he turned his attention to other pressing matters. Rumors circulated that the rift between the president and the secretary of the treasury would disrupt the cabinet and bring about Father's dismissal. The *New York Times* scoffed at such speculation, saying, "It does not follow that the Cabinet will dissolve on so small a point," but Kate felt as if she were holding her breath, waiting for the controversy to subside, hoping that her father would not do or say anything that would compel Mr. Lincoln to replace him as he had Secretary Cameron. Father's ambitions for the White House would be ruined if he were compelled to leave the cabinet in disgrace.

Eventually the press and the gossips found other controversies and events to occupy their thoughts, but Kate knew that Mr. Lincoln would not forget how, when Father did not get his way, he had chosen to air his grievances in public rather than in the privacy of the president's office, where they would not jeopardize his administration.

Kate could think of only two reasons why President Lincoln did not ask her father to resign over the conflict: He was a man of preternatural tolerance and forbearance, and he knew it would be disastrous for the Treasury if her father were not there to sustain it. As long as the president knew that he, and the nation, could not afford to lose Father, his position was secure.

While Father was airing his disagreement with President Lincoln in Radical Republican circles and in the press, Kate stumbled into a conflict of her own, bewildering, disheartening, and one she could not have foreseen.

William Sprague's letters had become less frequent with the passage of time, though no less ardent, but Kate knew the governor was exceptionally busy and did not worry that his affections had faded. Then, in early May, he sent her one chilly, brief, and strangely formal note, and then nothing more. Puzzled and concerned for his well-being, Kate continued to write to him as always, although she did not receive a reply. Eventually, citing his enjoinder that they must always be honest with each other, Kate wrote again to ask him plainly why she had not heard from him in so long. "I assume it is because you are occupied every moment with the business of Rhode Island, the Union, and your mills," she said. "You have enough work for three men, I know, and little time to spare for correspondence with a friend. However, if there is another reason, I trust you will tell me."

This time, her letter provoked an immediate reply: "Dear Miss Chase: I regret that I am unable to correspond with you at present. Please give my best regards to the Secretary of the Treasury. Sincerely, Gov. Wm. Sprague."

Astounded, Kate read the letter over twice more, her heart plummeting. If not for his familiar handwriting, she might have imagined he had dictated the letter to a secretary, so cold and distant was his tone. She considered leaving the matter alone, but curiosity compelled her to write back. "May I inquire as to the reason?"

A week dragged by while she waited, and just as she abandoned hope of ever understanding him, he replied, "I would have preferred to part amicably without belaboring the issue to the point of embarrassment, but since you persist, I will say that I have received news from an acquaintance in Columbus that suggests you have not represented your conduct honestly. In light of this, I find I can no longer continue the friendship we once enjoyed."

Shocked, Kate stared at the incomprehensible words as if they might rearrange themselves on the page into something that made sense. Then, with a flash of anger, she took her pen in hand and sent back an equally brief, direct note: "Tell me who has apparently disparaged my character, and what he has said. If I have been judged, I should at least know the nature of these accusations, and be afforded the opportunity to confront my accuser."

She sent the letter off to Rhode Island and waited impatiently for a reply, but William retreated into silence.

Stunned and heartbroken, Kate refrained from writing to him again, but his abrupt decision to accept someone else's condemning story without offering her the chance to defend herself confused and hurt her deeply. Although many of her peers in Columbus had been jealous of her and sometimes even spiteful, she could not imagine any of them carrying malicious tales about her to William. She told herself that if his feelings for her were so ephemeral that a stranger's stories could send them scattering like leaves in the wind, she was well rid of him. Nevertheless, her heart was heavy and she often caught herself brooding. Even Father noticed that she was dispirited, although he attributed it to the stifling summer heat and discouraging news from the battlefield.

It was he who suggested that she escape the sweltering air and strife of Washington for more pleasant climes and company, and, thinking that a change of scenery might indeed do her some good, she traveled to Ohio to visit her beloved grandmother and other relations. Amid the familiar landscape of home, within the affectionate circle of family and longtime friends, Kate began to feel somewhat restored to herself, although she was not truly happy. Her spirits rose when Nettie joined her there—her younger sister had been obliged to remain at school through the first week of July to make up for the weeks she had missed due to illness in January—but she missed the excitement and intrigue of Washington City even more than she missed William, whose absence had become a dull ache in her heart, one she fervently hoped would fade with time.

"You don't need him," Nettie declared after prying the truth out of her, if only part of it, after noticing her lingering sadness. "You have so many admirers, and Governor Sprague is too often away from Washington to be a suitable suitor anyway. You should like Mr. Hay instead. He is very nice and very amusing."

"Yes, he is," acknowledged Kate, allowing a small smile. She liked John Hay quite a lot, and she suspected that he had felt more than friendship for her for quite some time, but he did not capture her passions the way William Sprague had from the moment they had met. Also, although she would never admit it to anyone, and she did not like what it said about her, she was mindful that John was only the assistant secretary to the president, while William could be president himself someday.

"And let us not forget Lord Lyons," Nettie mused. "He is terribly old, but still handsome even so, and quite rich, I think. Wouldn't it be lovely to have everyone obliged to call you Lady Kate?"

Kate laughed. "Yes," she declared, embracing her younger sister. "You are absolutely right. What I need most out of marriage is wealth and a title. Mutual affection is a luxury I can well do without."

Nettie laughed and hugged her back, knowing that Kate didn't mean it—at least, not entirely.

While Kate was away from Washington, she followed the news of the war through the papers, and Father kept her well apprised of political machinations in the capital.

General McClellan had at last led his army deeper into Virginia toward Richmond, only to be driven back by Confederate General Robert E. Lee in seven days of brutal fighting that ended with the Union forces retreating to the James River.

Although Mrs. Lincoln was still deep in mourning, the Lincoln family had relocated to their summer residence on the grounds of the Soldiers' Home about two miles north of the city, a cool, wooded, secluded haven on a hilltop, far enough away from the Capitol and the White

House to act as a restful retreat, but near enough for Mr. Lincoln to travel back and forth as needed.

In the aftermath of emancipation becoming the law in Washington, thousands of contraband had flooded the city, arriving alone or with their families in tow, footsore, hungry, exhausted, most of them field hands with no trade or training except farm labor, almost all of them illiterate. Very few contraband could find or afford rooms in colored homes or boardinghouses, and so the first arrivals were accommodated in Camp Barker, a complex of empty soldiers' barracks, stables, and tents. When these places filled to overflowing, the refugees built shacks of blankets, mud, and scraps of wood in camps that sprouted up near military hospitals, beside the forts on the outskirts of the city, or tucked away in alleys. Diseases like dysentery, smallpox, and typhoid flourished in the overcrowded, filthy camps, and the dead were buried in makeshift cemeteries not far away. Mrs. Lincoln's dressmaker, Mrs. Keckley, founded the Contraband Relief Association to help provide for their needs, and Father made a generous contribution.

By the end of June, General McClellan's campaign on the Peninsula and increased military activity in the West had spent the entire first issue of greenbacks, so on July 11, the president signed the second Legal Tender Act to allow for the issue of another one and a half million dollars' worth of currency. Father and his allies in the House and Senate had battled mightily to get the measure through Congress, and as soon as it had passed, Father became responsible for designing the new greenbacks.

"If only I had your artistic skill, Nettie," Father wrote to her at Kate's grandmother's house in Ohio. "Of course, I will have artists and engravers at my disposal, but an artist's eye would help me provide the concepts. Others have determined that my visage must grace one of the bills, but I have been unable to decide which one. It seems the height of arrogance to put one's own face on currency at all."

"Father should appear on the hundred-dollar bill," Nettie declared after she finished reading the letter aloud to Kate. "Or the thousand. The highest value that is printed, is what I mean, since he is so important."

"No," said Kate thoughtfully, "I think not."

"You think he is not important?"

Kate laughed. "Of course that's not what I meant."

She promptly found pen, ink, and paper, and wrote to their father that he should arrange for his visage to appear on the one-dollar greenback.

"The one-dollar note?" protested Nettie, reading over her shoulder as she wrote. "Father's worth much more than that. He'll be president someday."

"That is indeed his ambition, and that is why he should do as I suggest."

Anticipating that her suggestion might hurt her father's feelings as they had Nettie's, Kate explained her reasoning: Many more people would use one-dollar notes, and use them more often, than those of significantly higher denominations. If Father's name and handsome face appeared on the one-dollar bill, the people would soon learn them by heart, and men tended to vote for candidates they felt they knew.

In a letter that arrived more quickly than Kate would have believed the mails capable of in wartime, Father praised her idea as ingenious and assured her he would see to it. "Your clever suggestion was to me a rare bright spot in a week saturated with gloom," he added. "The people are despondent over McClellan's losses. We ought to have won a victory and taken Richmond. Instead the country sinks to its lowest point since the birth of the Republic."

Kate's own mood mirrored the low spirits of the country, and although she tried to conceal her lingering sadness from her father, unhappiness must have cast faint shadows upon the pages of her letters. From his questions, it became apparent that he suspected she was hiding something from him, and when she pretended not to understand his circumspect inquiries, he became more direct. In one missive, after his usual complaints about the discrepancy between the date on her letter and the date of its arrival, he wrote:

> *Your appreciation of my long letter as a mark of love and*
> *confidence and the gratification it gave you are more than ample*
> *reward for the time & trouble of writing it. It is quite as agreeable to*
> *bestow love and confidence as it can be to receive it. You have my love*
> *always and I confide greatly in you on many points. My confidence*
> *will be entire when you entirely give me yours and when I feel—that*
> *is am made by your acts & words to feel that nothing is held back*

from me which a father should know of the thoughts, sentiments &
acts of a daughter. Cannot this entire confidence be given me? You
will, I am sure be happier and so shall I. One other thing now that I
am upon this subject. A daughter ought in all things to respect a
father's feelings and if wishes conflict and no moral principle is
compromised by yielding she ought to yield gracefully, kindly,
cordially. You will easily remember instances in which you have tried
me pretty severely by not doing so.

Kate could remember every one of them all too well, but although it pained her to worry her father and earn his stern rebuke, she simply could not tell him why she was so unhappy. Even as a child at boarding school when he had complained that her letters were not written "freely" enough, she had been unable to confide in him completely because the headmistress had read every one of her students' letters before they were sealed and put in the post. Now that she was older, Kate knew that some confessions would hurt him too much, and she must keep them to herself. If her mother had lived, perhaps she could have been the confidante that Father wanted to be, but his good opinion was too difficult to earn to jeopardize it by sharing her mistakes and weaknesses and uncertainties— especially where William Sprague was concerned. She shuddered to think her father might ever know the mistakes she had made with him.

Kate endeavored to make her letters more sprightly, but even as she did, she grew indignant as she mulled over his rebuke. Father wanted her confidence, and yet he did not give his own. She knew from mutual friends in Washington that Father had been paying frequent calls on her friend, the lovely widow Mrs. Douglas; that he corresponded regularly with two New England ladies, each of whom was probably unaware that he corresponded with the other; that he enjoyed a close friendship with Charlotte Eastman, the widow of a former congressman; and that he spent quite a lot of time with Miss Susan Walker, a remarkably intelligent and accomplished friend from Cincinnati, whenever her work for the abolitionist cause brought her to the nation's capital. Kate suspected that any one of those ladies would be happy to become the fourth Mrs. Chase, but she was not anxious for that to happen. Perhaps, Kate thought, somewhat miffed, she would consider confessing her secret romance when Father confessed his.

As midsummer passed, Mr. Lincoln surprised them both with a new resolution that made Father—and Kate too—forget her unhappiness.

Father wrote to Kate immediately, while the events were fresh in his mind. On July 21, a Monday morning, a messenger had brought word that the president had called a special cabinet meeting to convene at ten o'clock in the second floor library. "It has been so long since any consultation has been held that it struck me as a novelty," Father noted. There, President Lincoln read them several military orders under his consideration, which were intended to bring about a more vigorous prosecution of the war. When the discussions ran long, the president had decided to adjourn until the following day, and when the cabinet reconvened, Mr. Lincoln's primary reason for calling the cabinet together the previous day had quickly become apparent.

President Lincoln had decided to proclaim the emancipation of all slaves within states remaining in insurrection on the first day of January 1863.

"We listened in silence as the astonishing scope of his proposal sank in," Father wrote. "Steward and Welles displayed so little surprise that it was obvious the president had informed them already. Stanton immediately voiced his support, for he is an abolition man and understands the great advantage to be gained by depriving the Confederacy of their laborers. Surprisingly, our conservative friend Bates also supported the measure, although he did so on the condition that freed slaves would be obliged to emigrate to Africa, for he does not believe the two races can live and thrive in close proximity."

That was an opinion Mr. Lincoln shared, Kate recalled, or at least he had once believed so. His position on slavery had become so changeable that Kate hardly knew where he stood from one week to the next. It had been too long since she had seen John Hay. He always let little telling details slip, often inadvertently.

"As for myself," Father's letter continued, "I acknowledged that Mr. Lincoln's proposal went beyond anything I had recommended, and that I feared it would lead to depredation and massacre on the one hand, and support to the insurrection on the other. However, since I regarded the president's plan as far superior to inaction, I would give it my entire support."

Father next urged Kate to remember not to divulge the contents of his letter to anyone, as always. "I write you very freely," he admitted. "Say nothing of what I write unless the news is in the papers. I trust your sense of prudence." Her discretion was particularly important in this case, for Secretary Seward had convinced President Lincoln to wait until after a decisive Union victory to announce the proclamation to the American people, or it would be viewed "as the last measure of an exhausted government, a cry for help, our last shriek on the retreat." The president had mulled over Mr. Seward's words and agreed to delay.

Kate was again torn between rejoicing that the end of slavery was apparently nigh and apprehension that Mr. Lincoln seemed to be usurping Father's place as the strongest champion of the abolitionist cause in the government. With the Republican nominating convention two years away, the people would have ample time to forget that Mr. Lincoln had come late to the cause that Father had supported nearly all his life.

For the first time since leaving Washington, Kate felt frustrated and full of regret that she was not by her father's side to witness such astonishing, significant events unfolding. When she wrote back to her father to suggest that she and Nettie return home, he replied that the heat and humidity were so oppressive that he feared for her health if they did. Furthermore, in the aftermath of the disastrous loss at the Second Battle of Bull Run—during which the fighting had been so close to the capital that the distant thunder of cannon had been clearly audible, and when the wind had blown from the west, the smell of gunpowder had filled the air—Father worried that the city remained vulnerable to invasion, and thus too dangerous for his daughters. "Gen. McClellan is so certain that Washington will fall that he is making arrangements to ship his wife's silver out of the city," Father wrote. "Sec. Stanton is packing up documents and has ordered a steamer to be prepared to carry the Pres. to safety at a moment's notice." Father, and many others, blamed General McClellan's irresponsible delays and disgraceful conduct for the terrible defeat, and he had collaborated with an outraged Secretary Stanton, who considered General McClellan recklessly disobedient to the point of treason, to force President Lincoln to dismiss him. After much intrigue behind the scenes with other members of the cabinet, the faction's efforts to be rid of the recalcitrant General McClellan were thwarted when President Lincoln placed him in charge of the defense of Washington. "The president was extremely distressed to discover nearly his entire cabinet opposed to the idea," Father wrote to Kate, "but not enough to change his directive, which I believe will prove a national calamity. Needless to say, I would not have you and your sister return to this city until I am certain it is safe."

Instead Father made arrangements for Kate and Nettie to visit Mrs. McDowell, the general's wife, at their home at Buttermilk Falls in upstate New York. The beautiful countryside along the Hudson River enchanted Nettie, who rambled happily for miles around with her sketch pad and pencils, but Kate grew restless with so much quiet and serenity, and she longed for the quick pace and activity and intrigue of the city. When an opportunity came to accompany friends to Saratoga, where she would be assured of a more vivacious social life, Mrs. McDowell graciously allowed her to go, and wrote to Kate's father to explain the change in her itinerary. Kate worried about leaving Nettie, but her younger sister cheerfully assured her that she was perfectly content, and Mrs. McDowell promised to arrange for a trustworthy escort home when the time came.

In Saratoga, a lovely resort town in the southernmost foothills of the Adirondacks, Kate felt her spirits reviving in the company of lively friends. She took the waters and enjoyed cotillions and concerts, and at parties and receptions she danced and flirted and enjoyed herself as thoroughly and as determinedly as only a young woman with absolutely no attachments to any gentleman possibly could.

Summer drew to a close, and with each passing day Kate felt more restored to herself. Nettie returned to Washington before her, in mid-September, and Kate followed soon thereafter. Her father welcomed her home joyfully and proclaimed that the time away had certainly done her good, for she looked happier and more radiant than she had been in months.

"Thank you, Father," she said, embracing him. He could not possibly know how glad she was to be home, and how relieved she was to have left her foolish passion for William Sprague behind her.

Chapter Fourteen

*O*n September 17, while Kate was still in Saratoga, General McClellan had managed to repulse General Lee's advance into the North in a costly battle along Antietam Creek in Maryland. Although the president was displeased that General McClellan had allowed the battered Confederate army to withdraw to Virginia without pursuit, a stalemate was victory enough for his immediate purposes.

Two days after Kate returned to Washington, Mr. Lincoln called the cabinet together unexpectedly, so Father and the other secretaries suspected a matter of great importance was to be addressed. To begin, Mr. Lincoln attempted to lighten the serious mood, as he often did, by reading aloud a humorous chapter from a book by Artemus Ward; everyone except Secretary Stanton had laughed aloud, Father told Kate afterward. Then the president adopted a more serious tone and reminded them of the draft emancipation order he had presented in July. He told them that some time before, he had determined to issue the preliminary proclamation as soon as General Lee's army was driven out of Maryland, and that time at last had come. He was not seeking their advice on the matter, the president emphasized, for he had already taken their opinions into consideration while reaching his own conclusions and revising the draft. He would, however, welcome their suggestions regarding language.

Mr. Seward recommended a few changes to the section regarding colonization, to which all present agreed. Mr. Blair said that since the matter had already been decided he would make no objection, although he feared the proclamation would have an adverse effect in the army and the border states. Judge Bates felt much as Mr. Blair did. Father conceded that the president's course was not precisely what he would have set, but he was ready to accept the proclamation as written and to stand by it with all his heart.

The next day, the preliminary Emancipation Proclamation was published in newspapers throughout the Union. Soon the people, North and South, learned that "on the first day of January in the year of our Lord one thousand eight hundred and sixty-three, all persons held as slaves within any State or designated part of a State, the people whereof shall then be in rebellion against the United States, shall be then, thenceforward, and forever free."

In Washington City, people of color and abolitionists of all races rejoiced, but in the days that followed, as the preliminary proclamation was discussed and debated, their celebration was tempered by concerns that it did not do enough to ensure liberty for all. The proclamation called for the abolition of slavery only in states that were in rebellion as of January 1, 1863, so if a state agreed to return to the Union before then, slavery could continue there. The proclamation did nothing to free the enslaved people living within the loyal Union border states of Delaware, Kentucky, Maryland, and Missouri, as well as Confederate territory that had come under Union control in Tennessee and parts of Louisiana. It seemed to Kate that Mr. Lincoln had emancipated slaves where the Union could not free them and had kept them enslaved in places where the Union did enjoy the power to give them liberty, a sentiment Mr. Greeley soon echoed in the pages of the *New York Tribune*.

And yet, despite its weaknesses, the proclamation was proof that the nation was moving toward freedom and liberty for all. The old Union was gone forever. When the nation was restored, it would be a new United States.

In the evening of the day after the proclamation was published, a large crowd complete with a band gathered outside the White House to serenade the president and make laudatory speeches in his honor. The president came to an upstairs window to thank them, saying, "I have not been distinctly informed why it is this occasion you appear to do me this honor, though I suppose it is because of the proclamation." The crowd applauded and shouted back that he was absolutely right. The president then declared, "What I did, I did after very full deliberation, and under a very heavy and solemn sense of responsibility. I can only trust in God I have made no mistake."

The crowd roared back their assurances that he had not.

After noting that it was now for the country and the world to pass judgment on his actions, Mr. Lincoln acknowledged that although his high office confronted him with many challenges, they were "scarcely so great as the difficulties of those who, upon the battlefield, are endeavoring to purchase with their blood and their lives the future happiness and prosperity of this country." Long and sustained applause interrupted him. "Let us never forget them. On the fourteenth and seventeenth days of the present month there have been battles bravely, skillfully and successfully fought. We do not yet know the particulars. Let us be sure that in giving praise to particular individuals we do no injustice to others. I only ask you at the conclusion of these few remarks to give three hearty cheers to all good and brave officers and men who fought these successful battles."

The crowd cheerfully and boisterously complied, and the White House lawn rang with their cheers.

All this Kate learned from John Hay soon thereafter, for he was among the serenaders, and after Mr. Lincoln withdrew from the window, the lively crowd, cheering and singing, moved on to the Chase residence. The household heard them coming from blocks away, but Nettie was first to the window. "Come quick," she called, gesturing excitedly to her sister and father without turning away from the scene outside. "We are either going to be serenaded or stoned, and I don't know which."

"If you really think it might be the latter," Kate remarked, joining her at the window, "perhaps we should draw the curtains and pretend we're not home." Then she glanced outside, and her gaze fell upon John Hay, grinning up at her as he sang with the others, banging what looked to be a tin plate with a wooden spoon. She nudged her sister. "Look. There's Mr. Hay. So it is to be a serenade after all."

"Mr. Hay," Nettie exclaimed, throwing Kate a mischievous grin. "So it is to be a love song."

"Nettie!"

As Nettie laughed, Father came to the window, and as soon as the crowd saw him, they called out loudly for a speech. "Well, although it is late, I suppose I must appease them," Father said, looking immensely pleased. "I haven't prepared anything."

"They know that." Smiling, Kate adjusted her father's coat and straightened his tie. "You will rise to the occasion as you always do."

Kissing her quickly on the cheek and ruffling Nettie's blond curls, Father excused himself and hurried downstairs, and a moment later, his daughters watched him emerge onto the pedimented entrance just outside the front door. In the twilight, with a hint of autumn in the air, he conferred briefly with a dark-haired young man at the front of the crowd, then raised his hands for their attention. Before he could speak, someone called for him to put on the gaslight so they could see him better.

"My friends," Father replied, "I believe all the light you need this evening is the light reflected from the great act of the president."

"Good, good," shouted someone in the crowd, and applause rang out.

"I understand that you have just paid your respects to the chief magistrate of the Republic, to assure him that the proclamation he has recently issued finds a welcome response in the hearts of the American people." Father nodded to the affirmative applause. "No one can rejoice more sincerely in the belief that the judgment you have expressed of that act will be the judgment of the whole people of the United States."

"The *whole* people?" echoed Nettie as her father paused for the people's cheers. "But he said he expects lots of people to be angry about it."

"True," said Kate quickly, as the cheers went on and her father, his hands raised to quiet them, prepared to continue. "But as a rhetorical strategy, that would be a particularly unwise idea to introduce at the moment. Hush now, and listen."

"I am, fellow citizens," Father said, "more accustomed to work than to speak. I love acts better than words."

As the crowd applauded in acknowledgment, Kate nodded approvingly. Yes, Abraham Lincoln was the far superior speaker, so Father would do well to present himself as a man of deeds instead, turning a deficiency into an advantage.

"But, fellow citizens, nothing has ever given me more sincere pleasure than to say Amen for the last great act of the chief magistrate."

242 · JENNIFER CHIAVERINI

"Amen, amen!" the people chorused in reply.

"In my judgment, it is the dawn of a new era."

"That's so," a man shouted back. A loud clanging rang out as if to underscore the sentiment, and when Kate turned instinctively toward the sound, her gaze lit upon John Hay, banging wildly upon his tin plate with the spoon and grinning wickedly up at her. She smiled broadly and shook her head at him, but her heart grew lighter, lifted by his merriment. He was, as Nettie had said, very nice indeed. He was handsome and clever and well educated, and all the young ladies of society adored him. While it was true that he was only an assistant secretary now, he was the assistant secretary of the president of the United States, and that was no small accomplishment. He was also a young man of not quite twenty-four with a promising future ahead of him—not an aging adolescent of thirty-two, playing at soldier, racing giddily between the statehouse and the battlefield as the whim struck.

He was in many respects far superior to the man upon whom Kate had until recently squandered her affections. Why should Kate not allow something deeper than friendship to develop between her and John instead?

Father had continued his speech as Kate stood at the window lost in thought. Suddenly she realized that she had kept her gaze locked on John's for far too long, so after giving him a gracious nod, she returned her attention to her father.

"The time has come," her father declared, "when all jealousies and divisions, all personal aims and aspirations should be banished so that we may unite in one common resolve to stand by the integrity of the Republic."

Cries of "Good!" and "Hear, hear!" rang out amid tremendous applause, and with a wince of guilt, Kate thought of Mrs. Lincoln. They were both political creatures, both Republicans, both women for the Union. Why should they be rivals when they had so many reasons to be friends?

"Dismissing all the past, let us look to the future," urged Father, "and henceforth let the time of dissension and discord be ended. Let us do nothing but work for our country, in whatever sphere God in his providence has called upon us to work."

To thunderous applause, Father nodded to the crowd, stepped aside, and gestured to invite Cassius Clay, who had arrived with the serenaders, to take his place on the makeshift stage. The Kentucky abolitionist and politician did not speak as long as Father had, but his fiery oration made quite an impression nonetheless, for he declared that anyone who did not stand by the president's proclamation was a traitor.

"That might be overstating it just a bit," said Kate. "We are a democracy, after all. Our Constitution provides for civil disagreement and debate."

"Mr. Lincoln doesn't like it when Father disagrees with him," Nettie pointed out.

"No, but he cannot forbid Father from doing it."

"But he *could* ask Father to leave the cabinet."

"He could," Kate acknowledged, "but that would be a terrible mistake."

When Mr. Clay finished speaking, he and Father acknowledged their listeners' adulation with dignified bows before withdrawing into the house. Kate and Nettie left the window and hurried downstairs to meet them, only to find that several other gentlemen they knew well had accompanied them inside, while the rest of the serenaders moved on to Secretary Bates's residence. Kate was pleased to see that John Hay was among those who had remained.

Kate had only time enough to smile at him from the other side of the vestibule before hurrying off to the kitchen to arrange refreshments for the impromptu party. Everyone was in a grand, celebratory mood, and they became even more lively after Kate served the wine. She and her father did not drink alcohol, of course, but Father had resigned himself to the necessity of keeping a modest wine cellar for his guests, although he never kept hard spirits in the house.

Father held court in the drawing room, where he led a toast to the president and his proclamation. The conversation soon turned to how the news of emancipation would be received in the South, and depending upon the speaker, the tone ranged from worried to maliciously gleeful.

"If the rebels don't like it, what can they do?" Mr. Clay called out. "Secede a second time?"

The gentlemen laughed uproariously, but Kate could only smile. Her imagination could conceive of many terrible ways the South could express their intense disapproval—retaliation against prisoners, for example.

"Secession," began Father in what Nettie called his "speechifying voice," and the raucous conversation quieted expectantly. "Secession was the most wonderful display of the insanity of a particular class that the world had ever seen."

"How so?" called out a gentleman, more to encourage than to challenge him.

"If the slaveholders had stayed in the Union," Father explained, "they might have kept their peculiar institution going for many years to come." He shook his head, marveling at their foolishness. "And now look what their rebellion has wrought. Slavery, which no political party and no public feeling in the North could ever have hoped to touch, so long as we needed to appease the Southern people in the Congress and at the polls, they madly placed in the very path of destruction."

"You've got that right, General Greenbacks," someone else called out, and the gentlemen roared with laughter. Father smiled and raised his glass of cider to them. Kate knew he rather enjoyed the nickname his new legal tender had earned him.

"The old fogies seem to be enjoying themselves," someone said close to her ear, and she whirled about to find John Hay smiling at her. She had not heard him approach over the din.

"Mr. Hay," she said, smiling and offering her hand. "I'm very pleased to see you. I had no idea you were such a talented musician. Have you been playing the tin plate and wooden spoon long?"

"As it happens, I took up the instrument only this morning."

"So recently! You're quite the virtuoso."

"Thank you."

"And to answer your question, yes, the *gentlemen*"—she gave him a look of teasing rebuke as she corrected his pejorative—"seem to be having a wonderful time."

"They seem to feel . . . a sort of new and exhilarated life," he said thoughtfully, with no trace of his usual sardonic wit. "They breathe more freely, as if the proclamation had freed them as well as the slaves."

"Indeed they do," said Kate. "It's true that an enormous burden has been lifted from their shoulders. Many of them, especially my father, having been working for this day, or a day like it, for decades."

John studied her. "You seem somehow freer too."

"And why not? Am I not an abolitionist myself?"

"I'm sure that's part of it, but you seem—" He paused, regarding her fondly but speculatively, his brow slightly furrowed. "You seem happier than when I last saw you. Unburdened somehow."

Kate spread her hands and shrugged helplessly, although she knew very well what burden she had discarded during her time away. "Perhaps my travels reminded me of all I had waiting for me here at home, and not to take it for granted."

He smiled, a little curious, a little skeptical. "You mean, of course, your family and your comfortable home."

"Not at all. I was referring to a lovely bit of embroidery I had left behind in my sewing basket. I'm thrilled beyond measure to take it up again."

John had chosen that moment to take a drink of his cider, and he nearly choked on it. "That was ill timed, Miss Chase," he scolded, laughing and spluttering as he groped in his pocket for his handkerchief.

"On the contrary," she said as she smiled, lifted her chin, and took his arm. "I would say it was perfectly timed."

John came to supper the following evening, and the day after that, he and Kate went riding together. The late-September air had turned pleasantly temperate, and John's company was even more amusing than she remembered. There was a new easiness between them, a comfortable friendship and mutual admiration that made it possible for them to tease each other about their differences, subjects they once had been obliged to avoid.

Kate had returned to a city transformed by the ongoing war. When she left Washington, it had resembled a vast army camp, but over the summer it had become one boundless, sprawling military hospital. Every morning since Antietam, steamships had brought hundreds of wounded soldiers to the Sixth Street Wharf, some disembarking on foot with bandages wrapped around their torsos or arms, others carried on stretchers, still more stumbling awkwardly on makeshift crutches. Ambulances distributed the sick and injured among the dozens of hastily organized hospitals established in converted schools, hotels, churches, clubs, and private residences. The wife of secretary of the interior, Elizabeth Smith, had transformed the second floor of the Patent Office into a hospital ward for hundreds of soldiers, and Father had told Kate that Mrs. Douglas had established a hospital in her own mansion. She was an "angel of mercy," he had rhapsodized, so fondly that Kate had looked askance at him. He had not called on the lovely widow since Kate's return, as far as she knew, and to her secret relief. Although Kate loved them both dearly, she did not want them to become too fond of each other.

Kate was astonished when John mentioned that Mrs. Lincoln visited the wounded soldiers almost every day. "That cannot be," exclaimed Kate. "Does she not remain in mourning?"

"She does," John said, "but nevertheless, shrouded in so much black crepe that you can scarcely tell there is a lady swathed within the vast acres of fabric, she fills her carriage with baskets of food, fresh fruit, and flowers, buying whatever the White House gardens cannot grow. She spends hours distributing her bounty to the wounded men."

Kate shook her head. "This contradicts everything I've read in the papers."

"Whom are you going to trust, me or some newspaperman?" he protested with a grin, and then, reconsidering, he added, "Unless you're referring to the accounts of a certain well-known lady reporter?"

Kate nodded, for she remembered Mary Clemmer Ames's scathing rebuke quite well, as it had provoked her righteous indignation. "While her sister-women scraped lint, sewed bandages, put on nurses' caps and gave their all to country and death," Mrs. Ames had written recently in the *New York Independent*, "the wife of the president spent her time in rolling to and fro between Washington and New York, intent on extravagant purchases for herself and the White House."

"You cannot believe everything Mrs. Ames writes," John said. "You know I would be the last person to heap praise upon the Hellcat if I was not certain she had earned it."

"Perhaps not the *last* person," said Kate, thinking somewhat abashedly that she might deserve that title.

"The penultimate, then. It is the absolute truth, Kate. Nearly every day Mrs. Lincoln can be found walking along the rows of bloodied, ailing men, offering them delicacies from the White House garden and kitchen with her own soft, plump hands. She sits at the bedsides of the lonely soldiers, talking with them, reading to them, helping them write letters home."

"I had no idea."

"I say she ought to make her rounds with a few newspaper correspondents in tow," John remarked, bringing his horse to a halt in the spreading shade of a chestnut tree on the bank of a particularly scenic bend in the river. "She should have them take shorthand notes of all her sweet, comforting remarks to the suffering men, and their grateful replies. Nothing would raise her in the esteem of a critical public faster than that."

"And yet she does not." Kate pondered the enigma. "Perhaps she doesn't want to draw attention to her visits out of concern that the curious public would flock to see her and would get in the physicians' way. Perhaps she's one of those who thinks it's improper for ladies to visit the hospitals because—" She felt a faint blush rise to her cheeks. "Because the patients are so often in a state of, that is to say, in order to facilitate the tending of their injuries—"

"The patients are not appropriately attired for company?" John offered helpfully.

"Yes, thank you, that's it."

"I don't think that's the reason," said John. "I believe she finds solace for her own grief in caring for the suffering men."

Kate gave him an appraising look from the corner of her eye. "Careful," she warned, nudging her mare with her heels to set her into a walk. "That sounded dangerously approving, perhaps even sympathetic."

"Then I have expressed myself very badly indeed," said John, feigning alarm as he urged his horse forward to catch up with her.

Kate smiled at him over her shoulder, but as she turned back around, her mirth quickly faded into puzzlement. Why would Mrs. Lincoln squander a perfect opportunity to do some politicking for her husband and polish her own oft-tarnished public image at the same time? Whenever Kate visited the hospitals—which was apparently far less often than the First Lady did, she thought with a twinge of guilt—she carefully ensured that at least one member of the press happened to hear of it before she carried her basket across the threshold.

Perhaps, she mused, Mrs. Lincoln received as her reward something more profound, more deeply fulfilling than the noisy praise of the irredeemably fickle public.

With the return of autumn, Nettie's summer holiday came to an end. Instead of sending her back to Brook Hall, Father enrolled her in boarding school in Manhattan, where he hoped she would receive a more rigorous program of study, especially in foreign languages, and develop a better regulation of her habits. Mrs. Eastman, her previous headmistress, had said that Nettie possessed a quick and comprehensive intellect, but she was woefully lacking in self-discipline. When Father determined that a girls' school in Manhattan would correct her of that fault, he asked Kate her opinion regarding schools. He was very much surprised when Kate recommended not her own alma mater, Miss Haines's School, but the French and English boarding and day school of her strongest competitor, Mrs. Mary Macaulay, at Madison Avenue and Fortieth Street. If he had been able to read between the lines of her censored letters so many years ago, he would have understood why.

Kate missed her dear little sister, who at fifteen was blossoming into quite a pretty young lady, sweet and endearing, beloved by everyone. Kate wrote to her often and promised to visit her at school when she could, but the change of seasons had also ushered in the Washington social season, and so she was soon caught up in the familiar, exciting whirlwind of balls, receptions, breakfasts, trips to the Senate gallery to observe important debates, and excursions into the nearby countryside to visit the troops. The most contentious talk in the drawing rooms and parlors centered around General McClellan's ongoing ineffectiveness in Virginia, terrible clashes between opposing armies, and the preliminary Emancipation Proclamation, which had stirred up resentment, in the border states especially but elsewhere in the Union too.

Father always found a receptive audience in Kate when he returned home from the Treasury Department at the end of a difficult day, and the days were all difficult. Father doggedly pursued General McClellan's removal from the head of the Army of the Potomac, and he even had a replacement in mind: General Joseph Hooker. On the day after the preliminary Emancipation Proclamation had been published, Father and Kate had visited General Hooker in the asylum where he was recovering from an injury to the foot he had suffered at Antietam, to wish him good health, to deliver a basket of fresh fruits and flowers, and to take his measure. The general had been unable to rise from his bed to welcome them, but even reclining with his leg propped up he had made an impressive figure, tall, with wavy blond hair, blue eyes, and a high complexion. His manner was gallant with a bit of braggadocio, and he had readily criticized General McClellan when Father had asked his opinion of what had gone wrong with the Seven Days Battles.

"General," Father had told him soberly, "if my advice had been followed, you would have commanded after the retreat to the James River, if not before."

"If I had commanded," General Hooker had replied stoutly, "Richmond would have been ours."

Afterward, Father and Kate had conferred over a game of chess, and by the time Father had placed her in checkmate, they had agreed that General Hooker would make a fine replacement for General McClellan. They had both liked that he spoke as a soldier rather than an aspiring politician, and although he had struck them as less intellectually gifted than they had expected, he had seemed quick, clear, and active. "All that remains," Father had said as they arranged the pieces on the chessboard for another game, "is to convince the president that replacing McClellan is necessary."

Father confided in Kate so freely and enlisted her aid so often that she was caught by surprise when he did not. One afternoon he met her at the door after she returned from a ride with John Hay in the brilliant, clear autumn sunshine. "Katie, dear," he said as she untied her bonnet, his expression pensive, "would you take a turn with me in the garden?"

Though cheerful from her pleasant outing, she was rather tired and badly in need of refreshment, but something in her father's manner told her the conversation could not wait. So she smiled, put her bonnet back on, and took his arm.

They had not wandered far from the house when Father asked if she had heard from Governor Sprague recently. "No," she replied, her heart leaping curiously at the sound of the name she had tried to forget, and deliberately ignored whenever it appeared in the papers. "His last letter to me came in the spring."

"I see." Father looked somewhat relieved, but then he halted abruptly. "Did you quarrel?"

"Not exactly." Kate fervently hoped that her father would not connect the timing of William's last letter to the advent of her inexplicable unhappiness. "Let's just say that there are other gentlemen I prefer at the moment."

Father nodded in a distracted, puzzled sort of way and resumed their stroll. "I thought perhaps he had called on you, since he has occasionally called on me, and I wondered why you had not mentioned it."

"There was nothing to mention," Kate replied, her curiosity rising. "I was not aware Governor Sprague came so frequently to the capital. Why has he called on you? Is he seeking your expert advice on how to run his state?"

Father allowed a small smile and patted her hand where it rested on his arm. "A bit of that, but mostly to discuss military matters, and politics in Washington." He hesitated. "He called on me this afternoon, and he talked so incessantly that I fear the only way I could see to get rid of him was to invite him to supper."

Kate fought back the urge to sigh. "When?"

"Tonight."

It was just as she had suspected. "Very well. I'll go now to speak to Addie and Mrs. Vaudry, if you haven't already."

"I have." Father looked pained. "I hope I haven't incurred their wrath, or yours."

"Nonsense! It's just as easy to prepare supper for three as for two. As long as he isn't bringing along the entire First Rhode Island Regiment, the servants should not be put to any extra trouble." A sinking feeling compelled Kate to ask, "He isn't bringing along the entire regiment, is he?"

"He didn't mention them." Father halted again and turned to face her. "Katie, dear, it isn't only because of the inconvenience that I thought this news might upset you. If there is some reason you don't wish to see the governor, you don't have to attend. I could tell him you are indisposed."

"And leave you without a hostess?" Amused, she shook her head. "I'm always happy to help you entertain your friends, Father. You know that."

"If the governor has offended you, I cannot call him my friend."

Kate felt a flutter of worry in her chest, but she concealed it with a loving smile. "I'm happy to entertain your enemies too. In fact, I daresay that is a skill worth mastering. It is surely at least as important to be able to entertain one's enemies well, as it is to entertain one's friends."

"I would not call Governor Sprague my enemy," Father said, "unless, of course, he has become yours."

"He has not," Kate assured him, patting his arm. Governor Sprague was not her enemy. He was nothing to her anymore except her father's political acquaintance and potential ally. That was the only role the Boy Governor would ever again play in her life.

Addie had already gone to and from the market by the time Father concluded his abashed warning about their altered plans for the evening, and she had the supper preparations well under way by the time Kate went downstairs to the kitchen to apologize on her father's behalf for the late notice, just in case he had forgotten to do so.

"It's nothing at all to make a supper for three, Miss Kate," Addie assured her, but she wore a frown as her cleaver came down with a solid whack on the neck of a plucked chicken. "If I had more time, I would have made you that roast duck with oysters you like so much, and peanut soup. I'd be happy to do that as soon as tomorrow, if you like, but it's too much food without Nettie here to take her portion." Another forceful whack sounded as the cleaver struck the cutting board. "Maybe you might see if that nice Mr. Hay would like to come so nothing goes to waste."

"Addie?"

"Yes, Miss Kate?"

"Governor Sprague is not my suitor."

Addie regarded her from beneath raised brows, her expression a study in skepticism. "If you say so, Miss Kate."

With a laugh and a sigh, Kate hurried off to inspect the china and the silver, and to contemplate the crucial matter of what to wear.

At seven o'clock, Governor Sprague arrived, clad in a fine black suit rather than his military garb, bearing flowers for Kate and a box of cigars for her father, which she knew he would keep untouched in a desk drawer until he found a suitable occasion to give them away. Considering his last letter, Kate had expected the governor to act cold and distant, but astonishingly, he seemed pleased to see her and made all the usual, appropriate compliments with something that bore a remarkable resemblance to sincerity. Addie's dinner of chicken stuffed with apples and sausage was delicious, but Governor Sprague took two glasses of wine with it, which Kate knew would earn her father's disapproval, as it had hers.

Encouraged by the wine, perhaps, Governor Sprague spoke expansively about a recent trip to Altoona, Pennsylvania, where he had attended the Loyal War Governors' Conference at the Logan House Hotel. "Thirteen of us convened," he said, "to discuss the war effort, state recruitment quotas, and the like."

"How very interesting," Kate said politely.

The governor smiled as proudly as if she had burst into applause. "We also spoke at length about General McClellan's appalling performance on the battlefield and the necessity for his immediate removal as the leader of any Union army."

"Now, that is a conversation I would have enjoyed immensely," said Father.

"Not all of us agreed on that point," Governor Sprague admitted, "but the vast majority would rejoice if Mr. Lincoln ousted McClellan tomorrow."

Father nodded. "A vast majority of the cabinet would as well."

"We also affirmed our support of President Lincoln and his Emancipation Proclamation, and debated a number of other topics, all to the effect of how our separate states could best support the Union cause." The governor was clearly proud of all they had accomplished, which to Kate seemed little more than a lot of talk—though to be fair, she was displeased with him and was unlikely to regard anything he did in a favorable light. "When our debates ended, we drafted an address expressing our positions, and all but Governor Bradford consented to the final document."

"I assume Governor Bradford's dissent rested on some matter of slavery," said Kate. It was the most logical conclusion, since Maryland remained a slave state.

"Exactly so. Immediately after we adjourned, the conference sent a delegation to the White House to present our deliberations to the president." Governor Sprague shook his head, frowning. "The president welcomed our suggestions regarding the states' support of the war effort, but he refused even to discuss replacing McClellan."

"He puts too much misplaced faith in that man," said Father. "I will never understand it, but I'm pleased to find, Governor, that you and I concur on so many important matters regarding the conduct of the war."

"You and I, and Miss Chase too, I believe," the governor remarked, raising his glass to Kate.

Kate gave him a gracious nod in reply, the picture of serenity, but her thoughts were in a whirl. He was incomprehensible. It was impossible to believe that this cordial dinner guest was the same man who had written her that dreadful, cold, accusing letter. Sometimes it was as if he were two men, and she never knew which one she would meet on any given day.

"While I was with the president," the governor said, pausing dramatically, "I asked permission to organize a Negro regiment."

Father and Kate exchanged a look, startled. "How did the president respond?" Kate inquired, although she suspected she knew the answer.

"He said he was against arming the Negroes, and he declined to discuss the issue further."

"Would you really do it?" Kate pressed him. "Would you outfit a regiment of colored men as you did the First Rhode Island, and ride at the head of the column as you did for the white soldiers you recruited?"

"I would," he replied so staunchly, so puzzled that she needed to ask, that she believed him, and for a brief moment she was impressed. Then she reminded herself of his changeable moods, and imagined him abandoning his Negro regiment in the field after a fellow white officer criticized them for some imagined disrespect. That, she thought scathingly, was the Boy Governor she knew.

The governor went on to describe the difficulties of his journey to Altoona, turning it into the sort of comical tale Mr. Lincoln enjoyed— how he and an aide had been obliged to travel by boxcar for three days; how they had slept on the rough floor wrapped in military blankets; how whenever they became hungry they would notify the conductor, who would stop the train at the nearest hospitable-looking farmhouse, where they would cajole the inhabitants into letting them buy a hearty meal. Several times Southern sympathizers fired upon the train, but its passengers and crew had always escaped unharmed.

Father enjoyed the evening tremendously, and Kate managed to appear as if she did by pretending William Sprague was a stranger, a patronage seeker whom she would never see again after that night, but whose goodwill Father needed.

"How long will you remain in the capital, Governor?" Father asked later, as they were saying good night at the door.

"Only a few days," he replied, and his gaze fell warmly upon Kate's face, searching for some remnant of affection. She felt a strange wrenching, and to her dismay the old longings began to rise to the surface from the depths where she had buried them in midsummer. "I hope that I might see you both again before then."

Father cordially echoed his wishes, but Kate merely smiled politely and expressed no preference one way or another, which a gentleman ought to recognize as a strong disinclination.

Either he understood, or he was too preoccupied with business, or he simply forgot, but he did not call again, and a few days later she was relieved to read in the papers that he had returned to Providence.

On a rainy evening soon thereafter, Father lingered at the supper table long after he usually retired to his study. "Kate," he said just as she was about to suggest they have a game of chess, "may I have a word?"

He could have had a word at any time throughout the meal, and in fact, they had exchanged a great many, but his expression had turned pensive, so she did not tease him. "Of course."

"Governor Sprague came to see me at the Treasury the morning after he dined with us."

Kate inhaled steadily, concealing her sudden disquiet. "To seek your help persuading Mr. Lincoln to allow him to recruit a Negro regiment?" Father had long advocated such measures, and he would be an eminent ally to enlist for the governor's mission.

"To discuss the cotton trade," said Father. "You know it has become much more difficult for him to keep his mills going."

"I didn't know, but of course that makes perfect sense." The Sprague mills needed cotton to weave their cloth, but after war erupted, embargoes and blockades had served to make that a rare commodity in the North. In November of 1861, after the federal navy had captured numerous South Carolina Sea Islands in the Battle of Port Royal, Father had established an experiment there in which the cotton plantations, hastily abandoned by their white owners as they fled the Union incursion, were turned over to the use of their former slaves. With the government and private charities providing food, clothing, medical care, and training, the freedmen were employed in growing, harvesting, and processing the valuable Sea Island cotton, all under the jurisdiction of the Department of the Treasury. The Port Royal experiment had thus far proven to be a resounding success, with the former slaves convincing all but the most ardent skeptics that they could work the land efficiently and manage their own affairs. Kate was tremendously proud of her father's accomplishments there, and she hoped the Sea Islands would become a model for administrators of other Southern regions that were restored to federal control.

But the Port Royal experiment was not the only source of cotton for the North. Since a significant portion of the northeastern economy depended upon cotton, early in the war, President Lincoln, Father, and the rest of the cabinet had devised a system for Northern manufacturers to purchase cotton from loyal Unionists in the South, but only if they obtained the necessary permits. Father had insisted upon that measure in order to prevent unmonitored cotton trading across the border, which could inadvertently provide aid and comfort to the Confederacy. The authority to grant cotton trading permits resided with Father, as secretary of the treasury, and he dispensed them scrupulously, wary of schemes that could benefit rebellious slaveholders falsely representing themselves as loyal Union men.

"You may remember," Father said, "that Governor Sprague sought a cotton trading permit from me quite a long while ago."

"Yes, but he didn't receive one, if I recall correctly."

"There were only so many to go around, and other companies put forth better applications." He added, almost apologetically, "I could not let his friendly acquaintance with you—with us—outweigh other factors."

Kate nodded, unsure where the conversation was leading. "Is he presenting his case again?"

"He does inquire from time to time, and he'd be a very bad businessman if he did not." Father fell silent for a moment. "But that is not the crux of the problem."

Kate steeled herself. "What is, then?"

"Do you know of a gentleman named Harris Hoyt?"

Kate thought for a moment. "I don't believe so. Is he related to Governor Sprague? I believe he has cousins named Hoyt."

Father shook his head. "I think this Mr. Hoyt would have told me if he were a relation. This fellow is a Texan, and over the past month or more he's carried a rather wild tale around the capital. He claims that he was banished from Texas for being a loyal Union man, and that he was forced to leave behind his wife, children, and property, most of which is cotton."

"I see," said Kate, although she wasn't quite sure what this Mr. Hoyt had to do with Governor Sprague or herself.

"He says there are many Union men like himself in Texas with plenty of cotton to sell in the North, if only they could get around the blockade enforced by the Union navy."

"I'm sure there are many men with cotton to sell," said Kate, "but whether they're Union men is another matter entirely."

"And very difficult to prove from so great a distance. Well, our Mr. Hoyt claims he has that proof. He carries with him what he says is a recommendation from President Lincoln attesting to his loyalty."

"An impressive credential."

"Yes, if it were real. Mr. Hoyt made the rounds of the cabinet offices, brandished his letter of recommendation, and asked for a permit to bring cotton through the blockade. Secretary Welles and Secretary Stanton refused him in no uncertain terms."

"Why did he go to the departments of Navy and of War instead of coming to you?"

"I suppose he did not understand the proper jurisdiction." Father frowned deeply, brooding. "Or perhaps he assumed they were the men to see about a troublesome naval blockade. Eventually Mr. Hoyt made his way to me, and I discovered at once why my fellow secretaries rebuffed him. The so-called letter of recommendation from the White House was not *from* the president at all, but a letter of introduction *to* the president, written by John Hay."

"John Hay?" Kate echoed, dismayed to hear his name mixed up in what sounded like suspicious dealings.

"My dear Katie, don't worry," Father assured her. "Your friend has done nothing untoward. The letter was a matter of form, written at Mr. Hoyt's request, commending him to the confidence and kind offices of whatever Union people he may meet as he travels home."

"Oh, good," said Kate, much relieved.

"But that is not how Mr. Hoyt represented the letter to me," Father emphasized, "or to Welles or Stanton, and I presume whomever else he may have harassed. In fact, I'm not even certain that Mr. Hay wrote the letter attributed to him—or rather, attributed to President Lincoln, though it has Mr. Hay's name on it."

Kate managed a laugh. "I believe I understand why Mr. Stanton and Mr. Welles rejected his suit."

"And why I did as well. I never heard such a strange, implausible story. You would think that would have been the end of the matter, but yesterday afternoon, who should appear at my office door but the indefatigable Mr. Hoyt, undaunted and curious to see if I had changed my mind."

"Not a man to give up easily, I see."

"I again refused him, and for the same reasons as before, and then I returned to the work on my desk, because as far as I was concerned, the matter was settled. In a sudden burst of anger, Hoyt threatened that if I did not issue him a permit at once, he would report me to Sprague and his partners."

"I beg your pardon?" said Kate, incredulous. "Report *you* to *them*?"

"For a moment, all I could do was stare at him, but then I said, coldly, 'I wish you to understand that those gentlemen don't control me.' Then I summarily turned him out of my office."

Kate could not believe what she was hearing. Who was this Mr. Hoyt, and how had Governor Sprague become entangled with him? Then she had another thought. "You don't suppose," she said carefully, "that Governor Sprague's interest in a . . . friendship, with me, and with you, has all been for the sake of securing a cotton trading permit?"

Father looked terribly unhappy. "I'm sorry, my dear Katie, but I think we both must consider that possibility."

Kate took a deep, shaky breath, pressing her palm to her waist. That would certainly explain why the governor had come back around, so friendly and courteous, deliberately ignoring his own parting letter. "That is the way of Washington, isn't it?" she said flatly. "People become friends for all sorts of expedient reasons. I confess there are ladies in this city who bore me almost to tears, but I summon up my patience and call on them nevertheless because it is the proper thing to do, and because it will foster goodwill between their gentlemen and you. This is, I suppose, much the same thing."

"This is far more serious than to be polite to ladies you would rather not see. That is simply good manners." Father took one of her hands in both of his. "But we should give Governor Sprague the benefit of the doubt, regarding both his intentions and his ties to Mr. Hoyt, to which thus far only Mr. Hoyt has alluded. He may know the governor even less well than he knows the president, which is to say, not at all."

Kate managed a wan smile. "Who knows what tenuous acquaintance he may attempt to benefit from next? At this very moment, he may be at a bank attempting to withdraw a wheelbarrow full of greenbacks from the vault because they have his good friend Secretary Chase's image on them."

"I almost hope he tries, so we will have cause to arrest him." Father regarded her steadily, his expression full of concern and affection. "I would not have burdened you with these worries, but as your loving parent, it is my duty to look out for your welfare, and in this case to urge you to be careful where you place your trust, until we know more."

Kate agreed that his advice was prudent, and she promised to take heed, but the necessity left her feeling disappointed and forlorn. Even though she and William Sprague were no longer friends, she hated to think that her feelings for him had been based upon a deception.

She sustained her hopes until the middle of October, when Father brought home a letter William had sent to him at the Treasury Department and studied her worriedly while she read it.

State of Rhode Island
Executive Department
Providence, October 14, 1862

Sir:

Mr. Harris Hoyt, a Union man of Texas, has made a proposition to the Government, as I understand, to go to Texas for the purpose of bringing away a portion of his family now there, relieving his Union friends, and at the same time getting important information for the benefit of our Government. He has letters from the President and others vouching for his good faith. He has proposed to some of our dealers, among whom is Colonel Reynolds, known to the Treasury Department, to put a few goods on board his vessel, which he will exchange with his Union friends for cotton. They desire to procure for Mr. Hoyt a document from the Secretary of the Navy which would enable him to pass the blockading squadron uninterrupted.

It is, of course, important to the Government to get the information
which Mr. Hoyt would be able to procure from them; and there can be
no objection raised to the relieving the Union men of Texas.

Kate was almost too disgusted and disappointed to read on. So Governor Sprague not only knew Mr. Hoyt, but he had become his advocate. Her heart thudded with apprehension as she skimmed the rest of the letter, a self-serving argument for the necessity of cotton to the economy, and the importance of keeping its price down, and the responsibility of the people of the North to support loyal Unionists in the South. "I shall esteem any aid you can give Mr. Hoyt an advantage to our whole people," Governor Sprague concluded, "as it will also be to those directly interested."

The governor was certainly included among those, although he neglected to mention exactly how Mr. Hoyt's scheme might benefit the A. & W. Sprague Company.

"Why, Father, I don't see why you have not already granted this eloquent and ingenious request," Kate said, shaking her head in exaggerated amazement. "It is entirely to the country's benefit, what with Mr. Hoyt intending to spy for the Union while he conducts his business. Business—perhaps I should have said charity, they intend to give so much to the country while profiting so little themselves."

"Katie—"

"It's all right, Father." She managed a tremulous smile. "We wondered if Mr. Hoyt and Governor Sprague were conspiring, and it appears almost certain that they were. How fortunate it is that the truth came out before either of us made any firm commitments to either of them."

"Yes," Father said, and he looked both outraged and sad. "How fortunate indeed."

Chapter Fifteen

NOVEMBER 1862–MARCH 1863

On November 4, discontented voters went to the polls for the midterm elections and made their unhappiness with the Union army's inaction and the forthcoming Emancipation Proclamation abundantly clear, with disastrous results for the Lincoln administration. Although Republicans held on to a slim majority in the Congress, Peace Democrats, who advocated conciliation with the Confederacy even at the expense of emancipation, won important offices in Illinois, Indiana, New York, Pennsylvania, and Ohio.

The following day, President Lincoln, safely clear of the elections, dismissed General McClellan as the commander of the Army of the Potomac. Father, Kate, and countless others rejoiced, but within the Chase household, their celebration was tempered by misgivings about the president's choice to succeed him—not General Hooker, as they had hoped and recommended, but General Ambrose Burnside, whose loyalty to General McClellan had twice compelled him to reject the command when it was offered to him after the debacles in the Peninsula Campaign and the Second Battle of Bull Run. Though General Burnside had performed adequately well for most of the war, Kate could not forget how the First Rhode Island Regiment had fallen apart under his command at Manassas in the early days.

More than a month later, her concerns proved prescient when General Burnside suffered a terrible defeat when—acting against president Lincoln's advice—he led one hundred twenty-two thousand troops across the Rappahannock to Fredericksburg, only to discover General Lee had already claimed the high ground and was waiting for him. When the trap was sprung, the Union suffered nearly thirteen thousand casualties, more than twice Lee's losses, and General Burnside was forced to make a humiliating retreat.

Though Kate imagined President Lincoln must have been thoroughly demoralized by the loss, he nevertheless released a public letter of commendation to the troops, declaring that they possessed "all the qualities of a great army, which will yet give victory to the cause of the country and of popular government." But the rumblings of discontent continued, echoing loudest in the halls of Congress. On the afternoon of December 16, the Republican senators caucused in the reception room of the Senate, determined to compose a unified response to the ongoing calamity. Unwilling to attack the commander in chief and further imperil the struggling army, they blamed Secretary Seward instead—and Father was at least in part responsible for making him the target of their fury.

For months Father had insisted, in private letters and in all-too-public conversations, that a "malign influence" controlled the president and overruled all the decisions of his cabinet—and it was obvious that he referred to Secretary Seward. Equally clear were Father's numerous complaints that Mr. Lincoln had failed, time and time again, to consult the cabinet on matters of significant national interest. If the president had heeded Father's councils instead of Mr. Seward's, Father implied, the catastrophes facing the nation and the party would have been prevented.

Rumors spread throughout Washington City and in Republican circles beyond the capital that Mr. Seward was responsible for any grievance anyone had with nearly anything President Lincoln had done since taking office—and the Republican caucus was determined to do something about it. The majority voted in favor of a resolution declaring a lack of confidence in the secretary of state and asserting that Mr. Lincoln should remove him from the cabinet.

The meeting was meant to be secret, but Mr. Seward had friends among the Republican senators, and one of them hurried to his home that evening to warn him about what had transpired. Unwilling to force the president into a painful, untenable position, Mr. Seward composed a letter of resignation, which his son and the senator immediately delivered to the White House. The president, though pained and surprised, grieved Mr. Seward by not immediately refusing to accept the resignation.

Father and Kate learned all this in the days that followed, from friends and eager acquaintances who hoped to win their friendship. They learned a few hours ahead of time that the Republican caucus had selected a Committee of Nine to present their resolutions to the president at the White House on the evening of December 18. The next day, although he was perfectly courteous, John Hay seemed none too pleased with Kate and her father when he admitted to her that Mr. Lincoln was greatly upset by the Republican caucus's machinations, but he had hidden his distress and had granted the Committee of Nine a three-hour audience to air their grievances.

"I hope you don't think my father instigated this," said Kate when John's righteous indignation and unspoken censure became a bit much. They were alone in the best parlor, ostensibly enjoying tea, but the pot had cooled and the plate of cakes had gone untasted while their conversation became more heated.

"Not directly, perhaps," John acknowledged. "But he had to know that his ongoing criticism would eventually have this effect. He had to know that this movement against Seward would shock and grieve the president."

"I learned long ago that it is a waste of breath to ask my father to be silent when he feels compelled to point out one's faults to them." Through the years she had been the reluctant audience of more of these monologues about herself than she cared to count.

"That's the problem. He hasn't pointed out the president's alleged faults to him, but to everyone else within the sound of his voice and the reach of his pen." John shook his head, exasperated. "The secretary of the treasury is no common bootblack. Did he really think his words wouldn't be repeated over and over until they made their way back to the president?"

Greatly displeased, Kate fixed him with a stony look. "My father is a man of exacting ethical standards. He does nothing in secrecy that would disgrace him were it made public."

John immediately calmed himself. "I didn't mean to suggest otherwise."

"Then you should say what you mean," Kate countered, "and perhaps you should say it to my father rather than me."

"If you think your father should know something that I confide in you," John said wearily as he rose to go, "you will tell him, as you always do."

Stung by the implication that she abused his trust, she accompanied him to the door without a word and shut it firmly behind him, heartsick and angry.

Early the next morning, before Father left for the Treasury Department, he received a request to attend a special cabinet meeting at half past ten. When he returned home later that day for a hasty supper, he looked rather shaken as he told Kate that Mr. Seward had not been invited to the meeting, because he had been the subject of it—for Mr. Lincoln had presented the entire history of the conflict to his abashed partial cabinet. "We are all—except Seward, of course—to return to the White House this evening to meet with the Committee of Nine," said Father, agitated. "I argued against it, but when all the others agreed, I had no choice but to acquiesce."

Kate felt faint, but she steeled herself and kept her voice steady. "What is the worst that could happen at this meeting?"

"All of my complaints about the president, and Mr. Seward, and the functioning of the cabinet—they could all come out into the open."

"Aren't your grievances already well-known?"

"Perhaps the substance of them, but not the scope and the sheer volume."

"I see." Kate thought in silence for a long moment. "Do you stand by your remarks?"

"The content, yes, but I certainly could have been more circumspect, and followed proper channels."

"Then if it seems appropriate, you can apologize for that oversight, even while you affirm that your criticism is valid."

Father heaved a sigh and agreed that there was nothing else to be done.

He left for the White House shortly before seven o'clock. As the hours dragged by, Kate tried to wait up for him, but she kept drifting off to sleep in her chair, and eventually she went upstairs to bed. The sound of the front door woke her about half past one, and she would have met her father in his study except she heard his slow, weary tread upon the staircase and knew he was going straight to his bedchamber.

The next morning, Father was still the first of the family to the breakfast table, his Bible open on the table, his plate untouched, his coffee cooling beside it, his gaze distant. He glanced up when Kate entered and wished him good morning, but her voice trailed off at the sight of his haggard face and shadowed eyes. Before she could ask him how the meeting had gone, he said, "I am going to submit my resignation."

"Father, no!" she exclaimed, hurrying to his side and taking his hand in both of hers. "What would compel you to cast aside—"

"The talk is that I am responsible for the movement to oust Seward," he interrupted, his voice dull from exhaustion and defeat. "The senators say I conspired against him because I wish to control the cabinet myself. If Seward goes and I stay, I'll face the wrath of Seward's friends, and they are legion. The only way to clear my name is if I offer to join Seward in resigning." He gave her a wan look. "Naturally, I hope the president will refuse to accept my resignation."

"As do I," said Kate fervently. "Are you sure such a drastic step is necessary? Is there no other way?"

Father replied that he had considered every other course and that he was resolved to follow this one, and he rebuffed all her attempts to ply him with alternatives. She convinced him to eat some breakfast to strengthen himself before he set out, but that was the most he would concede.

When Father returned from the White House, Kate's heart plummeted at the sight of his forlorn, indignant expression. "The president did not refuse your resignation?"

"He did not, but he did not exactly accept it either." Father sank wearily into a chair and clasped a hand to his brow. "His eyes lit up with delight as he took the page from my hand, and as he read it over, he said, 'This is all I want. This relieves me. My way is clear; the trouble is ended.'"

Kate supported herself on the back of his chair. "And now you must await his response?"

Father nodded.

"Then you shall have something to eat while you wait." Blinking back tears, Kate hurried from the room and off to the kitchen, taking slow, even breaths to calm herself. They could be hours away from the end of all their ambitions. Tomorrow at that time, they could be packing cartons for the move back to Columbus—for Father would not want to remain at the scene of his embarrassment, and where else would they go?

The hours passed slowly, but President Lincoln's reply came before supper, in a letter addressed to both him and Mr. Seward:

> *Executive Mansion, Washington.*
> *December 20, 1862.*
>
> *Hon. William H. Seward, &*
> *Hon. Salmon P. Chase.*
>   *Gentlemen: You have respectively tendered me your resignations, as Secretary of State, and Secretary of the Treasury of the United States. I am apprised of the circumstances which may render this course personally desirable to each of you; but, after most anxious consideration, my deliberate judgment is, that the public interest does not admit of it. I therefore have to request that you will resume the duties of your Departments respectively.*
>   *Your Obt. Servt.*
>   *A. LINCOLN.*

"He does not say he *wants* to retain me," Father observed after reading the letter aloud. "He says he has to, for the public interest."

"But he has refused your resignation," Kate pointed out happily. "That is the important thing."

"Yes, and now I must decide whether to accept. I think I shall not."

Kate stared at him, her relief swiftly fading. "Why?"

"If you had seen the sheer gratification on his face when I handed him my letter, you would not need to ask."

"He was gratified that you provided him with a way out of his conundrum without losing either of his most important cabinet members, that's all."

Father grudgingly allowed that she could be right, but he desired to think the matter over nonetheless. Kate felt as if she were holding her breath while she waited for him to make up his mind, fearful that if she said too much to push him in one direction, he would obstinately choose the other. Later that day, he told her that he had written to the president declining to remain in the cabinet, but then he received a note from Mr. Seward announcing his intention to heed the president's wishes and stay—and knowing that, Father did not see how he could do otherwise. He informed Mr. Lincoln that his desire to resign had not changed, but he would submit to the needs of his country and his president and return to the Treasury Department.

Mr. Seward was clearly pleased with the outcome, and, by nature a congenial, resilient man, he seemed to hope that he and Father could put the conflict behind them and cooperate for the good of the Union. As a sign of his willing friendship, he invited the Chases to join his family for supper on Christmas Eve, but the anxiety and strain of the weeks of discord had taken their toll on Father's health, and he was too ill to accept the invitation. He sent a gracious note instead, begging Mr. Seward's indulgence for his unwilling absence and explaining that he was too unwell to venture upon his hospitality.

Soon Nettie's school holidays began. Kate traveled to New York to bring her home, and after a brief delay there while Kate recovered from a bad chest cold, the sisters returned to Washington, where Nettie's cheerful, loving presence eased the tension and worry that had afflicted the household for far too long. Kate celebrated Christmas with a heart more relieved than merry, for she felt that they had narrowly escaped disaster, and she feared that the next time Father heedlessly sailed too close to the treacherous shore, they might not be able to steer the ship to safe waters before they wrecked upon the rocks.

On December 30, President Lincoln distributed to the members of his cabinet copies of the Emancipation Proclamation, which he intended to sign into law two days thereafter. At ten o'clock the next morning, the cabinet convened so the secretaries could advise the president on any final revisions. Mr. Seward and Mr. Welles suggested a few minor changes, but Father wanted to drastically revise the section that stipulated where slaves would be declared free, arguing that entire states should be included, with no piecemeal regions or sections omitted. He also submitted a complete draft of an alternative Emancipation Proclamation he had written himself, but when the president seemed disinclined to accept it, Father urged him to at the very least adopt his closing sentence, which he thought struck the proper reverential tone: "And upon this act, sincerely believed to be an act of justice warranted by the Constitution, and an act of duty demanded by the circumstances of the country, I invoke the considerate judgment of mankind, and the gracious favor of Almighty God." The president agreed that it was quite a good conclusion, and with a few minor alterations, he added it to his own draft.

The morning of New Year's Day dawned beautiful and sunny. At eleven o'clock, Father escorted Kate, Nettie, a friend of Nettie's from school, and Father's youngest sister, Mrs. Helen Chase Walbridge, to the traditional reception at the White House. Mrs. Lincoln had not yet emerged from mourning, but she had dutifully resumed her role as hostess for the event. Pale and forlorn in a black bonnet and an exquisite dress of rich black velvet, she stood at her husband's side in the Blue Room to receive their visitors. The most illustrious guests— cabinet officers and their ladies, members of the Supreme Court, foreign dignitaries, and others—arrived at eleven o'clock, offered their respects to President and Mrs. Lincoln, wished one another a Happy New Year, and discussed the Emancipation Proclamation, which apparently the president had not yet signed.

Kate would have searched out John Hay, but he found her first, and she scarcely remembered to wish him a Happy New Year before she queried him about the rumors. "The Tycoon hasn't signed the proclamation yet, but he will," John assured her. He looked especially handsome that morning, in a new suit and haircut, although he seemed a bit tired. The bedchamber he shared with John Nicolay was on the second floor of the White House, directly across the waiting room from the president's office, and whenever Mr. Lincoln could not sleep, which was often, he would wander into their room in his nightclothes and slippers, find himself a seat, and read aloud passages from interesting books or regale them with his own stories. Kate would have been displeased to have her sleep regularly interrupted by an insomniac employer, but John enjoyed the president's companionship too much to feel the inconvenience.

"What accounts for his delay?" Kate asked. "People have been gathered in churches and meeting halls and telegraph office all across the North for hours already, awaiting word that emancipation is finally the law of the land."

"He's still revising it," said John, with affectionate exasperation. "Nothing too drastic—that was all done days ago. Just some fine changes here and there, with details from the latest reports from the field inserted in the proper places." He inclined his head to indicate the guests. "This little party interrupted him, but he'll finish soon, and he will sign it. Never fear."

"Tell that," said Kate archly, "to the thousands of colored people in Washington City alone who worry, not without justification, that he'll change his mind at the last minute."

"I understand their concern," John countered. "It's not official until it's signed. But to those of us who have labored over this document so long, the signing is merely the simplest and briefest formality. The real mental conflict and moral victory took place last July, when the Tycoon presented his preliminary draft to the cabinet, and when it was announced to the public."

Kate did not truly believe that the president would fail to sign the proclamation, but she would still feel much better after he had put pen to parchment.

Like most of the early arrivals, the Chase entourage departed by noon, before the event was opened to the public and vast throngs crammed into the White House. They, like many of the cabinet officials, had their own reception to prepare. At one o'clock, Kate and her father received their guests in the parlor, which soon became quite crowded with gentlemen and ladies. Kate had planned a sumptuous menu of oysters, salads, game pastries, fruits, cake, and punch, and as their guests enjoyed themselves, the fervent wish expressed by one and all was that 1863 would be the year that brought victory to the Union and peace to a reunited nation.

The reception was well under way when a messenger brought word from the White House that President Lincoln had signed the Emancipation Proclamation. Cheers and shouts of joy went up from the gathering, and distantly, Kate heard similar exultant outbursts as other households received the good news. Soon, throngs of triumphant people, white and colored, began streaming past the windows in the direction of the White House, where Kate supposed they intended to cheer and serenade the president, and call for a speech. Considering that he had spent more than three hours shaking hands with the public at the reception earlier that day, Kate hoped the people would be satisfied with a few brief remarks, and then let the president rest. She saw Mr. Lincoln fairly often, but that morning she had been startled by his gaunt, careworn appearance. His tall frame had become more stooped, and his eyes sunken and cavernous, and yet his compassion and interest for all the people who had come to wish him a good New Year remained unaltered by time or tragedy. Seeing that, she understood why people like John Hay admired him so, why his former fierce rival William Seward had become his most trusted and intimate friend in the cabinet. Abraham Lincoln drew others to himself and turned enemies into friends in a way that her father had never been able to do. The people respected Father, but they loved Mr. Lincoln.

Now that Mr. Lincoln had unquestionably usurped Father's place as the most eminent abolitionist in the land, Kate was not sure how Father would reclaim the people's esteem and confidence before the next presidential election.

In the early days of January, throughout the North, celebrations of the Emancipation Proclamation drowned out the grumblings of its detractors, but as the winter dragged on and the cheers and serenades and fanfares faded, an angry, sullen resistance rose and crested. Peace Democrats in the Congress, who protested that Mr. Lincoln's war measures had strayed too far from their professed objectives, used every trick and stratagem at their disposal to prevent the Republicans from enacting any more of the president's proposals. They fiercely opposed reform legislation, denounced the new conscription law, and contrived to suppress votes on key issues by attaching unacceptable amendments onto bills, keeping the Senate awake with interminable filibusters, and even hiding in the House lobbies and cloakrooms during quorum calls. To Kate's alarm, the Peace Democrats, or Copperheads as they were also known— not for their similarity to the poisonous snake, but from the Liberty heads they cut from copper pennies and wore as badges—were organizing a movement against the war.

Assisting the Copperheads as they stirred up discontent was the demoralizing lack of progress on the military front. Warfare customarily slowed in winter, but heavy rains in January and a series of fierce February snowstorms had forced the Army of the Potomac to settle in at winter quarters north of the Rappahannock. In the West, General Grant's Army of the Tennessee had tried and failed four times to capture Vicksburg, and thus could not seize control of the Mississippi River. At the end of January, General Burnside had attempted to cross the Rappahannock at Banks Ford and Fredericksburg to launch an ill-advised winter offensive, only to become deeply, helplessly mired in mud. In the aftermath of the embarrassing failure, President Lincoln accepted General Burnside's resignation and named as his replacement General Joseph Hooker. For Kate and her father, General Hooker's appointment to command the Army of the Potomac, a choice they heartily approved and had long desired, provided a rare bright spot in a gloomy season of war.

In the weary capital, people in Republican circles looked forward expectantly to spring, when fair weather would allow General Hooker to fully exercise his new authority and the commencement of a new Congress would welcome in new members to replace some of the pesky obstructionist Copperheads. Outwardly, Kate professed the same hopes and expectations for the new Congress as her acquaintances did, but secretly she dreaded its approach, for William Sprague intended to give up his governor's chair to become the newest senator from Rhode Island.

Weeks before, when Kate discovered his name in the election returns, she had felt a strange, anxious fluttering in the pit of her stomach. It was fairly easy to avoid William Sprague when he made only sporadic visits to the capital, but after he assumed his new office, he would surely reside in Washington most of the time. She might not have been concerned except that in the beginning of January he had sent her a note, strangely cordial and cheery, wishing her a happy New Year. Though she did not respond, he sent her another a week later describing the pleasant Christmas he had enjoyed with his family. She did not know what to make of it, and although she was tempted to write back a coolly concise reply asking him to give her regards to Mr. Harris Hoyt, Texas cotton farmer, she refrained, in part because she thought he might completely misunderstand her meaning and do exactly as she asked in hopes of pleasing her.

She was thrown into more confusion thanks to an older and trusted friend. When she accompanied Nettie to Manhattan at the end of her school holiday, Kate stayed with Mr. and Mrs. Barney for a few days, where Mr. Barney utterly confounded her by mentioning Governor

Sprague, not merely once in passing but several times, and always to praise him. "I had no idea you and the governor were friends," Kate replied after Mr. Barney offered a lengthy description of William's many charitable ventures in Providence and Narragansett, where the Sprague family kept a summer home on a rambling farm.

"Indeed, yes," Mr. Barney replied, smiling. "His accomplishments speak for themselves, but we gentlemen require our friends to speak to our other qualities on our behalf, since it is unseemly to boast."

Kate smiled back, hiding her uncertainty. Why would Mr. Barney want to praise William to her? If they were such fond acquaintances, wouldn't William have told Mr. Barney about the mysterious information that had compelled him to end their courtship so abruptly? Perhaps the governor still entertained hopes of charming Kate into begging her father to grant him a cotton trading permit, and he had deceived Mr. Barney too.

She began to wonder if a plot was afoot when Father's friend Mr. Jay Cooke, the wealthy Philadelphia banker who had, with his wife, seen Nettie through her bout with scarlet fever, mentioned Governor Sprague favorably several times during a visit to confer with Father about loans and bonds to fund the war. Mystified, as soon as Kate found an opportunity to speak to Mr. Cooke alone, she inquired how well he knew the governor. He admitted that their acquaintance was limited to the realm of business, where Governor Sprague had always conducted himself honorably.

"I wonder," Kate said, "do you know his acquaintance Mr. Harris Hoyt?"

"I don't recall," Mr. Cooke said. "Is he a cousin, perhaps? I believe the Spragues are related to the New England Hoyts."

"This fellow is a Texas Hoyt," said Kate, feeling somewhat deflated, as if she had felt a tug on her line and reeled it in only to find the bait missing from the hook. "Please forgive my incessant curiosity, but since you know Governor Sprague through business, do you happen to know how he obtains cotton for his mills?"

"From Port Royal, South Carolina," Mr. Cooke said promptly. "He purchases through a distributor, of course, but it comes from the Sea Islands. That is how your name came up in our conversation. Governor Sprague rhapsodized at length about your father's successes there, but he wondered if the credit should go to his daughter instead." Mr. Cooke smiled, amused. "Perhaps I shouldn't tell you this, but he said you were not only a rare beauty, but also compassionate and wise, and he would not be surprised to learn that it was you who thought of turning over the captured plantations to the freed slaves."

Kate laughed shortly. "I hope you enlightened him."

Mr. Cooke, who had exchanged many letters with Father as he was devising his audacious plan, assured her that he had corrected the misunderstanding. "Even then, the governor insisted that your good influence must have inspired your father in some way."

"Perhaps I can take credit for that much," Kate said, but the conversation left her both more informed and more bewildered than before. If William Sprague already had a reliable source for cotton, he would not need to become entangled with a charlatan from Texas with dubious political inclinations. If he thought Kate compassionate and wise and a good influence, he could not also believe whatever scurrilous tales about her he had heard from some anonymous enemy.

Why, then, did he not apologize for his parting letter, if he no longer believed what he had written? She wanted so terribly to believe that their falling-out had been nothing more than an unfortunate misunderstanding, easily remedied by an earnest conversation, but she could not account for the cold, unkind tone of that letter, which she knew by heart from thinking of it too often.

Throughout the winter, at least once a week the inscrutable Governor Sprague sent Kate a pleasant, informative, undemanding, occasionally amusing missive. She replied to but one of them, and then only because he asked specific questions about particular senators whom he would soon call colleagues, she happened to know the answers, and it seemed politically prudent to advise him.

When the special session of the Senate convened on March 4, Kate was in the gallery, drawn by curiosity to see William again. To her surprise, he was not there. She did not understand it. Surely he could not be so indifferent to the honor of his high office that he did not wish to be sworn in on the momentous first day.

He was not the only new senator to fail to appear, she reminded herself as she walked home, but he was the only one whose absence disappointed her.

She was nearly home when she heard someone call out her name. She turned and looked up to see William Sprague approaching her on a magnificent stallion, the coal-black twin of his fallen white charger.

"Miss Chase," he said, raising his familiar black hat with the rakish rolled brim. The long yellow plume had been replaced by a feather of cardinal red.

"Governor Sprague," she replied, bowing gracefully to conceal her surprise.

"May I walk with you?"

When she nodded, he dismounted and walked beside her, leading his horse. "You look well."

"Thank you," she said. "You look late for your swearing in."

Too late, she realized that he would assume she had gone to the Senate to see him. He should not flatter himself, she thought indignantly. She often visited the Senate gallery to watch the workings of government, and she intended to continue regardless of his presence or absence.

"Yes," he said ruefully. "I was delayed in Providence, and have only just arrived. As it happens, it's a rather involved process to resign as governor, even of a state as efficiently run as Rhode Island."

"I can well imagine."

"I will be there tomorrow, if you should happen to return." He smiled, his gaze lighting warmly on hers, and she had to look away. "It would be good to know that I have an interested friend watching from the gallery."

"If I happen to be there," she said evenly, "I will look around and see if I find anyone who meets that description."

"You mean to say you do not?"

She halted and fixed him with a steady look. "I was not aware that we were friends any longer."

"Indeed?" he said, wounded. "What about all the letters we exchanged this past winter?"

"I don't believe that 'exchanged' describes it properly, but regardless, your recent letters could not have undone the letter you sent me last spring. Or have you truly forgotten it?"

"I have not forgotten it," William replied, with quiet calm, "but I do regret it."

"Then why have you not said so?"

"You have always understood me so well, I had hoped it would not be necessary."

"Even when apologies for dreadful behavior are not strictly necessary, they are very often desirable."

She started to walk away, but he quickly caught up to her. "Miss Chase, please. Let's go riding together and I will tell you everything."

She halted and looked him squarely in the eye. "I am not inclined to go riding with you today. If you have something to say to me, you should say it here and now."

He frowned, and glanced up and down the sidewalk warily, and drew closer. "I did not want to say this where anyone might overhear."

"Then lower your voice," she said, resolute.

He studied her, and when she did not flinch, he heaved a sigh of resignation. "Very well. A year ago, while traveling, I met a man from Columbus. Naturally I mentioned my acquaintance with Secretary Chase, and you, because you were prominent residents of that city. He knew Mr. Chase and had only praise for him, but he made an aside about your character that provoked my anger. When I demanded that he explain himself, he protested that it was common knowledge in Columbus that you had comported yourself inappropriately with a married man, much to the distress of his poor, scorned wife. He even named the gentleman—a Mr. Richard Nevins."

The sound of the horrid name made Kate's stomach lurch. "What exactly am I accused of?" she asked, but she quickly waved off the query. "Never mind. I don't want to know. A better question is why you peremptorily believed this stranger you had only just met instead of trusting what you knew of my character, why you simply accepted his word instead of asking me if there was any truth to his accusations."

"I was shocked and offended, and I acted in haste," William admitted. "But it's all right. I now know you did nothing wrong. When I was at the governors' conference in Altoona last September, I befriended a gentleman from the Ohio entourage, a native of Columbus. He told me that he was aware of the incident, and he insisted that although you were somewhat impetuous as a girl, your behavior was never unethical or immoral, and anyone who claims otherwise speaks either from jealousy, ignorance, or spite. He said everyone in Columbus, with the exception of an envious few, regarded you as a respectable young woman."

William clearly seemed to believe his explanation resolved the matter, but Kate fixed him with a steely gaze. "You mean to say that you've judged me innocent of these charges, not because your own observations of my deportment and character make them utterly impossible to believe, but because the testimony of yet another stranger persuaded you?"

William hesitated. "It was his testimony and my own observations together that persuaded me," he said. "I never should have listened to that first fellow, and I'm truly sorry I did."

"I'm sure you are," said Kate sharply, "now that you want a cotton trading permit for your friend Mr. Harris Hoyt."

"Who?" William's brow furrowed in confusion, until understanding dawned. "Oh, yes, that fellow. I would hardly call him a friend. We met at the Willard during one of my visits to the capital, and he told me such a sad tale of his longing for his wife and children and his worries about his cotton languishing in Texas that I was moved to write to your father on his behalf." He winced, chagrined. "At the risk of sounding like a fool, I trusted him in part because he shares a last name with some of my cousins, although of course there is no family connection."

Kate studied him intently, searching his face for the smallest nervous flicker that would betray a lie, but his expression was so pained and earnest that she felt her anger ebbing. "I don't know whether I should believe you."

"Kate, listen." He shifted the reins to one hand and took her hand with the other. "I swear to you, my interest in your friendship has not been some scheme to win a cotton permit. Surely you remember that my . . . fascination with you began not only before your father was in a position to dispense permits, but before the war, when none of us could have conceived that permits would ever be necessary."

Kate thought back to the ball in Cleveland in September before the presidential election and felt her resistance wavering. It was true; his romantic interest had preceded any economic necessity. Even then, she might not have believed him on his own, but Mr. Barney's and Mr. Cooke's recent remarks corroborated William's version of events.

"You said that you wanted us always to be honest with each other," she reminded him. "If you had done that, no estrangement would have come between us."

"And I'll regret that every day of my life, if you don't forgive me now."

The intensity of his words left her speechless for a moment, but she quickly regained her composure. "As a Christian, I must forgive you, and I do, but that does not mean I must accept your friendship again, or anything else."

"If you give me a second chance, I swear I will not disappoint you again." William pulled her closer, but she was mindful of passersby even if he was not, and she did not let him draw her too near. "Kate, I know I've made mistakes, but I'm certain that with your womanly moral influence, and your esteemed father's noble example, I can be a better man."

Kate felt a rush of gladness and heat and longing rise within her, but she was careful not to let it sweep her away. The prudent course would be to remember how he had hurt and disappointed her, and to ask him never to speak to her again. But although she had many admirers, and she enjoyed the friendship and company of other men, none of them made her feel the heady, powerful rush of passion that William made her feel. And William was the only man she had ever met who revered her father as much as she did.

"I will come to see you take your oath in the Senate tomorrow," she told him. "Afterward, you may escort me home. The day after, you may call, and if you make a favorable impression, my father might invite you to supper the following evening. That is where we will begin. Prove that you will be a true, enduring friend to me, and I may be willing to consider whether someday you could become something more."

"I will prove myself to you," William said fervently. "I swear it."

"You must promise me one thing more," said Kate. "If, whether after a few weeks or mere days, I conclude that you are no true friend to me, we will part amicably, and you will not trouble me again."

The hopeful light in his eyes dimmed somewhat, but he nodded. "I accept your condition," he said. "I'm not afraid of it, because I know you will not invoke it."

"Time will tell," she told him, hoping with all her heart that he was right.

Chapter Sixteen

$\mathcal{T}$he next day, Kate wore a new dress of lilac silk trimmed in purple ribbon and a bonnet adorned with wood violets and lilac tulle to the Senate gallery, where she sat in the front row and witnessed William Sprague being sworn in as the newest senator from Rhode Island. Afterward, when he walked her home, Kate found his conversation so engaging that she deliberately slowed her pace to prolong their time together. He called on her and Father at home the following day, and after he departed, Father admitted that he'd had some reservations about allowing him into their home, but Kate's explanation about his connection to Harris Hoyt had sufficiently eased his worries. Now, after seeing William again and looking into his eyes as they conversed, Father could not believe that he was unscrupulous. "He seems a good and decent man, at heart," said Father. "He should choose better friends and not squander his recommendations on men he scarcely knows, but I think he has a promising future and may do much good in the Senate." Almost as an aside, he added, "It's a pity he enjoys his tobacco and whiskey so much."

Kate agreed. Nearly all the men she admired most, including her father, abstained. Whiskey made William loud and boastful, and she wrinkled her nose at the odor of tobacco in his clothes and on his breath, but what troubled her most was what his habits said about his self-control. A man was not truly his own master if he could not refrain from indulging his appetites.

As spring brought blossoms and birdsong to Washington, so too did it illuminate the war-weary spirits of the people of the North. As soon as the sunshine dried the muddy roads and made them passable, General Hooker would be able to march the Army of the Potomac on to Richmond at last. In the meantime, enormous rallies sprang up in cities throughout the Union, loud outcries of support for President Lincoln and their brave soldiers—cheering crowds, rousing speeches, stirring martial music, thunderous artillery salutes—all to drown out the misery and defeatism of the Copperheads. On the last day of March, Kate and her father attended a massive Union rally at the Capitol, observing the speeches and the vast, cheering crowds from the dignitaries' platform alongside President Lincoln and his family, the other members of the cabinet, and William Sprague. Kate hoped word of their staunch support would reach the soldiers on the battlefield and the sailors at sea and hearten them, for she imagined very little else did.

William fulfilled her conditions, so when her father raised no objections, Kate allowed William to resume courting her. With every hour they spent together, every letter they exchanged, Kate found her faith in him growing, her confidence in his affection restored. And she observed that the more she trusted him, the more he endeavored to deserve that trust. She felt lighthearted and breathless when she heard his footsteps on their front stairs; when he was obliged to return to Rhode Island, she felt downcast and lonely and she counted the days until his return. She longed for his touch and treasured stolen kisses. Surely, she thought, she was falling in love, but her glow of delight was shadowed with apprehension.

In early April, when William asked her to marry him, she demurred and asked him if he had spoken to her father.

"I wanted to ask you first," he said. "If you refuse me, there's no point in asking your father."

"I regret that I can't accept your proposal today," she told him as kindly as she could. "You know that you have several habits I cannot abide."

William nodded unhappily. "Tobacco and whiskey."

"If you truly wish to marry me," she said, "abandon these vices and ask me again."

For a moment he only glared at her, mutinous and angry, and she thought he might storm away, but then he heaved a sigh of resignation and agreed.

Kate was impressed by how diligently he went about reforming his habits, although he was unbearable company during his first week without tobacco, irritable and scathing, but with soothing patience, she could usually cheer him out of his bad tempers. Eventually, as his physical vigor increased, his good spirits returned and he became quite companionable again. And so, in the middle of May, William asked her a second time to marry him.

His timing could not have been worse. Back in March, Father had again threatened to resign from the cabinet, this time because President Lincoln had decided not to renominate one of Father's appointees for the collector of internal revenue in Hartford, Connecticut. Furious, Father had declared that unless he was granted authority over his own appointments, he could not be useful to the president or the country in the Treasury and thus he would be obliged to resign. Thankfully, the president had managed to assuage Father's injured pride, but the underlying problem remained unresolved.

Then, in early May, the president instructed Father to investigate another one of his appointees, a Mr. Victor Smith, collector of the Puget Sound district in Washington territory, who had been accused of mismanaging his office, not through corruption but sheer bad judgment. Father entrusted the investigation to his assistant secretary, but before it was complete, and while Father was away from Washington on another campaign to raise money for the war, Mr. Lincoln dismissed Mr. Smith and appointed a successor. Enraged anew, and disregarding Kate's urgent pleas that he wait until the next day to allow his temper to cool, Father sent the president a solemn, caustic letter expressing his profound disappointment and anger that he had not been consulted. "If you find anything in my views to which your own sense of duty will not permit you to assent," he wrote, "I will unhesitatingly relieve you from all embarrassment, so far as I am concerned, by tendering you my resignation."

Kate agreed absolutely that Mr. Lincoln should have consulted Father about replacing his subordinates, and the president's timing was suspicious, but she wished her father would not so quickly threaten to resign whenever he was affronted. On May 11, she and Father waited at home for Mr. Lincoln to read the letter and respond—Father pacing grumpily in his study, Kate sewing trim on a new spring bonnet and mentally composing a letter of her own to persuade the president to reject her father's resignation.

The hours passed, their gloom deepening as twilight descended. Then, suddenly, a knock sounded on the door. Expecting a messenger from the White House, Kate bounded from her chair and reached the door before Will. Opening it, she discovered that the White House messenger was Mr. Lincoln himself.

"Mr. President," she said graciously, opening the door wider and noting, with a quick glance, that he carried her father's resignation letter. "What a pleasure it is to see you. Please, do come in."

"Thank you, Miss Chase," he said, his morose features forming a kindly smile as he removed his hat and entered.

By that time Father had reached the foyer. "Good evening, Mr. President," he greeted him stiffly.

Mr. Lincoln's brow furrowed and his eyes conveyed wounded regret. "Chase," he said, shaking his head. He placed his hands on Father's shoulders, the letter crinkling between his palm and Father's suitcoat. "Chase, here is a paper with which I wish to have nothing to do; take it back, and be reasonable."

Silently Kate inhaled deeply, pressing her hand flat against her waist to settle her nervous stomach. Father too was silent as Mr. Lincoln explained that he had been compelled by troubling reports from the Puget Sound district to remove Mr. Smith immediately, and it was by unfortunate coincidence, not design, that Father had happened to be away from Washington at the time. "I will leave the authority to name his successor entirely in your hands," he promised, but although Father looked mollified, Mr. Lincoln was obliged to plead awhile longer before Father agreed to withdraw his resignation.

Thrice now Father had submitted his resignation and thrice Mr. Lincoln had persuaded him to stay, but Kate knew even the president's vaunted patience was not infinite. Eventually the day would come when Father would loftily offer to quit and the president would gladly accept.

It was the next day, when her nerves were still raw from her latest narrow escape, that William asked her again to marry him.

"Speak to my father," she said. "If he does not object, then you may ask me again."

Two days later, William came to her, every line of his face arranged in determination. "I have reformed my habits, as you required," he said. "I have spoken to your father, and have received his blessing. Our bond has been tested by adversity and has grown stronger because of it."

Trembling, Kate nodded.

"Miss Kate Chase, my dearest darling, will you marry me?"

She took a deep, shaky breath. "I thank you for the honor you have shown me. I'll consider your proposal very carefully, and I'll give you my answer soon."

He regarded her for a long moment in silence, disappointed and incredulous. "I must say I expected you to have your answer ready. If you don't know whether you want to marry me today, how will you be any more certain in a week?"

She didn't know that she would be, but it would be cruel to tell him that. "My father approves, we know," she said, a slight tremor in her voice, "but now that this moment has come, I find myself at a loss, and in great need of a woman's counsel."

His face softened. "Of course," he said, taking her hand in both of his. "At a time like this, you wish you could seek your mother's guidance. I understand completely."

She knew he did—William, who had lost his father, would always understand that part of her that felt forever bereft and abandoned, beyond consolation.

"One week," she said, managing a smile. She did love him dearly. "One week and you will have your answer, for better or for worse."

He smiled wanly at her inadvertent echo of the marriage vow.

She wrote to the two aunts whose opinions she valued most, pouring her heart out to them, her hopes and her fears, all that she admired and cherished about William and all that worried her and left her uncertain. They wrote back immediately, with kindness and affection, and both separately told her that they did not know William well enough to judge his character, but he seemed to have a promising future and it spoke well for him that he had given up his most objectionable habits for her. They found no reason to urge her to refuse him, but in the end she must make up her own mind, trusting in her father's counsel and her own conscience.

Although Kate was grateful for their loving advice, she knew that their responses had sprung from generous hearts. What she truly needed was the counsel of someone who could examine the match with cool objectivity and pragmatism, and help her determine not only how happy she would be on her wedding day, but also how contented she was likely to be every year thereafter.

She called on Adele Douglas, described her plight, and confessed her uncertainties. "I love him," Kate concluded, "but I don't know if I should marry him."

Mrs. Douglas nodded and sank into a thoughtful silence, which she broke with the same question everyone asked: "What does your father say?"

"He gave his blessing, but he has some reservations. In all fairness to William, I suspect my father would have reservations regardless of the suitor in question."

"Of course. He's a loving, protective father, and you're his pride and joy." Mrs. Douglas studied Kate fondly. "Oh, my dear girl. You have so many excellent men in love with you. Some are more handsome than Senator Sprague, quite a few are similarly accomplished, and others are more intellectually equal to yourself. What is it about William Sprague that makes you consider marrying him instead of another?"

"It's something I cannot explain or define," she admitted. "When we're together—and even when we're not—I feel a . . . a sort of passion that I've never felt for any other man."

"I see." Mrs. Douglas looked amused. "Tell me, Miss Chase. I know your mother and your stepmother passed away when you were quite young, so I can only assume you never discussed marriage with them. What do you know of the marriage bed?"

"Very little," Kate admitted, a flush rising in her cheeks. "I know about my monthly cycles, of course, and about how children are brought into the world. I know something of kissing. My aunts tell me that my husband will teach me what else I need to know on our wedding night."

"Is that what they said?" Mrs. Douglas's smile deepened. "Well, my dear, whether you choose Senator Sprague or another gentleman, you and I will need to have another lengthy chat before your wedding night."

"I do not dread the embraces of a husband, as some young ladies do," Kate said in a rush, her face aflame.

Mrs. Douglas patted her hand. "And you should not discount that attraction, especially if it is mutual, but let us examine the practical facts with cool heads free of giddy romanticism."

"Yes," said Kate, relieved. "Yes, that's precisely why I came to you."

"The senator has satisfied your concerns about his abrupt severing of your friendship a year ago, as well as his involvement with Mr. Hoyt, has he not?" When Kate nodded, she said, "He has abandoned his worst vices at your request—as far as you know."

"As far as I know they are his worst vices," Kate echoed, startled, "or as far as I know, he has abandoned them?"

"I meant the latter, although I suppose the other is true too. In any event, he has shown that he will sacrifice to deserve your love. Not all men are willing to do that, and of those who are willing, not all are able."

"His triumph over his vices has raised him even higher in my esteem."

"It speaks well for his self-discipline," Mrs. Douglas acknowledged. "However, there is another, entirely unromantic matter that you must also consider: Senator Sprague's fortune."

"I would never marry a man solely for his wealth."

"No, of course you wouldn't, but you must consider his prospects." Mrs. Douglas paused. "I wish there were a more delicate way to put this, but I am aware that you do not have a personal fortune."

"That is so." Father must have told her—although perhaps his indebtedness was not quite the secret they supposed. It was ironic, she often thought ruefully, that her father ran the Treasury masterfully but his own finances very badly indeed. "I have only a very small bequest from my mother."

"Your future security, and that of your children, will depend upon how well Senator Sprague will provide for you," Mrs. Douglas said. "Not only does he possess considerable wealth, but he has proven himself to be industrious, persevering, and determined. His accomplishments suggest that you need not fear poverty."

Kate laughed shakily. "That would be a great relief, one that I confess is unfamiliar to me."

"I know we ladies prefer to speak of true love, but there is more to a successful marriage than affection and passion, although without them marriage can be very dull indeed."

Kate nodded, knowing she was right. "There is one more consideration."

Mrs. Douglas peered at her questioningly over the rim of her teacup.

"I cannot bear to leave my father."

Mrs. Douglas's hand froze for a moment, but then she carefully set her cup down upon its saucer. "I see," she said, her expression curiously guarded.

"For years I've devoted myself to helping him achieve his life's ambitions," Kate explained. "I can't bring myself to abandon him, or his noble cause, not when he is closer than he has ever been to fulfilling his destiny."

"When a young woman marries," Mrs. Douglas said carefully, "her husband should come first in her life, not second to her father."

"I know that," Kate replied miserably. "And yet, these are unusual circumstances. My father should be president—not for his own self-aggrandizement, but for the good of the country."

"I share your opinion."

"Senator Sprague reveres my father," Kate added. "I sincerely believe there is no reason why I cannot serve my husband's interests as well as my father's. Senator Sprague might agree that I should continue in my present role, for the good of all."

"He might," Mrs. Douglas admitted, with a little shrug and a wistful smile. "Your marriage might even help your father gain the White House, if Senator Sprague is as generous and devoted to your father as it seems. You can but ask him, and base your decision upon his reply."

Suddenly Kate felt inordinately happy. "I shall do exactly that," she vowed, and she thanked Mrs. Douglas profusely for her motherly advice. She knew what to do and say. The rest depended upon William.

A week after his third proposal, William called for Kate and they went riding together along the Potomac, and when they reached the secluded stand of willows, they dismounted and walked together in the shade, leading their horses. There Kate told him frankly that she would marry him, if he agreed that she need not relinquish the role she played in her father's life.

William frowned, dubious. "I had thought when I married to be master of my own household."

"My father will not command you," Kate assured him, reaching for his hand. "That is not why I ask this of you. You must see how I cannot abandon my duty to my father. He needs me." When William appeared unmoved, she quickly added, "If you prefer, we could have a long engagement. Perhaps we could marry in December after the presidential election."

"That's almost two years away."

She attempted a teasing smile. "Do you think you'll change your mind between now and then?"

"No, but I fear you might."

"I will not," Kate told him emphatically. "However, if you cannot abide my condition, I understand, and if you need more time to consider—"

"No." Suddenly he took her in his arms, his voice a rough, warm caress close to her ear. "If that's what I must do to have you, then that's how it will be."

Breathless, she tried to thank him, to tell him of her joy and gratitude, but his lips were upon hers, stealing the words from her mouth.

Afterward, they rode back to the Chase residence, happy and contented, and together they told Father that the matter was decided. With tears in his eyes, Father embraced Kate, and shook William's hand vigorously, and declared that it was his most ardent wish that they make each other very happy.

"God bear me witness that it will be the object of my life to see that Kate receives no detriment in my hands," William vowed solemnly. "If a life of devotion to her, and to yourself, can make me worthy of it all, I shall deem it well spent."

Father smiled beneficently, clearly moved, and Kate welled up with joy to see them together, the two men she loved so dearly. She had never before felt so happy, so blessed, so certain of her future contentment.

William departed soon thereafter, parting from her with a discreet kiss at the door. Still glowing with delight, Kate hurried off to fetch pen and paper so that she could keep her promise to Nettie that no one else would learn of her engagement before her dear sister.

In the days that followed, Father, Kate, and William shared the happy news with their family and closest friends. While all congratulated the couple, many of Kate's friends and acquaintances expressed surprise, if not outright shock. Worse yet, as Kate had expected, the friend whom she most dreaded to tell of her engagement proved to be the least happy to learn of it.

She had seen less of John Hay that spring as she had seen more of William, and John had noticed the difference, and had made half-hearted jokes about her neglect. She had hoped the news would not come as a complete surprise to him, but as she spoke, his expression became so thunderstruck and dejected that her announcement trailed off into silence.

"I hope you will be very happy together," John said stiffly, guessing the rest. "Sprague is a very fortunate man. I suspect he has no idea how fortunate."

"That is very kind of you to say."

"Not at all." He sounded almost angry. "Have you set a date yet?"

"No." She managed a light laugh. "Father and I would prefer a long engagement. William would not."

"I don't blame him. Sprague would be mad to give you any time at all to change your mind." Abruptly John rose. "Thank you for the honor of including me in the close circle of acquaintances to hear the news from you directly."

"Of course." She remained seated, studying him. "Are you leaving already?"

"Is there reason for me to stay?"

"I should say so," said Kate tearfully. "You are still my very good friend, John, and I think I'm going to need friends in the years to come."

In a moment he was by her side, holding her hands in his own as she bent her head to hide her tears. "Kate," he said, astonished. "Are you quite all right? Why are you so unhappy?"

"I—I don't know."

"I'm sorry I was a brute. Please don't weep on account of my careless cruelty."

"I'm not weeping, and you weren't a brute." She took a deep breath. "I'm all right. Please don't mention this to my father."

John snorted. "Of course not, but Kate—you seem profoundly unhappy."

She shook her head and tried to smile. "I'm merely overwrought. Making this decision, sharing the news, seeing the shock and worry on my loved ones' faces—"

"Not shock and worry, surely," said John. "Surprise, perhaps—"

"Perhaps. But I can't help suspecting that people believe I've made a terrible mistake."

"Well," John said carefully, "if *you* think you have, it's not too late. You've been engaged only a handful of days."

"I can't break off the engagement now, nor do I wish to," said Kate. "I love William. I'm just . . . anxious. I'm sure all brides feel this way, don't you suppose?"

John looked skeptical. "I know very little about the temperament of brides, but I do think you should insist upon a long engagement."

Kate agreed. She had seen so much of William lately that she was beginning to yearn for solitude, and that too contributed to her unusual bouts of nervous strain. So it was with mixed feelings that Kate bade farewell to William when the special session of the Senate ended and he returned to Rhode Island to look after his business. "I wish you were coming with me," he said, caressing her cheek with the backs of his fingers.

"I wish I were too, but I have obligations here." She gave him a teasing smile. "And you know we can't travel together unchaperoned."

"Of course not," he said, feigning alarm. "Who knows what sort of mischief we would get into?"

"I think *you* know, and that's precisely why a chaperone is required."

"But at the end of the summer, you're coming to Rhode Island to visit. If I have to do without you any longer than that I'll go mad."

"I'll come as soon as I can," she promised. "Nettie and Father too."

"Are we never to be alone?"

"On our wedding night."

"Then let us be married tomorrow."

"You know that isn't possible," she scolded teasingly. "I must have a new gown, and flowers, and I must plan the party—"

"You shall have everything you want. I swear it. Your wedding day must be as perfect as you desire. Fulfill your every wish. Spare no expense."

"You know I can't do that," said Kate, as startled by his vehemence as she was touched by his generosity. "I must be frugal. The bills will go to my father."

"Why should they, when I can easily pay them?"

"Darling William," said Kate tenderly. "He claims a father's right. Remember, that will be the last day he provides for me." She smiled mischievously. "After we are married, however, I give you permission to spoil me with as many trinkets and treasures as you wish."

"You will have them all," he vowed, kissing her cheek, and her neck, and the hollow of her throat. "And I will have you."

"Not quite yet," she said breathlessly, prying herself free from his embrace.

"Such exquisite torture," he lamented, but he let her go.

William's departure brought Kate a curious sensation of painful relief. She missed him, but in his absence she felt as if she could finally catch her breath and think. They wrote to each other every day, and as the early weeks of summer passed, their letters grew more affectionate, more passionate, more full of longing to be reunited. Father still had not agreed to set a wedding date—in fact, he would not even settle upon a time to travel to Rhode Island to meet William's family. Even after Nettie returned to Washington from school for her long summer holiday, brightening the home with her sweet ebullience, Father was often grumpy and petulant, and the more he insisted that he expected Kate to bestow the greatest measure of her loyalty upon her husband, the more she doubted his sincerity. As the days grew more sweltering, Kate showered her father in attention and affection, reassuring him whenever he made sorrowful asides about his impending loneliness, which he seemed to believe would descend like a shroud upon him the moment Kate and William exchanged vows.

As if to prove his willingness to relinquish the most prominent place in her heart, at the end of June, Father reluctantly agreed to allow Kate and William to meet for a brief, well-chaperoned visit with Mrs. McDowell at Buttermilk Falls in Upstate New York. It was an idyllic respite from the stifling heat of Washington and the grim miasma of war—and Father's exasperating, exhausting complaints. Although Mrs. McDowell rarely left them alone, the couple found that their separation had inflamed their desire, and they took sweet pleasure in stolen kisses and caresses whenever they could.

Kate returned home to find Father more peevish and gloomy than when she had left. It was then that she proposed the idea she had mulled over for weeks, awaiting the most opportune occasion to present it. As William had no permanent residence in Washington—like many bachelors in Congress, he had simply taken a suite of rooms at the Willard—it was impractical for Kate to give up her beloved home for her bridegroom's. After they married, the newlyweds could instead reside with Father in the mansion at Sixth and E streets, which was more than large enough to accommodate them all, as well as Nettie when she was home from school and their ever-shifting company of houseguests. At first William expressed some reluctance, but after Kate reassured him that he would not be subject to Father's commands, William satisfied another point of pride by purchasing the mansion from their landlord, for he insisted he could not make his home in another man's house. He and Father, who had his own pride to satisfy, worked out a scheme whereby Father would pay a certain amount of rent depending upon whether he was in residence or traveling, and they arranged to divide the other household expenses equitably. Kate's heart soared to see how cheerfully her gentlemen agreed to the arrangements, once she and William convinced Father that they truly would miss him if he moved elsewhere.

Resolving that troublesome matter made Father more amenable to setting a wedding date, and before long they chose November 12. Much relieved, Kate happily threw herself into the delightful toil of planning the ceremony and reception, ordering invitation cards from Tiffany, and choosing the menu, the flowers, and the guests with scrupulous care. She arranged for the Marine Band to serenade the guests, and it was with great pleasure that she accepted the talented Frederick Kroell's request to compose a new wedding march in her honor.

After a lifetime of worrying about extravagance and debt, she often veered from the path of sensible frugality in purchasing her trousseau, most of which she ordered from Paris. Of all the dresses and linens and lingerie she selected, she lavished the most care and attention to the design of her wedding costume—a splendid gown from Madame Hermantine du Riez of the Place Vendôme, fashioned of white velvet trimmed in white point lace, with a snug bodice and a long, elegant train. Her rich lace veil would be held in place by a dazzling parure of diamonds and pearls in an orange blossom pattern, a magnificent piece of jewelry William had commissioned for her wedding gift.

It was too important that the jewels be absolutely perfect for them to remain a surprise, William explained, and so he had asked General and Mrs. McDowell to accompany him to Tiffany in New York City to advise him on the design. It was Mrs. McDowell who suggested certain alterations so that parts of the tiara could be worn separately as a brooch and a necklace. William encouraged Kate to visit the jewelers to see how it was coming along, which Kate eventually did. The lavish beauty of the piece rendered her breathless and enchanted, but she nevertheless worried about the exorbitant expense and wrote to William to assure him she would be perfectly content with something less extravagant. "It is not extravagant in the general sense," he replied, although it certainly was, and he begged her to allow him to indulge her. "You know I am but gratifying my own desires when I contribute to your pleasure. I have earned the right to do this."

Secretly she was pleased he insisted, and she refused to feel even the slightest twinge of chagrin when newspapers ran sketches and descriptions of the jewelry—including the price, often wildly exaggerated as much as ten times its value. The days of reluctantly settling for linen and flowers were behind her.

Her bridegroom's generous gift was far from the only aspect of the wedding that fascinated the press, and in turn, their readers. Newspapers throughout the North and even some in the Confederacy eagerly reported new details as they emerged, often without bothering to confirm their veracity. Kate found their accounts amusing, but she turned away from the other, uglier stories carried in whispers throughout Washington. She knew that a few cynical, ignorant, envious gossips insisted that she cared nothing for the unworthy William, but craved only his millions; other, more offensive tales claimed that her father had arranged the match, sacrificing his dutiful daughter on the altar of his ambition so that his new son-in-law would bankroll his next bid for the presidency. For his part, the gossips said, the former Boy Governor enjoyed the ladies too much to devote himself faithfully to any particular one, even so great a prize as the Belle of Washington, and he had sought the alliance only in order to further his own political ambitions. It was all utter nonsense, and Kate disliked hearing the men she loved so unfairly vilified, but she had long ago learned not to allow the spiteful grumblings of the jealous throng to influence her.

William, ever more frustrated by their separation, continued to urge Kate to come to Rhode Island. The fresh sea air and sunshine would invigorate her, he insisted, and his family was eager to meet his bride and her illustrious father. Kate and Nettie prevailed upon Father to take a holiday from Washington, which was suffering its hottest summer in years. "Even the *New York Times* thinks you've earned a few days off," Kate reminded him, referring to a laudatory article they had printed in early May. In two months, the reporter noted, Father had persuaded the American people to purchase more than forty-five million dollars' worth of bonds to support the war effort, with demand for such investments ever increasing. In such favorable circumstances, the reporter declared, "Mr. CHASE may well spend a few leisure days away from his Department. Never before did the finances of any nation, in the midst of a great war, work so admirably as do ours."

At last, near the end of July, Father managed to extricate himself from his innumerable duties to make the trip north to Providence with Kate, Nettie, and their cousin Alice Skinner. Along the way they stopped in Newport and Boston, where the secretary of the treasury was appropriately received by local dignitaries, and where he and Kate renewed friendships with prominent gentlemen whose support Father would need at the Republican National Convention, now less than a year away.

From there they traveled to Providence, where William welcomed them enthusiastically. There too they were honored with a reception at City Hall and received by the first families of Rhode Island. Kate was well pleased to observe the influential gentlemen's keen interest in Father's potential candidacy, and her heart warmed to see William basking in his reflected glow. With Father's wise guidance, William could become a truly great man. When she regarded them together, she was struck by their differences—Father tall, fair, and dignified; William lithe, dark, and passionate—but within both men was the spark of greatness, and her ardent pride soared to think that she could be looking upon not one but two future presidents.

Naturally, as the daughter of the secretary of the treasury and the celebrated Belle of Washington, Kate received an abundant share of the dignitaries' attention, but in Providence she drew particular interest as the bride-to-be of their former governor. She received many warm regards and polite good wishes for her future happiness, but one spindly, white-haired grandmother leaned on her cane, peered at her curiously, and said, "So, you have a mind to become Mrs. William Sprague."

"Yes, I do," Kate replied.

Instead of offering the usual congratulatory remarks, the elderly woman nodded knowingly. "Have you met the family, then?"

"That great pleasure yet awaits me."

"Great pleasure?" The woman's eyebrows, two thin slashes of frost above cloudy blue eyes, rose in her wrinkled brow. "I see you've set your expectations high."

Kate felt mildly annoyed at her arch tone, but she reminded herself of the woman's age and smiled politely. "I have no reason not to."

"You do know about Hamlet, do you not?"

"*Hamlet*?" Kate echoed. "Shakespeare's tragedy?"

The white-haired woman studied her for a moment, her expression becoming oddly sympathetic. "I believe Mr. Shakespeare inspired the name, yes." She reached out and lay a gnarled hand on Kate's forearm. "Ask your betrothed to tell you about Hamlet before you marry him, dear. I cannot say any more than that, but I could not say any less either."

With that, the elderly woman hobbled off on her cane, leaving Kate staring after her, utterly astonished. Was her cryptic remark meant as a slight against William's limited formal education? She and William never discussed literature, for he was not much of a reader and Kate carefully avoided reminding him of the differences in their schooling.

The encounter so bewildered her that she wanted to ask William about the woman immediately, but when she glanced around the room, she could not find him. A few of his gentlemen friends were also absent, so she concluded that they had sequestered themselves in a drawing room somewhere to discuss business and politics confidentially. She did not see him again until the reception was ending, at which time she suggested they walk the half mile to their inn and allow Father, Nettie, and Alice to precede them in the carriage.

"I had an unusual conversation with a certain Mrs. Sloane," Kate began, taking his arm as they exited City Hall.

"The judge's widow?"

"I believe that is how she was introduced." Kate paused for a moment, and continued, lightly. "She made the most unusual request. She said I should ask you to tell me about Hamlet."

William stopped short. "Did she say why?" he asked, his voice strangely brittle.

"No, she didn't. It was all very mysterious. I wasn't aware that you were fond of Shakespeare."

"I'm not." William abruptly began walking again, and Kate was obliged to hurry or be dragged after him. "Did she say anything else?"

"No."

"Then don't give her another thought. She's a doddering old crone, not quite right in the head. Never believe a word she speaks."

"Consider me duly warned." Kate studied his profile as he strode along. His voice was husky, his eyes were red, and although they had left the reception far behind, the odor of cigars lingered about them. "You were smoking," she said, dismayed. "And drinking too, I suppose."

"What of it?" he said roughly, and then she smelled the brandy on his breath.

"You said you gave up those vices." They had reached their inn, but Kate halted at the foot of the front steps, unwilling to face Father and Nettie when she was so upset. "I would not have agreed to marry you otherwise."

"I did give them up," he replied. "I never promised I wouldn't take them up again from time to time."

"My condition was that you give them up entirely and for good," she said sharply. "I did not mean for you merely to set them on a shelf to take down again the next time the whim to indulge yourself seized you."

"I have proven that I can give up tobacco and drink when I choose," he countered. "Today, I chose not to. I am still the master of my habits, and that is what you wished me to prove. I have not violated your infernal conditions."

She stared at him, shaking her head, incredulous. "I cannot believe you think me gullible enough to accept that."

Setting his jaw, he seized her by the upper arm and propelled her through the front doors of the inn. "We're not going to debate the matter on the streets where all the world can stare and mock."

"You're hurting me," she said in a low voice, trying to walk as sedately as she could past the clerks and guests in the foyer.

His grip loosened as he steered her down the hall into the first unoccupied parlor he found. There he shut the door behind them, heedless of propriety. "It's not your place to command me."

"But it is my place to decide what sort of man I shall marry," she said, her voice rising, "and it is your obligation not to misrepresent yourself."

William shot back a sharp, sneering retort, and she replied in kind, and a terrible row ignited, and there were shouts and tears and insults hurled on both sides. Only later did Kate reflect that it was odd the concierge had not come running to find out what was the matter. Uninterrupted and undeterred, they argued on and on until they were spent, until they had almost forgotten the impetus for their fight.

Then a cold, tense silence descended upon the parlor.

For a long time they stood without speaking, Kate by the door with her hands clasped at her waist, William with his head bowed, supporting his weight on the back of an armchair.

"Perhaps," Kate eventually said, remembering how easy John Hay had made it sound weeks earlier, "we should break off our engagement."

William spun to look at her, shocked and wounded. "You would cast me aside over a single disagreement?"

"This was no mere disagreement," Kate replied, astonished that he did not see it. "There are fundamental differences of understanding between us that I fear we cannot overcome."

"It was a lovers' quarrel, nothing more." William strode across the room and tried to take her in his arms, but she delicately stepped out of his embrace. "If all betrothed couples broke it off after their first argument, no one would ever marry."

But it was not their first argument, Kate almost said, merely the first of such virulence and fire.

"Birdie," he said, managing a smile, the familiar endearment so tender on his lips that her tears resumed. "We let our tempers get the better of us, but that doesn't mean we love each other any less. We must learn to disagree, and even argue, without fearing that it will mean the end of us."

"I've never fought with anyone the way we fought today," Kate said shakily.

He put his hands on her shoulders and drew her close, and this time, desperate for comfort, she let him. "That's because we've never felt for anyone else what we feel for each other. Our passions inspire our love, but we will learn to master our tempers." She stiffened, and he must have felt it, for he added, "As we must master other vices. Kate, darling, I misunderstood your intention. I thought you only meant for me to prove that I could give up drink and tobacco, and once I proved my mastery, I was free to indulge or abstain as I desired."

She pulled away just enough to look him in the eye, and she let her look of supreme skepticism speak for her.

He smothered a laugh. "I understand how ridiculous that sounds, but it's the truth. Now that I understand you better, I will abstain forthwith and forevermore."

Her spirits lifted a trifle, but her disappointment lingered. "You were excessively ill-tempered when you first gave up your vices. Now we shall have to endure that unpleasantness all over again."

"No, actually, we shall not." He winced, chagrined. "Dearest little birdie, I scarcely tasted the brandy. After one swallow I discovered that it had lost all its appeal for me. And I did not smoke at all. The fumes that permeate my clothing come from other men's cigars, not mine."

"Then why did you not say so from the beginning?" Kate protested. "We could have avoided this entire ugly scene."

"I was too proud," he admitted. "When you came at me with your accusations, I didn't care for your presumption that I am yours to command—or for your apparent lack of faith in me."

The rebuke stung. Father had often complained that she was too willful, that she too often tried to command when she ought to submit, that she possessed an unwomanly desire for dominion, or worse, that it possessed her. Those were her greatest failings, he had admonished her on more than one occasion, and they were why she would never be as inherently lovable and adored as sweet, cheerful, compliant Nettie.

Had she attacked William with accusations, as he said? The argument had scraped her mind raw and she could not clearly recall the words they had exchanged before it. Perhaps if she had asked him why he smelled of liquor and cigars, rather than declaring what she thought she knew, he would have told her ruefully how the other gentlemen had made him seem complicit in their vices, and they would have had a good laugh about it.

"I'm sorry I didn't give you a chance to explain before I believed the worst," she said, drained and exhausted and unwilling to prolong the discord a moment longer. "It will not happen again."

"Can you promise me that?" His gaze was upon her, searching her face as if afraid of what he might find there. "Will you always keep faith in me? Because, Kate, if you cannot—I half believe your doubts will turn me into the man you fear I am, rather than the good man I could be with your constant, faithful, loving influence."

"I can promise you that, and I do," she said. "But in turn I ask that in the years to come, if any shadow of suspicion should fall upon you, you'll explain the truth to me before doubt has time to take root."

"That seems fair." William kissed her, tentatively. "Are we reconciled, then?"

She nodded. Perhaps she should have felt relieved and happy that their terrible quarrel had been resolved, but she felt upset and nervous and tense, sensations unfamiliar and unwelcome.

If Father, Nettie, and Alice were aware of the couple's disagreement, they gave no indication. Kate was relieved that she did not have to explain away the misunderstanding or justify their explosive tempers.

The next morning, when they departed for the Sprague family summer residence in Narragansett Pier, William was so kind and solicitous that Kate almost could not believe he was the same man with whom she had been embattled in a shouting match the day before. As for herself, she felt subdued and exhausted to the marrow. When her father began to fret that she seemed to have taken ill, she feigned liveliness for his sake, wondering how it could be that no one detected the strain between her and William.

It was little wonder, she thought later, that her introduction to the Sprague family was stilted and uncomfortable. She made a far less dazzling impression than any of them had expected, but in her listlessness, she did not care. William's mother—Madame Fanny, as she preferred to be addressed—was likable enough, a weathered yet spirited woman of strong opinions and independent thought, but Kate found her future mother-in-law's constant scrutiny wearying. William's sisters, Almyra Sprague and Mary Ann Nichols, were so awestruck by the illustrious Chases that they could scarcely stammer out complete sentences, rendering conversation impossible and their company tiresome. Kate was torn in her opinion of Amasa Sprague, William's elder brother, his ostensible business partner who was too preoccupied with his first love, horses, to involve himself very much in A. & W. Sprague Company. Amasa could be amusing and genial when he made the effort, and he evidently had a great many friends, but Kate found him crude and ill-mannered, with a bad habit of making critical jokes at everyone else's expense. When Kate grew tired of pretending to find his constant stream of comic invective entertaining, she snapped at him, which startled William and plunged the gathering into an awkward, painful silence.

It came as a great relief a few days later when Father returned to Washington and other young people from William's extended family joined them, making up a younger, merrier party than the one that had witnessed Kate losing her temper with Amasa. As the days passed, the sunshine and ocean breezes revived Kate's spirits and restored her fresh bloom of health just as William had promised. They still felt bruised from their terrible row, but they treated each other gently, and before long their old affection and desire returned—strengthened, it seemed, by their relief that they had survived a frightening test of their bond.

It was a glorious summer. Kate loved cruising along the Atlantic coast in the Sprague yacht, her skin warm and blushing from the sun, her auburn locks dancing free of her bonnet in the refreshing breezes. At night the young people would sit out beneath the stars and sing, or call out musicians and dance on the piazza. In their company the war faded away, and Kate could almost forget the dashing young soldiers with whom she had danced and flirted before they met their gruesome deaths on the battlefield. For a time she did not have to think about the stench of death and decay permeating Washington City, or about the thousands of grievously wounded soldiers suffering in makeshift hospitals in private homes and public edifices, or the thousands of poor, desperate contraband who eked out a shabby living in the refugee camps that had sprung up in alleyways in the colored neighborhoods. She could put aside for the moment worries about her father's conflicts with Mr. Lincoln, and Mr. Seward, and for that matter most of the cabinet with the exception of Mr. Stanton. She allowed herself to be seduced by luxury, comfort, and the ineffable sense of safety that only great wealth could bestow.

But the war, and her father's work, and her awareness of her responsibilities never entirely left her thoughts, and as summer faded and an autumn chill infused the ocean mists, she knew it was time to go home.

On their last night in Rhode Island, Kate was packing her trunk for the return journey when William came by her room to see if she needed his help, and took advantage of her solitude to steal a quick, discreet kiss. "I think you may need another trunk for all this," he said, eyeing the garments draped over the bed and folded in neat piles upon the chairs.

"Everything fit on the way here," she retorted, smiling. "Everything will fit on the way home."

"How many trunks would we need for your glorious trousseau, I wonder?" he teased. "It's a very good thing you decided not to break our engagement that day in Providence. I can't imagine how you would pay for everything you've already acquired if you were suddenly no longer the future Mrs. William Sprague."

Kate's hands froze in the middle of folding a soft cotton chemise. "My father is responsible for my expenses until we marry," she said stiffly. "He sold the farm in Cincinnati to pay for the wedding. You know that."

William laughed. "Of course I do. I also know that your father will defer many of those bills until after we are wed, at which time they will become my responsibility." He took her hands. "Birdie, don't be upset. It's my great pleasure to indulge you. You know that."

"I do." She managed a smile. "You are the very soul of generosity."

And as long as she was his, he would continue to be.

The next day, they departed Rhode Island for New York, where Kate and William left Nettie at school and spent a few days with the Barneys before continuing on to Washington. Father welcomed them gladly, though not without admonishing them for delivering Nettie to Miss Macaulay's school several days late.

William remained in Washington for less than a week before returning to Rhode Island, his family, and his mills. Kate missed him very much, but she took comfort in knowing that after they were married, and the next session of Congress began, he would surely be obliged to reside in the capital and make only sporadic visits to Rhode Island rather than the other way around.

Embracing any distraction from her worries and loneliness, Kate resumed her role as her father's hostess with renewed vigor even as her wedding preparations continued. The war had dragged on in Kate's absence, and political maneuvering had continued to alternately promote and thwart her father's ambitions. Father was intensely dissatisfied with the ineffective workings of the cabinet, for rather than present war matters to the entire group for discussion, the president consulted only Secretary Stanton and General Henry Halleck. "I look on from the outside," Father grumbled, "and, as well as I can, furnish the means to enact the strategies they alone decide." Disgruntled, he had embarked on a speaking tour of the West ostensibly to escape the strife, but also to enlist support for his own presidential run. His audacity had earned him the ire of Mr. Lincoln's allies, though not, apparently, the president himself, who seemed incapable of hatred.

General Hooker had suffered a crushing defeat at Chancellorsville in late June, and afterward, in a bit of theater Kate found uncomfortably familiar, he had submitted his resignation in protest over a dispute with army headquarters. President Lincoln had accepted it and appointed General George Meade as his successor. The surprising turn of events greatly distressed Father, who had long supported General Hooker and had recently returned from visiting him in the field.

Father was also displeased with rumors from Vicksburg that, perhaps out of sheer boredom from the siege, General Grant had fallen back into his old habits of excessive drinking. The general was, a journalist warned Father in a private letter, "Most of the time more than half drunk, and much of the time idiotically drunk." Mr. Lincoln had heard similar reports, but when he and Secretary Stanton ordered an investigation, they concluded that General Grant's habits had been greatly exaggerated and evidently did not interfere with his ability to win battles, and so no action was taken against him. To Father's disgust, Mr. Lincoln even joked that if he knew what brand of whiskey the general favored, he would immediately distribute bottles of it to his other generals.

But thankfully, not all news of the war was distressing. A few days after General Hooker had been relieved of his post, General Lee's invasion of the North was halted in a tremendously bloody battle at Gettysburg. Then, on Independence Day, word reached the capital that General Grant had taken Vicksburg after a long and wearying siege, and five days later, Port Hudson, the last remaining Confederate fort on the Mississippi, had surrendered. Most heartening of all, Negro regiments were marching in Washington and on to the battlefield, where they fought as courageously as any of their white comrades. Father, who had argued for putting rifles in the hands of colored men from the outset of the war, and had long supported his friend Frederick Douglass's efforts to organize colored regiments, regarded the president's newfound approval with wry amusement. "The President is now thoroughly in earnest in this business," he wrote to a friend, "and sees it much as I saw it nearly two years ago."

Thanks in no small part to the fierce determination of the new regiments, at long last the war seemed to be turning in favor of the Union, but at a terrible cost, with the tallies of the wounded and the dead so staggering they defied comprehension.

Then, just as her hopes for a future of peace and contentment were rising, Kate received a letter from William that threw her back into uncertainty, only three weeks before the wedding. "I fear I shall be very cross for a few days as I have stopped the use of the weed which stills but does not satisfy," he warned her. Tobacco was a dangerous indulgence, he admitted, because after it followed "brandies and whiskies, then dyspepsia and an unhappy life. Look out for this won't you my love."

Kate did not know what to think. Had William resumed his old vices after their quarrel, or had he never relinquished them at all? She did not know which possibility was worse—that he had lied to her in Providence or that he had returned to drink and cigars despite the assurances he had given her in the aftermath of their terrible row. Either way, William seemed to have forgotten what he had told her then, or else he believed *she* had.

After brooding over his letter, she told herself resignedly that he intended to abandon his vices before the wedding, and that was what mattered most. She could not ask more of him than that, and in any case it was too late to end their engagement over something anyone else would regard as a small matter.

On the day she received William's letter, Kate attended the theater with John Hay, where they watched Maggie Mitchell perform in *The Pearl of Savoy*. The story told of Marie, a lovely young peasant girl whose love for a peasant boy was thwarted by a licentious nobleman who desired her for himself. Through his cruel manipulations, Marie's family would lose their farm unless she consented to be his, and, torn between her innocent love for the peasant boy and her devotion to her virtuous father, the tormented Marie went mad. Thoroughly absorbed, Kate was unaware that she wept until she felt John's hand upon hers and realized her face was wet with tears.

"Are you quite well?" John asked quietly, his sympathy and concern evident in every line of his face. Suddenly she was struck by the unexpected, impossible thought that if she were engaged to him instead, she might never know the intense passion she felt with William, but she would never find herself shaken by uncertainty or doubt either.

But it was too late for such considerations—much too late.

"I was merely swept away by the melodrama," she murmured, managing a smile and drying her tears on a handkerchief trimmed in elegant lace. It was another lovely trifle she had purchased as part of her trousseau, something William would eventually pay for—and she would too, in a very different sense.

Chapter Seventeen

NOVEMBER–DECEMBER 1863

$\mathcal{K}$ate's first thought when she woke on the morning of November 8 was that in exactly a year's time, her marriage would be approaching its anniversary, and her father would be elected president of the United States. She did not allow herself to consider that either event was anything less than a certainty. She loved William and longed to be his wife, and she had faith that as soon as they were united, all of their petty little squabbles and disagreements and doubts would fall away.

As for her father's great ambition, there was no reason to believe he would not win the presidency in 1864. No president had won a second term since Andrew Jackson in 1832, so Mr. Lincoln's status as the incumbent was more likely to work against him than in his favor. Father was also second only to the president as the most prominent Republican in the nation, with the possible exception of Mr. Seward, who had become too good a friend of Mr. Lincoln's to challenge him for his office.

Not so Father, and despite the demands of his responsibilities in the Treasury, he had not neglected his politicking. Although the most illustrious and ambitious people in Washington eagerly sought invitations to dinners at the Chase residence, Kate always found a place at the table for humbler gentlemen who came to the capital on the business of their modest cities and tiny hamlets, if the slightest possibility existed that they might be delegates to the Republican National Convention the following June. Father spent many a late night alone in his study composing hundreds of letters to provincial officials, influential generals, congressional leaders, and sympathetic newspapermen, reminding them of the regrettable failures of the Lincoln administration and suggesting how his own would differ. Whenever he addressed potential supporters, however, he was careful never to explicitly acknowledge that he intended to run. Instead he denied that he coveted the presidential chair, but said that he would accept it if that was the will of the people.

Earlier that autumn, Father and the other cabinet secretaries had observed Mr. Lincoln's growing anxiety as crucial October elections in Ohio and Pennsylvania had approached, to be followed by congressional elections in other states in November. The midterm elections the previous year had been disastrous for the Republicans, and if the Peace Democrats gained more high offices that year, it would be an unmistakable sign that Northern support for the war had drastically eroded—a revelation that would surely demoralize the Union army and hearten the enemy. With the Ohio election a week away, Father had spoken to the president and offered to return to his home state to promote Republican candidates there. Mr. Lincoln had agreed, and so Father had traveled throughout Ohio, meeting with eager supporters at every stop, attending rallies, and urging Republicans to the polls. Wherever he spoke he addressed the pressing issues of the war, slavery, and Reconstruction, but even as he championed the local ticket, he denigrated the president. Mr. Lincoln was honestly and earnestly doing his best, he would declare, even if the war was not being prosecuted as swiftly as it ought, and if under a different leader, mistakes might have been avoided and misfortunes averted. Father had invited a journalist from the Associated Press to accompany him, so Mr. Lincoln had been well aware of the content of Father's speeches, and yet he had offered not even the smallest rebuke, which Kate found astonishing and remarkably shortsighted. Although Father's tour drove Republicans to the polls in record numbers, giving Mr. Lincoln the decisive victories in Ohio he desperately needed, Father had also taken the opportunity to advance his own presidential ambitions, which Mr. Lincoln could not afford. It was almost as if Mr. Lincoln was not inclined to seek a second term, or he was unaware that the election was only a year away.

Kate knew how swiftly a year could pass, which was why her first thought on the morning of November 8 was of the election, but her second thought, as she threw back the quilt and hurried to wash and dress, was that she had a great deal to do before her wedding in four days' time, and lolling in bed would accomplish none of it.

The wedding of Kate Chase and William Sprague would be, as every newspaper throughout the North concurred, the social event of the season, perhaps of the decade. Fifty of their closest friends and relations would gather in the Chases' parlor for the ceremony, which would be presided over by Episcopalian bishop Thomas Clark of Rhode Island, and nearly five hundred more would join them for the reception immediately following. President and Mrs. Lincoln would attend, as would the most celebrated members of the Washington elite, including all of the cabinet secretaries and their wives, with the exception of Postmaster General Montgomery Blair, who bore a particularly virulent grudge against Father and had recently made ridiculous, incendiary speeches falsely accusing Father of all manner of outrageous crimes. His absence would be remarked upon in the press, naturally, but he would not be missed.

Kate was never happier than when she was planning and hosting a grand event, and the wedding would surely be her triumph, ushering in what she had resolved would be a glorious period culminating in her father's inauguration in March of 1865. She only wished that William were there to enjoy those last few days of anticipation and excitement by her side, but business kept him in Rhode Island, as it had for most of their engagement. Kate missed him terribly and longed to see him again, and from his letters, she knew he felt the same. His passion for her seemed to drive him nearly mad sometimes, and when she thought of how they would at last consummate their long-denied yearnings, she grew weak and faint from desire.

Two days before the wedding, while William was en route to Washington City with an entourage of more than fifty Rhode Island friends and relatives, her true and faithful friend John Hay put together an excursion for Kate, her bridesmaids, and several mutual friends. The merry group spent a delightful day at Mount Vernon, which was adorned in the full radiance of its autumn beauty.

As the steamer carried them back to Washington, Kate stood at the railing, savoring the sunshine and bracing river winds while her companions told stories and jokes nearby. The beautiful scenery had made her contemplative, her thoughts circling around her impending transformation from bride to wife. She understood well that she had risen high in her career as her father's official hostess, but although she enjoyed independence and success, she felt certain that she had not yet reached the pinnacle of all that she could become. She was surrounded by kind friends and many others who were ready to flatter and do her homage. She was accustomed to command and be obeyed, to wish and be anticipated—and yet she was prepared, without a sigh of regret, to lay everything upon the altar of her love in exchange for a more earnest and truer life, one long dream of happiness and devotion. That was what she wanted, and yet she felt a stir of trepidation and impending loss.

It was a relief when John interrupted her reverie. "You look so lost in thought I hate to disturb you," he said, resting his elbows upon the railing and grinning up at her. "Especially since I come bearing bad news— but also, I hope, some good news."

She smiled fondly back. "Tell me the bad news first, and then comfort me with the good."

"As you wish." He hesitated, grimaced, then plunged ahead. "Mrs. Lincoln is unlikely to attend your wedding."

"But she and Mr. Lincoln are expected," Kate protested. "Why would they not come?"

"The Tycoon will be there," John quickly assured her, "but I overheard the Hellcat tell her dressmaker that she expects to be struck down with a bad headache that day."

"Does she indeed?" Indignant, Kate folded her arms and turned around to lean back against the railing. "She would snub me on my wedding day?"

"I'm afraid so. Nicolay overheard her sneer that she would not 'bow in reverence to the twin gods, Chase and daughter.'"

The insult stung. "Quickly, tell me the good news before I say something unbecoming a lady."

John grinned as if he wished she would. "The good news is the same as the bad. Her Satanic Majesty will not be present to spoil your wedding with her imperious scowls and demands."

Kate laughed, her anger dispelled. "There is that. Well, her absence won't ruin the day for me, and in fact is likely to improve it. I know she's fond of William, but if she wants to deny herself the pleasure of what is sure to be a wonderful party out of the spite she bears me, that's her prerogative."

"She would rather gouge out her own eyes, I think, than to behold you in all your bridal glory." He hesitated. "I confess it will pain me somewhat too, and you know why, but I won't embarrass either of us by saying any more than that."

"Thank you, John." She clasped his hand in both of hers, grateful that he would not again remind her she still had time to change her mind. "You're a true friend."

It seemed too much to hope that John and William could become friends someday too, but Kate would hope for it nonetheless.

Later that evening, William and his traveling companions arrived in Washington, and after settling into their rooms at the Willard, they gathered at the Chase residence for a late reception. The moment William saw her, his face lit up with love and joy and yearning, and when he embraced her and murmured affectionate words in her ear, her spirits soared. He bore not a trace of whiskey or tobacco on his breath or in his clothing; his eyes were bright, his voice clear. Her heart welled up with love and gratitude to know that he had kept his promise to abandon his vices. She would marry a good and sober man, a man who adored her, and whom she adored in return.

The next day passed in a swift, dizzying blur of welcomes, reunions, and last-minute preparations, but the bride and groom spent it mostly apart. The Chase residence was so full of family from Ohio and New Hampshire that throughout the morning and afternoon Kate never had a moment to herself. That was an unexpected blessing, for she did not want to be alone with her thoughts. As thrilled as she was by the fuss and celebration, the irrevocability of the solemn vows she and William would soon exchange filled her with nervous excitement and apprehension, and if she dwelled upon it too long, her chest constricted until she almost could not take a breath.

As twilight approached and the house quieted, Kate found herself restless and brooding, her mind racing with the details of the ceremony and reception. Earlier that day, John, anticipating her need for distraction, had invited her to accompany him and a few friends to the theater to see Mr. John Wilkes Booth perform the starring role in *Romeo and Ju-*

liet. "Thank you, but no," Kate had replied dryly. "I intend to retire early, and a tragic romance that ends in death is unlikely to induce sweet dreams on the eve of my wedding." But as she climbed the stairs to her chamber on her last night as a maiden, with Mrs. Douglas's startling revelations about the marriage bed crowding into the forefront of her thoughts, she almost wished she had accepted.

Just as she was beginning to undress, she heard outside on the street below the faint but mellow sound of men's voices raised in song. William's smiling face appeared in her mind's eye, and her heart leapt with delight as she hurried to the window to find a crowd of men gathered around the front stairs offering up a beautifully harmonized rendition of "Aura Lee." Searching the faces of the singers, she did not see William, but she quickly recognized the men as soldiers from the Seventeenth Infantry, with John Hay in the middle of the throng, singing with tender gusto.

Warmth and happiness flooded her as she enjoyed the serenade, smiling down upon the singers, exchanging smiles with Nettie and Alice and others as they appeared at the windows, beckoned by the song. Her gaze often lingered upon John, and when he grinned mischievously up at her, she knew that he wished her well.

The singers next performed "When the Corn is Waving, Annie Dear," and concluded their concert with "I Will Be True to Thee." Then they all doffed their hats, bowed, and strolled on. John lingered to hold her gaze for a long moment, and to offer her an encouraging smile. Then he too replaced his hat and walked away.

Kate watched until he caught up with his friends and they rounded the corner and disappeared, and then she drew the curtains and finished preparing for bed. Nettie, who had been displaced from her own chamber by visiting cousins, soon joined her, as bright and happy and as unready for sleep as the first robin of spring. "It's all so lovely and romantic," she gushed as she climbed into bed and drew the quilt up to her chin. "If Mr. Hay were not so very old, I should like to marry him."

Kate felt an inexplicable sting of jealousy. "He's not 'so very old.' He's only a year older than I. Goodness, you must think William is practically ancient."

Nettie's guilty look told her that was not far from the truth. Kate laughed and turned out the light.

She put her arm around her sister when Nettie snugged up close, but although she closed her eyes, sleep was slow in coming. Her thoughts swirled with all that the next day would bring, and her heart was alive with reverence. For an hour, perhaps two, she lay awake praying that she would completely fulfill her new role as wife, and that to William, her dearest beloved, she might become companion, friend, and advocate, so that he would be a husband entirely satisfied. All that existed of love and beauty, nobleness and gentleness, were woven into her fair dream, and she believed with all her heart that no future could be brighter than that of their two lives united as one.

And when she thought of their wedding night, when she would be folded at last in her husband's loving arms—oh, the sense of ineffable rest, joy, and completeness that would fill her then, a glimpse of heaven for purity and peace. All strife ended, all regret silenced, in William's strong arms she would find a lover, a protector, a husband to be cherished. Every thought, every desire, every feeling merged with her one longing to make him happy—William, the first and only man who had found lodging in her heart.

It was a glorious wedding.

No matter what followed after, nothing would ever tarnish her memories of that perfect, golden evening when all of Washington celebrated the union of the Belle of Washington and the Boy Governor.

By half past seven o'clock, carriages lined Sixth and E streets, bringing traffic to a standstill as the Washington elite awaited entrance to the Chase residence and the social event of the season. A large, good-natured crowd of spectators filled the sidewalks, eager to admire the distinguished guests in all their finery. Many onlookers craned their necks to peer through the Chases' windows, hoping for a glimpse of the lovely bride in her gown and jewels, but their attempts were thwarted by large mirrors that had been hung inside the window frames, turned inward to reflect and enhance the scene and give the illusion of more expansive rooms. Cabinet secretaries, generals, diplomats, dignitaries, and their ladies arrived, smartly attired in dashing uniforms or splendid gowns of silk or satin or velvet in a dazzling array of colors.

Mr. Lincoln arrived in a private carriage alone and unheralded, his shoulders bent with the burden of his office, his expression careworn and weary, acknowledging with a gracious bow the burst of cheers and applause that greeted him. He was quickly ushered into the drawing room, where William, clad in rich, elegant black, and the most intimate circle of friends and family awaited the appearance of the bride.

When Kate entered the room on her father's arm, she knew by the murmurs and the intake of breath that she had rendered them awestruck, resplendent in her white velvet gown and magnificent jewels. The Marine Band struck up the newly composed "Kate Chase Wedding March" as she processed down the aisle after her lovely bridesmaids—Nettie, her cousin Alice Skinner, and Ida Nichols, one of William's nieces. When they reached the front of the room where Bishop Clarke stood smiling benevolently, his open Bible in hand, Father kissed her on the cheek and entrusted her to William, who regarded her with shining eyes as he took her hands, as awestruck as all the rest.

The bishop led them in prayer, spoke on the profound nature of the marriage bond, and guided the exchange of vows. Then, with a final benediction and a sweet, chaste kiss, they became husband and wife.

Applause rang out, and as the couple accepted warm embraces and congratulations from those dearest to them, the doors to the parlors were flung open so that all their guests could enjoy the wonderful moment. Before Kate was whisked off to open the reception, Mr. Lincoln bent to kiss her cheek and offer his warm good wishes. "I am sorry Mrs. Lincoln could not attend," he said. "She would be here, but her heart is too mournful yet for such a merry celebration."

"I understand," Kate assured him, sensing his discomfort with the half-truth. Not even a deliberate snub from the First Lady could diminish her joy on such a glorious occasion. "I hope that her sufferings will ease with time."

The president thanked her and moved on to congratulate her father, while Kate took her husband's arm and let him escort her into the reception. The doors between two adjacent parlors had been opened to create one grand hall, elegantly draped in the national colors and glowing in the warm gaslight, made even more brilliant by the reflecting mirrors. While the Marine Band serenaded them from a rear alcove, Kate, William, Father, and Madame Fanny met at the top of the room and accepted congratulations and good wishes from the hundreds of guests who passed through the receiving line. "You are magnificent, my darling," William told Kate in a brief respite between handshakes and greetings, and thereafter he murmured tender endearments whenever a guest's slower pace afforded a momentary lull.

When all the guests had been properly received, the servants cleared the rear parlor for dancing. With the long train of her luxurious gown swept over her arm, Kate led the first dance, a lancers, with her father's friend Mr. Richard Parsons, who had introduced her to William in Cleveland years before. The band played for hours, and the rooms were filled with laughter and music, and champagne and cider flowed and toasts were offered in abundance. When the revelers needed refreshments they proceeded upstairs to the dining room to partake of the lavish buffet arranged by the Washington caterer F. P. Crutchet—galantines of truffles, patés, terrines, aspics, veal salad, oysters, rolls, and fourteen dozen roast partridges.

Mr. Lincoln honored them with his presence until eleven o'clock, and around midnight, the other guests began to disperse, fatigued but exhilarated from the wonderful evening. John Hay was among the last to go, and when he came to bid Kate good-bye, he seemed content, and with a wicked grin he assured her that Mrs. Lincoln would seethe with jealousy when she heard how splendid the wedding had been.

William found her as the last guests departed, and she felt her pulse quicken as he took her hand. Before long only their houseguests remained, but they graciously withdrew after bidding the newlyweds good night.

"At last," William murmured as he and Kate retired to their bridal chamber alone. There, with the doors shut tight against the cares of the world, Kate discovered the bliss and fire of William's embraces, and as she fell asleep in his arms afterward, she felt whole, and wholly loved, for the first time.

The next evening at five o'clock, Kate and William embarked on their wedding trip accompanied by a large bridal party—Nettie; cousin Alice Skinner; Madame Fanny; William's two sisters, Almyra and Mary Ann; his brother, Amasa; Amasa's wife, Mary; and William's three groomsmen. So that they might be shielded from curious gawkers, Mr. William Prescott Smith of the Baltimore and Ohio Railroad had provided them with a private railcar, a courtesy he had extended to Father on several previous occasions, though usually only for official business. They spent the night in Philadelphia before continuing on to New York City, where they took rooms at the Fifth Avenue Hotel.

On Sunday morning, after attending church services with the Barney family, the wedding party spent the day sightseeing and paying calls, with Nettie in particularly high spirits, knowing that only a few blocks away, her classmates were toiling over their books while she ran free. Supper was another lavish, lighthearted affair, with jokes and merry stories and happy reminiscences of the marvelous wedding. Kate was obliged to guide the conversation elsewhere whenever William and Amasa boorishly bandied about the value of the great many wedding gifts the couple had received, which the newspapers estimated to be in excess of one hundred thousand dollars, but otherwise all was pleasant. Afterward, when she and William withdrew to their private chamber, his caresses made her forget anything he ever might have done to annoy her.

She drifted off to sleep in his arms, sated and content, only to wake abruptly in the darkness. "Kate, darling," William said urgently, shaking her. "Get up and dress as quickly as you can. We must flee."

"What's wrong?" she asked groggily, crawling out from beneath the covers. Before he could reply, the distant clanging of the alarm bell registered and shocked her fully awake. The hotel was on fire.

Quickly they threw on their clothes and raced into the hall, pounding on the doors of their companions' chambers in case they had not heard the warning. Outside on the pavement, breathless and frightened, Kate embraced Nettie and Alice and counted heads to be sure all of their loved ones were safe.

For two hours they stood outside watching and shivering in the cold as the firefighters battled the blaze, sharing cloaks and shawls with those who had neglected to snatch up their warm wraps in their haste to evacuate. Eventually only smoke and the odor of charred wood remained to mark the defeated blaze. William learned from the fire chief that the fire had begun in the boiler room and had quickly spread to the laundry, drying, and engine rooms within the hotel basement. An insufficient amount of hose had prevented the firemen from extinguishing the blaze sooner, but the chief was satisfied that it had been put out, and the guests were allowed to return to their rooms.

After all the excitement Kate found it difficult to settle down to sleep again, but eventually she did—only to be jarred awake not two hours later by more clanging alarms. "There must be some mistake," she said, scrambling back into her clothes, but she and William nevertheless again hurried down the hallway pounding on friends' doors, down the stairs, and outside, where the hotel guests mingled in consternation and confusion. The firemen quickly determined that a fire had been set to the woodwork beneath the stairway on Twenty-Fourth Street, and after it was extinguished, the chief told William grimly that it was evidently the work of an incendiary. "Thieves take advantage of the confusion to make off with whatever they can carry," he said, quickly adding that the police had prevented anyone from leaving the hotel with any parcels or luggage, thus thwarting the villains.

It was some time before the guests were again allowed to return to their rooms, but by then Kate, William, and their companions were so shaken that they only hesitantly went inside, and once there, they stayed awake until morning. Dread had stolen over Kate as soon as the fear of immediate danger had passed, inexplicably strong and steadily increasing, until with a sudden shock of recognition she understood its source.

"William, darling," she said shakily. "This fire—it is a terrible omen. Something dreadful is going to happen."

Bleary-eyed and half-asleep in his chair, William regarded her in bewilderment. "Something dreadful *has* happened, I would say. The hotel has suffered some expensive damage thanks to those malicious would-be thieves, and we've all lost a good night's sleep."

"Yes, that's dreadful too, but something else, something even more dire, awaits us." She knew she sounded foolish and hysterical, but she could not be silent. "I've witnessed terrible hotel fires before, and each was followed by a dreadful calamity. On the night Mr. Lincoln was elected, the Neil House in Columbus burned to the ground, and soon thereafter, the South seceded from the Union and war began. Early in the war, you'll remember, the Willard Hotel caught fire. The New York Fire Zouaves successfully fought it and saved the building, but Colonel Ellsworth was killed in the taking of Alexandria only weeks later, shot to death in a hotel." She pressed her hand to her heart and willed it to stop racing, all in vain. "And now, two fires in one night—surely that portends some terrible disaster."

"Birdie," protested William, rising from his chair to take her in his arms. "Don't be distressed. You describe coincidences, nothing more."

"How can you be so sure?"

"Because signs and omens are the stuff of superstition. They have no power beyond what frightened minds give them." William took her hands and smiled encouragingly. "Come, now. You're too clever to fall prey to such nonsense. If you weren't so tired and frightened, you would not indulge in such unhappy speculation."

It was true that she was exhausted and nervous, straining her ears, expecting the tocsin to sound again at any moment. "Perhaps you're right."

"A little logic will defuse your argument," said William, pleased that his words were having the desired effect. "The Willard didn't catch fire. It was the building next door."

"That's true," Kate admitted.

"As for the other, the war was an inevitable consequence of a long chain of events stretching back years. Astute men needed no fiery omens to tell them it was coming."

She nodded and gave him a wan smile, embarrassed by her foolishness.

"My dear little frightened birdie." William raised her hands to his lips, kissed them, and embraced her. "Hotel fires aren't portents of terrible calamity, Kate. They *are* the calamity."

"I'm sure you're right," said Kate, managing a shaky laugh, "but nevertheless, I'll be glad to leave as soon as the sun rises, and gladder still to reach Providence."

The next day, the tired but obligingly cheerful wedding party departed the Fifth Avenue Hotel, assuring one another that the exciting story of their misadventure would eventually prove to be ample compensation for the loss of one night's sleep. Their spirits rose further as they boarded the ferry that would take them across the Long Island Sound and up Narragansett Bay to Providence. Madame Fanny assured them that a pleasant family welcome awaited them at her home, Young Orchard, and that she would host a more formal public reception in honor of the newlyweds on Friday evening.

Kate was glad to hear that the day of their arrival would be limited to family, for she was looking forward to some restorative tranquility after the whirlwind of celebration and travel and fire alarms. Her hopes to find a peaceful haven were dashed, however, when Young Orchard came into view through the carriage window. An enormous, garish WELCOME HOME sign hung from the archway above the front entrance, which was lavishly festooned in red, white, and blue bunting. Streamers in the national colors hung from the eaves and all around the central tower, with more bunting and flags adorning the doors and windows. Above the front door hung a large banner inexplicably decorated with the flags of many nations. Kate drew in her breath slowly, shocked and dismayed. Rather than making her feel welcomed into the Sprague family circle, the gaudy display instead gave her the odd sensation that she had arrived at some sort of international regatta.

Cousin Alice had another take on the tawdry scene. "It looks like they're preparing for a horse fair," she murmured in horrified wonder.

Nettie smothered a laugh, but Kate felt faintly ill. It was a small mercy that their party was so large that they had been obliged to divide themselves between two carriages when they departed from the ferry dock, and that William, Madame Fanny, and the rest of the Spragues were in the other. Kate had time to compose herself and to warn Nettie and Alice to stop giggling into their handkerchiefs before she had to face the perpetrators of the horrific crime against good taste and refinement.

As the carriage pulled into the front drive, she found William waiting for her, beaming. "Welcome home, indeed," he declared, taking her hand and helping her alight from the carriage. She managed a tight smile as he admired the nightmare of ribbon and banners and bunting, while nearby, Madame Fanny and her daughters watched him, fairly bursting with pride.

"Were you surprised?" inquired Mary, Amasa's wife.

"Oh, yes, more than you can possibly imagine." Turning to William, Kate implored, "Would you please show me to my room? I'm feeling quite unwell."

His brow furrowed in concern, and while his family looked on, surprised and uncertain, William quickly led her inside and upstairs to the bedchamber they would share. "What's the matter?" he asked, assisting her to a seat on the bed. "Can I fetch anything for you—a glass of water, smelling salts?"

"A glass of water would be lovely, thank you."

With a solicitous nod, William hurried off, and by the time he returned, she had decided that the best course of action was simply to tell him, straight out, that the gaudy decorations had overwhelmed her and that she would be grateful if they were removed. "My mother and sisters thought a little fuss would please you," he said, bewildered and disappointed. "The housemen and gardeners have gone to a lot of trouble. Their feelings will be badly hurt."

"I do regret that," Kate said, "but after our harrowing night, I require peace and calm, and that display is anything but. Surely you see that."

William agreed, but uncertainly, and her heart sank when she realized that he thought the decorations were perfectly fine. Apparently she would have to redouble her efforts to refine his taste.

William left her alone to rest with the curtains drawn and a scented handkerchief covering her eyes and forehead. Later he returned to report, somewhat brusquely, that he had excused her lack of enthusiasm as fatigue, and that the decorations had been removed. Kate thanked him, but he merely nodded and left her alone in the darkened room. When she emerged for supper, she realized that the pragmatic, equanimous Madame Fanny had taken her implicit criticism well in stride, but that William and Amasa were disconcerted and offended.

The next day, after a good rest and time to reflect, Kate endeavored to make it up to the brothers by being a gracious and charming houseguest, a dutiful daughter-in-law, and a fond sister. William's good spirits quickly returned, but Amasa and Mary were not so easily won over. Privately Kate resolved that no matter what tasteless decor adorned Young Orchard on the night of the reception, she would hold her tongue for the sake of family harmony.

When Friday evening came, however, Kate was pleasantly surprised to discover that all had been stylishly arrayed. Dozens of Chinese lanterns had been hung from the trees in front of the residence, beautifully illuminating the expansive grounds and transforming them into something from the realm of fairy. Inside, the hall and dining room were adorned with fragrant flowers tastefully arranged, with nary a scrap of bunting to be seen. A quintet of musicians provided excellent music, and the banquet proved to be a delectable feast, the seafood succulent and almost impossibly fresh, the confections artful and light and airy. Hundreds of guests attired in their finest suits and silks and satins graced the halls, and everyone was so gracious and agreeable and obviously pleased to make her acquaintance that it was some time before she realized that something was amiss.

But something was.

As the reception went on, Kate smiled and laughed and chatted and danced, her joyful demeanor concealing her increasing confusion. At first she thought—she hoped—she was mistaken, but a careful study confirmed her suspicions: None of the first families of Providence had attended the reception. The ladies and gentlemen of the Rhode Island social and political elite who had welcomed her and Father and Nettie so cordially the previous summer were nowhere to be seen. The last time Kate had witnessed such an obvious snub was when the elite of Washington City had spurned invitations to Mrs. Lincoln's earliest receptions at the Willard and the White House. More puzzled than upset, Kate resolved to enjoy the party nonetheless and solve the mystery of the guest list later.

The next day, William exulted in rapturous review of the gala that appeared in the *Providence Evening Press*. "Young Orchard was 'the scene of one of the most superb affairs that ever graced our city,'" William read, his voice ringing with triumph. "Listen to this: 'Beauty and fashion were allied with solid worth in the brilliant throng whose assemblage was a fitting acknowledgment of the happy circumstances'—our marriage, of course—'which contrast so pleasantly with war's alarms.'"

"I'm sure your mother's guests will be flattered by such charming praise," said Kate carefully, "but did it not seem to you that many friends were absent?"

William's eyebrows drew together, though his gaze did not leave the paper. "As far as I could tell, everyone who had accepted my mother's invitations was present, although there were so many hundreds here I suppose I could have overlooked one or two absences."

Kate had counted far more than one or two local dignitaries who had been, to her thinking at least, conspicuously absent. "What about Judge MacDonald?"

"He sent his regrets a week ago. Oh, this is well said: 'The banquet which ministered to appetites heightened by the general pleasure, was fairly unsurpassable in its elegant profusion.'"

"Yes, the food was superb. William, darling, only a very few of the ladies and gentlemen my father and I met at City Hall last summer attended us last night. Did your mother not invite them?"

William's happiness dimmed. "Mother knows how to compose a guest list, and she knows the character and conviviality of the people here more than you."

"Of course she does," Kate said, taken aback, "but that doesn't preclude the possibility of an oversight—"

"Hundreds of friends wished us well last night," William interrupted. "As I recall you never lacked company."

"I didn't, but—"

"Then be content." William returned his attention to the paper, and soon his smile reappeared. " 'The youthful senator and his lovely bride contributed very decidedly to the enjoyment of the evening by their graceful cordiality. None could help rejoicing that Rhode Island has such a son, and that in the event which secures his domestic happiness, she gains a charming daughter.' "

"I have never heard anything more obsequious," Kate said under her breath.

"What was that?" asked William.

Kate smiled innocently. "I have never heard any sing more lovingly of us."

Knowing she was unlikely to get anything more out of William, or anything at all out of his mother or sisters, Kate turned her attention to the servants, quickly picking out the newest and youngest chambermaid, a fair-haired, peaked, rather frightened-looking Irish girl. Still learning her trade, she surely listened to every word uttered in the household lest she commit an embarrassing mistake, and she would not have yet formed loyalties that would prevent her from sharing unflattering gossip about her employers.

Kate easily managed to catch her alone by hasting back to her bedchamber when she was meant to be out so that the servants could tend to the linens and the fires. "Why, good morning," she exclaimed brightly, startling the poor girl. "And who might you be?"

The girl scrambled to her feet and gave a small curtsy. "Katie, ma'am."

"How delightful! I'm a Katie too."

The girl nodded, looking as if she couldn't imagine ever addressing her by that name.

"How long have you been in service here, Katie?"

"Since August, ma'am."

"And is this your first situation?"

"No, ma'am. I worked for the Johnsons on Galbraith Street from February until May. That was my first."

"Why did you leave their employ?"

Her cheeks reddened. "I dropped the lamb while serving table at Easter."

"Oh, dear."

"But it wasn't my fault," she added with a burst of spirit, "and it won't ever happen again."

"I'm sure it won't," said Kate soothingly. "The Johnson family . . . I don't recall meeting them at the reception last night. Do you happen to know if they were here?"

She shook her head. "They wouldn't have been, ma'am."

"Wouldn't have been?" Kate echoed. "Why *wouldn't* have been?"

The girl looked uneasy. "I only meant they weren't here, ma'am."

"No," Kate replied, smiling. "That isn't what you meant. You're a clever girl, I can tell, and you meant what you said. Why were you so certain that your former employers would not have been here?"

"I—I really shouldn't say."

"On the contrary." Kate leaned forward and lowered her voice conspiratorially. "You really should."

The housemaid hesitated again, glanced over her shoulder, and gulped air. "Everyone knows the Spragues aren't received in society, ma'am."

"How very curious," said Kate, masking her sharp dismay. "The family of the former governor of Rhode Island, the current United States senator, a military hero, and one of the most successful businessmen in the state is not received in society?"

Miserable, the poor cornered housemaid nodded.

"Why on earth not?"

At that, tears pooled in her eyes. "That's not for me to say, ma'am," she said, distressed. "I—I really should get back to my work, ma'am, if you please, or the housekeeper will box my ears—"

"Of course," said Kate. "I apologize for detaining you." With one last gracious smile, she swept from the room.

The revelation defied all logic, but it confirmed what Kate had observed the night before. For some reason, which William either did not know or was reluctant to divulge, the Sprague family was not accepted among the social elite of Rhode Island, in spite of their wealth and William's position, marks of status that usually guaranteed admittance to the highest circles of any community. The gracious and the good of Providence would receive Miss Kate Chase, daughter of the secretary of the treasury, but they would not receive Mrs. William Sprague, and she meant to discover why.

Kate had little time to pursue the question on their wedding trip, however, for on the Monday after the reception, she and William left Nettie at school, glum but resigned to her fate, and embarked on their honeymoon, a tour of Ohio during which they would visit some of Kate's dearest family and friends. Traveling alone with her husband at last, Kate felt alive and blissful and free. William was in such congenial, tender, and affectionate spirits that Kate could not bear to deflate him by pricking him with questions about the Providence snub, so she set the puzzle aside, although she never completely forgot it.

Their travels took them to Cincinnati, Columbus, and on to Cleveland, where they stayed with Mr. and Mrs. Parsons, who hosted a grand party in their honor. Early December found them in Loveland, Ohio, in the home of Kate's cousin Jane Auld, both suffering from bad colds contracted along the way, but still determinedly cheerful. "A red nose does not diminish your beauty," William told her, interrupted by a sneeze, "and my watery eyes cannot prevent me from appreciating that." In reply, Kate laughed and embraced him, and gave him a fresh handkerchief.

They had almost entirely recovered by the time they departed for Washington a few days later. Father welcomed them home with such great joy that Kate felt a stab of guilt for their long absence. Pleasantly weary from travel, she happily settled back into the routine of home, content and thankful that it had become William's home too.

She had barely finished unpacking and they had only just settled into the comfortable companionship of a trio when William announced that he was obliged to return to Providence to attend to business matters.

"So soon?" Kate protested. "When must you go?"

"The day after tomorrow."

Kate was disconsolate, but she did not want to spoil their newlywed joy with complaints, so she cheerfully asked what she could do to help him prepare for the trip. After he departed, she tried to forget her loneliness by occupying herself with her father's business and preparing for the holidays, which were sure to be wonderful, since they would be the first she and William would celebrate as husband and wife.

She wrote to William at least once a day, sometimes twice, and she could not always keep her ardent yearning from the penned lines. "Shall I tell you how much I miss you," she wrote a few days after his departure, "and how the sunshine has all gone from our beautiful home? My life is indeed deserted in my longing for my own darling. I prayed to God very earnestly before going to rest for your protection and safe return." A few days later, she concluded a summary of the news from Washington with the wistful lament, "There are letters lying for you unopened upon the table and I feel every now and then that you will come in with your accustomed smile and I shall have the joy of welcoming my husband home again. Oh darling I hope these separations will not come very often. They are hard to bear."

The pain of separation was augmented by the paucity of William's letters, which, when they came at all, resembled in no fashion the passionate, affectionate, tender notes he had sent her with endearing regularity throughout their engagement, even when he resided at the Willard Hotel only a few blocks away. William offered little more than terse descriptions of his work and sent along perfunctory greetings from his mother, brother, and sisters, and nothing in his words suggested that he missed her the way she ached for him.

Shortly before Christmas, Nettie returned home for her school holiday, and Kate anxiously awaited a letter from William telling her when she could expect him to complete the new family circle. Instead he sent her a lovely ashes-of-rose silk shawl for her Christmas gift along with his regrets, for he had decided to spend the holiday with his family at Young Orchard.

Shocked, Kate immediately wrote back to remind him that she couldn't possibly get away. They were expecting a houseful of guests, like every year, and they had already invited dozens of friends and colleagues to several festive gatherings. William responded by assuring her that he had not expected her to come, and that she should remain in Washington and carry on as she always had.

Heartbroken that they would not spend their first Christmas as a married couple together, and deeply troubled that this bothered William not at all, Kate made the mistake of complaining to her father. Clearly uncomfortable to be thrust into the middle, he took William's side and urged her to submit to her husband's will with good cheer and Christian forbearance. Although she knew her father was probably right, his advice grated, so instead she tried to bring William home by inviting his entire family to spend the holidays in Washington with the Chases. Her hopes were dashed when William's sister Mary Ann wrote to decline politely on behalf of the family, whom she said remained too exhausted from their trip to the capital for the wedding to attempt the journey again so soon.

Her last gambit thwarted, Kate resolved to try following Father's advice, and so she sent along gifts to Young Orchard for William and his family and told him she would count the days until his return. They would welcome the New Year together, and all would be well.

As Christmas drew closer, Kate wrote faithfully to William at least once a day, knowing that due to the vagaries of the mails he might receive them out of order and some not at all. She endeavored not to reproach him for his absence, or for the scarcity of his terse letters, and so she was especially hurt when he wrote to complain that she did not write to him enough. Her long-simmering anger boiled over. "I received your *brief* note written 'Sunday' this morning just as I was leaving home, and was a good deal grieved by the imputed reproach of 'forgetfulness' it contained," she quickly responded, barely keeping her indignation in check. "Of one thing always rest assured, if a promise I have made does not *appear* to have been kept, the fault is not mine. The day after you left home—Thursday—I wrote you *twice*, a hasty note in the morning when posting some official communications as you directed, and a longer letter in the evening. Since, I have written *every day* and in the *morning* until now, in order as I thought, to have my letters get off in the noon mails. I can only regret the delay that has prevented your receiving them darling for they were sent in such good faith."

On Christmas Day William made no mention of her explanation in a telegram he sent wishing her a Merry Christmas. And then, two days later, Kate received a thick envelope with his beloved inscription, but when she opened it, she discovered nothing more than official documents he needed her to deliver to various departments on his behalf. Later that afternoon, another envelope arrived containing a letter for Father and a brief but very welcome note for her—or at least it was welcome until Father wordlessly handed her his letter and she read it only to discover that William did not intend to return for New Year's Day either.

"He tells you," she said numbly. "Why did he not tell me?"

Father shrugged, looking pained. "I'm sure he knew I would inform you."

That was not the point, but Kate did not bother to tell him what he already knew. Instead she shut herself away in the study, paced until she had quite composed herself, and then seized pen and paper and dashed out a reply. "Forgotten so soon?" she wrote. "Oh darling how could you serve me so? Father has only just received your letter saying you will not return for New Year's Day. That it was a bitter disappointment to me you well know. New Year's Day with us this year promises to be a great failure."

She considered burning the letter instead of sending it, but indignant anger compelled her to put it in the mail. She had been as patient and forbearing as any bride could be expected to be under the circumstances, and he ought to know how angry and disappointed he had made her so he could put things right. But in this regard too she was disappointed, for on the last day of the year she received his coldest letter by far.

> *My dear wife:*
>
> *It is almost to the day twenty years ago that my good father was murdered and your letter brought further vexation and disappointment to a sorrowful anniversary. That your January reception will promise a failure I very much regret. I would that you would make it a success despite my inability to be with you and you would lighten my burden this much by exhibiting a willingness to deny yourself for that purpose. I am in every moment engaged in large & numerous duties & engagements and try to do my duty in every way and I have a right to ask your aid and sympathy. You my love are not I hope to prove an additional burden to me, as you will certainly do if you consider my acts as the cause of any unhappiness.*

The rebuke stung. She had not deliberately arranged for her letter to arrive on a particularly melancholy day—as if she could have done, when not even Postmaster General Montgomery Blair commanded such precise control over the mails—and she knew from his mother's letters describing the many pleasurable ways he was taking his leisure that he was certainly not working "every moment." As for his warning that she not become a burden, she did not know whether to laugh or weep. No man of her acquaintance had ever considered her a burden or likely to become one, and none had thought of her companionship as something to be patiently endured when he was not occupied with business. William's cold contempt was unbearable. Kate knew many married couples who lived apart, allowing their marriages to drift along in a state of benign estrangement for years, but she had not expected that to happen to her and William, and certainly not so soon.

Despondent and angry and hurt, Kate did not understand William's behavior or know how to restore his tender affection, and she had no one in whom to confide. Father's instinct was to side with William, and at sixteen Nettie was still too young to understand. Her most reliable friend was John Hay, but obviously she could not complain about her husband to him without suffering the worst of mortifications, and telling anyone else, even her dearest cousins, seemed like a betrayal of William's trust, of their marriage bond itself.

There was another reason she endured her unhappiness in silence as the old year drew to a melancholy close.

It was profoundly humiliating and shameful to admit that she, who had always been so proud and admired and loved and cherished, was not treasured by the one man to whom she had given her heart completely, the one man who knew her better than any other.

Chapter Eighteen

JANUARY–JUNE 1864

$\mathcal{T}$he first day of January dawned cold and overcast, with nipping frosts and blustery winds that scattered the clouds by midmorning, revealing a bright sun that mirrored the people's good cheer. Over breakfast, many Washingtonians found good tidings in the *National Republican*, which published a long list of the victories won by the Union army throughout the previous twelve months. The general consensus, or perhaps it was merely a fervent wish, was that 1864 would surely be the year the war would end and peace would descend upon a newly united, reconciled nation.

At ten o'clock, Father, Kate, and Nettie attended the traditional New Year's Day reception at the White House with the dignitaries and officials, an occasion that Kate discovered would mark Mrs. Lincoln's transition to half-mourning, which some believed was long overdue. The First Lady wore a beautiful gown of rich purple velvet, exquisitely fashioned, adorned with Valenciennes lace and white satin fluting, with a sweeping train, finished with a headdress boasting a large white plume. Although she greeted the Chases with frosty concision, Kate could sense the steely determination beneath. While Mrs. Lincoln surely still felt the pain of Willie's death acutely, she must have realized that the demands of the upcoming election obliged her to put aside the solace of mourning ritual for the sake of her husband's political future—and her own.

Perhaps too, Kate surmised, Mrs. Lincoln wanted to make a defiant show of resilience in the face of renewed controversy over her family's Confederate ties. Back in December, Mrs. Lincoln's younger half sister, Emilie Todd Helm, had come to stay at the White House. Mrs. Helm, the young widow of a Confederate general killed at the Battle of Chickamauga, had been traveling with her daughter from Atlanta to Mrs. Lincoln's stepmother's home in Kentucky, until she had been detained at the border for refusing to take the oath of allegiance to the United States. When her resolve had not faltered, the stymied border guards had telegraphed President Lincoln, who promptly telegraphed back, "Send her to me." Word had spread throughout Washington that the Lincolns were secretly harboring an unrepentant rebel beneath the White House roof, stirring up displeasure and contempt and more aspersions about Mrs. Lincoln's suspect loyalties.

As for Mr. Lincoln, on that first day of the New Year he greeted Father, Kate, and Nettie with his customary warmth and familiarity. He seemed to be in unusually excellent health and spirits as he received the Washington dignitaries, his eyes clear and shining with good humor, his handshake firm and cordial. Still, he must have shared some of Mrs. Lincoln's evident worry about what the year might bring, for his nomination and reelection were by no means certain—especially when his secretary of the treasury offered a viable alternative.

Following established tradition as well as their own preferences, the Chases left the White House before the doors opened to the general public at noon and a crush of eight thousand eager citizens packed the reception rooms. Later that afternoon they hosted their own New Year's gala, welcoming particular friends and colleagues and potential allies to an elegant, lively affair graced by excellent music, delicious food and drink, and sparkling conversation. Kate presided over everything with her usual grace and charm, but although she knew her guests were enjoying themselves thoroughly and no one would have guessed that anything was amiss, she felt her husband's absence keenly. She wished he were by her side so that they could greet the New Year properly, together as husband and wife.

Soon thereafter, William wrote to tell her he would return by the end of the first week of January. On the day of his arrival, she fussed and prepared as if Father were entertaining foreign diplomats with an important trade agreement hanging in the balance.

She did not know what to expect from him—until the moment he crossed the threshold, eagerly called her name, and swept her into his arms when she came running to meet him. It was her own dear, loving William who had come home to her, and when he kissed her tenderly she felt as if she would melt into him. She was so relieved and happy to have her beloved husband restored to her that she could almost forget the other William existed.

She was doubly thankful to have her darling husband home again because of the sudden surge in political intrigue that swept through the capital that month. Winter's cold had held the two armies almost to a standstill except for minor raids and skirmishes, and with the Union army camped firmly between Washington and the rebels, the people of Washington felt safer, if no closer to the end of the war. With the threat of invasion quite remote, and with the victories at Gettysburg and Vicksburg indicating that the end of the war was near, they were free to turn their attention to politics and the upcoming election.

No one knew what candidate the Peace Democrats or the Whigs might put forth in the race for the presidency, although General McClellan was occasionally whispered about as a possibility. But within Republican circles, it was generally understood that moderates and conservatives would cleave loyally to Mr. Lincoln, while Radical Republicans would rally around Father. After the Emancipation Proclamation had rendered it impossible for Father to distinguish himself from Mr. Lincoln by his stronger stance on abolition, Father chose Reconstruction as his new great cause. He believed, and he was confident voters would agree, that his experience leading the Treasury through its wartime crises made him better suited than the wartime president for the great endeavor of putting the divided nation back together.

While Father wished to remain above the fray, he did not discourage his supporters among the Radical Republicans from promoting his cause. Several friends, including the wealthy banker Jay Cooke, who had helped look after Nettie when she had been afflicted with scarlet fever two years before, paid thousands of dollars to the publisher of the Philadelphia magazine *American Exchange and Review* to produce a brief, laudatory biography of Father. Mr. Lincoln usually ignored such politicking, but to Kate's surprise, the president questioned

Father about the pamphlet, as well as Mr. Cooke's role in its publication, which had an unseemly appearance since Mr. Cooke and his brother were official agents for selling government bonds. Father wrote Mr. Lincoln a lengthy, heartfelt letter disavowing any wrongdoing, and as far as Kate knew Mr. Lincoln accepted his explanation and the matter was forgotten.

The president's tolerance did nothing to discourage Father from continuing to cultivate support, however, and he soon commenced writing a series of twenty-five long letters to the Boston author Mr. John Trowbridge, who intended to write a small, inspirational book about Father's life to place him more favorably before the public. Father wrote many private letters too, corresponding vigorously with friends and allies throughout the North, but it was his more public efforts that raised the ire of Mr. Lincoln's staunch supporters. No one disputed Father's right to criticize President Lincoln and to pursue his own presidential ambitions, but to do so from within the cabinet rather than honorably resigning and challenging Mr. Lincoln openly struck many observers as duplicitous and unethical.

No one was more outraged by Father's preludes to a campaign than Mrs. Lincoln. John Hay, who did not call on Kate as often as he once had but remained her confidant, told her that the Hellcat had resolved to do nothing that might promote the ambitious Secretary Chase. "You're aware she's preparing for the first state dinner of the year," John said.

"Yes, for the evening of the twenty-first. Father, William, and I plan to attend."

"Well, you almost weren't invited."

"What?" Kate exclaimed. By well-established tradition, the first state dinner of the year was held for members of the cabinet, justices of the Supreme Court, and their families, a group in which Father ranked among the highest. "An innocent oversight, I dare hope?"

"Not at all. John Nicolay is always involved in planning these affairs, and he composed the appropriate guest list as usual. He told me that Her Satanic Majesty demanded that your names be struck. Naturally, Nicolay told her that he couldn't possibly exclude one of the secretaries, not only because it went against custom, but also because it would make the president appear spiteful and overly wary of a potential rival."

"And, of course, Mr. Lincoln is neither of those things."

"He isn't," said John emphatically, "although I wish he were the latter. So Mrs. Lincoln insisted, and Nicolay refused, and back and forth the argument went, off and on for days. Finally the Tycoon caught wind of the conflict, and he settled it by ordering Nicolay to invite you three and telling his wife to drop the matter."

"I'm sure that pleased her immensely."

"You have no idea. The Hellcat went on quite a rampage, and she banished Nicolay not only from her little planning committee but from the dinner itself. Nicolay took his revenge, though. He ordered William Stoddard not to help her, and I have no intention of volunteering, so she's going to have to flounder about on her own."

"This should make for an interesting evening," Kate mused, smiling.

"Never fear. I expect her to come down with a serious case of contrition soon, and go humbly back to Nicolay to beg for his help."

"Will he give it?"

"Yes, but for the president's sake, not hers."

It did indeed come to pass as John had predicted, as he told Kate later. On the afternoon of the dinner, after two sleepless, worrisome nights, Mrs. Lincoln sent Mr. Nicolay a contrite note of apology through the White House doorman and requested his help, which he dutifully provided. Kate was expecting utter disarray when she, Father, and William arrived at the White House on the evening of January 21, but the dinner was actually quite pleasant, except for some stiffness between various bickering members of the cabinet. They also patiently endured constant dour looks from the prolifically bearded Secretary of the Navy Gideon Welles, who could not bring himself to partake of the renewed enjoyment of parties, receptions, and fairs that had infused the capital that winter. "It's like merrymaking at a funeral," Kate overheard him grumble to his wife.

There were moments when Kate felt as Secretary Welles did, but she knew that policies were created over dinners and alliances forged in drawing rooms as often as in the halls of Congress or the White House, and that the art of masterful entertaining contributed as much to the machinery of government as the press and the lecture hall.

Kate had never been happier than she was that winter. Father was actively pursuing his great ambition and had allowed his romantic correspondence with several lady friends to diminish. William was attentive and loving, and after he settled back into the routine of the Senate he only rarely complained to her that he ought to be back in Rhode Island overseeing his business empire instead. Kate often watched the proceedings from the Senate gallery, proud to see her husband in his official chair, although she wished he would take the floor more often to introduce new legislation or participate in debate. Privately she encouraged him to make his mark, and although he seemed to be in no hurry, he assured her he would do when the time was right. She realized that he was somewhat intimidated by the great political minds all around him, but she was impatient for him to gain confidence before his colleagues decided he was a man of no consequence. Several sneering articles had already appeared in the papers mocking his absences and inactivity, and Kate knew that sort of nonsense had to be uprooted before it dug itself into the bedrock.

Kate had been preoccupied with her wedding and honeymoon—and then with William's heartbreaking absence—to pay much attention at the time, but late in the previous year, a Kansas senator named Samuel Pomeroy had launched a clandestine "Chase for President" movement even as he publicly pledged his loyalty to Mr. Lincoln. John Hay had heard rumors of the campaign and had questioned Kate about it, but she had been able to tell him in all honesty that she was unaware of anything Mr. Pomeroy might be doing outside of the Senate, and that her father had not endorsed any campaign organization. By early February, if John had asked, Kate would have had to confess an entirely different answer. A few days after the Lincolns' state dinner, Father and William together informed Kate that Senator Pomeroy had indeed formed a campaign committee, and that William and Mr. Cooke were its most generous contributors.

Kate was at first startled to discover that her father and her husband had collaborated on a political scheme without including her, but the feeling soon gave way to dismay when they informed her that the committee intended to publish an anonymous pamphlet titled "The Next Presidential Election." Without mentioning Father by name, it painted Mr. Lincoln as an uncertain, ineffective administrator who wrongly arrested innocent citizens, and it argued that he must be replaced on the Republican ticket at the convention in June. While the pamphlet accurately expressed Father's opinions about President Lincoln's shortcomings, it did so in harsher terms than Kate had ever heard him use.

Father and William had confided in Kate, they explained, because the pamphlet was already in the mail, on its way to hundreds of newspaper editors and other influential personages throughout the North, and they wanted her to know about it before anyone else. The admission rendered Kate speechless for a moment, but when she composed herself, she told them heatedly that she wished they had confided in her sooner, for she never would have allowed such a diatribe to be published. "At least Senator Pomeroy had the good sense to leave your name off of it," she snapped. "Vitriol of this nature often damages the reputation of the author more than the subject. I hope you'll advise them not to repeat this experiment." Startled by her fierce indignation, Father and William somewhat meekly concurred.

Thankfully, the pamphlet garnered little attention and no one publicly linked it to Father, but Kate's relief was short-lived. In the second week of February, Republican circles buzzed with rumors that a confidential circular issued in Senator Pomeroy's name had been distributed to one hundred prominent Republicans throughout the North. The Pomeroy Circular, as it became known, sharply criticized President Lincoln, predicted that his second-term policies would be even more disastrous than those of his first term, and declared that "even were the reelection of Mr. Lincoln desirable, it is practically impossible." Salmon P. Chase, in contrast, was "a statesman of rare ability, and an administrator of the highest order" who possessed "more of the qualities needed in a President during the next four years, than are combined in any other available candidate." The only way to avoid the disaster of a Peace Democrat victory in November, it asserted, would be for all loyal Republicans to make certain that Salmon P. Chase won the nomination in June.

Father acquired a copy of the circular soon after the rumors began, and when Kate read it, her heart plummeted. She dared not ask her father or William if they had known about the document before it was distributed, for she was afraid of the answer. "I can't imagine how Senator Pomeroy expects to keep such a volatile document confidential," she said instead, "or what good he expects to come of it."

Leaving the offensive pamphlet on her father's desk, she swept from his study, trembling with suppressed anger. Her father's presidential aspirations were her life's work, and it grieved her to watch others bungle his campaign so badly while she was inexplicably left out. From the time she was sixteen her father had consulted her in nearly everything regarding his political aspirations, and she did not understand why he was apparently excluding her now.

To make matters worse, her remarks about Senator Pomeroy's foolhardy expectations of confidentiality proved prescient. On February 11, the *National Intelligencer* printed the Pomeroy Circular in its entirety, and a few days later the *Constitutional Union* did as well, and soon thereafter it was reprinted in papers through the North. The effect on public opinion was swift and explosive. Outraged Lincoln loyalists who received the memo by mail in envelopes marked with the congressional frank of Father's supporters forwarded their copies to the White House, often including personal notes expressing their disgust with Father and their steadfast allegiance to the president. Mr. Lincoln's friends denounced Father and Senator Pomeroy, and Democrats gleefully celebrated the division within the Republican Party.

It was the worst political disaster of Father's entire career, and neither he nor Kate nor William knew how to stop it from hurtling out of control.

Frantic, Father wrote to the curiously silent president to disavow any knowledge of the Pomeroy Circular until it was published in the papers, a claim Kate knew to be not entirely accurate. Father insisted that although ambitious friends had asked to use his name in the upcoming election, he had not authorized the formation of the Pomeroy Committee and he did not know which gentlemen comprised it. This too Kate knew to be only partially true. "I have thought this explanation due to you as well as to myself," Father wrote. "If there is anything in my action or position which, in your judgment, will prejudice the public interest under my charge, I beg you to say so. I do not wish to administer the Treasury Department one day without your entire confidence." He concluded the letter by emphasizing that their differences of opinion had never diminished his strong personal feelings for Mr. Lincoln. "For yourself I cherish sincere respect and esteem; and, permit me to add, affection," he asserted, adding hopefully, "You are not responsible for acts not your own; nor will you hold me responsible except for what I do or say myself."

Father sent off the letter with dim hopes that it would be well received, and the entire household seemed to hold its breath until a reply came the following day.

> *Executive Mansion,*
> *Washington,*
> *Feb. 23. 1864.*
> *Hon. Sec. of Treasury*
>
> *My dear Sir:*
> *Yours of yesterday in relation to the paper issued by Senator Pomeroy was duly received; and I write this note merely to say I will answer a little more fully when I can find time to do so.*
> *Yours truly,*
> *A. LINCOLN*

Kate never would have expected such a dispassionate reply, even from the preternaturally tolerant Mr. Lincoln, nor such a calculated maneuver. The president clearly meant to keep Father suffering in suspense, deferring his response until he could take his measure of the people's reaction to the Pomeroy Circular. Then and only then would he decide what to do.

The response of the people was unmistakably the opposite of what Senator Pomeroy had intended, for throughout the North, the circular roused Mr. Lincoln's supporters from their complacency. Opposing circulars were published denouncing Father and his political machinations, and in one state after another, Republicans met and passed unanimous resolutions calling for Mr. Lincoln's renomination. Even the usually sympathetic *New York Times* declared that the circular was unworthy of the party, proclaiming, "We protest against the spirit of this movement."

Following the unfolding nightmare in the press, Kate absorbed each devastating blow with outward stoicism and secret despair. All that she and Father and even William had worked for seemed to be crumbling to ruin all around them. The worst moment came when Father's friends in the Union caucus of the Ohio state legislature, who had previously blocked efforts to endorse Mr. Lincoln's reelection, repudiated their support, allowing a resolution in favor of the president to pass unanimously.

As in 1860, her father's chances to win the Republican nomination depended upon strong support from his home state of Ohio. For Father, the resolution meant that he had lost the election before it had truly begun.

On the last day of February, Father at last received Mr. Lincoln's response.

Executive Mansion,
Washington,
February 29. 1864.
Hon. Secretary of the Treasury

My dear Sir:
I would have taken time to answer yours of the 22d sooner, only that I did not suppose any evil could result from the delay, especially as, by a note, I promptly acknowledged the receipt of yours, and promised a fuller answer. Now, on consideration I find there is really very little to say. My knowledge of Mr. Pomeroy's letter having been made public came to me only the day you wrote, but I had, in spite of myself, known of its existence several days before. I have not yet read it, and I think I shall not. I was not shocked or surprised by the appearance of the letter, because I had had knowledge of Mr. Pomeroy's committee and of secret issues which, I supposed, came from it and of secret agents who, I supposed, were sent out by it, for several weeks. I have known just as little of these things as my friends have allowed me to know. They bring the documents to me, but I do not read them; they tell me what they think fit to tell me, but I do not inquire for more. I fully concur with you that neither of us can be justly held responsible for what our respective friends may do without our instigation or countenance; and I assure you, as you have assured me, that no assault has been made upon you by my instigation or with my countenance.
Whether you shall remain at the head of the Treasury Department is a question which I will not allow myself to consider from any standpoint other than my judgment of the public service, and, in that view, I do not perceive occasion for a change.
Yours truly,
A. Lincoln

The entire Chase household accepted the president's decision with shock and muted relief. William alone seemed entirely reassured that Father retained Mr. Lincoln's friendship and confidence along with his cabinet position, but Kate suspected that was because William did not fully comprehend the more dire implications of all that the circular had done and undone. Without Ohio behind him, Father had no chance to win the nomination, and long before the scandal broke, he had publicly expressed that if he did not gain the support of his home state, he would withdraw from the race.

A week after receiving Mr. Lincoln's letter, Father wrote a public letter to the influential Ohio state senator James C. Hall, a personal friend, solemnly declaring that since the legislature had vowed to support Mr. Lincoln instead of himself, "it becomes my duty, therefore, and I count it more a privilege than a duty, to ask that no further consideration be given to my name." Ever patriotic and mindful of his loyalty to the Union cause, Father emphatically concluded, "It was never more important than now that all our efforts and energies should be devoted to the suppression of the rebellion, and to the restoration of order and prosperity on the solid and sure foundations of Union, freedom, and impartial justice, and I earnestly urge all with whom my counsels may have weight, to allow nothing to divide them while this great work—in comparison with which, persons and even parties are nothing—remains unaccomplished."

In the aftermath of Father's withdrawal, Kate knew, Mr. Lincoln would surely claim the vast majority of Father's supporters as his own, for Father had all but urged them to rally to his rival's side.

Father was profoundly disappointed, but Kate was devastated. His presidential aspirations had been resoundingly thwarted, and she knew that the only reason Mr. Lincoln allowed him to retain his post at the Treasury was because Mr. Lincoln wanted and needed him there.

The moment the president believed he no longer did, Father would be peremptorily dismissed.

While Father's star precipitously declined, Ulysses S. Grant's was on the rise. On the same March day that Father wrote to Mr. Lincoln to confirm his withdrawal from the presidential race, he was among the witnesses at the White House ceremony in which Mr. Lincoln awarded the celebrated, taciturn officer a commission as lieutenant general. The next day, after the restless General Grant had already departed Washington to rejoin his troops, the president appointed him general in chief of the armies of the United States.

At the end of March, when the transfer of his command in the West to General William Tecumseh Sherman was complete, General Grant returned to Washington accompanied by his wife, Julia. She was said to be a devoted mother of four, much beloved of her husband, and a pleasant conversationalist, though not much given to politics. Despite her preoccupation with her father's troubles, Kate immediately recognized the Grants as people the Chases ought to know, and she successfully contended with the general's resistant chief of staff to arrange for the general to call on her father. Kate found Mrs. Grant to be a pleasant, dark-haired woman in her late thirties, whose plain features were made prettier by her ready smile and unassuming, friendly manner. Mrs. Grant delighted in the attention and praise showered upon her husband, who seemed uncomfortable with the fuss and eager to return to the field. Before he could escape, he was obliged to make the rounds of Washington society, where he was cheered and serenaded and toasted with such fervor that Kate was not surprised to hear him whispered about as a potential presidential candidate. Kate hid her concerns behind a dazzling smile, was gracious to the matronly Mrs. Grant, and must have succeeded in charming the general, for although his dislike of music and dancing was well-known, on one occasion he took a few turns with her on the dance floor. "You made him look much less awkward than he usually does in such circumstances," an officer who had known General Grant since his West Point days remarked.

When the general departed Washington for his new headquarters near Culpeper, Virginia, Mrs. Grant remained at the Willard, but Kate had little opportunity to further their acquaintance. Stress about Father's misfortunes and worry and lack of sleep had conspired to make her so desperately ill with various afflictions of the lungs that she required constant care. Since neither Father nor William had the time, ability, or inclination to nurse her properly, General McDowell and his wife invited her to convalesce at their home at Buttermilk Falls in Upstate New York. There, far from the strife of Washington and the incessant scenes of war's terrible toll on its soldiers, Kate slowly regained her health, thanks to enforced rest and Mrs. McDowell's adept ministrations.

Father, William, and various friends kept Kate apprised of events in Washington, and so she was in her sickbed when she first learned of the shocking tales of improprieties in the Treasury Department.

For several months, rumors had whispered of irregularities in business and immorality among the Treasury staff, but Father and Kate had dismissed them as the usual malicious gossip. Even Father's political enemies considered him morally above reproach—in fact, some muttered that he would be more agreeable company if he were not so pious and righteous. Then one outraged citizen wrote to President Lincoln accusing Secretary Chase of speculation in stocks, gold, and cotton, an outrageous allegation that the president gave no credence whatsoever. That fuss had scarcely died down when complaints emerged that women employees of the Treasury Department were reportedly hired for their personal attractions rather than their skills. Several young ladies claimed that they were refused employment until they yielded to the passionate embraces of the superintendent of the Bureau of Engraving and Printing. More shocking yet, dozens of the department's young, unmarried female employees were said to be with child.

Alarmed, Father brought in a detective from the War Department to investigate the allegations, and when the detective found outrage and scandal everywhere he looked, a special congressional committee began a formal inquiry. After hearing the testimony of a series of witnesses, including two young clerks who swore that they had been coerced into intimate encounters with their employer, the committee could not unanimously conclude whether the charges were true or false. The public preferred to believe the most scandalous, salacious version of events, and so even if the Department of the Treasury was not the "most extensive Whorehouse in the nation," as one critic claimed, its reputation was tarnished—and Father's was tarnished further, at a time when he was struggling to redeem himself in the eyes of the people.

Certain political enemies were determined to see that he never did. Father had long been embroiled in a feud with the Blairs, a family of conservative Republicans that included Postmaster General Montgomery Blair. That winter his brother, Missouri congressman Francis Blair, denounced Father from the House floor in one of the most bitter and hateful verbal assaults ever delivered in the halls of Congress. For two hours he castigated Father's character, charging him with corruption in high office, with treason, and with "grasping at all power and patronage for the purpose of providing a fund to carry on his war against the administration which gave him place."

The blistering litany of outlandish charges had gone on and on, and when Father had learned of them, he had been shocked and deeply offended. Mr. Blair had attacked his integrity and honor, which Father prized above all earthly possessions. He waited for his colleagues to defend him, and for President Lincoln to renounce Mr. Blair, and he grew ever more distressed and affronted when none rallied to his side.

Father was still waiting in vain for satisfaction at the end of May when Kate recovered enough to return home. Still weakened from her long illness, she nevertheless tried to arbitrate her father's latest political crisis. She arranged meetings between him and leading Republicans in an attempt to mend the ever-widening chasms dividing different factions within the party, and eventually a tentative truce was forged. Even so, Mr. Blair refused to withdraw his accusations, the Speaker of the House appointed a Committee of Nine to investigate the allegations, and Father remained outraged by the president's refusal to discipline Mr. Blair.

All was in a dreadful, tumultuous disarray, but before Kate could wrest control of the situation, William's attempts to defend his father-in-law made everything worse. His loyalty to his father-in-law had set him at odds with other senators, especially the Radical Republicans, whom William felt had betrayed Father by abandoning him at his time of greatest crisis. One evening, while attempting to resolve their differences over dinner, they all drank far too much, and the evening deteriorated into an undignified drunken brawl.

Kate was more upset about William's drinking than the fight. "You swore to give it up," she said, trembling with anger and distress.

"Everyone was drinking," he shouted back, though she stood within arm's reach. Wincing, she turned away, but he grabbed her by the shoulders and forced her to face him. "You would unman me. You would have me say I cannot toast my fellow senators' health because my wife forbids it!"

"I would have you toast them with cider or water not because I demand it but because you know liquor is your weakness," Kate snapped. "You've said yourself that it leads you to dissipation and bad decisions, as it very clearly did tonight, for you to come home with your face bruised and clothes torn as if you were a common street hoodlum!"

He struck her hard across the face with the back of his hand, and she staggered back, reeling.

"You are not the master here," he said, quietly and with preternatural calm.

Stunned, she pressed her cool palm to her hot, stinging cheek and groped for a chair. As she collapsed into it, she felt his gaze boring into her, but he said nothing, only stood watching her silently, radiating triumph. Then, without a word, he turned and strode unsteadily from the room.

Kate sat alone in the foyer, listening to his footsteps fading and the blood rushing in her ears. That would be the last day William touched liquor, she told herself firmly as tears trickled down her face. They had argued furiously before, but he had never struck her. In the morning, when he was sober, the memory of what he had done would so horrify him that he would swear off alcohol forever. It was a terrible thing he had done, but a greater good would come of it.

But the next morning, William greeted her pleasantly at breakfast as if nothing had happened, and if not for the faint bruise on her cheekbone and his bloodshot eyes, she might have convinced herself that she had dreamed the whole shameful incident. She ate slowly, waiting for an apology, for some sign of contrition, but he offered nothing to suggest he felt any remorse whatsoever. He did not want Father to know what had happened, she concluded uncertainly, and so she waited for him to find a more opportune moment; but although the day passed and chances to speak to her alone came and went, still he made no apology. It was as if he had no memory of striking her, or that striking her was not significant enough to remark upon.

Weakened from her recent illness, distressed by the precipitous downturn in Father's political fortunes, Kate found herself overwhelmed by a desperate need to escape Washington. The family had already arranged for Kate to pick up Nettie at the end of her last term at Miss Macaulay's school and take her to Newport, Rhode Island, where William had rented a quiet, seaside retreat for the summer. After a week of barely speaking to her husband, Kate announced that she would be leaving the capital early, so that she might visit friends in New York City while Nettie completed her final exams.

William agreed, perfectly amiable, smiling as he instructed her to indulge herself to her heart's content at her favorite shops on Fifth Avenue. Less reluctantly than she had expected, Father conceded that she ought to go as soon as possible, before the worsening heat and humidity of summer damaged her still-fragile health. She knew that was not the only reason he wanted her away from the capital. In his scathing critiques of her father, Mr. Blair had hinted that Kate was implicated in his worst offenses, and ever since, Father had admonished her to avoid involvement in politics. He might as well have asked her to stop breathing, or to stop being his daughter.

She left the next morning, wordlessly enduring William's farewell kiss on the platform before boarding her train. She wondered if he realized that he had kissed the same cheek he had struck only a few days before.

Soon after Kate and Nettie arrived in Newport, moderate and conservative Republican delegates gathered in Baltimore to establish a party platform and to nominate candidates for the upcoming general election. The Radical Republicans did not attend; at the end of May, their faction had split off from the party proper, renamed themselves the Radical Democracy Party, and convened in Cleveland, where they had chosen General Frémont as their nominee. In response, the delegates in Baltimore renamed themselves the National Union Party—not only to distinguish themselves from the radicals, but also to appeal to disgruntled Democrats who supported the war and rejected the Peace Democrat platform, but could not bring themselves to vote for a Republican.

Kate followed the proceedings in the papers with a heavy heart, knowing that if not for a few critical mistakes, her father's trusted deputies would be in the middle of the convention fray, securing endorsements and gathering delegates around him. Instead, the Republicans and War Democrats united to nominate Mr. Lincoln on the National Union Party ticket. The nomination would have been unopposed but for a delegation of twenty-two Radical Republicans from Missouri, who first nominated General Grant before changing their votes so Mr. Lincoln's nomination would be unanimous. Afterward, the delegates also established their party platform, which praised the president for his management of the war and called for, among other important measures, the pursuit of the war until the Confederacy surrendered unconditionally, a constitutional amendment to abolish slavery, assistance for disabled Union veterans, and the construction of a transcontinental railroad.

Next the agenda turned to the selection of a vice-president. Previously Mr. Lincoln had expressed his desire to let the convention decide without his interference, and once the debate began, he stuck to his resolution. Father knew that Vice-President Hannibal Hamlin wanted to be renominated, but many delegates believed that they should select a War Democrat from a border state to broaden the appeal of the ticket. After much heated debate, they eventually chose Andrew Johnson, the Union military governor of Tennessee, a War Democrat and Southern Unionist.

Mr. Lincoln's nomination had been certain, but Kate was surprised by the choice of Mr. Johnson. She understood the desire to make the ticket more appealing to War Democrats, but she never would have chosen someone who had been so outspoken in the defense of slavery before the war, and so opposed to abolition after it. While serving as the military governor of Tennessee, Mr. Johnson had asked President Lincoln to exempt the state from the provision in the Emancipation Proclamation that freed slaves in areas under rebel control, and the president had complied. Kate hardly dared imagine what other schemes against people of color Mr. Johnson might encourage President Lincoln to enact, once emboldened by his new authority as the highest member of the cabinet.

News from private letters offered Kate at least as much insight as the papers. William wrote to her at Newport, his letters warm and affectionate, which would have delighted her once but bewildered her then. More troublingly, scattered among his inexplicably tender declarations of love were hints that not all was well with Father. Kate knew that Father had clung to vain hopes that he would garner a respectable number of votes on the first ballot at the convention, but as soon as Mr. Lincoln had been nominated, Father had been forced to reconcile himself to his diminished status. Worsening matters, he was apparently embroiled in yet another conflict with President Lincoln regarding appointments.

Since Father wrote little about it, Kate was obliged to piece together

her understanding of the situation from the incomplete stories each man offered in his letters. Shortly after the convention in Baltimore, the assistant treasurer of New York had resigned his post, and selecting his replacement was a matter fraught with the potential to offend important factions within the state Republican Party. Since the post fell within the jurisdiction of the Treasury Department, choosing a successor was Father's responsibility, but Mr. Lincoln instructed him to consult with New York senator Edwin Morgan to be sure that all sides were satisfied with his nominee. Instead Father had submitted a formal nomination for his own favorite candidate, though well aware that Senator Morgan strongly disapproved of his choice. Soon thereafter, Mr. Lincoln informed Father that he could not make the appointment and asked him to try harder to find a nominee he and the senator could agree upon. Determined to press his case, Father requested an interview with the president, and when he received no response, he persuaded the outgoing assistant treasurer to remain in his post three months longer in order to buy time. Then, annoyed that the president had refused to meet with him and that he had been obliged yet again to assert his authority over his own department, he submitted his own resignation, certain that Mr. Lincoln would again refuse to accept it. "I cannot help feeling that my position here is not altogether agreeable to you," he wrote, "and it is certainly too full of embarrassment and difficulty and painful responsibility to allow in me the least desire to retain it. I think it my duty therefore to enclose to you my resignation."

If Kate had been in Washington, or if her father had sent her a draft of the letter beforehand, she would have strongly urged him not to send it. But she was in Newport, and her father had been too confident in the security of his position to consult her.

She did not see the terse letter the president sent in response until much later, nor did Father himself see it until after Mr. Lincoln had sent John Hay to deliver the news of Father's resignation to the Senate and to announce his recommendation for his successor.

As William later explained it, Father went to his office at the Treasury Department after breakfast that morning, fully expecting Mr. Lincoln to send a note begging him to reconsider. Instead he received an urgent request from Senator Fessenden of Maine, the chairman of the Finance Committee, to call on him immediately at the Capitol.

"Have you resigned?" Senator Fessenden frantically demanded when Father arrived. "I am called to the Senate and told that the president has sent in the nomination of your successor."

Thus it was from a distraught colleague that Father learned President Lincoln had accepted his resignation. Salmon P. Chase was out of the Treasury, neither secretary nor candidate but a private citizen like any other far more ordinary man.

Chapter Nineteen

*W*hen the devastating news reached Kate and Nettie in Newport, it rendered them shocked and dismayed and disbelieving. Nettie wept openly, but Kate, mindful that her reaction would likely be remarked upon in the press, bore it stoically in public and reserved her grief for her letters to William. As faithful and steadfast as she could possibly want, he reported the news from Washington with unfailing frank sympathy. She was so relieved to find him once again assuming the role of her protector that her heart, desperate for consolation, warmed to him anew.

She found hope too in William's account of the immediate aftermath of her father's dismissal from the cabinet, confided to him by trustworthy witnesses. As word of Father's departure had spread on Capitol Hill, the members of the Senate Finance Committee had held an emergency meeting and had called on the president as a group to lodge a vehement protest. The president had listened patiently while they explained their serious concerns about removing Father from the helm and setting the Treasury Department adrift at a time when Father's incomparable leadership was most necessary, and they also expressed grave reservations about the man Mr. Lincoln had chosen to replace him. What the president had said in reply William did not know, but although the committee had left the White House unsatisfied, other officials had called on the president throughout the day to register their anxiety and dismay, including Massachusetts congressman Samuel Hooper and Treasury registrar Lucius Chittenden. Mr. Chittenden was particularly upset, and he had insisted that the loss of Father as the head of the Treasury was worse than another defeat at Bull Run. Calm and unperturbed, Mr. Lincoln had explained why Father's position in the cabinet had become untenable. "And yet," he had mused, "there is not a man in the Union who would make as good a chief justice as Chase, and, if I have the opportunity, I will make him chief justice of the United States."

At this revelation Kate's hopes soared, and she prayed William's informant was not mistaken—and that Mr. Lincoln had not let the remark fall merely to appease the stream of worried petitioners. Her father, William wrote, had been greatly moved when Congressman Hooper told him that the president had made a similar comment to him. Father also had admitted that if the president had tendered any such expressions of goodwill before he had resigned, he might not have done so.

As the days passed, newspapers throughout the North lamented Father's departure from the Treasury. "Mr. Chase is one of the very few great men left in public life," declared the *New York Tribune*. But the president did not give in to the upswell of regret and dismay, except to reconsider his choice for Father's successor. When his first choice declined, citing poor health, Mr. Lincoln asked Senator Fessenden, who adamantly declared that he could not possibly accept. Later, when Senator Fessenden returned to Capitol Hill and met with the hearty congratulations of his Senate colleagues, he discovered, much as Father had three years before, that the president had already submitted his nomination, rendering it all but impossible for him to decline.

In a state of numb disbelief, Father introduced his friend and successor to the department, and stayed on long enough to see him settled. Then he vacated his beautiful offices, a private citizen for the first time in years, though one with aspirations of returning to public life as soon as the right circumstances arose. In a letter to Kate, Father noted sorrowfully that only Secretary Stanton, "warm & cordial as ever," had bothered to call on him after his resignation, and no one else in the cabinet seemed very sorry to see him go. As she read the words, Kate suddenly imagined Mrs. Lincoln in the elegantly refurbished East Room of the

White House, clad in a sumptuous gown made by the incomparable Mrs. Keckley, gloating because her rival's father had been brought low. She had never wanted Father in the cabinet, and she had pestered her husband to dismiss him almost from the moment he had assumed the post. It nettled Kate to imagine Mrs. Lincoln glorying in her triumph, and she was thankful for the many miles between them that prevented her from witnessing it.

On Independence Day, just before the congressional session concluded, William earned her gratitude by making a speech in the Senate defending her father and rebutting the accusations Senator Blair had made in his diatribe weeks before. Soon thereafter, Father traveled to New York City, where after a conference with Mr. Cooke and other friends, he met his daughters for dinner at the Astor House on Broadway. That evening, the three departed together for Newport, where Father spent a week's vacation enjoying his daughters' sympathetic company, recovering from his recent ordeals, and contemplating his future. Retirement did not suit him, not with the country still mired in crisis, and although the position of chief justice was enticing, it had not been offered to him, nor did the ancient and ailing Justice Taney seem in any haste to vacate it.

On July 22, Father departed for Boston, where he met with friends and was honored with a dinner at the Union Club, with Senator Sumter, Mr. Emerson, Mr. Tennyson, Mr. Lowell, and Mr. Agassiz in attendance. To Kate's consternation, Father then moved on to visit his longtime dear friend the widow Mrs. Eastman, who of all the attractive, mature ladies who had caught his eye through the years seemed most likely to become the fourth Mrs. Chase. Kate did not complain. She adamantly did not want her father to remarry, but if Mrs. Eastman was able to comfort him in his disappointment, Kate could not bring herself to begrudge him that.

While Father continued his travels, visiting Salem, Naushon Island, and other charming locales in New England, William joined Kate and Nettie in Newport. He had recently purchased several hundred acres on the western shore of Narragansett Bay with the intention of transforming the rambling farmhouse on the property into a gracious mansion. Kate had been eagerly anticipating his arrival for weeks, warmed by his affectionate letters and hopeful that the conflicts of their newlywed days were at last behind them. But when she met him at the station, she quickly took in his bloodshot eyes, his flushed cheeks, the slight tremble of his hands, the faint slur in his voice, and she knew he was drinking again.

Bitterly disappointed, she blinked away her tears and forced a smile. "How were your travels?" she asked, kissing him on the cheek. "Pleasant, I hope."

"The journey was more stomach-churning than usual," he complained wearily, "but I am much better for getting off that train."

Kate murmured sympathetically as she beckoned the porter to stow William's bags on the carriage. As they set out to meet Nettie at the hotel, he looked so queasy that Kate was sorely tempted to point out that it seemed to her that the cause of his sour stomach was his dissipation, not any particular vehicle.

After dinner that evening, William, much recovered, invited her to accompany him on a stroll along the beach. As they walked, he held her hand and talked enthusiastically about his plans for the construction on their new estate, and how he intended for her to decorate the mansion as beautifully as their home in Washington City. She promised to do so, but she suspected he had given her the pleasurable task—along with the promise that he would grant her a generous allowance for it—in order to distract her from his return to intemperance.

It did not work, of course; she managed to contain her anger for a few days, reminding herself constantly of her father's repeated admonitions to submit and to endure all with Christian forbearance, but eventually her anger and disappointment boiled over, and she and William argued more furiously than they ever had. He did not strike her, although he seemed close to it, but as soon as their anger was spent, they reconciled with excuses for their tempers and promises on both sides to do better, to be more loving and patient.

For days on end, peace and tenderness and affection would rule over the household. William would contend with matters of business, Kate would supervise the building of their new home, Nettie would swim and sail and sketch and spend time with William's younger cousins, and at the close of day they would gather around the dinner table happy and full of stories of how they had spent the hours since breakfast. Then the glass would fall, and the ominous thunderclouds would roll in, and the storm would burst—and Nettie would seek shelter out of sight while her sister and brother-in-law raged at each other, waiting for the downpour to cease and the clouds to drift away, borne away on a wind of tearful apologies.

All summer long, as the refurbishing and construction on the Narragansett property progressed enough that they were able to move into one wing of the house, Kate and William struggled to reclaim the affection and amity they had achieved through the mails. Through Confederate general Jubal Early's frightening raid into the North, the Battle of the Monocacy, the ongoing stalemate around Petersburg, the Battle of the Crater, and more skirmishes than they could keep track of, the pattern of argument and reconciliation continued until even Nettie grew accustomed to it.

To Kate it seemed that their frayed tempers reflected the mood of the nation. With General Grant unable to advance upon Richmond and General Sherman stalled near Atlanta, the war had ground to a dispiriting halt, and dissatisfaction with the Lincoln administration was on the rise. Kate found it tragically ironic that one significant element of the dreadful Pomeroy Circular seemed to have been remarkably prescient: As the summer passed and disgruntlement grew, Mr. Lincoln's reelection seemed ever more unlikely.

She was not the only one to think so. Everywhere Father traveled, as he confided in his letters to Kate, he was called upon to speak, and afterward he invariably was approached by gentlemen who would disparage the president and denounce Father's removal from the cabinet. A few Union organizations in New York had demanded a new convention to nominate "a man who would put an end to the war," but when they had tried to draft Father as their candidate, he had flatly refused. It pained Kate to read her father's matter-of-fact, stoic descriptions of the state of things, for they both knew that if Father were in the race he very likely would have claimed the Republican nomination; but if Mr. Lincoln lost in November, Father's chance to be named chief justice would vanish like mist in the August sunshine.

Other political opportunities to return to public service had come Father's way that summer, none promising enough for him to accept. Early in August, several of Father's friends in Ohio had, without his knowledge, submitted his name for consideration as the Republican nominee for Congress from Cincinnati's first district. Father was intrigued, but he informed his friends that only if the district convention nominated him unanimously would he accept. The caveat turned out to be unnecessary, for another candidate won the nomination. Soon after that humiliating loss of an office Father had not even sought, Secretary Fessenden had met him in Boston to consult him on various Treasury Department matters, and also to suggest somewhat obliquely that Father might be offered an ambassador's post in Europe. It was only the vague, indefinite shadow of an offer, but Father firmly declined, unwilling to absent himself from his beloved country before its great crisis was resolved.

On the second day of September, Father took the train from Boston to Providence; William met him at the station and escorted him to Narragansett, where Kate and Nettie welcomed their father joyously. In unmistakable but unintended contrast, Kate greeted her husband with polite reserve. She and William had not yet reconciled from their most recent squabble, and although they were careful not to argue in front of her father, they were abrupt and sometimes hostile to each other. They could not seem to help it. Father was clearly shocked to witness how poorly they were getting along, and for his sake Kate endeavored not to engage William in argument for the duration of her father's visit, even if that meant ignoring her husband entirely.

But the next day, their ongoing quarrel was driven from their thoughts by the news from the South: General Sherman had captured Atlanta.

The people of the North were jubilant. After a dismal summer marked by stalemate, discouragement, and defeat, the Union army suddenly surged toward victory—and so too did Mr. Lincoln. Overnight he had become a victorious commander in chief, and in the transformed political environment, the Radical Republican effort to put forth another candidate seemed foolhardy, even dangerous. Father and Kate speculated that unless the National Union and Radical Democracy parties united around a single candidate, it was entirely possible that the Republican voters would divide their ballots between Mr. Lincoln and General Frémont, and thereby allow the Democrats to seize the presidency. At the end of August, the Democratic National Convention met in Chicago to nominate General McClellan on a peace platform that called for a cease-fire and negotiated settlement with the Confederacy. This, the family agreed, would be disastrous for the Union cause—but with Father out of the cabinet, he was unable to advise the president on a better course.

But that did not mean he was powerless to help. In mid-September, a few days before Nettie's seventeenth birthday, the Spragues and Chases returned to Washington City, where Father made the perfunctory round of calls to his remaining loyal friends, all of whom urged Father to campaign yet again for Mr. Lincoln. Secretary Fessenden promised to speak to Mr. Lincoln on his behalf, and he encouraged Father to call at the White House himself as soon as possible. Father eventually did, albeit reluctantly, but as Kate had privately foreseen, the meeting was stiff and awkward and uncomfortable despite Mr. Lincoln's attempts to welcome Father with his usual cordiality. Afterward, Father decided to endorse his former rival, and he promptly began writing letters to friends and allies declaring that he wholeheartedly supported Mr. Lincoln for president, and if they cared at all about saving the Union, they would too.

Not long after Father joined the campaign, Postmaster General Montgomery Blair resigned from the cabinet. "A late birthday present for me," exclaimed Nettie when Father broke the surprising news of his enemy's ouster.

Kate, William, and Father laughed, but their mirth quickly turned to speculation. Mr. Lincoln was fond of Mr. Blair, he needed the support of the powerful Blair family among conservatives, and Mr. Blair had seemed to relish his position in the cabinet. "I cannot fathom why he would resign unless the president requested it," said Father, "but I cannot imagine Mr. Lincoln doing so." They were all pleased when Mr. Lincoln named as Mr. Blair's replacement Father's own successor, the former governor of Ohio William Dennison, who remained Father's friend even though he had stood firmly with Mr. Lincoln in the wake of the Pomeroy Circular fiasco.

Soon thereafter, an intriguing possible explanation for Mr. Blair's removal emerged when General Frémont, the Radical Democracy candidate, abruptly withdrew from the race. Although the Chases could not prove any reciprocity, they agreed that the timing was too suspect to be a coincidence, considering that the Radical Republicans had particularly despised Mr. Blair and had long wanted him excised from the cabinet.

Now the separate factions of the divided Republican Party were almost certain to rally around Mr. Lincoln, for the political distinction between the two remaining candidates could not have been more clear. President Lincoln was the leader of a victorious army and the savior of the Union, while General McClellan was remembered as a perpetually hesitant military officer whose party insisted upon a platform of peace at any price, a position most loyal Unionists could not abide.

Although Mr. Lincoln's prospects had greatly improved, Father campaigned for him as vigorously as ever, traveling to Ohio, Kentucky, Illinois, Missouri, and Michigan to urge voters to reelect him. Kate and Nettie accompanied their father as far as Cincinnati, where Kate was heartened to see him addressing the crowds, dignified and earnest, enjoining them to show up in record numbers at the polls on election day. Kate knew well that a lesser man would have sulked at home, bitterly wishing for his rival to fail, but Father cared too much about the survival of the Union to sacrifice it to his vanity. She wished his detractors knew this about him, but they had closed their hearts and minds to his nobility of spirit long ago.

On October 11, exultant Republicans celebrated victories in state elections in Ohio, Pennsylvania, and Indiana, races that were considered auguries of the presidential contest to follow a month later. The next day, a more somber mood prevailed when it was announced that Chief Justice Roger Brooke Taney had passed away at the age of eighty-seven, leaving a vacancy on the Supreme Court. By then Kate and Nettie had returned to Washington, but Kate gleaned from her father's letters that he fervently hoped Mr. Lincoln would nominate him for the position immediately. Neither she nor her father was surprised when the president deferred his decision until after the election.

In the anxious, frenzied month between the state and national elections, Secretary of War Edwin Stanton made sure that soldiers were given absentee ballots, if the laws of their states permitted, or furloughs so they could travel home to vote. President Lincoln wrote to several of his generals asking them to grant leave to soldiers from states where the election would likely be close—Missouri, Indiana, Pennsylvania, and New York—assuming that the Union soldiers would overwhelmingly support the Republican ticket as they had in the off-year elections.

In the end, the steadfast, devoted soldiers made all the difference.

The early returns suggested even larger Republican majorities than in the state elections, and by midnight on Election Day, November 8, Mr. Lincoln's triumph was certain.

In the days that followed, as the final tallies were recorded, the people learned that Mr. Lincoln had won all but three states—New Jersey, Delaware, and Kentucky—and that he had captured an overwhelming majority of the electoral votes, 212 versus 21 for General McClellan. Moreover, the newly reunited Republican Party had elected twelve governors and had acquired thirty-seven additional seats in Congress.

It was a tremendous victory, the only outcome that allowed for the preservation of the Union; but although relief pervaded the Chase household, their joy was muted, for they all believed the triumph should have been Father's.

Four days later, Kate came down to breakfast with happy expectations of a joyful, romantic Saturday with her husband. They had been getting along better than usual of late, their shared apprehensions about the election and their new hopes for Father's prospects drawing them together, as the extremes of mutual joy and worry always had. William had said nothing about any special plans, which gave her pause, but she decided to give him the benefit of the doubt and assume he meant to surprise her. That suited her just fine, because she had a surprise for him as well.

But there were no flowers or loving proclamations at breakfast, nor did William suggest that they go riding or walking together later. As the hours passed, and William seemed content to treat the day as if it were as ordinary as any other, her anger and unhappiness grew in equal measures. She endured it as long as she possibly could, even lingering in the study after nightfall while he read the evening news. She ordered herself not to reproach him, but when he finally folded up the papers, rose from his chair, and bent to kiss her good night, she could not restrain herself any longer. "You forgot our anniversary."

He froze, wide-eyed with dismay and guilt. "Happy anniversary, darling," he said weakly.

"How could you have forgotten our first anniversary?"

"I didn't forget," he said quickly. "I meant to celebrate tomorrow, to mark the first full year of our married lives. That always seemed to me the better day to honor. I suppose I should have told you my plans."

"You," she said distinctly, her anger surging, "are a liar." She rose from her chair, turned her back upon him, and said over her shoulder as she left the room, "And you are going to be a father."

She slept alone in Nettie's vacant room that night, leaving their bedchamber to William. The next morning, she found a bouquet of beautiful autumn flowers outside the door, and when she met William at the breakfast table, he looked pale and contrite. "I'm sorry, my darling," he whispered in her ear as he clumsily kissed her cheek. Expressionless, she endured the kiss rather than upset her father, who sat at the head of the table with his coffee cup and Bible, closed upon a black velvet ribbon to mark his place.

"Katie, dear," he said, quickly rising and coming over to kiss her too. "Happy anniversary, daughter—somewhat belatedly, I regret. And to you too, William," he added, shaking his son-in-law's hand.

Father looked abashed, but Kate was so accustomed to his forgetting his daughters' birthdays that she had not expected him to remember her wedding anniversary. "Thank you, Father," she said, more surprised than touched by his remorse.

They all sat down together at the table, where, ever the gracious hostess, Kate steered the conversation to Mr. Lincoln's lengthy delay in appointing a new chief justice, a subject of keen interest to them all and one upon which they all agreed. Afterward, they parted company to attend to their own duties, but long after she had assumed William had left for Capitol Hill, he found her alone in the kitchen, where she and Addie were discussing the menu for their Thanksgiving feast.

When she saw William in the doorway, Kate nodded to Addie as a sign to leave them alone. The servants would never admit to knowing William hurt her, but they often arranged to be discreetly present whenever William came upon her unexpectedly. He never hit her when Father was in the house, or at least he had not yet, but she was grateful for the servants' loyalty, their compassionate desire to protect her.

"Are you feeling well?" he asked quietly when they were alone.

She nodded.

"How long have you known?"

"Almost two weeks."

"And that means the baby will come . . ."

"In June."

"June," he echoed, a note of wonder in his voice. "Will you have the baby here, do you think, or in Rhode Island?"

"I honestly haven't thought that far ahead."

William nodded and fell silent. After a long moment, he said, "But you are feeling quite well?"

"Yes, thank you." Such a strange conversation, so formal and polite, when they should be laughing tearfully and embracing over the good news. "A little queasiness in the mornings, but nothing too dreadful."

"You must be sure to take care of yourself," he said, and then, after a momentary pause, he added, "If you are feeling well enough to bear my absence, I thought I should go away for a little while."

With practiced care, she sat perfectly still, not permitting even the barest trace of her sudden distress to show. "I see. Where will you go, and when?"

"I thought I would spend Thanksgiving with my mother and family in Providence."

"I have a feast planned," she said steadily. "Many friends and family are coming."

"Then I'm reassured, for with so many guests around you, my absence will scarcely be noticed. Besides, it is you and your father the people come to see, not me."

"I think they come to see us all, together," she said carefully, "but perhaps . . . perhaps some time apart would be good for us."

He nodded, haggard and mournful, and then he gave her a slight bow and left her alone.

On Thursday, November 24, Father and Kate entertained a houseful of friends and family in fine style, marking the day with solemn joy and gratitude as the president had urged the nation to do in his Thanksgiving Proclamation issued the year before, when he had established the national holiday on the fourth Thursday in November. As she found comfort in the kind words and fond embraces of those she loved, Kate imagined William sitting at his mother's table and felt profoundly sad that they seemed unable to be happy together.

Suddenly Kate realized with shock that her vaunted poise had abandoned her, and if she brooded over her absent husband and inexplicably fractious marriage a moment longer, she would burst into sobs in front of all her guests. Determinedly, she drove William from her mind and turned her thoughts to Mr. Lincoln, the founder of the new national holiday. She imagined him and Mrs. Lincoln presiding over a sumptuous banquet in the White House, for despite their personal losses and the trials of their high offices, surely no one in the country had greater reason to be thankful than they.

But within a few days, Kate learned that Mr. and Mrs. Lincoln had probably celebrated less happily than she had supposed. Mr. Lincoln had spent the day in his sickbed, still suffering from the effects of the varioloid he had contracted on his way home from the dedication of the new national cemetery at Gettysburg. It was there that he had received an unwelcome letter from Attorney General Edward Bates. With Mr. Lincoln safely reelected, citing illness, fatigue, and the overwhelming yearning to retire to St. Louis to enjoy the company of his wife, children, and grandchildren, Mr. Bates had submitted his resignation, and President Lincoln had regretfully accepted it.

On December 1, the day Mr. Bates's resignation took effect, Mr. Lincoln appointed as his successor Kentucky lawyer and abolitionist James Speed, the elder brother of his dear friend Joshua Speed. "Would that all the president's appointments were made so swiftly," Father said unhappily when the news broke. President Lincoln still had not chosen a new chief justice, and while Father waited with increasing desire and diminishing hopes, his loyal friends tirelessly campaigned for him. They had warned Father that three of Mr. Lincoln's most loyal cabinet members also coveted the post—Secretary Stanton, the recently retired Mr. Bates, and the mysteriously ousted former postmaster Mr. Blair. To Kate, who was admittedly hardly an objective observer, Father seemed a far better choice than any of the three, and not only because of his qualifications: Secretary Stanton was absolutely indispensable at his current post as secretary of war, Mr. Bates had only just retired and had expressed great desire to return to St. Louis, and whatever political circumstances had compelled the president to accept Mr. Blair's resignation as postmaster general likely remained to complicate his nomination. Mr. Lincoln had proven to be an astute judge of character, he clearly respected Father as a statesman and lawyer, and he had always shown a remarkable ability to put aside personal disagreements for the greater good of the country. Why, then, Kate wondered, did he delay?

Massachusetts Senator Henry Wilson, a mutual friend who had been advocating Father's cause, soon provided an answer. "Of Mr. Chase's ability and of his soundness on the general issues of the war there is, of course, no question," President Lincoln had told him. "I have only one doubt about his appointment. He is a man of unbounded ambition, and has been working all his life to become president. That he can never be; and I fear that if I make him chief justice he will simply become more restless and uneasy and neglect the place in his strife and intrigue to make himself president. If I were sure that he would go on the bench and give up his aspirations and do nothing but make himself a great judge, I would not hesitate a moment."

Kate waited, tense and watchful, while Father mulled over his friend's words. "Thank you for this confidence," he said, but when he promptly changed the subject to a finance bill under debate in the Senate, Kate understood that he was not quite ready to relinquish his presidential ambitions.

The following day, William returned from Providence, so contrite and affectionate and concerned for her and their unborn child that Kate was inclined to forgive him every slight, every misunderstanding. And yet there was a strange undercurrent of apprehension in his manner that every instinct told her had nothing to do with the state of their marriage.

At dinner, William spoke so earnestly with Father on the subject of the Supreme Court that she concluded that he was simply anxious about Mr. Lincoln's delay in naming a new chief justice, as they all were. Father had heard nothing new from Senator Wilson or any of his other friends who had been appealing to the president on his behalf. "I've put off a trip to Ohio in expectation of a summons from the president," Father told William, "but now that you are here to watch over our Katie, I have decided to go. If the president discovers he has something important to ask me, he can send a telegram."

At that Kate and William exchanged a smile, and when their eyes met, Kate felt the same familiar warmth and longing he had once inspired in her so easily. She knew then that she still loved him dearly, and she wished with all her heart that they could turn back the clock and begin anew on their wedding day, fresh and bright and hopeful. She would do so many things differently. She would be patient and tolerant and vigilant, so that William would have no reason to slip back into his indolent ways. She would soften her sharp words and sweeten her bitter remonstrances. And while she was at it, she thought with wry amusement, she would warn them both to have nothing to do with Senator Pomeroy and his "Chase for President" gang, and she would intervene before they published their disastrous pamphlet and circular. Above all, she would prevent Father from submitting his resignation. What a different, happier quartet she, Father, William, and Nettie would be if she could do it all over again, but possessing the wisdom of the hard lessons learned that year.

Kate could do nothing about the poor decisions that had led to her father's downfall, but she could strive to advise him better in the future, and she could dedicate herself to improving her marriage, for their child's sake as well as their own.

When the meal was finished, they lingered at the table to hear about William's business enterprises, which were all thriving, and to discuss the progress of the war. Their lively conversation was interrupted when Will announced a visitor, Speaker of the House Schuyler Colfax, whom he had shown to Father's study.

"Please have coffee brought up to us," Father instructed, and as Will nodded and hurried off to the kitchen, Kate and William followed Father to his study, where Mr. Colfax waited, his hands clasped behind his back as he examined a shelf of books, scanning the spines for their titles.

Father greeted him cordially and invited him to sit, and before the usual exchange of pleasantries was concluded, Addie appeared with coffee and apple tart. Mr. Colfax, who had just come from the White House and confessed that he had had no dinner, accepted the refreshments with great satisfaction. "I apologize for the late hour," he said, after quickly savoring two bites, "but I understand you are off to Ohio in the morning, and it was essential that I speak with you before you depart."

Kate and William exchanged a quick, hopeful glance, but Father said only, "It is not too late, and you're always welcome here. To what do I owe the pleasure of your visit?"

"Mr. Lincoln and I enjoyed an interesting conversation about you this evening," Mr. Colfax said. "He is still considering you for chief justice."

"Did he offer a reason for his interminable delay?" William queried.

"In a manner of speaking. First he assured me that there is no question in his mind about your abilities, Chase, and of your soundness on the general issues of the war. He also said that he should despise himself if he allowed personal differences to affect his judgment of your fitness for the office of chief justice."

"He has always been fair-minded in that way," admitted Kate.

"His only concern is that you would be a politician first and a judge second," Mr. Colfax said. "In his estimation, you would make an excellent judge if you devoted yourself exclusively to the duties of your office and didn't meddle in politics. If instead you kept on with the notion that you're destined to be president of the United States, you would never acquire that fame and usefulness as chief justice that you would otherwise certainly attain." He winced and quickly added, "Do bear in mind that this is my poor paraphrase of his statements, and not my own opinion."

"Of course," Father replied automatically, but his gaze was faraway.

Mr. Colfax's message from the president—for that is certainly what it was, although decorum required that no one acknowledge it as such— echoed Mr. Lincoln's remarks to Senator Wilson, and the consistent emphasis told Kate that he was resolute. Perhaps he truly did believe that the distraction of other ambitions would prevent Father from fulfilling his duties on the Supreme Court as perfectly as he otherwise could, but it was also very likely that Mr. Lincoln simply wanted his strongest rival out of the way, never again to contend for the White House. Assurances that Father would never again campaign against Mr. Lincoln for the presidency was the price he would pay to become chief justice.

Kate remembered well what Father had told Senator Wilson, but the days of anxious waiting and uncertainty had forced him to reflect, so she was not surprised when he soberly replied, "I would be honored and content to dedicate the remainder of my life to the bench."

Relief flooded Kate, and William broke out in a grin, and even Mr. Colfax smiled as he took up his plate and fork again and said he would make certain the president knew that.

After Mr. Colfax departed, Nettie joined them in the study, and the family sat up chatting animatedly until the hour grew quite late, more cheerful than they had been in months. When they finally bade one another good night, Kate's pulse quickened as William took her hand and led her off to their bedchamber.

He was gentle and tender, but whether it was their estrangement or the child in her womb that made him cautious, she did not know. Afterward, as she lay in his arms, her eyes full of blissful tears, her heart of love and relief, she silently vowed never again to let anger and resentment divide them.

Later she would reflect ruefully upon how quickly fate tested her resolve.

"My darling birdie," he said, just as she was drifting off to sleep. "I'm sorry, my love, but I have something I must tell you, and I know I shall not sleep until I do."

She rested her hand on his chest above his heart. "What is it, dear?"

"You may remember a certain gentleman named Harris Hoyt."

"The Texan," said Kate, with a stir of trepidation. "That professed Union loyalist who sought a cotton trading permit from Father more than two years ago."

"That's the one," said William. "I don't want to alarm you, but recently one of his ships was apprehended as it attempted to run the blockade with a load of guns to trade for cotton. The captain, Charles Prescott, has been arrested."

"I knew Mr. Hoyt was up to no good," declared Kate, but then the full weight of his words sank in. "Why would this alarm me?"

William said nothing.

Kate steeled herself and kept her voice even. "You weren't involved in this scheme, were you?"

"No," he replied vehemently, and then, calmer but more earnest, "No, I was not, but my cousin Byron Sprague and a friend, William Reynolds, were."

Reynolds. Kate thought quickly. Yes, a Colonel Reynolds had been mentioned in the letter Father had shown her, the one William had written recommending Mr. Hoyt for a cotton permit. "Do you think their actions will reflect badly upon you, or is it worse than that?"

"It could be much worse." William heaved a sigh. "I fear they may implicate me in their crimes—if they have committed any—even though I had nothing to do with it."

Kate fervently hoped he did not. Trading weapons to Confederates for cotton—for anything—without proper authorization was treason. She felt a sudden chill of fear and foreboding. William must not be arrested for treason. Even if he was found not guilty, the charge alone was enough to ruin a man, and his family. Her father would never be chosen chief justice; her child would live out his life in the shadow of shame and disgrace.

"Shall we tell your father?" William asked tentatively. "Perhaps he could make it all go away."

Kate's thoughts raced. "No," she decided. "Not yet. As of this moment, there is nothing to tell. You cannot be prosecuted for the crimes of a cousin, a friend, and a passing acquaintance. If they cast blame on others in a vain attempt to save themselves, and your name comes up, then we'll seek Father's counsel. Until then, we shall wait and see, and hope they have the decency not to condemn the innocent."

But how much decency, really, could they expect from traitors?

"I knew you would offer me sensible advice," said William, sounding much relieved, and very tired. "Thank you for standing beside me, dearest birdie."

"I would say lying beside you, rather," Kate remarked. He chuckled and hugged her, but as he sighed and settled down to sleep, she grew pensive. "William?"

"Yes, my love?"

"I want to help you, and I will, but I cannot unless you are perfectly frank with me," she said. "Is there anything else you want to tell me—or rather, is there anything else I would want to know that I don't? Anything that you have kept from me, perhaps out of a kindhearted wish to protect me?"

He stiffened. "Why? What have you heard?"

"Nothing," said Kate, taken aback. "What is there for me to hear?"

"Exactly that, nothing," he replied, quickly and firmly, "but we both know that doesn't prevent malicious gossips from spreading lies. You mustn't listen to any scurrilous tales anyone might tell you of me."

"I won't, of course." He had asked her that once before, she recalled, and she had made him the same promise. "You must not believe slanderous gossip about me either."

"I never have," he said through a deep yawn. "I never will."

But he had, Kate recalled. Nearly three years before, someone from Columbus had given him an exaggerated account of the incident with the married Mr. Nevins—an impropriety, but not as terrible as William had been told—and he had believed it, until another acquaintance refuted her accuser. Yet again she found herself puzzled by her husband's inaccurate memory of his own words and actions. Was he truly that forgetful, or did he think that by deciding to accept a particular version of events as true, he could make it so by sheer force of belief?

Wondering, full of doubt, she lay awake long after William fell sound asleep beside her.

In the morning Father bade Kate, William, and Nettie farewell and left for the train station, fretful about the ongoing silence from the White House, worried about leaving Kate in her delicate condition, but clearly happy to see her and William reconciled.

Despite their intimacy of William's homecoming night, in the days that followed he and Kate were tentative around each other, overly polite and formal, wary of giving offense that might hurl them back into rancorous discord. Nettie, aware only that they were speaking kindly to each other rather than arguing, fairly danced through the house with delight. She had good reason to be cheerful. Where the rest of them harbored doubts, she was absolutely certain that Mr. Lincoln would choose Father for chief justice eventually, and she knew nothing of Mr. Hoyt's alleged crimes. Kate wished she could be so confident and carefree.

Father's trip to Ohio was rewarding, but in a letter home he confessed his anxiety about being away with Mr. Lincoln's decision still pending, and so he decided to cut his travels short. Shortly after breakfast on the day they expected him home, William returned unexpectedly from the Senate, which had convened a new session the day before. Ashen-faced, he told Kate he had learned that Captain Prescott had confessed his illicit activities in great detail, and that Harris Hoyt, Byron Sprague, and William Reynolds, implicated as partners in his schemes, had been arrested in Providence. "What should I do?" he asked, frantic.

"Has your name come up in the investigation?"

"I don't know."

"Well, there's no reason that it should," she reassured him as he paced. "Why should the accused men mention you at all, if you were not involved?"

"Because of my cousin," he said, agitated, as if she should have known. "The Sprague name will naturally turn the investigators' thoughts to me, the most prominent Sprague in the nation."

Kate did not think that was necessarily so. "All the same, let's refrain from acting hastily. Keep silent and watchful rather than do anything to draw their attention."

"No." William shook his head, scowling in worry. "No. I must write to the officer in charge and explain that I had absolutely nothing to do with their scheme. I'll explain that I have no connection to Hoyt, and that this whole affair is nothing more than a partisan attack on me through my cousin and friend."

"Do nothing yet," Kate said emphatically, laying a hand on his arm. "If you adamantly deny that you were involved when they have no reason to believe you were, placing yourself before the investigators will only raise their suspicions."

He threw her a mutinous look and set his jaw, but she persisted, and eventually she persuaded him to defer writing his letter of self-defense. He had no time at present anyway, she reminded him. The Senate was in recess only until one o'clock, at which time John Nicolay would deliver the president's annual message to Congress. William ought to be there, and Kate certainly intended to be, and avoiding his duties in order to compose an unnecessary refutation to charges that did not exist only made him look guilty.

Reluctantly, William agreed to wait. Together they went to the Capitol, where Kate assumed her favorite seat in the gallery and William took his place at the table beside Henry B. Anthony, the senior senator from Rhode Island.

Soon thereafter, Mr. Nicolay arrived with President Lincoln's address. Kate thought it lacked his usual eloquence and poetry, especially in the beginning, perhaps because he had composed it on his sickbed. It was certainly more optimistic than any of his previous State of the Union addresses. The Union army was steadily advancing, the president had noted, and the results of the November elections proved that the people of the North were resolved to see the war through to victory. Despite their significant losses, the North still overmatched the South in men and resources. "The financial affairs of the government have been successfully administered during the last year," the president also asserted, which Kate took as a compliment to Father, for he was responsible for that success even though he was no longer secretary of the treasury.

As if Mr. Lincoln anticipated that his address would be read in the Confederate capital—and indeed it likely would be printed in the Richmond papers within days—he emphasized that the overmatched South could have peace the moment they decided to lay down their arms and submit to federal authority. His administration would not, however, acquiesce in any way to any demands to perpetuate slavery; in fact, the president called on the House to approve the constitutional amendment abolishing slavery that the Senate had already passed. "In stating a single condition of peace," he concluded, "I mean simply to say that the war will cease on the part of the government whenever it shall have ceased on the part of those who began it."

If only it were that simple, Kate thought. If only it were a matter of deciding to stop fighting, laying down one's arms, and going home.

She mulled over the president's words as other business was introduced—a motion by Senator Anthony that thousands of copies of the message be printed, a reading of Secretary Fessenden's report on the state of the nation's finances, a resolution from Senator Sumner that the Department of State furnish to the Senate any information they possessed regarding British subjects supporting the rebellion—and then executive business was considered.

Kate was studying her husband from above and considering what she might do to encourage him to speak more often in the chamber when the clerk commenced reading other messages Mr. Nicolay had brought from the White House. "To the Senate of the United States," he began the first, "I nominate Salmon P. Chase, of Ohio, to be Chief Justice of the Supreme Court of the United States, vice Roger B. Taney, deceased. Signed, Abraham Lincoln."

Kate smothered a gasp. She had lived all this before, she thought faintly, nodding with practiced grace as others in the gallery congratulated her in hushed voices. Her eyes met William's, wide with shock, and as she watched, a slow grin spread over his face. A fellow senator clapped him heartily on the back and shook his hand, but elsewhere in the chamber, Kate spotted others scowling and shaking their heads. In the meantime, Governor Dennison's nomination as postmaster general and Mr. Speed's as attorney general were also announced, but in the motion that followed, only Father's appointment was immediately and unanimously approved, even though Kate knew that more than a few men in that room would have preferred another in his place.

Father surely did not know yet, Kate realized. He was traveling home, and it was unlikely that a telegram could reach him along the way.

The moment the Senate adjourned, before any eager petitioners could detain her, Kate hurried off to meet William in the rotunda. "At last," he declared, exultant. "Finally your father has received his just reward for his years of loyalty to the Republican Party and his thankless efforts on Mr. Lincoln's behalf. This honor is long overdue."

"I cannot wait to tell him," Kate said, smiling as she took his arm. "I do hope I shall be the one to give him the good news."

"He'll probably hear it from some railroad porter first," William said airily as he escorted her outside. "Kate, darling, this changes everything. No one will prosecute the son-in-law of the chief justice of the Supreme Court. They wouldn't dare attempt it, not even if they had caught me with my pockets stuffed with rebel cotton."

Kate regarded him askance. "It is your innocence that shields you, not Father's new position, is it not?"

"Oh, yes," he hastened to agree. "Yes, of course. However, I'm not sorry to have this extra measure of protection too."

Kate fell silent, suddenly wary—and worried that in his jubilation he might say more than he should within earshot of men who would not hesitate to use that information against him.

Later that evening, when Father returned home, Kate met him at the door. "Good evening, Honorable Chief Justice," she greeted him, beaming.

A weary but joyful smile lit up his face. "It's official, then?"

"It is," she said, and threw herself into his arms, relieved and proud and happy.

After accepting congratulations from the entire household, Father promptly retired to his study to write to Mr. Lincoln. "Do you think this will suit the occasion?" he asked Kate, as he handed her the letter almost shyly.

Washington, Decr. 6, 1864

My dear Sir,
*   On reaching home tonight I was saluted with the intelligence that you this day nominated me to the Senate for the office of Chief Justice. I cannot sleep before I thank you for this mark of your confidence, & especially for the manner in which the nomination was made. I shall never forget either and trust that you will never regret either. Be assured that I prize your confidence & good will more than nomination or office.*
*   Faithfully yours*
*   S. P. Chase*

"As for myself, I would not have thanked him so profusely for the manner in which he nominated you," Kate admitted with a little laugh, "but otherwise I think it suits perfectly."

So Father summoned a messenger and sent it off straight away.

Nine days later, William, Nettie, and Kate—elegantly coiffed and exquisitely attired for the momentous occasion in a beautiful gown by Parisian couturier Charles Frederick Worth, adjusted to fit her *enceinte* figure—accompanied Father to the Supreme Court for his swearing-in ceremony. While Father was escorted to an anteroom where the justices awaited him, his family took their places of honor in the chamber. Already it was crowded with dignitaries, Father's friends, allies, and political enemies alike, all determined to witness history, the first installment of a chief justice since 1836.

Soon after the family seated themselves, an usher announced, "The Honorable Justices of the Supreme Court of the United States." Nettie seized Kate's hand and let out a little gasp of excitement as Father entered the room through an entrance behind the bench. The senior associate justice—James M. Wayne, a frail septuagenarian in poor health—accompanied him, and the other eight justices followed close behind. Bowing formally to one another, they took their seats according to tenure, and then Father and Justice Wayne approached. Steadily and distinctly, Father read the oath aloud from a paper Justice Wayne provided him, and when he had finished, Father set the document aside, gazed up at the rotunda, and in a voice thick with emotion but as strong as his faith, declared, "So help me God."

Overwhelmed with pride and love—and only the most fleeting sting of disappointment that her father's presidential dreams were almost certainly over—Kate squeezed her sister's hand and echoed his fervent prayer in the silence of her own heart.

Chapter Twenty

*F*ather's proud achievement lifted the spirits of the entire household and boded well for the merriest Christmas the family had known in years, despite William's ongoing worries about the arrests of Mr. Hoyt and his cohorts. Against Kate's advice, soon after Father's installment as chief justice, William wrote to General John A. Dix, the officer in charge of the investigation, presumably to clear his name, but the content of his letter remained a frustrating mystery to Kate, for he refused to let her read it. "I have been assisting Father with his professional correspondence since I was sixteen years old," she reminded him, to no avail. Full of misgivings, every afternoon she awaited the mail with breathless dread, expecting each delivery to bring a summons commanding William to appear before a court of inquiry. When no ominous document appeared, her fears lessened with the passage of time, leaving behind a residue of anxiety and unhappiness. It saddened her terribly that William delegated innumerable little tasks to her, but excluded her from the more significant aspects of his business and political life. What she wanted most was to help him in everything, as she had always helped her father. She would have thought that she had proven herself in her long career as Father's hostess and domestic secretary, but William either thought she was not quite capable enough, or he did not trust her enough to confide his secrets, or some insulting combination of the two.

Kate was pleased and relieved when William decided to spend Christmas with her, Father, and Nettie in Washington, but she was—childishly, she knew—rather disappointed with his gift. For weeks she had hinted very strongly that either of two gifts would please her immensely—a comfortable settee for her sitting room, if he preferred to give her something practical, or a stunning diamond brooch from Tiffany, if he was feeling more extravagant and romantic. Instead, on Christmas morning, she discovered a thick envelope containing money and a note. "I place in your stocking tonight this token," he had written. "Let it stand in place of a reminder of power for happiness and of usefulness, yet not powerful enough or rich enough in resources to purchase from you the smallest particle of my affection or to represent, with all its power a millionth part of the strength of my love to my wife."

It was a pleasant enough note, if rambling in a troubling way that suggested he had been drinking when he wrote it, but his ardent phrases could not disguise the hasty, impersonal nature of the gift. Even so, Kate knew it was selfish and spoiled of her to resent him for the imperfect present—which indeed was quite generous—so she said nothing. She did not want to seem petty, and she did not want to diminish the family's Christmas joy, which had been multiplied by the good news that General Sherman's march across Georgia had concluded at the Atlantic. All of Washington City exulted in reports that the general had sent the president a telegram that day declaring, "I beg to present to you, as a Christmas gift, the city of Savannah, with 150 heavy guns and plenty of ammunition, and also about 25,000 bales of cotton."

But good news from the war did little to console Kate when William left Washington to welcome the New Year with his family at Young Orchard. Then grief and sorrow compounded her loneliness, for Father's younger sister, Helen Chase Walbridge, died in Ohio, leaving Father and Uncle Edward the only survivors of their ten siblings. Aunt Helen was buried on New Year's Day, and with the household in mourning, they canceled their usual celebration and did not attend Mr. and Mrs. Lincoln's traditional reception. Grief-stricken, Father wrote to send his regrets and to explain that the death of his beloved sister precluded them from attending. Later, Kate was moved when she read the gracious, sympathetic letter of condolence Mr. Lincoln sent in reply. For her part, Mrs.

Lincoln remained silent. Not even tragedy would inspire her to show compassion for a rival.

On January 6, Ohio congressman James M. Ashley reintroduced the Thirteenth Amendment abolishing slavery throughout the United States, which had already passed the Senate, into the House. On the last day of the month, Father and the other Supreme Court justices attended the final debates before the vote. Dozens of senators, including William, had come to witness the historic moment, as had members of many foreign ministries and Secretaries Seward, Fessenden, and Dennison, representing the cabinet. Kate and Nettie arrived early to claim good seats in the gallery, which for the first time also admitted people of color. The Negro men and women watched the final speeches and heard the vote taken in solemn, breathless quiet, breaking into cheers and joyful weeping when the measure passed. Although three-fourths of the states would have to ratify the amendment before it would become the law of the land, people of color and abolitionists rejoiced, certain that slavery had been dealt a fatal blow.

Father and Kate knew that President Lincoln had appointed him to be chief justice in part because of his certainty that Father would use his exalted position to help secure rights for people of color. Soon after Father ascended to the Supreme Court, Senator Charles Sumner wrote to him on behalf of John Rock, a Negro lawyer from Massachusetts who had long sought to practice before the Supreme Court but had been rejected solely because of his race. Father was well pleased to open the court to people of color, and the day after the Thirteenth Amendment passed the House, he welcomed Senator Sumner to stand before the bench as Mr. Rock's sponsor. "May it please the court," Senator Sumner declared, "I move that John S. Rock, a member of the Supreme Court of the State of Massachusetts, be admitted to practice as a member of this court." While Kate and Nettie looked on proudly, Father summoned Mr. Rock forward to swear the oath that would permit him to practice before the highest court in the land.

A Peace Convention at Hampton Roads in early February resolved nothing despite President Lincoln's unexpected appearance at the bargaining table, but elsewhere, upon the battlefields and in the halls of government, the first months of the New Year brought about promising developments. In mid-January, the Union navy captured Fort Fisher, which closed the port of Wilmington, North Carolina, and severed supply lines to the Confederacy from abroad. Farther south, General Sherman had moved on from Savannah to Columbia, and on February 17 his forces captured the state capital of South Carolina. The following day, the Confederates surrendered Fort Sumter and evacuated Charleston, and all the while, General Grant was tightening his stranglehold on Petersburg and threatening the Confederate capital of Richmond twenty-five miles to the north.

Kate hardly dared believe it, but a Union victory seemed more certain than ever before. Perhaps, she thought, stroking her swelling abdomen, perhaps her son or daughter would be born into peace—into a nation no longer torn asunder by war and into a home reconciled in love.

The mood in Washington was hopeful and ebullient as the capital prepared for Mr. Lincoln's second inauguration. In scenes reminiscent of four years before, thousands of visitors flooded the city, citizens eager to enjoy the revelries and politicians determined to promote themselves and their favorite causes. Again the hotels and boardinghouses were packed to overflowing, and at the Willard, ladies and gentlemen alike sat up all night in the crowded parlors because no beds could be found for them.

On the evening before the inauguration, a welcome guest from Boston called on the Chase family, Father's friend and fellow abolitionist Frederick Douglass. Kate was making some last-minute alterations to the new robe Father would wear when he administered the oath to Mr. Lincoln, but she quickly set aside her pins and needles and shears to welcome the renowned orator and former slave into the parlor, where for the better part of an hour, Father had obediently donned or removed the garment as instructed so Kate could fit it to his imposing form.

"I decided to join the grand procession of citizens from all parts of the country who have come to witness this historic occasion," Mr. Douglass said as he settled into an armchair and accepted a cup of tea. When Kate and her father exchanged a troubled glance, he smiled knowingly. "Yes, my people have always been excluded from these inaugural celebrations, but when I contemplate how much blood of both white and Negro soldiers has been spilled in our common cause, and lies forever intermingled upon the battlefields, I believe it is not too great an assumption for a colored man to think he might offer his congratulations to the president in the company of white citizens."

"I hope you aren't turned away at the door," said Kate, pursing her lips as she threaded a needle.

"That would be a great outrage," Father fairly growled.

"I've been turned away at doors before and have survived," Mr. Douglass said easily. "And yet I don't think I'll be sent away tomorrow."

"But if you are," Father said, "find me and I will get you in."

"Thank you, but I want to get myself in, on the merits of my own citizenship, not because I am accompanied by the chief justice of the Supreme Court."

"I was your friend long before I assumed that lofty title," said Father, "and your friend, first and foremost, I remain."

"Of that I have no doubt," said Mr. Douglass. "I remember well our early antislavery days, when you welcomed me to your home and your table when to do so was a strange thing."

Kate smiled as she made tiny, even stitches in the hem of the robe. "To Father, it was always a strange thing to consider it strange." She finished the last stitch and deftly tied an almost-invisible knot. "There. It's done. Father, will you try this on one more time? You've been infinitely patient and if I've done this right, I promise to cease plaguing you."

Obligingly Father stood. "You are no plague, my dear."

As Kate stretched to lift the robe over his head, she felt a sudden strong twinge in her abdomen, and with an involuntary gasp, she bent forward, clutching her side.

"Katie," her father exclaimed, alarmed, and Mr. Douglass too was on his feet.

She smiled, waving off the men's concern. "It's nothing, just a little kick. I was surprised, not hurt."

Uncertain, Father asked, "Are you sure?"

"Very sure."

"Nevertheless, please allow me," said Mr. Douglass, holding out his hands for the robe. Kate gave it to him with her thanks, and as Father stood tall and still, Mr. Douglass placed the robe over his shoulders. Kate made a few adjustments here and there so that it draped better upon him, and then she declared it perfect.

She doubted Mr. Lincoln would look half as well as her father did when they stood upon the platform together the next day.

That night a terrible storm struck Washington City, and Kate was dragged from sleep by the crash of thunder and the scour of hail upon the roof. Scarcely awake, heart pounding, she propped herself up on her elbows, confused and wondering whether the tumult was a storm or an attack. When the truth dawned, she lay down wearily and hoped the tempest would soon subside and allow her to drift back to sleep. It was not an ominous portent for the president's second term, she told herself as she rolled carefully onto her side and drew the quilt up to her chin. If a hotel had caught fire somewhere nearby, she might be tempted to consider *that* an ill omen, but not a mere storm, even if it was the most severe one that had struck the capital in that damp early spring.

The morning dawned gray and drizzly, and a glance out the window revealed that the night's torrential downpour had turned the streets into thick rivers of mud. Kate hoped the streets would dry somewhat in time for the grand parade for the sake of the fifty thousand citizens who were predicted to gather at the Capitol and the thousands more who would line the parade route. It was expected to be a glorious procession, with soldiers and cavalry and bands, representatives from fire departments, civic organizations, and fraternal lodges from across the North marching proudly carrying banners and flags, and much more adding to the spectacle. Kate would not see it, for she, Nettie, and William would accompany Father to the Senate ahead of time, as they had been granted places of honor in the galleries thanks to Father's important role in the proceedings. When they arrived, Kate learned that Mr. Lincoln had missed the entire procession too, for he had so many bills pending that he had gone to the Capitol early, and was signing them still. Kate imagined Mrs. Lincoln riding in the closed carriage alone, proudly accepting the joyful cheers meant for her husband.

After the Senate adjourned at noon, Kate watched as Mr. Lincoln entered the chamber accompanied by his cabinet, his expression grave and melancholy, his eyes shadowed, his cheeks cavernous. As they took their appointed seats to the left of the rostrum, Father led the other justices into the Senate chamber and to their places opposite the president and his cabinet.

The ceremony began with the traditional valedictory address of the outgoing vice-president, and Mr. Hamlin's remarks to bid the senators farewell and introduce his successor were appropriately warm, gracious, and brief. Next Mr. Johnson took the rostrum, and he had uttered barely two sentences in a thick, slurred voice before Kate realized that he was either very ill or very drunk. As Mr. Johnson rambled incoherently, red-faced and barely coherent, a murmur of puzzlement stirred the gallery and Kate and Nettie exchanged a look of alarm. Mr. Lincoln bowed his head in what Kate could only imagine was profound embarrassment, enduring the startling harangue in dignified silence and waiting patiently for Mr. Johnson to finish. After an excruciatingly uncomfortable twenty minutes in which the vice-president-elect lauded his humble roots and proclaimed the power of the people, his unfocused gaze fell upon the members of the cabinet, each of whom he addressed in turn, although he forgot several of their names and which offices they occupied. Then, wheeling upon the Supreme Court justices, he reminded them that they derived their power from the people, and fixing a red-rimmed, blood-shot eye upon Father, he declared, "You too got your power from the people, whose creature you are!" Turning back to the audience, he changed subjects abruptly to the nature of the solemn vow he was about to take, but when he paused for breath, Mr. Hamlin quickly took advantage of the momentary lull and administered the oath.

"How dreadful," Nettie murmured as she and Kate rose and filed from the gallery with the other guests. "The poor man."

Kate nodded her assent, although she was not sure whether Nettie meant Mr. Johnson, Mr. Lincoln, or Father.

Holding hands so they would not be separated in the crowd, the sisters proceeded to the east front of the Capitol, where they took their seats on the platform with the other honored guests to observe Mr. Lincoln's oath. An eager audience thousands strong had packed the muddy Capitol grounds beneath overcast skies, and when the president emerged onto the East Portico with Father by his side, a sheet of paper in his hand, the newly completed dome rising in magnificent splendor high above, the people let out a great roar of welcome and gladness. As Mr. Lincoln came forward to offer his speech, the clouds suddenly parted and the sun broke through, and a bright shaft of sunlight shone down upon him like a benediction from heaven.

"How lovely," Nettie said, sighing. "How perfect."

"It *would* be perfect, if Father were taking the oath instead of administering it," Kate murmured in reply, but Nettie's gaze was fixed on the portico with such eagerness that Kate wasn't sure she heard.

Kate supposed she was not alone in expecting a great deal from the president's address, but his brief speech surpassed even her elevated expectations. It was a brief, simple, and profoundly beautiful address, clear and poignant and warm, full of forgiveness and reconciliation. The president spoke of the war, and how slavery was the undeniable cause of it, and how four years earlier everyone, North and South alike, had wanted to avoid war, but one side would make war rather than let the nation survive, and the other would accept war rather than let it perish. He spoke of their shared belief in the Lord, and how peculiar it was that each side prayed to the same God and invoked His aid against the other. "It may seem strange that any men should dare to ask a just God's assistance in wringing their bread from the sweat of other men's faces," he noted, "but let us judge not that we be not judged. The prayers of both could not be answered; that of neither has been answered fully. The Almighty has His own purposes."

The president went on to suggest that God had sent them the terrible war as punishment for the offense of slavery, and that the war could be a mighty scourge to rid them of it. People North and South alike hoped, and fervently prayed, that the war would swiftly pass away, but if God willed that it should continue "until all the wealth piled by the bond-man's two hundred and fifty years of unrequited toil shall be sunk, and until every drop of blood drawn with the lash, shall be paid by another drawn with the sword," they must accept that the Lord's judgment was true and righteous.

In closing Mr. Lincoln displayed the extraordinary magnanimity and forgiveness that had at first astonished, and later had come to deeply impress Kate. "With malice toward none," he urged his listeners, "with charity for all, with firmness in the right, as God gives us to see the right, let us strive on to finish the work we are in; to bind up the nation's wounds; to care for him who shall have borne the battle, and for his widow, and his orphan, to do all which may achieve and cherish a just, and a lasting peace, among ourselves, and with all nations."

Her throat constricting with emotion, Kate watched as Mr. Lincoln turned to Father, who stepped forward and beckoned for the clerk to hand him an open Bible. Father set it on a stand, and Mr. Lincoln placed his right hand upon it, and Father solemnly administered the oath of office. Then the president bent and kissed the holy book, and as the multitudes roared their approval, an artillery salute boomed and the Marine Band played a stirring tune—but Kate barely heard it, for her ears and heart and thoughts were full of President Lincoln's powerful oration.

She did not think Father could have done any better.

After acknowledging with courteous bows the ardent cheers and thunderous applause of the people, Mr. Lincoln left the portico for the lower entrance, where a carriage waited to carry him in joyful procession back to the White House. As the crowd dispersed, William was nowhere to be seen, but Nettie and Kate spotted Father easily thanks to his imposing stature. Working their way to him was more difficult, even though people who recognized them quickly gave way, and those who didn't kindly stepped aside when they noticed Kate's delicate condition. They arrived to find him talking earnestly with two other justices and a senator, and Kate noticed that he still held the Bible, closed upon a scarlet ribbon, which she supposed marked the place where Mr. Lincoln had kissed the pages. Kate and Nettie chatted with other ladies on the platform while they waited for Father to finish his conversation, and just as he did, William appeared, laughing heartily, his arms flung over the shoulders of a senator and a congressman, their faces as merry and flushed as his. They had evidently slipped off to the Capitol commissary immediately after the ceremony in order to toast President Lincoln's second term in their own fashion.

Kate turned away before her husband saw the disgust and anger in her eyes.

The Chases and Spragues, like most of the Washington elite, did not attend the public reception at the White House that evening, for they found little appeal in the thought of standing in line for hours with six thousand eager citizens to shake the president's hand and exchange a few brief pleasantries, not when they knew they would be able to pay their respects more pleasantly at the Inaugural Ball two evenings later. Instead they returned home, where Father promptly went to his study to write a letter, which he asked Kate to read. "I intend to send this to Mrs.

Lincoln," he said, handing her the paper, "along with the Bible the president used to take his oath."

Washington, March 4, 1865

My dear Mrs. Lincoln,

I hope the Sacred Book will be to you an acceptable souvenir of a memorable day; and I most earnestly pray Him, by whose Inspiration it was given, that the beautiful sunshine which just at the time the oath was taken dispersed the clouds that had previously darkened the sky may prove an auspicious omen of the dispersion of the clouds of war and the restoration of the clear sunlight of prosperous peace under the wise and just administration of him who took it.

   Yours very truly,

   S. P. Chase

Kate was mildly surprised to discover that Father had apparently come to believe in omens, but she supposed he could have meant it merely as a rhetorical device. "It's a lovely gesture," she told him sincerely. "I hope she'll appreciate it."

Father smiled agreeably, but Kate knew Mrs. Lincoln hated her father, and she could more easily imagine the First Lady shelving the Bible in some dark, dusty corner of the White House attic than cherishing the memento and the spirit in which it was given.

At ten o'clock on Monday evening, Kate, Father, William, and Nettie arrived at the Patent Office for the grand Inaugural Ball. Nettie looked delightfully sweet and pretty in her ashes-of-rose satin trimmed in white lace, but Kate felt enormous and bloated and cumbersome in her lavender moire antique, even though William assured her that she looked as beautiful as ever. Nettie promptly agreed, although she added the unfortunate qualifier, "*almost* as pretty."

The marble hall appropriated for dancing was about two hundred and eighty feet long and about a quarter that in width, with blue-and-white marble floors, an elaborately frescoed ceiling, and walls tastefully appointed with emblems, banners, and devices among which the Stars and Stripes and flags of various army corps were prominently featured. At the north end of the room, sofas and chairs furnished in blue and gold were arranged on a dais for the comfort of the president and his family. A fine brass band occupied a gallery at the east end, ready to provide music for the promenade, while in the center on the south side, a splendid string ensemble would furnish music for the dance.

At half past ten, a vaunt-courier cleared a path from the main entrance, and the nearly five thousand already assembled in the vast marble hall turned to watch as President Lincoln entered, accompanied by Speaker Colfax, with Mrs. Lincoln following close behind on the arm of Senator Sumner. To sustained applause they proceeded down the center of the hall and seated themselves on the dais. Mr. Lincoln looked rather smart in a plain black suit and white gloves, but he struck Kate as terribly weary and much aged, though he appeared to be making a valiant effort to forget his cares for the night, and he seemed pleased and gratified by the warm good wishes of his guests. Mrs. Lincoln's strain showed only around her eyes, for she otherwise looked extremely well, attired in the most elegant manner in a low-necked, short-sleeved gown of ample, rich white satin adorned with an overskirt of the finest point appliqué and passementerie of narrow fluted satin ribbon. Over her fair, smooth shoulders she wore an exquisite shawl of the same rich lace as the overskirt; her necklace, earrings, brooch, and bracelets were fashioned of the rarest pearls; and her hair, drawn back simply from her face, was gracefully ornamented with trailing jasmine and clustering violets. Despite the usual signs of middle age, which in Mrs. Lincoln's case were worsened by care and prolonged mourning, she looked elegant and fine, and her manners were easy and affable. As she took her seat, she smiled proudly up at her eldest son, Robert, who was dashing in his spotless dress uniform of an army captain, for despite his mother's best efforts to keep him out of the military, he had enlisted upon graduating from Harvard, and presently served as an assistant adjutant general on General Grant's own staff.

The music was excellent, the gentlemen handsome and gallant, the ladies splendid in their finery, which Kate was in a frustratingly excellent position to behold from her seat near the dance floor. She loved to dance, and excelled at it, but because of her delicate condition she had resigned herself to the role of spectator, her feet tapping in time to the music beneath her long skirts. She was not idle, though, for even seated she was graceful and lovely, and she held court as if she were hosting her own salon. Throughout the evening she was always surrounded by a throng of admirers—handsome soldiers, prominent senators, foreign dignitaries, witty intellectuals, the most brilliant political minds of the age. From her comfortable chair she observed Nettie enjoying herself thoroughly as she whirled and glided through the quadrilles and lancers, the schottisches and polkas and waltzes, smiling up at the young gentlemen who sought her as their partner as eagerly as they had once sought Kate. Wistful, and a trifle envious, Kate searched the crowd for her husband instead, and found him enjoying himself perhaps a little too much as he danced with pretty young belles from Indiana and Pennsylvania and elsewhere, and filled his cup with spirits more often than she liked to see.

Of late, when Kate wasn't nauseous she was ravenous, and as the hours passed she waited with increasing hunger and impatience for the buffet to be opened. The printed bill of fare was enticing and quite expansive—oyster stews, terrapin stews, pickled oysters; roast beef, fillet de beef, beef à la mode, beef à l'Anglais; leg of veal, fricandeau, veal Malakoff; roast turkey, boned turkey, roast chicken; grouse, boned and roasted; pheasant, quail, and venison; pâtés of duck en gelée and of foie gras; smoked ham; tongue en gelée and plain; and salads of chicken and of lobster. The confections surpassed the entrées in number and variety—ornamental pyramids of nougat, orange, caramel with fancy cream, coconut, macaroon, croquant, and chocolate sweets; cake trees boasting confections of almond sponge, belle alliance, dame blanche, macaroon tart, tart à la Nelson, tarte à l'Orleans, tarte à la Portuguese, tarte à la Vienne, pound cake, sponge cake, lady cake, and a multitude of fancy small cakes; jellies and creams including calf's foot and wine jelly, charlotte à la Russe, charlotte à la vanille, blanc mange, crème Neapolitane, crème à la Nelson, crème Chateaubriand, crème à la Smyrna, crème à la Nesselrode, bombe à la vanille; vanilla, lemon, white coffee, chocolate, burnt almond, and maraschino ice creams; fruit ices of strawberry, orange, and lemon; dishes of grapes, almonds, and raisins; and coffee and chocolate.

Since Kate was not occupied with dancing, shortly before midnight she caught John Hay's eye and beckoned him over. "Would you care to accompany me on a stroll?"

"Certainly," he said, offering her his hand and helping her to her feet. "Where shall we go?"

"Very far." She took his arm and smiled up at him. "All the way to the west hall, to see how our supper is coming along."

"If you insist," he said, grinning. "But I wasn't expecting such a long journey. I might not have the strength to bring you all the way back."

She laughed as they made their way around the dancers to the west hall, where other hungry guests were watching the waiters race back and forth between the rear doors and the buffet table, which seemed to stretch more than two hundred feet long, placed in a corridor only twenty feet wide between patent model cases. The aromas of roast meats and sugary confections made her mouth water, and the sight of the heavily laden table made her stomach rumble. After reading the bill of fare she would have thought no table could have held anything more, and yet it was ornamented with three remarkable pieces of confectionary art—a spun-sugar tribute to the army at the one end of the table, marked by a tasteful profusion of all the insignia of war, the paraphernalia of battle, and the emblems of victory; a monument to the navy's glorious achievements at the other, represented by Admiral Farragut's flagship *Hartford*, riding white-crested sugar waves; and in the center, an imposing and impressive sculpture of the Capitol, a perfect reconstruction down to the smallest detail from columns to majestic dome to the Goddess of Liberty towering above all.

Everything was beautifully arrayed, but the space seemed too narrow when she considered the thousands of guests dancing and making merry in the grand halls. "This could be a disaster in the making," mused John, as if he had read her thoughts. "I can't imagine this corridor accommodating more than a few hundred people at a time."

"When they call us to dinner," Kate advised, "either be sure you're at the front of the pack, or stay well out of the way of the stampede."

"You should stay out of the crowd altogether. Why don't you find yourself a place at a table, if you can, and I'll bring you a plate?" He caught himself. "Or perhaps you would prefer to entrust that task to your husband."

Kate felt a sudden, sharp pang of loss and regret. From the look of things, her husband was already well on his way to intoxication, and at that moment she would not trust him to remember her name. But she hid her consternation behind a smile and said lightly, "I'm famished, and you're much closer to the buffet than he, so I think you're the man for the job."

John escorted her to a seat in one of the alcoves arranged for diners between the display cabinets—there were few enough of those, and most were already occupied—and then he joined the crowd massing near the doors. At midnight, the president and his party were escorted by a private entrance to privileged places, where they all seated themselves comfortably and were served at table. Mrs. Lincoln happened to glance Kate's way, and she returned Kate's gracious bow with a chilly nod.

Soon thereafter, the doors were opened and the guests called to supper, and immediately they began flooding in by the hundreds, eagerly rushing the table to claim the choicest victuals. Kate watched with increasing alarm as the crush of hungry revelers descended into utter mayhem. Ladies and gentlemen snatched up plates and fought to fill them, knocking over the exquisite spun-sugar sculptures and sometimes breaking off pieces to carry home as souvenirs. Cutlery, plates, and wine cups became accidental weapons in the frantic scramble for viands, although some abandoned the custom of table settings altogether and fed themselves with their hands as they perused the table. Some gentlemen were inspired to seize entire platters of meats or fowl or game, hoist them over the heads of the mob, and carry them back to their friends, spilling jellies and stews on fine raiment and coiffures along the way. Glasses were shattered and plates smashed as waiters frantically rushed to and fro carrying replenished trays of food, but they immediately were swarmed by guests who had abandoned all pretense of dignity in the pandemonium. By the time John suddenly reappeared at her side, breathless and carrying two hard-won plates of tasty delicacies, the buffet was an utter ruin, the floor a sticky, pasty, and oily mess from mashed cake, scattered confections, and the debris of fowl and meat.

"Be careful as you go," said John, standing at the table beside her, for someone had made off with his chair. "That floor is treacherous underfoot."

Kate thanked him and fed herself with as much serene grace as she could manage, pretending they were not a small island of calm civility in the midst of a sea of confusion and grasping and gluttony. At that moment John threw her a grin of such good-natured enjoyment that she burst out laughing. Trust him to find even that scene of astonishing bedlam just another problem to solve with cheerful efficiency.

There were times she could not imagine what she would do without him. She was by turns astonished and deeply touched that it did not seem to matter to him that she was not his.

The chaos had subsided somewhat by the time Kate and John finished eating, but John still sheltered her protectively as he escorted her back to the main hall, his strong arm steadying her as they crossed the perilously sticky and slippery floor. "I imagine that more food will be spoiled tonight than eaten," Kate remarked, her mouth close to his ear so he could hear her over the din, and John nodded ruefully, no doubt imagining how the wasteful frenzy would play in the papers.

Out of the fray and back to her comfortable chair near the dancers, John left her with apologies, for he had engaged another young lady for a dance and could not keep her waiting. As she watched him go, she realized that he had probably ignored a good portion of his dance card for her sake. She hoped the ladies he had slighted would not make him suffer too badly for it.

Soon thereafter, Father and Nettie joined her, having managed to obtain a little supper for themselves. From the grumbling and protestations Kate overheard, it seemed that little more than half of the guests had been able to get anything to eat, but that was not even the worst of it. Dresses had been stained, uniforms torn, the corridor left in appalling disarray. And yet in the grand hall, all was elegant and graceful, glorious and celebratory. With the ugliness and mess and greed out of sight, she could almost imagine that all had been lovely and good.

The president and his entourage left the ball shortly after one o'clock, and many other guests took this as their cue to depart, alleviating the crush of the crowd and making promenading and dancing easier for those who remained. It was evident that Nettie and William would have been happy to stay until the ball concluded shortly before dawn, but Father was ready to go and Kate was fatigued, so Father sent word for their carriage to be brought around.

Just as they were about to depart, John caught her at the door. "I have some news I wanted to share with you," he said after the others had continued on ahead, out of hearing. "Now that Mr. Lincoln has been returned to office, I've decided it's time for me to resign."

"What?" she exclaimed. "But why? You love Mr. Lincoln, and you love working for him, or so I thought."

"I do," he said earnestly, lowering his voice and glancing over his shoulder, "but this position, which I esteem so highly, leaves me no time for anything or anyone else." He managed a grin. "Also, I can't endure Her Satanic Majesty any longer. I intend to admit defeat and quit the field."

Kate knew John, and John Nicolay too, had seen their responsibilities increase throughout President Lincoln's first term. They were not only secretaries; they were gatekeepers, emissaries, companions, and surrogate sons. When John Hay had first come to work for Mr. Lincoln, he had regarded the Tycoon with more than a hint of intellectual superiority and condescension, but time and close observation had soon inspired him to reconsider his opinion. Not long before Kate married, John confided to her that he believed the hand of God had put Mr. Lincoln in the White House, and shortly before the election, he had declared that if the "patent leather kid glove set" could not recognize his genius, it was because they knew "no more of him than an owl does of a comet, blazing into its blinking eyes."

"What will you do?" Kate steeled herself and asked the more pertinent question. "Where will you go?"

"I haven't decided. I haven't even told Mr. Lincoln yet, so please don't say a word to anyone."

She promised him she would not, and wished him well, and made him swear not to leave Washington without bidding her good-bye, without sharing one more ride along the Potomac. Then, with a heavy heart, she joined her family in the waiting carriage.

"What a glorious night," Nettie exclaimed as they rode home, her eyes shining, her cheeks flushed and glowing.

Kate smiled, remembering how she had enjoyed her first balls, when everything was new and unexpected and full of promise. She recalled how badly Nettie had wanted to attend Mr. Lincoln's first inauguration four years before, and how Kate had reassured her that she would be old enough for the next Inaugural Ball. Kate had once been so certain that 1865 would be the year her father assumed the presidency, and that the ball she promised her sister would be in his honor.

How much had changed, she thought, her gaze traveling from her bright-eyed sister, to her proud father, to her husband, asleep and snoring faintly, his head lolled back against the seat, his mouth open.

She studied him a long moment in silence, then turned her face to the carriage window and watched the moonlit streets of Washington rush by, thick with mud and glistening with rain.

A few days after the inauguration, William's sister Almyra paid the family a visit, and when it came time to escort her home, William suggested that Kate and Nettie accompany them. He was eager for Kate to see the progress of the renovations to their home in Narragansett, over which he had kept careful watch on his many and frequent journeys back to Rhode Island, but which she knew only from his descriptions. Privately William confided that he also wanted her to see if she did not agree that it would be better to deliver her child in the fresh sea air of Narragansett rather than in the sickly heat and stench of summertime Washington. She could interview doctors and midwives while they were there, he suggested, and speak with his mother and sisters, who had already promised to tend to her in her confinement.

Nettie was eager to go; she loved travel and, Kate suspected, she had developed quite a fancy for one of William's cousins. When Father gloomily noted that he had a great deal of reading of the laws to occupy him in their absence, Kate agreed to the plan. She wanted an excursion away from the capital while she was not yet too far along to travel in relative comfort and safety, and William wanted so badly for his son or daughter to be born in Rhode Island that she thought she must give the idea serious consideration.

The mid-March weather was fair and fine as they boarded the train, and William could afford the best accommodations, so they made a pleasant party as they traveled north, stopping overnight in New York to visit friends and continuing on to Providence in the morning. When they reached the city they were famished, so they decided to send their luggage ahead to Young Orchard and dine at a favorite hotel before escorting Almyra home. William wanted them to spend a day or two with Madame Fanny before traveling to Narragansett Pier with a few of William's cousins, including the young man Nettie admired, an arrangement that had disconcerted Father until Kate privately assured him she would be a vigilant chaperone.

The hotel was lovely and elegant, and the lobby smelled of fresh flowers and whitewash. Nearly all the staff recognized them from previous visits, and as William led the way into the dining room, the proprietor descended upon them so swiftly that Kate and Almyra jumped, startled, and laughed at themselves.

"Perhaps the governor and his enchanting ladies would prefer to dine in a private parlor," the proprietor suggested. "Chef will prepare something special just for you, something not on the menu."

Almyra, the most reserved of the party, looked hopefully at her brother, but Kate knew he would refuse. In Providence, he liked to see and be seen, and Kate encouraged this, knowing it was important for his constituents to feel as if he were one of them, despite his status and wealth.

"Thank you, but that's not necessary," William replied. "We like the view from your dining room, and your regular menu has never disappointed us."

When William took another step forward, the proprietor moved smoothly to block his path. "Perhaps the governor and his ladies would care to take the air on the porch for ten minutes, while we prepare our very best table for you."

"The second best table is good enough," Nettie assured him, glancing past him to the dining room, where families and couples were enjoying themselves and the delicious aromas of luncheon drifted on the gentle breeze through the open windows.

The proprietor smiled indulgently. "Miss Chase is gracious indeed, but I insist, only the best for you." To William he added, "Mrs. Anderson is within, and I believe she occupies your favorite table. If you will allow me to—"

"No," William said quickly. "No, that's quite all right. You mustn't displace anyone on our account. A private parlor will be best, I think."

"Oh, let's stay," Nettie protested, turning in place but not following after as the proprietor led William away. "A private room will be so dull. Forgive me, but we've been closed up in a train together for almost two days, and we've run out of things to say to one another. In the dining room we can watch the other guests and talk about them."

Though she had begun to follow the men, Kate was inclined to agree with her sister. Surely the second- or even third-best table would more than suffice, but before she could speak, she heard a woman say, "William?"

William halted and slowly turned, his face ashen. Quickly Kate glanced over her shoulder and discovered a woman frozen in place in the doorway of the dining room, staring at William with wide brown eyes. She seemed closer to William's age than her own, slender and brown-haired, and she clutched the hand of a young boy who looked to be no more than five years of age. The child had fine, silky dark-brown hair, and brown eyes that turned down at the corners. He stared up at William with shy recognition and put his fingers in his mouth.

"Good afternoon, Mrs. Anderson," said William in a strangled voice.

She blinked at him, as bewildered as if he had addressed her in an ancient foreign tongue. "William?" she repeated, and then her gaze fell upon Kate. "Oh. I see."

"This is my wife, Mrs. Sprague." William scarcely looked at the mother and child. "This is her sister, Miss Chase."

"How do you do," said Mrs. Anderson flatly.

Kate scarcely heard her over the strange roaring in her ears. She could not tear her gaze away from the boy. That silky dark hair, those eyes . . .

She had addressed William by his given name. He had not introduced his sister, which meant that Mrs. Anderson knew her too.

"How *you* do?" asked Nettie, a trifle sharply.

"William," said Almyra quickly, "I find that I'm feeling indisposed. Will you take me home?"

"Yes, I too am feeling quite unwell," said Kate faintly, instinctively resting her hand upon her abdomen.

With a nod for Mrs. Anderson but not another word, William offered his arms to his wife and sister and quickly led them from the hotel, with Nettie following close behind. He summoned a carriage and helped the ladies into it, and soon they were speeding off to Young Orchard. No one spoke. William glared furiously, Almyra wrung her hands and glanced furtively from her brother to Kate and back, and sweet Nettie frowned, looking as suspicious and confused and worried as Kate felt.

When Kate could bear the brittle silence no longer, she asked, "Who was that woman?"

"She is no one you need concern yourself about," William snapped.

"Brother," exclaimed Almyra, but one sharp look silenced her again.

Suddenly Kate knew—not *who* Mrs. Anderson was, or the exact circumstances of her acquaintance with William, but she knew very well *what* Mrs. Anderson was to him, or had been, around five years before.

She was too shocked and distressed to weep. As soon as they reached Young Orchard, Kate climbed awkwardly down from the carriage without waiting for assistance and fled inside and upstairs to the room she and William shared when they visited his mother's house. She did not know that Nettie had followed until she turned to shut the door and discovered her sister there. Unable to speak, she gestured for Nettie to enter and quickly locked the door behind them.

She flung herself on the bed, silently weeping. Nettie sat down beside her, took her head on her lap, and stroked her hair. Wordlessly, Kate clutched her other hand, tears streaming down her face, trembling and heartsick.

Kate lost track of time, so it could have been minutes or perhaps hours before a knock sounded on the door.

"Who's there?" Nettie called.

"It is I," said Madame Fanny, her voice muffled by the door. "May I come in?"

When Kate stiffened, Nettie squeezed her hand reassuringly. "Are you alone?"

"I am."

Nettie raised her eyebrows in a question, and Kate took a deep breath and nodded. As Nettie went to unlock the door, Kate sat up, head spinning, and quickly dried her eyes with her handkerchief.

Madame Fanny entered; she regarded Kate sympathetically before seating herself in a chair by the window. "So, you have met Mrs. Anderson."

Neither of the sisters replied.

Madame Fanny sighed. "I urged my son to tell you before you wed to avoid this unfortunate situation."

"What situation," asked Nettie clearly, "is this, precisely?"

Kate braced herself, praying that the truth would be no worse than what she imagined.

"Mrs. Anderson was born Mary Viall," said Madame Fanny after a preamble of a long, weary sigh. "Her family is one of the most prominent in Richmond, but as a younger woman, Mary's ideas of—what do they call it—'free love' put her at odds with the Vialls' conservative ways. She fell in love with my son and, well, she was quite enticing, and he succumbed to her wiles. Eventually she was discovered to be in a delicate condition."

At last Kate understood why the Spragues were not received in Providence society.

"Why did he not marry her?"

"As to that"—Madame Fanny shrugged—"he never had any intention of marrying her, as he had made clear to her from the very beginning, but she insisted she did not mind. Love without wedlock was perfectly in keeping with her philosophy. Her kind believes that 'instincts of love' are what legitimize acts of intimacy, not the law or the church."

"Her kind?" Nettie echoed skeptically.

"Believers in free love," Madame Fanny clarified. "I did not mean to suggest she was a fallen woman. She was a good girl from a respectable family."

Perhaps she had been, Kate thought, until William came into her life. "He ruined her and then abandoned her."

"He did not abandon her. He did not marry her, but he provides for her and the child." Madame Fanny paused before adding, "Of course, we are not certain the boy is even his."

That hair, those eyes. "Of course the child is his. I can see that. Anyone can see that. Everyone must have known." Everyone but Kate.

"Not necessarily. When William departed for Europe soon after Miss Viall discovered her condition, her parents quickly arranged for her to marry a military officer by the name of Anderson." A flicker of embarrassment appeared on her face before she added, defensively, "Mr. Anderson left her soon afterward, but she is properly married, and as far as the world knows, Mr. Anderson is the child's father."

"Why did William never tell me?" Kate fought back a sob, and Nettie held her shoulders, lending her strength. "Why did no one tell me?"

"This all happened long before my son met you. It belongs to the past."

"And yet I still had a right to know."

"This does not change William's love for you."

"Perhaps not, but it changes everything about the man I thought I married." How could he have kept such a secret from her? Why had no kindhearted person told her?

And then memory flooded her—the spindly, white-haired woman at the reception in City Hall, leaning on her cane and studying her with sympathetic curiosity.

"What is the child's name?" Kate asked.

Madame Fanny frowned. "What could that possibly matter?"

"I want to know."

"He is not called William Sprague, Junior, if that's what you're afraid of."

Insistent, Kate said, "Tell me his name."

"Hamlet," Madame Fanny snapped. "His name is Hamlet Anderson. A foolish, fanciful, poetical name, bestowed upon him by a flighty, poetical mother."

"Hamlet," Kate echoed numbly, lying back down on the bed and wrapping her arms protectively around the child in her womb.

Chapter Twenty-one

*I*n the inevitable row that followed, William was by turns imploring and hostile, begging Kate's forgiveness in one breath and in the next insisting that the affair was irrelevant, for it had begun and ended long before they met. "You do not command me," he growled, seizing her by the upper arm and shaking her so roughly that she knew he would leave bruises.

"It has nothing to do with command," she cried, tearing herself free of his grasp. "It's bad enough that you sired a child out of wedlock and abandoned his mother—that is your crime against them. Your crime against me is that you concealed it. It is a lie by omission, and it was wrong, and you know it."

"Who are you to judge me?" he snapped. "You've had your own indiscretions and your own lies. I know you were no virgin when you married me. You were but a seductive and licentious girl when you gave to Richard Nevins what you should have saved for me."

"How could you even think such a thing?"

"How could you have hoped to fool me?" he countered. "You knew too much when we took to our bridal chamber, and you've enjoyed it more than is proper for a lady ever since. That, coupled with the liberties you allowed me before we wed, is evidence enough of your impurity."

"I knew the little I did on our wedding night because of what you had shown me during our courtship," she protested, deliberately omitting Mrs. Douglas's role in her education for her friend's sake. "I've enjoyed it, but with *you*, and only with you. Would you have me shrink from your embrace?"

He did not bother to respond. "The boy is none of your concern," he snarled instead, and stormed from the room.

As soon as he left, Nettie darted back in and held her until she stopped shaking. Kate had no idea how an argument sparked by William's sin and deception had turned into an inquisition into her sexual purity, but it was clear that there was apparently no limit to the ways her husband was able to wound her.

She wanted to go home to Washington, but William forbade it. When several days passed with no lessening of her resolve, William adopted a more conciliatory tone, encouraging her to come with him to Narragansett as they had planned, to enjoy the spring sea air and to tour the mansion, which he assured her was coming along magnificently. "We are husband and wife," he reminded her. "That is irrevocable, so let us forget the past and think instead of our future. We could still be very happy, Kate, in our beautiful home with our precious child."

She knew he meant to entice her with beauty and comfort, but she was too heartsick to be tempted. When he still refused to pay the train fare, she resignedly told him that she would telegraph Father and have him make travel arrangements for her and Nettie instead. At that, such a look of shock came over William's face that Kate knew he had only just realized that Father, whom he greatly admired, would soon know of his lies and indiscretions. He attempted to bargain with her, offering to pay the sisters' travel expenses in exchange for her promise not to tell Father about young Hamlet. "I will not conspire to conceal your secret from my father," said Kate, astonished. "The truth will come out. You must know that."

William looked so stricken that in any other circumstances Kate would have felt sorry for him.

Later that afternoon, he relented, and the next day when he saw Kate and Nettie off at the train station, he seemed genuinely remorseful. "I'm truly very sorry I didn't tell you the truth from the beginning," he said, seizing her hand as she was about to board. "My family has kept this secret so long that it didn't occur to me to reveal it, not even to you—nor, I admit, did I see the necessity."

Kate knew that in this he was being utterly truthful—but it was an uncomfortable truth, revealing how little honesty and frankness he thought he owed her.

Nettie had written to tell Father they were coming home early, but not why, and so soon after their arrival, they sat down together in his study and Kate revealed the whole unhappy tale. Father was greatly distressed and angry, and he was grievously sorry that he had not inquired into William's past more thoroughly before giving his consent to the marriage. "But what is done is done," he said resignedly. "You must find a way to reconcile with him. Your Christian forgiveness and uncomplaining submission will compel him to be a better man. I am sure of it."

Kate was far less certain, and when her eyes met Nettie's, she knew her sister felt the same. And yet she knew she had little choice but to make the best peace she could, for her child's sake.

Soon after his daughters returned to Washington, Father left for Baltimore to attend to his duties on the circuit court. Baltimore was close enough that he would be able to return home from time to time, and yet Kate felt bereft, even with Nettie for company.

In the last week of March, John Hay invited her to go driving, and she gladly agreed. Even though he had confided his intentions at the Inaugural Ball, she was surprised and saddened when he told her that he had submitted his resignation to the president. "I've been appointed secretary of legation of the United States in Paris," he announced proudly. "I'll sail for France as soon as the president can spare me."

"I hope that won't be soon," said Kate as the carriage rolled slowly along the riverbank. They sat on the same side, so close that John could have taken her hand if he wanted.

"June, I think," said John. "Of course, I won't go as long as my services here seem essential."

Kate managed a laugh. "I suspect Mr. Lincoln would argue that your services are essential in perpetuity. Indeed, I have no doubt that they are."

"I'm sure the Tycoon will replace me easily enough."

"I think you underestimate how much he relies upon you. Don't you feel even the smallest twinge of conscience for abandoning him to gad about Paris?"

"Abandoning him? Gad about?" John echoed, astonished. "I think you accuse me unfairly. Paris is indeed a pleasant place, but I go for study and observation. I shall no doubt enjoy it for a year or so—but not very long, as I don't wish to exile myself in these important and interesting times."

"They are certainly interesting," agreed Kate, unable to keep the regret from her voice.

"I go away only to fit myself for more serious work when I return." His brow furrowed; he had not missed the subtle shift in her tone. "I will come back, and when I do, I'll call on you, and you can introduce me to your little bundle of joy, and I'll marvel at what a wonderful, doting mother you have become."

Tears filled her eyes, and she turned her head away. "My parlor will seem very dull to you after Paris, I think."

"Anyplace in your company, dull?" A note of amusement in his voice compelled her to turn back to him, and the fondness and admiration in his eyes brought her both comfort and ineffable grief. "Never, Kate. Never that."

As the Senate had adjourned *sine die* before the Spragues' ill-fated excursion to Rhode Island, William had no compelling reason to return to Washington City except to see Kate, and to her relief, he seemed eager to establish a truce through the mail first. His letters were tentative but kind, free of the recriminations that had marked their arguments. Gradually they became warmer, more wistful and loving. Kate responded to his letters dutifully, but she wrote to him less often than he wrote to her. Her shock and anger had subsided, but a dull melancholy replaced them as she grappled with the disappointing truth that the child within her womb was *her* first, but not her husband's. They would not share the joy and wonder of new parenthood in the way she had fondly imagined, and she could not help feeling that William and his paramour had stolen something precious from her. From time to time, William strongly hinted that he remained in Rhode Island only because she had not asked him to come home. She was not ready to do so quite yet, but she hoped that in time she could be.

While Father and William were away from the capital, so too was Mr. Lincoln. At the end of March, the president, Mrs. Lincoln, and Tad had traveled by steamer to City Point to visit General Grant and his wife, Julia. According to John Hay, the president wanted to review the troops and confer with his general in chief before what was expected to be a climactic battle. "I fancy he will do very little except satisfy his own curiosity and gratify in some measure that of the public, by sending telegrams to Stanton," Father told Kate, with some disdain. "What little he may do besides that will be, I fear, not well done."

Based upon the newspaper reports printed upon their departure, Kate had expected the Lincolns to remain in Virginia for a week or more, but to her surprise, Mrs. Lincoln returned a few days later without her husband and son—and rumors swirled about of an embarrassing altercation between her and another lady in the party.

Intrigued, Kate was delighted when John called on her and told her the story of "The Hellcat's Escapade," as he titled it, a tale he had pieced together from conversations between Mrs. Lincoln and her dressmaker and gossip shared by trusted eyewitnesses. Escorted by General Grant, Mr. and Mrs. Lincoln had gone out to review the troops with a small party of companions. The president had ridden ahead on horseback with General Grant and two officers' wives, but Mrs. Lincoln and Mrs. Grant had been obliged to follow in an ambulance slowed to a crawl by a rough corduroyed road and shin-deep mud. After much delay and hassle, the carriage caught up to the horseback riders—and Mrs. Lincoln discovered that the review had begun without her and that the attractive wife of Major General Edward Ord was riding alongside Mr. Lincoln in her place. Seized by jealousy, the Hellcat gave Mrs. Ord a terrible tongue lashing, turned her fury upon the astonished Mrs. Grant when she tried to intervene, and demanded that her husband immediately relieve Major General Ord of his duties.

"How terrible," exclaimed Kate, delighted. "Did Mr. Lincoln banish her from City Point, or did she return home out of shame on her own?"

"I'm not sure. You'd have to ask her."

Kate laughed. "Oh, I dare not."

When John threw back his head and laughed, she was reminded so vividly of happier times that she could almost forget her estrangement from her husband and John's impending departure. She could almost believe that the worst had passed, and that better days yet awaited her.

Shortly after noon on April 3, Kate and Nettie were upstairs in Kate's room making plans for the nursery and the baby's layette when the sudden cacophony of passing artillery forced them to raise their voices to be heard. When whistles and cheers joined the ruckus outside, Kate and Nettie abandoned their conversation, and Nettie darted to the window.

"What's going on out there?" Kate asked, waddling after her.

"An artillery salute to celebrate one achievement or another, I assume." Nettie frowned thoughtfully as she peered outside. "The streets are filling with people, and they're tossing their hats in the air and—oh, my goodness, embracing and kissing and weeping. For joy, I hope."

Kate had joined her at the window, and as she watched the celebration in the street below, she remembered John's passing remark that General Grant had been preparing for a climactic battle. "Dare we hope this celebration marks exceptionally good news?"

"Oh, I think we should dare," said Nettie fervently.

They hurried downstairs and reached the foyer just as Will burst in, breathless from excitement. "Richmond has fallen," he shouted, forgetting all decorum. "The Union army has taken the city!"

Nettie shrieked and flung her arms around Kate, and then, completely disregarding her sister's delicate condition, she seized her hand and pulled her out the front door. Arm in arm, they joined the celebration already spilling over into the streets, their hearts overflowing with joy, their happiness reflected in the faces of the people they passed, ladies and gentlemen, soldiers and nurses, clerks and shopkeepers and housemaids and waiters, all rejoicing together. Citizens draped patriotic banners and bunting from their windows, and bands quickly formed on street corners and parks to play spirited marches and merry jigs. Thankful crowds gathered outside the War Department and called for Secretary Stanton to address them, and the sisters would have stayed to listen but Kate was wary of being jostled by the crowd. Nettie solicitously escorted her home, and they watched the rest of the celebration from their parlor window, drinking apple cider toasts to all the officers whose names they could remember and wishing that Father were there to enjoy the glorious moment with them.

Later they felt the roar and thunder as an eight-hundred-gun salute shook the city, three hundred booms for the fall of Petersburg, five hundred for Richmond. As the afternoon passed, Kate observed many men celebrating by indulging in too much liquor, tottering down the streets, singing and proclaiming the glory of President Lincoln, General Grant, and the Union army in loud, slurring voices. Tomorrow they would regret their overindulgence, but for the moment, nothing could diminish their rejoicing. Repulsed by the sight, too reminiscent of William at his worst, Kate left the window and went to her father's study, where she wrote him a letter describing the scenes of merrymaking she and Nettie had observed, and expressing her heartfelt joy that the war was surely almost over.

The realization struck her with such force that she had to set down her pen and blink tears from her eyes. This time it was not an empty hope, a prayer unheard. After years of suffering and discord and thousands upon thousands of dead and maimed, the war truly was in its final hours.

The next day, word came to the capital that President Lincoln had entered Richmond early that morning, while flames of the fires the fleeing Confederates had set to destroy precious stores of cotton and liquor still flickered among the ruins. A group of colored workmen had recognized the president from a distance as he approached and, to his embarrassment, had shouted, "Glory, hallelujah!" and had fallen to their knees to kiss his feet. "Please don't kneel to me," President Lincoln had urged them, or so the stories told. "You must kneel only to God and thank Him for your freedom."

Escorted by General Godfrey Weitzel, whose troops had occupied the fallen city, Mr. Lincoln had toured the Confederate Executive Mansion and had sat at Jefferson Davis's desk. Later he and his escort had passed the infamous Libby Prison, where thousands of captured Union soldiers had suffered starvation, disease, and unimaginable cruelty—and where Mr. Lincoln's own brother-in-law, Confederate captain David Humphreys Todd, had served as a warden.

Father came home unexpectedly at midafternoon, having departed Baltimore for the capital as soon as he could put his docket in order. "Oh, my dear girls," he said, embracing them in turn. "How wonderful it is to see you both, on such a glorious, long-awaited day."

As Nettie happily described for him the celebrations they had seen in his absence, he listened dutifully, nodding, but whenever his eyes met Kate's, his worry was evident. Her smile trembled, but she nodded to assure him she was well. The fall of Richmond heralded an inevitable

Union victory, and if peace and reconciliation could come to a nation divided by war, surely they could fill her own heart and William's.

That evening, Secretary Seward ordered all the public buildings in Washington to be illuminated by thousands of candles to celebrate the glorious Union victories. Once again disregarding her delicate condition and the custom of confinement, Kate ventured out with Father and Nettie in the carriage to witness the city alight with rockets, fireworks, and dazzling lights. The streets were full of people and music, laughter and rejoicing. It was a brilliant spectacle, the likes of which Kate never expected to witness again.

She was wonderfully mistaken.

The following day, Father was obliged to return to Baltimore and his duties on the circuit court, so he was absent from the capital on Saturday evening, April 9, as rumors flew through the capital that the Union army had cut off General Lee's retreat and had surrounded the Army of Northern Virginia. Citizens filled the streets, full of anticipation and eager for news, and bonfires burned on every street corner. A young clerk who came to the house on an errand for the court informed them that President Lincoln and his party had returned from Virginia that evening, but the sisters could only speculate what that meant for the progress of the battle.

The next morning at daybreak, Kate woke to a five-hundred-gun salute that shook her bed and rattled the windows. She heard Nettie shriek from the next room, and answering shouts from Will and Addie and Mrs. Vaudry, and then Nettie burst into joyful laughter.

She climbed out of bed as quickly as she could and hurried to wash and dress, her heart pounding with hope and happiness. Surely the artillery salute meant that General Grant had at last triumphed over the Army of Northern Virginia.

She went downstairs to the front parlor window and was gazing outside at the misty streets when Nettie joined her. "Does this mean the war is over?" her sister asked, tucking her arm through Kate's and resting her head on her shoulder.

"I hope and pray it does," she replied, putting her arm around her sister. "But even if General Lee has surrendered, as far as we know, General Sherman is still battling General Johnston in North Carolina. I thought I should send Will to the telegraph office for official word."

At that moment, a loud thunderclap interrupted her and a heavy rain began to pelt the dusty streets. Kate decided to delay sending Will out until after breakfast, in hopes that a court messenger would be dispatched to bring them word in the meantime. Instead it was the morning papers that delivered the glorious news: The previous day, in a solemn ceremony at Appomattox Court House, General Lee had surrendered to General Grant.

Washington again resounded with celebration. Kate and Nettie watched from the upstairs windows as thousands of citizens took to the streets despite the storm, laughing and embracing and cheering. Impromptu parades formed as civilians linked arms with soldiers and sang "Rally Round the Flag" and "Hail, Columbia," cheering as they followed the bands through the muddy streets. Steam fire engines adorned with flags and bunting shrilled their whistles. Soldiers and mechanics towed a battery of six howitzers in from the navy yard and fired off thunderous salutes.

Later, the evening papers would describe how an ecstatic, thankful crowd had gathered outside the White House to serenade the president with a chorus of "The Star-Spangled Banner." The people had shouted for the president to address them, and a cheer had rung out when Tad poked his head out of a window, and a louder cheer had followed when he returned to wave a captured rebel flag. Before long Mr. Lincoln had appeared, and a great roar had gone up, and hundreds of hats were flung into the air. When the din subsided enough for the president to be heard, he had addressed them briefly, promising a longer, more formal speech in the days to come.

"I have always thought 'Dixie' one of the best tunes I have ever heard," the president had said then, according to the papers. "Our adversaries over the way attempted to appropriate it, but I insisted yesterday that we fairly captured it." A great shout of assent had met his words. "I presented the question to the attorney general, and he gave it as his legal opinion that it is our lawful prize." As laughter and applause again rang out, the president had raised his hand to the musicians and called for them to perform "Dixie." Afterward, he had led the crowd in giving three cheers for General Grant and all the soldiers under his command, and then three more for the gallant navy. Then, with a final bow, the president had withdrawn from the window, and the crowd had moved on to the Department of War to honor Secretary Stanton.

A smaller crowd had come to serenade Father that evening, unaware that he was not at home, so Kate and Nettie had accepted their ardent praise graciously on his behalf. Kate was pleased that Father's role in the triumph had not been forgotten, at least not by everyone.

The rejoicing continued into the next day, when again the city was gloriously illuminated in anticipation of the president's speech. Kate did not attend, but the following day she read the president's address in the papers and found it by turns moving and astonishing. "We meet this evening, not in sorrow, but in gladness of heart," the president had begun. "The evacuation of Petersburg and Richmond, and the surrender of the principal insurgent army, give hope of a righteous and speedy peace whose joyous expression can not be restrained." He praised the valiant troops, and addressed the contentious subject of Reconstruction, mentioning in particular criticism of the new Louisiana State constitution. "It is also unsatisfactory to some that the elective franchise is not given to the colored man," Mr. Lincoln had said. "I would myself prefer that it were now conferred on the very intelligent, and on those who serve our cause as soldiers."

Kate read the lines with particular interest, knowing Father was one of the critics to whom the president referred. She marveled at the revelation that President Lincoln approved of enfranchisement for Union soldiers and certain other men of color, fervently hoping that the correspondent had not misunderstood the speech. "Once again," she said to Nettie after reading the passage aloud, "Mr. Lincoln has finally embraced ideas that Father has long advocated."

"Father will be very pleased to hear this," Nettie observed, "but I cannot help thinking that a great many others will be outraged."

"Yes," Kate replied with spirit. "The same people who wanted to appease the secessionists rather than fight to preserve the nation, who protested that emancipation would destroy the country, the same obstructionists who stubbornly cling to the tired old ways of oppression and injustice—yes, I'm certain they will object to this too. But with Father leading the Supreme Court and—very well, I'll say it—Mr. Lincoln in the White House, their vain attempts to prevent the inevitable will come to nothing. One day soon the light of freedom and justice and peace will illuminate the country. You'll see."

"My goodness." Nettie regarded her from beneath raised brows, amused. "That was quite an impassioned speech. Perhaps *you* should run for the Senate next."

"Well, why not?" Kate countered. "Who is to say what is impossible anymore?"

The next day, General Grant came to Washington to meet with the president and attend a celebration Secretary Stanton had arranged in his honor. Kate knew when the boat carrying the general and Mrs. Grant arrived, for it seemed that every gun in the capital burst forth in a salvo of welcome and every bell rang out salutations and grateful thanks. She had heard that while General Grant visited Mr. Lincoln at the White House, Mrs. Grant and Mrs. Stanton would receive callers at the Willard Hotel. She wanted to call on them, and had intended to, but her pregnancy was in its seventh month and she did not wish to invite rebuke and scandal by defying the custom of confinement again merely to pay a social visit. Later that evening, Father returned from Baltimore on the evening train, and the family enjoyed a happy reunion. "The city is absolutely swathed in flags and bunting," he marveled. "I have never seen such rejoicing."

"We have never had such great reason," Kate said, and Father agreed, although he added that the war was not yet over and that a great deal of work awaited them before the divided nation would be whole once more. Before departing Baltimore, he had sent the president a lengthy letter advising him on Reconstruction, drawing upon his success with the Port Royal Experiment. He hoped to speak with Mr. Lincoln on the subject soon.

Another grand illumination had been called for that evening in honor of General Grant's triumphant visit, but when Father declared himself too weary from travel to go, Nettie prevailed upon Kate to accompany her instead. "We need never leave the carriage," she promised. "No one will see you. Anyway, I think it's foolish to shut up a woman in her house just because she is in a delicate condition, if her health is otherwise good."

Kate was inclined to agree, for she was becoming quite frustrated wandering about the house peering out of windows while all of Washington rejoiced. And so at twilight she and Nettie set out, merry and content, gazing through the windows at the city transformed by light and bunting and banners. The windows of government buildings dazzled with the light of hundreds of candles, and every heart seemed overflowing with hope and with a deep, profound longing for peace that seemed soon to be fulfilled.

As they rambled through the familiar streets of the capital, Kate marveled at the transformations the city had experienced over the previous four years—and even just in the previous week. The exuberant rejoicing of the first days after General Lee's surrender had settled into a calm sense of hope, gratitude, and peace, despite the ever-present concerns about what yet lay ahead. In all but the most radical, punitive hearts, Mr. Lincoln's speech of April 11 had inspired a mood of forgiveness and clemency—and Kate's own heart had not remained unmoved. That very morning she had written a long, heartfelt letter to William, expressing her regret for their past discord, forgiving him for his deception, and expressing hope that they could begin anew. "I would be happy to see you soon," she had written in closing. It was not an explicit invitation for him to come home, and yet she hoped his longing for her would inspire him to return nevertheless.

On Good Friday, Father was restless from the moment he woke, and after their religious observances he took to pacing in his study, puttering idly in the garden, and complaining about trivialities whenever he crossed paths with his daughters. Nettie gathered her sketch pad and crayons and disappeared into some nook of the house to wait out his peevish mood, but Kate decided to distract him with a game of chess. Father somewhat testily agreed, but after they set up the board and he became engrossed in the game, he relaxed enough to tell her what was bothering him.

"The end of the war is imminent, and soon Reconstruction will begin in earnest," he said, capturing her pawn with his knight. "I shouldn't have mailed my letter from Baltimore. I should have brought it home with me and had a messenger carry it to the White House. Now the president may not receive it for days, but I had hoped to discuss my ideas with him immediately."

"You could write another copy and send that over," said Kate, moving a rook to protect her queen. "Or deliver it to him yourself."

He shook his head. "I would look forgetful and foolish, or worse yet, hectoring, when the original letter arrives bearing all the same information and suggestions."

"Perhaps you could call on Mr. Lincoln to congratulate him for the success of his armies, and the talk could naturally turn to Reconstruction."

"Perhaps," Father replied thoughtfully, capturing another pawn, then frowning as Kate claimed his rook.

He must have concluded that her suggestion was a good one, for later that afternoon, he announced that he intended to ride to the White House and present his views to the president. Nettie asked if she might accompany him and go on a few errands of her own after dropping him off. When Father agreed, she asked Kate to join them. "No one will see you in the carriage," she said. "The fresh air will do you good."

Kate was tempted, but her stomach was unsettled, her hips and back ached, her feet had swollen so much that it was an effort to squeeze into her shoes, and she needed to visit the necessary far too frequently to risk a lengthy outing. So she thanked her sister but declined, and after they departed she went upstairs and lay down for a nap. What she did not admit to Father and Nettie was that she was feeling downcast, not because of her physical discomfort or worries about the baby but because of a recent letter from William. He told her with apparent good cheer that he was perfectly well and was pronounced handsome by all the ladies in Narragansett—an appallingly insensitive remark even if he had meant it in jest. He claimed that he had eschewed all liquor and cigars since her departure except for a single glass at Senator Anthony's residence, which had given him a touch of dyspepsia and had persuaded him that he was better off without it. So breezy and careless was his tone that she wondered if she had imprudently erred in abandoning him to his hometown and his onetime lover. Plagued by doubts and worries, she slept fitfully, waking with a start when she heard Nettie and Father return.

She straightened her dress and hair and hurried downstairs to meet them. "What did Mr. Lincoln think of your ideas?" she asked Father after welcoming them home.

"He didn't call on Mr. Lincoln after all," Nettie said, untying her bonnet. "As we approached the White House, he told the driver to keep going."

"I thought an unannounced visit might annoy the president and do more harm than good," said Father, a trifle sheepishly. "I've written him two lengthy letters on Reconstruction and suffrage in recent days, and I've made my views known to him on countless other occasions over the last two years. I'm not in the cabinet anymore, and I forget that I'm no longer welcome as one of his official advisors."

"But your ideas are sound," Kate protested. "I've never known you to be shy about sharing them."

Father took her hand and patted it. "I am not shy now, and my confidence in my ideas is unshaken, but they will still be good ideas tomorrow. I'll call on him then."

His mind seemed made up, so Kate said no more. Instead they spent a quiet evening at home together, reading, chatting, playing chess. Kate retired early, but she woke around ten o'clock to the sound of her father climbing the stairs on his way to bed.

She drifted off to sleep, her hands resting on her abdomen, where her child gently rocked, as if sensing the protective presence of the great man he, or she, would call Grandfather.

An hour later the doorbell rang.

Kate woke immediately, listening in the darkness to a curious and worrisome tread of feet on the stairs—Will ascending to report the caller's identity to Father, Will descending, Will going up again accompanied by another man, and at last, all three men returning downstairs. Puzzled, Kate rose and used the necessary, listening all the while, curious and increasingly worried. She heard men's voices rumbling from the direction of Father's study, and after a time, when the sound of the front door closing was not followed by that of Father returning upstairs, she drew on her dressing gown and carefully made her way downstairs to his study.

She found her father alone, standing at the window, gazing outside through his own reflection. The sound of her footsteps pulled him from his reverie, and when he turned and she glimpsed his stricken expression, her heart plummeted and her thoughts flew to William and her far-flung family. "Who called at such an hour?" she asked. "What's wrong?"

"Katie, dear," he said, his voice shaking, "perhaps you should sit."

Obediently, she sank into a chair, one hand clutching the arm rest, the other resting on her belly. "Is it William?"

"No, my dear." Steadily, but with evident worry, he said, "The man who called is a former clerk of mine from the Treasury Department. He brought grievous news, terrible news."

"Tell me."

"He had just come from Ford's Theatre. The president was in attendance, seated in the State Box with his wife and another couple. The president—" He paused to gulp air. "A man stole into the president's private box and shot him."

A sudden chill of horror froze Kate to the marrow. "Does Mr. Lincoln yet live?"

"I don't know." Father sank heavily into the chair beside her and clasped one strong hand to his brow. "The clerk could give no particulars. I hope—I pray—he is mistaken altogether."

He reached out his other hand to her, and she took it, but almost immediately thereafter, a knock sounded upon the front door. "Wait here," Father instructed, and he quickly rose to answer.

She followed him as far as the study doorway, clutching her dressing gown closed at the neck; but although she heard him conversing with two or more gentlemen, she could not make out their words. When Father returned to her, his eyes were full of such grim horror that she knew the clerk had spoken true.

The new callers were Mr. Mellon, Mr. Plantz, and Mr. Walker, Treasury Department employees Father trusted implicitly. They reported that President Lincoln had been shot but was expected to survive, but Secretary Seward had been assassinated in his sickbed, where he had been recovering from a terrible carriage accident, and his son had been seriously wounded. "Guards are being stationed at the houses of all prominent officials," Father said. "It is suspected that the plot may have a wider range." Suddenly his face drained of all color. "My God. Seward, dead. I cannot believe it." He shook his head as if to clear it, and a look of anguished determination came into his eye. "I must go to the president at once, and see how I might be of service."

"Father, no." Kate seized the sleeve of his dressing gown. "The assassins have already struck twice. You too could be one of their intended victims. You must not go out."

"If I can help the president, I must try, even at risk to myself."

"What could you do?" protested Kate, tightening her hold on his sleeve. "Are you a physician or a Pinkerton agent? You're far more likely to get in the way than to help, and in the meantime, you would recklessly expose yourself to danger."

Father hesitated, and in that moment three loud knocks sounded on the front door. Will soon appeared in the study doorway, haggard and grief-stricken, to report that soldiers had taken up positions around the house and would stand guard throughout the night. His sorrow was so palpable that Kate's heart went out to him. Mr. Lincoln was revered in the colored community as their Great Emancipator, as their Moses. If he perished, their lamentations would be heart-wrenching.

"So it seems I will remain at home," said Father wearily after Will left them. "Go back to bed, daughter. I will sit up and wait for more news."

"How could I possibly sleep?"

"Katie—" He cleared his throat, dropped back into his chair, and covered his face with his hands. "I would rest easier knowing you and my grandchild are safe upstairs in bed."

She hadn't the heart to argue, but as she turned to go, she said, "You should try to sleep too. You'll be needed in the morning, whatever else happens tonight."

He nodded, but she did not hear him come upstairs until much later.

Throughout the long night, grief and worry and the sound of soldiers' boots on the pavement below her window precluded restful sleep. Morning came at last, gray and somber, with a steady downpour as if the heavens wept. At half past seven, a distant church bell began to toll, and then another joined it, and another, until all the bells in Washington resounded with the terrible pealing. Kate knew at once the dire news they proclaimed.

The president was dead.

She lay in bed, listening to the bells, paralyzed by grief and worry. Then she heard stirring downstairs, and a cry of shock and grief from Nettie. Reminded of her responsibilities, she roused herself from bed, numb and dazed and disbelieving, to wash and dress.

Downstairs, she found Nettie curled up on the sofa in the front parlor, sobbing as if her heart had irreparably broken, while Mrs. Vaudry stroked her back and murmured words of consolation, her own face streaked with tears. Nettie had always liked Mr. Lincoln more than anyone else in the family, Kate reflected, and suddenly a memory sprang to mind—Mr. Lincoln bending from his great height to confess to a concerned young girl that he had freed the terrapins intended for his supper table. The Great Emancipator indeed, she thought giddily, and suddenly the room spun around her, and she grabbed on to the back of a chair to steady herself. "Where's Father?" Kate asked when she had recovered enough to speak.

"He went to see Mr. Lincoln," Nettie choked out, sitting up and wiping her eyes. "He was gone before I woke."

Kate felt a tremor of worry. She wished Father had stayed safely home behind locked, well-guarded doors. "Is there any news?"

While Nettie fought back sobs, Mrs. Vaudry shared the few details she had acquired from the soldiers who had relieved the nighttime guards at dawn. With his wife sitting beside him in their private box at Ford's Theatre, Mr. Lincoln had been shot in the back of the head at close range by the actor John Wilkes Booth, who had leapt down to the stage, apparently injuring himself upon landing, and made his escape through a rear exit. Mortally wounded, the president had been carried across the street to the Peterson boardinghouse, which was where Father had gone to see him, and where he had apparently breathed his last.

The sound of their voices must have alerted Will, for he came to the parlor, took Kate aside, and informed her in a quiet, hollow voice that he had learned from a servant in the Seward household that the secretary of state had been grievously injured, but yet lived. At nearly the same time Mr. Lincoln had been shot, a tall, powerfully built man had appeared at Mr. Seward's front door, where he informed a servant that Mr. Seward's physician had sent him with medicine. Suspicious, the servant told him to leave the medicine and instructions so he could tell Mr. Seward how to take it, but the stranger pushed his way into the house, insisting that he had been ordered to deliver it in person. Mr. Seward's son Fred stopped him on the staircase, demanded the medicine, and refused to grant the stranger admittance to the sickroom. The man turned as if to descend, but suddenly he whirled around, leveled a revolver at Fred Seward's head, and pulled the trigger. The gun misfired. Muttering an oath, the intruder struck him with the revolver with such force that his skull was fractured in two places, exposing his fragile brain matter and rendering him unconscious. The vicious attacker then forced his way into Secretary Seward's bedchamber, where a soldier and Mr. Seward's daughter Fanny kept vigil. Slashing the soldier across the forehead with the knife, the intruder turned upon Mr. Seward, and while Fanny bravely pleaded for him to spare her father's life, he plunged a bowie knife into the invalid's neck and face, again and again. Fanny's screams had brought another brother running, and with the soldier's help he managed to pull the intruder away, taking a knife wound to the face in the struggle. Before they could stop him, the intruder fled down the stairs, stabbing a young State Department messenger in the back in his urgency to escape.

At first it was believed Mr. Seward could not survive, but according to Will's friend, all of the injured, even Fred with his terrible head wound, were considered out of immediate danger. Only the neck brace Secretary Seward wore due to the injuries he had sustained in the carriage accident saved him from being stabbed to death.

Kate and Nettie waited anxiously for word from Father, and finally, shortly before noon, he returned home, his eyes bloodshot, his face distorted. Embracing his daughters tightly, he allowed Kate to lead him to the parlor, where she begged him to explain where he had been and what he had learned.

He had left the house at dawn and walked with Mr. Mellon through the rain to Ford's Theatre and the Peterson boardinghouse facing it across Tenth Street. A crowd of grieving civilians had gathered there, kept at bay by grim-faced soldiers. Father had spotted Assistant Treasury Secretary Maunsell Field among the throng, and from him Father learned that he had arrived too late. The president was dead, and those who had been with him in his final moments—his cabinet save Mr. Seward, his wife and son Robert, a few others—had dispersed.

Stunned, uncertain what to do, Father and Mr. Mellon had walked to Secretary Steward's residence. Recognizing the chief justice, the guards had allowed them to enter the lower hall. "There the doctors told me that Mr. Seward has partially recovered, and although he is in critical condition, he might live," Father said. "His son Frederick's case, however, is considered hopeless."

"We must pray nonetheless that they both survive," said Kate, her voice shaking, and Nettie's tears began anew.

"From there I went to the Kirkwood House, Mr. Johnson's residence in Washington," said Father, his voice thick with grief. "I found him calm, but very grave. Stanton had already told him that Mr. Lincoln had perished. We met in the small parlor, and before long a few others joined us—the new Secretary of the Treasury McCulloch and Attorney General Speed. After conferring briefly, we agreed to meet again there at ten o'clock, at which time I would administer the oath of office to Mr. Johnson."

"Oh, my goodness," said Nettie, startled. "I had not thought—I mean, of course I knew, but—we have a new president now."

And a new First Lady, Kate realized. Ashamed that she had not thought of her before, she asked, "How is Mrs. Lincoln?"

Father shook his head. "I don't know. I haven't seen her, or heard from anyone who has. She was with Mr. Lincoln when he was shot, so I must imagine she is extremely distraught."

Kate nodded, her thoughts flying to little Tad, who had so recently suffered the loss of a cherished brother, and to Robert, who had suddenly become the head of a grieving family, and John Hay, her dear friend, who had loved Mr. Lincoln with steadfast but clear-eyed devotion—how they all must be suffering at that moment.

After the gentlemen agreed to reconvene at ten o'clock, Father and Mr. Speed had gone to the attorney general's office to examine the Constitution, the precedents of vice-presidents Tyler and Fillmore, and the law regarding the succession. "On our way back to the Kirkwood House, Mr. Speed recounted for me their last cabinet meeting. He told me that he had never—" Father paused to compose himself. "He said he had never seen the president in better spirits. The principal subject was Reconstruction, and Mr. Lincoln showed Mr. Speed the letter I had sent him from Baltimore the day of my departure. Mr. Speed said the president complimented it highly." The last words dissolved into a mournful sob.

Kate reached out to take his hand and clasped it in both of her own.

Father cleared his throat. "We returned to the Kirkwood House, and just inside the entrance, I encountered Montgomery Blair and his father."

"Oh, dear," murmured Kate without thinking. What an inopportune moment for Father to cross paths with his longtime enemies.

"I was determined to bury old resentments, so I took the elder Blair's hand and said that I hoped that from this day forward all anger and bitterness between us would cease." He managed a small, forlorn smile. "The old gentleman replied with equal warmth and kindness."

"It would be wonderful if that old feud could be put to rest at last," said Nettie, her voice trembling. "Mr. Lincoln would have liked that, I think."

"A dozen gentlemen looked on as I administered the oath to Mr. Johnson," Father said. "After he said, 'So help me God,' I was compelled to reply, 'May God guide, support, and bless you in your arduous duties.'"

Kate silently echoed his prayer. In the wake of such a devastating national tragedy, with the end of a divisive bloody war in sight but not yet achieved, President Johnson would need all the divine guidance the Lord could provide.

It was a time of unprecedented shock and loss and sorrow.

Never had a nation plummeted so suddenly from joyful triumph to utter despair. Grief-stricken citizens sought comfort in churches and in the company of friends. Others took refuge in righteous anger, demanding justice and retribution. Flags that had waved proudly in victory were slowly lowered to half-staff. The merry bands fell silent. Government offices and shops that only days before had been illuminated by the light of thousands of candles were darkened and closed. Every grand public building, every gracious mansion, every humble residence was draped in the black crepe of mourning.

Moved by Father's reconciliation with his own bitter rivals, Kate wrote a heartfelt letter to Mrs. Lincoln to express her sincere condolences. She would have called on the grieving widow in person, but she had learned that in her desolation Mrs. Lincoln refused to see anyone but Secretary Welles's wife and her faithful friend the dressmaker Elizabeth Keckley. Kate received no immediate reply to her letter, nor did she expect to until Mrs. Lincoln emerged from the sharp, raw anguish of new widowhood. Kate hoped that Mrs. Lincoln would, in time, find some comfort in her words of peace and sympathy, and perhaps respond in kind.

As officials made plans for President Lincoln's funeral, Kate stroked her swelling abdomen, quietly celebrated the strong kicks and vigor of her unborn child, and brooded over the too-brief span between birth and death. Life was too fleeting to harbor resentments, to take offense instead of practicing tolerance and forgiveness, to engage in rivalries over matters of pride, without substance.

Kate knew that her rivalry with Mrs. Lincoln had diminished them both. It was too late to start anew with the grieving widow, but it was not too late to seek reconciliation where else it was needed—where it was even more necessary.

She could not heal the breach between her and William without his help, but someone had to begin it; someone had to reach a hand across the chasm first.

A letter would not reach William swiftly enough. Suddenly, desperately eager to reconcile before it was too late, Kate quickly wrote a brief note imploring William to come to her as soon as he possibly could. She found Nettie in the garden, gave her the precious paper, and tearfully begged her to take the message to the telegraph office at once. Too overcome to speak, Nettie agreed with a nod and immediately set out.

Kate returned inside to the parlor, where she sat alone, watching the clock and listening for her sister's footsteps on the front stairs. She knew Nettie would not return with a message from William, but she was overwrought and hopeful and apprehensive all at once, and she longed for the small consolation of knowing that her telegram was on its way.

When Kate heard the front door open, she hurried to the foyer as quickly as her newly cumbersome body would allow, but there, instead of her lively young sister she discovered her husband, gazing at her with grief-stricken hope and trepidation.

For a long moment they stood regarding each other in the full awareness of the gulf between them, and the great effort it would require to cross it.

Then Kate held open her arms to him, and sobbed out his name, and he rushed to embrace her, as if she and their child were all he had ever wanted in the world.

Epilogue

*T*he day after Kate and William reunited, President Abraham Lincoln lay in state in the East Room of the White House, watched over by an honor guard of two generals and ten other officers. At half past nine o'clock in the morning, nearly thirty thousand shocked and grieving citizens began to file past the coffin to pay their last respects in a slow procession that lasted into the evening.

On Wednesday morning, April 19, a warm, gentle spring day, Father, William, Nettie, and Kate were among the dignitaries invited to attend the private funeral ceremony. Many thousands of grieving citizens had assembled outside the White House, but a strong cavalry guard kept the Avenue clear for the official mourners' arrivals and for the procession that would follow after.

Kate and her family were ushered to their places in an East Room transformed by mourning. Mirrors and chandeliers were draped with black crepe, risers had been erected and lined with chairs covered in black muslin, and the president's casket, richly ornamented in silver, rested upon a black catafalque beneath a black canopy. Swathed in mourning black, Kate watched John Hay through her veil as he entered, pale and stricken, and took a seat of honor near the foot of the casket. Robert Lincoln alone represented the family, for Mrs. Lincoln and Tad were too distraught to attend.

There were sermons and prayers but no music.

After the service, a funeral procession carried the president's remains to the Capitol, where he lay in state in the rotunda so that thousands more could pay their respects. On Friday, April 21, nearly a week after the president's death, a nine-car funeral train bedecked with bunting, crepe, and a portrait of Mr. Lincoln left Washington on a seventeen-hundred-mile journey west to Springfield, carrying three hundred passengers and the remains of the president and his young son Willie. The Lincoln Special traveled at only five to twenty miles per hour out of respect for the thousands of mourners who had assembled along the rail lines. The train made scheduled stops in twelve cities, where tens of thousands gathered to mourn and to bid farewell to their fallen leader.

For six weeks Mrs. Lincoln and young Tad remained at the White House. It was said that the esteemed Mrs. Keckley rarely left her side, sleeping on a lounge in the distraught widow's chamber at night, comforting and soothing her as best she could throughout the long, sorrowful days. Mrs. Lincoln's closest friends in Washington, Mrs. Mary Jane Welles and Mrs. Elizabeth Blair Lee, attended her sometimes too, but she denied admittance to nearly everyone else. John Hay had told Kate, in a voice taut with indignant anger, that President Johnson had not called on her, nor had he sent a single note to express his sympathies. Kate had heard rumors that on the night Mr. Lincoln had been killed, Mr. Johnson had gone to the Peterson boardinghouse to visit the president on his deathbed, but had been turned away lest the sight of him upset the First Lady, who had never forgiven him for his outrageous performance at the inauguration. Apparently the new president could hold a grudge as firmly as the former First Lady.

Kate thought it was unbecoming a gentleman to show so little forgiveness for a grieving widow, and yet, in a singular act of generosity, he did not demand that Mrs. Lincoln vacate the White House promptly so that he might move in. Instead he lived under guard at a residence on Fifteenth and H streets and worked out of a small office in the Treasury Building, forgoing the use of the White House residence, offices, and reception rooms that were rightfully his.

Week after week, Mrs. Lincoln lingered in the home she loved so well, too prostrate from grief to leave, too uncertain about the future to decide where to go. At first it was assumed that she would return to Springfield, then it was rumored that she intended to go abroad, and finally it was confirmed that she had decided to settle in Chicago. Mr. Lincoln had hoped to retire there after his second term, Mrs. Lincoln reportedly claimed, and it was a city that had always been kind to him. It was in Chicago that he had received his first nomination as the Republican candidate for president, and so it was a city reminiscent of triumph, not despair and loss. It was also near Mr. Lincoln's tomb in Springfield, where Mrs. Lincoln might visit him in the years to come, and find comfort in his silent presence.

Although Mrs. Lincoln desperately clung to the vestiges of her former life as long as she could, the White House was no longer hers, and eventually, reluctantly, she chose May 22 as the day of her departure. Kate heard this first from John Hay, but since it was soon announced in all the papers, she assumed a large crowd would line the circular drive in front of the mansion, people on foot and in carriages, waving handkerchiefs, tossing flowers, and calling out for God to bless the widow of the beloved martyred president as she departed the White House. Perhaps the crowds would be so vast that they would fill the sidewalks all the way to the train station.

Kate hoped so, for she meant to conceal herself within that crowd.

After all that had passed between her and Mrs. Lincoln, she felt compelled to see her rival one last time before she left Washington, but Kate was determined not to be recognized. If malicious gossips spotted her there, they would insist that she had come to gloat, and that was not her intention. If anyone had asked, she would have been unable to explain precisely what her intention was, but it was not to celebrate another woman's misery. It was, in fact, something closer to a tribute.

But when Kate arrived at the White House at the appointed hour, concealed beneath a heavy veil within a borrowed carriage, she was stunned to see the adjacent streets empty except for the usual traffic, and only a handful of people gathered around the front portico. The contrast between Mrs. Lincoln's departure from the White House and her husband's the month before was stark and astonishing, even shameful. Mr. Lincoln's casket had been carried from the Executive Mansion in a grand and solemn state. Thousands had gathered to bow their heads reverently as the plumed hearse bore him off to the Capitol rotunda surrounded by the mournful pomp of military display—battalions with re-versed arms, a riderless horse with boots turned about in the stirrups, the flags at half-staff, the melancholy strains of funeral dirges. Mrs. Lincoln left to complete indifference, the only music the chirping of birds, with scarcely anyone to bid her farewell. The silence was excruciating.

Kate watched through veil and carriage window as Mrs. Lincoln and a small entourage, including Tad, Robert, and Mrs. Keckley, emerged from the White House. On the threshold, she paused for a moment, drew a deep, shaky breath, and took Tad's hand in hers. She spoke briefly to him, then fixed her gaze straight ahead and left the White House without looking back. She boarded her carriage, the rest of her party climbed in after her, and at the driver's signal, they drove briskly past the bronze statue of Thomas Jefferson in the center of the driveway and turned in the direction of the train station. There, Kate knew, they would board the private railcar that had so often carried Mrs. Lincoln to and from the capital and New York City, in far happier days that were only memories now.

Kate watched until her rival's carriage disappeared around the corner and out of sight. Mrs. Lincoln might have been the first to quit the field, but Kate felt no sense of triumph, no victory, only sadness and loss and regret. It pained her to think of what might have been, and what never would be. Father might make another attempt to win the presidency, but Kate knew his chances to win even the nomination were slim. William, who had once seemed full of promise and ambition, had through his own lapses and failures diminished so precipitously in the view of the public and his fellow senators that Kate no longer believed he could win the White House, not even with her to direct him.

At that moment, Kate knew she would never be First Lady—and that she would never be as loved and honored by her husband as Mrs. Lincoln had been by hers.

For a brief season Kate and Mrs. Lincoln had both lived and loved, grieved and celebrated, schemed and triumphed in the great capital city of a nation at war. Now Mrs. Lincoln was gone and Kate alone remained—but Kate knew that although her star had burned brighter, Mrs. Lincoln's had shone higher in the firmament, and would forevermore, in the memory of the nation.

AUTHOR'S NOTE

Mrs. Lincoln's Rival is a work of fiction inspired by history. Many events and people from Kate Chase Sprague's life, though noted in the historical record, have been omitted from this book for the sake of the narrative. While many characters appearing in this novel are based upon historical figures, in some cases two or more individuals have been combined to form a single composite character. With a few exceptions, quotes from speeches, letters, and newspaper articles have retained the spelling, capitalization, and other stylistic features of the primary sources.

In June 1865, Kate gave birth to a son. She wanted to name him after her father, but Salmon P. Chase had always loathed what he called his "fishy name," and he urged her to name the child after her husband instead. "It is natural enough that you should want to name him after me in some way," Chase wrote to Kate from Cincinnati, "but my only tolerable name is my surname; and William is not only a better one; but is the name of one to whom *your first duties* belong, and it was the name of his father, was it not? It *should* be borne by his first boy." Chase was wrong on two counts—William's father was named Amasa, and Kate's newborn was not his first boy—but she named her son William even so.

In 1868, after presiding as chief justice over President Johnson's impeachment trial, Salmon P. Chase again sought the presidency. Realizing he had no chance of taking the Republican nomination from the tremendously popular General Ulysses S. Grant, he turned to the Democratic Party instead. In July, Kate attended the Democratic National Convention in New York as his de facto campaign manager, and although women were not allowed on the convention floor, she held court at the Fifth Avenue Hotel, where she wielded her considerable skill and influence on his behalf. Despite her best efforts, Chase was never really in contention, losing the nomination to former New York governor Horatio Seymour, who lost to General Grant in the general election in November.

In 1872, Chase was again put forward as a candidate, but he had suffered a stroke in August 1870, and although he still served as chief justice, his private correspondence reveals his reluctance to seek the presidency. "I do not desire it," he wrote to one eager supporter. "There has been a time when I did. I say this frankly, and say just as frankly that I have no such desire. If those who agree with me in principle think that my nomination will promote the interests of the country, I shall not refuse the use of my name. But I shall not seek a nomination, nor am I willing to seem to seek it." Chase had made such assertions before, of course, but that year he seemed to truly mean it, and he appeared more relieved than disappointed when he lost the Democratic nomination to Horace Greeley. Kate had hosted one magnificent reception for him in Washington, but otherwise she had seemed neither hopeful nor approving of his candidacy, for she was far more concerned with his health than his political career.

On May 7, 1873, almost six months after President Grant won reelection, Salmon P. Chase died of a stroke in New York at the home of Nettie, her husband, and their newborn daughter, ending his political ambitions forever.

Kate and William's marriage produced a son and three daughters, but ultimately ended in an acrimonious divorce in May 1882. While they had enjoyed a few periods of relative contentment, William's alcoholism, abusiveness, and repeated infidelities ruined any chance they might have had for lasting happiness. It was an act of great courage for Kate to leave her abusive husband in an era when divorce, for a woman, almost always meant scandal, ostracism, and poverty. She legally reclaimed her maiden name and was awarded custody of her three daughters, but to her great sorrow—and ultimately his own—her son, Willie, almost seventeen, chose to live with his father.

William passed on his worst traits and habits to his son, dragged him into his most notorious escapades, and ultimately left him feeling utterly unloved and betrayed. Willie eventually broke free of his father's influence and tried to reconcile with his relieved and grateful mother, but her faithful love, compassion, and encouragement could not overcome his deep depression, anger, and sense of futility. In October of 1890, William Sprague, Junior, committed suicide in Seattle, leaving behind a bitter, accusatory letter addressed to his father—and a devastated, heartbroken mother, who blamed her former husband for their son's despondency and never forgave him.

Kate lived out her final years quietly at Edgewood, an estate on the outskirts of Washington left to her by her father. (Chase had bequeathed it to both of his daughters, but Nettie much preferred her home in New York City and had gladly sold her share to her sister.) Near the end of her life, Kate supported herself and her second-eldest daughter—Kitty, who had special needs and would never live independently—on contributions from kindhearted friends, and also by selling vegetables, eggs, milk, and other produce she raised on the estate grounds.

Kate died at Edgewood on July 31, 1899, of acute kidney disease and was buried in Spring Grove Cemetery in Cincinnati, Ohio, near the graves of her beloved father and mother. "No name could possibly be spoken in this city among the older residents that would evoke the flood of reminiscence always accorded the mention of Kate Chase," the Washington *Evening Star* lauded her on the day of her death. "No woman as young ever held here the prominent and controlling position as leader which came to her as mistress of her father's household, nor has the most critical observer failed in according to her a brilliancy all her own and a queenship undisputed." From the time she arrived in the nation's capital, "here Kate Chase held a court of her own and her reputation spread far and wide as the most brilliant woman of her day . . . [N]one outshone her in grace of manner, nor the ability to attract and to hold all her admirers. She had rare personal magnetism, a faculty of drawing out the best traits in others, and while shining herself pre-eminently, she was able to keep about her the most prominent leaders in politics, in society or in fashionable life."

ACKNOWLEDGMENTS

I offer my sincere thanks to Denise Roy, Maria Massie, Liza Cassity, Christine Ball, Brian Tart, Kate Napolitano, and the outstanding sales teams at Dutton and Plume for their support of my work and their contributions to *Mrs. Lincoln's Rival.* I appreciate the generous assistance of my first readers, Geraldine Neidenbach, Marty Chiaverini, and Brian Grover, whose comments and questions were, as always, insightful and helpful. I also thank Heather Neidenbach, Nic Neidenbach, Marlene and Len Chiaverini, and friends for their ongoing support and encouragement.

I am indebted to the Wisconsin Historical Society and their librarians and staff for maintaining the excellent archives I have come to rely upon in my work. The resources I consulted most often are David Homer Bates, *Lincoln in the Telegraph Office: Recollections of the United States Military Telegraph Corps During the Civil War* (New York: The Century Company, 1907); Thomas Graham Belden and Marva Robins Belden, *So Fell the Angels* (Boston: Little, Brown, and Company, 1956); Michael Burlingame and John R. Turner Ettlinger, eds., *Inside Lincoln's White House: The Complete Civil War Diary of John Hay* (Carbondale and Edwardsville: Southern Illinois University Press, 1997); Catherine Clinton, *Mrs. Lincoln: A Life* (New York: HarperCollins, 2009); Columbia Historical Society, *Records of the Columbia Historical Society, Washington, D.C.* Vol. 13 (Washington, D.C.: Columbia Historical Society, 1910); Daniel Mark Epstein, *The Lincolns: Portrait of a Marriage* (New York: Ballantine Books, 2008); Jennifer Fleischner, *Mrs. Lincoln and Mrs. Keckly: The Remarkable Story of the Friendship Between a First Lady and a Former Slave* (New York: Broadway Books, 2003); Ernest B. Furgurson, *Freedom Rising: Washington in the Civil War* (New York: Knopf, 2004); James M. Goode, *Capital Losses: A Cultural History of Washington's Destroyed Buildings*, second edition (Washington and London: Smithsonian Books, 2003); Doris Kearns Goodwin, *Team of Rivals* (New York: Simon & Schuster, 2005); Horace Greeley, *Proceedings of the First Three Republican National Conventions of 1856, 1860 and 1864* (Minneapolis, MN: Charles W. Johnson, 1893); Janet Chase Hoyt, "Setting Free a Race: How the Emancipation Proclamation Was Made," *New York Tribune*, February 22, 1893: 8; Janet Chase Hoyt, "Sherman and Chase: An Interview at Beaufort," *New York Tribune*, February 22, 1891: 16; Janet Chase Hoyt, "A Woman's Memories: The Battle of Bull Run, General McDowell," *New York Tribune*, June 7, 1891: 16; Janet Chase Hoyt, "A Woman's Memories: A Privateer, General Scott, Charles Sumner," *New York Tribune*, April 5, 1891: 16; Janet Chase Hoyt, "A Woman's Memories: Washington in War Time," *New York Tribune*, March 8, 1891: 16; Virginia Jeans Laas, ed., *Wartime Washington: The Civil War Letters of Elizabeth Blair Lee* (Urbana and Chicago: University of Illinois Press, 1991); Peg A. Lamphier, *Kate Chase and William Sprague: Politics and Gender in a Civil War Marriage* (Lincoln, NE: University of Nebraska Press, 2003); Eba Anderson Lawton, *Major Robert Anderson and Fort Sumter 1861* (New York: The Knickerbocker Press, 1911); James P. McClure, Peg A. Lamphier, and Erika M. Kreger, eds., *Spur Up Your Pegasus: Family Letters of Salmon, Kate, and Nettie Chase, 1844–1873* (Kent, OH: The Kent State University Press, 2009); John Niven, *Salmon P. Chase: A Biography* (New York and Oxford: Oxford University Press, 1995); John Niven et al., eds., *The Salmon P. Chase Papers Volumes 1–5* (Kent, OH: The Kent State University Press, 1993); Mary Merwin Phelps, *Kate Chase, Dominant Daughter* (New York: Thomas Y. Crowell Company, 1935); Ishbel Ross, *Proud Kate: Portrait of an Ambitious Woman* (New York: Harper & Brothers, 1953); Carl Schurz, *The Reminiscences of Carl Schurz Volume 2 1852–1863* (London: John Murray, 1909); Frederick W. Seward, *Seward at Washington as Senator and Secretary of State: A Memoir of His Life, with Selections from His Letters, 1846–1861* (New York: Derby and Miller, 1891); Alice Hunt Sokoloff, *Kate Chase for the Defense* (New York: Dodd, Mead & Company, 1971); and Justin G. Turner and Linda Levitt Turner, *Mary Todd Lincoln: Her Life and Letters* (New York: Knopf, 1972). Unfortunately, I found that most early biographies about Kate Chase were written with such obvious contempt for their subject that it was a challenge to wade through the snark and find the facts. I encourage readers interested in learning more about Kate Chase to refer to primary sources such as the great many letters the Chase family exchanged, and secondary sources from the late twentieth and early twenty-first centuries.

As always and most of all, I thank my husband, Marty, and my sons, Nicholas and Michael, for their enduring love, tireless support, and inspiring faith in me. You make everything worthwhile, and I could not have written this book without you.

Also by bestselling author
Jennifer Chiaverini

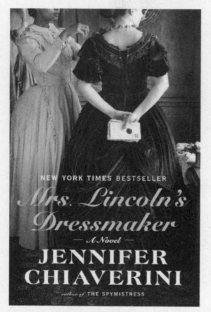

978-0-14-218035-8

978-0-14-218088-4

Available wherever books are sold.

Also by *New York Times* bestselling author
Jennifer Chiaverini

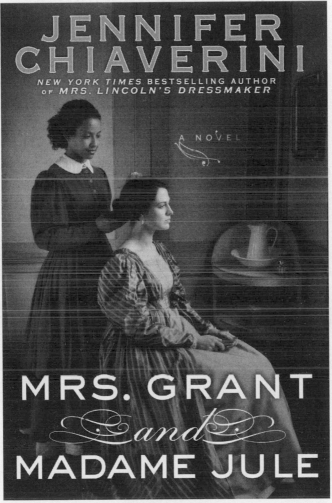

978-0-525-95429-3

Coming in March 2015